Pooh Bridge

by

Nigel Lampard

Also by Nigel Lampard

Naked Slaughter
Obsession
In Denial
Subliminal
The Loser Has To Fall

A Bardel Publication

Published by Bardel 2015
© Nigel Lampard 2004
Third Edition - Pooh Bridge

No part of this book may be reproduced or transmitted in any form or by any means, electronic or mechanical, including photocopying, recording, or by any information storage and retrieval system, without permission in writing from the publisher
This is a work of fiction. Names, places, businesses, characters, and incidents, are either the product of the author's imagination or are used fictitiously and any resemblance to any actual persons, living or dead, organisations, events or locales, or any other entity, is entirely coincidental.
The unauthorised reproduction or distribution of this copyrighted work is illegal.

Cover designed by Bardel
Image provided by www.123RF.com

Dedication

Pooh Bridge is dedicated to a close family friend, Nancy Blatherwick, who died in August 2000 after a long illness.

Nancy was an inspiration when she was alive and she still is.

Chapter One

She was lying in the undergrowth a little way off a well-trodden track.

If I had not chosen that particular track, in that particular wood, I would never have found her and someone else, by virtue of either diligence or their dog rooting around in the undergrowth, would have made the grim discovery.

It was early evening in late May with the sun setting on what had been a beautiful and warm day. Before entering the wooded valley, I had rested as I contemplated my next move.

Having bought what I needed for another week, I was looking for somewhere to spend the night. I suppose to some of the people in the crowded supermarket from which I had bought my provisions, I had looked like a vagrant but to others, a not so youthful-looking adventure scout. It was over a week since I had spent a night in a proper bed and although I had planned my isolation, there were things I had forgotten. My backpack was now heavy and I was looking forward to getting some of the weight off my weary shoulders.

It seemed a lot longer than a week. I had hardly spoken to anybody in that time; in fact, I had deliberately gone out of my way to make sure I did not speak to anybody. My mind needed sorting out before I even considered discussing what I was doing, or what I had done, with anybody else.

Was there anybody with whom I could discuss such things?

Would anybody understand?

Would anybody want to understand?

I was isolated within my own loneliness. There were parts of me that rebelled against what I was doing, but my subconscious understood. What I was doing was not wrong: I hadn't done any harm to anything or anybody. There were those who would be concerned that what I was doing was weird – the only word I can and maybe they could think of – but I hoped that the verbal and written explanations I had provided would be sufficient to justify my absence and the need to be on my own.

There had been plenty of time to come to terms with the creeping inevitability of Belinda's death and I had tried to make her last months, weeks and days on this earth as painless, both physically and mentally, as possible. She had been tremendous, which in many ways had made my own situation even worse. She was far, far better at facing up to her illness than I was.

I marvelled at her, the way she could smile when she was in a lot of pain, the way she could remain positive when she had every reason to be despondent.

She planned, she understood and she was tidy.

It was almost as though she had passed over to a different plain and was able to view from an entirely dissimilar perspective the fact that she was dying. Her life was ending but she did not want mine to end with hers: how hard that was to accept and it remains difficult to acknowledge. She made me make promises, promises that I would have great difficulty in keeping.

That was the reason why I was now in the middle of a dense and quickly darkening Derbyshire wood, looking down at another poor soul whose life was at an untimely end.

I had made sure before I left home that as many loose ends as possible were sorted so there was nothing to stop me from getting away. In many ways I thought that by being on my own I would be closer to her: the memories, both recent and distant could be with me. There would be nothing to distract me from being with her: hearing her laugh, seeing that look in her eyes when she did not agree with me but still allowed me to make my point.

It would give me time to think further back to when the

children were born and the way she made sure that I was never alone.

The twins were a handful but she always had time for me, she always had time for us. The children did not come between us because she always made me feel as though I was the most important person in her life.

However, I made it especially difficult for her because I was away a lot of the time and when I returned she had to make room for me in their routine – the private life she had with the children when I wasn't there. She constantly told me, when I felt conscience stricken about being away so much, that I did as much as I could. It helped but I always felt that I never did enough. The changes in the twins were so swift that even when my absence was shorter than normal, I would return to another transformation. Then as soon as we had established a routine that included me, I was off again and they had to revert to the world that was known to only the three of them.

It would have helped if the house had not been isolated. I worried about her and the children's safety and, although I spent a lot of money on securing the house, I knew Belinda rarely made use of the alarms and the sophisticated locking system when I was away.

She loved the country.

Once the children were older, she revelled in the hours the three of them spent exploring the many woods and valleys in the area, and what they had to offer. When I was at home, they would take me out and show me what they had discovered – a nest here, a badger's set there, the fallen old oak that had collapsed during the latest gale but still clung to life. They showed me the remnants of the dam they had built and asked whether they should have built it higher or thicker. Daddy built dams and that is what took him all over the world. Building one across the brook at the bottom of the field down from Elliot's farm, brought them closer to me, or so they said.

When we were out, reliving their experiences, Belinda would deliberately hang back to let David and Isabelle have me all to themselves. There were other times when Belinda and I could bury ourselves in each other and try to make up for lost time. There were never any recriminations. The time we had together during my brief re-appearances was too short to spend it arguing. I knew what the separation was doing to me and I could only guess what it was doing to her, but she never told me. We had agreed that I would have a career change when I was forty – a chance to be at home and lead a proper family life.

Then, three years before I was due to stop my wanderings and almost two years ago to the day, I returned home from a trip to Nigeria and it was obvious that something had happened.

By this time, the twins were ensconced in a boarding school in Hertfordshire. They had discussed what they wanted between themselves: they had not included Belinda or me. Then they announced one day – they said they deliberately waited until I was at home – that they wanted to go to boarding school. We were shocked: they had seemed happy going to the local school in the village a half mile down the lane from the house and we had assumed that the comprehensive a few miles further away held equal attractions.

Its reputation was the best.

However, according to the children, this wasn't the plan they wished to follow. If I could afford it, they wanted to go away to school and, they insisted, to the same one. Belinda had been to boarding school and, surprisingly, after getting over the initial uncertainty, she was all for it. She believed that academically both schools would be on an equal par, but for continuity and social awareness, nothing could beat a boarding school. I reluctantly agreed, and before I knew it, the twins had gone. That same weekend Belinda told me not to worry; she would fill her time by getting a part-time job somewhere.

"After all," she said, "I do have a degree and it's about time I made use of it."

Belinda and I met at Leeds University and we married the year after we both graduated, she with a 2nd Class Honours in sociology and me with a 1st Class Honours in marine engineering. We had scraped a living initially, but then I was fortunate to get a job with an American international company that planned, designed, built and maintained many of the dams in the Third World. Once with them I never looked back, *we* never looked back. The money was excellent but the downside was that I was away a lot. Fortunately, Belinda fell pregnant after we had been married for three years and the twins, David and Isabelle, were the result.

Originally, we bought a house in Warwickshire but then moved across into Leicestershire which meant when I was away Belinda could be closer to her parents who lived in Market Harborough.

I had been in Nigeria for a month and arrived home in the middle of the twins' summer holidays. Having taken a month off, and within two days of my return, all four of us were on an aircraft destined for Florida and Disney World.

Neither Belinda nor I were in the holiday mood, but of course, we had to disguise our concerns for the children's sake. The evening before we flew, we had all gone out for a meal and then the twins had reluctantly gone to bed early because we would have to get up at five o'clock in the morning.

Having poured a couple of strong gin and tonics, Belinda and I went into the conservatory.

"What's the matter?" I asked, sitting next to her on the wicker two-seater sofa.

She kicked off her shoes and put her feet on the small table in front of her. "What makes you think there's something the matter with me?" she replied morosely.

"Your answer confirms that there is something."

She stood up, her anxiety obvious in her inability to sit still, and went over to the window, clutching her glass to her chest. She turned to face me and there were tears in her eyes.

I started to get up but she held up her hand and shook her head.

"No, Richard, stay where you are please. There is something I have to tell you but …"

"Come on, love, what is it?"

She took a sip of her drink and bowed her head.

"A couple of weeks after you flew to Nigeria, I went to the doctor and the results came through the other day."

"Results? What results?" I thought the penny had dropped. I smiled. "You're not are you?"

Belinda did not return my smile.

"No, I'm not, Richard, and even if I were pregnant it would be the last thing on my mind at the moment." She peered into her glass as she spoke and ran her index finger round its rim. "I've got cancer," she added quickly without looking up.

A silence fell as what she had said tried to drill itself into my brain. I felt my heartbeat quicken and I could hear the pulse beating in my ears. Belinda lifted her head and looked at me. The tears were now rolling down her cheeks. I crossed the few feet between us and took her in my arms. Burying her face in my shoulder, she cried. I pressed her head against me, the view through the window becoming a blur as my eyes became glazed with my own tears.

It was something we had never discussed: it was something we believed would never happen to either of us, so why did we need to discuss it?

Apart from my long absences, we had been rather lucky. The twins were coping well with their young lives and had not presented us with many of the problems experienced by other families. Belinda and I had been married for thirteen years and our love for each other had grown almost daily. I regarded her as my best friend and I was hers. We had become lovers a month after we met, and twenty years later, we were still lovers. I missed her terribly when I was away. Sometimes I would lie in a lonely hotel bed on the opposite side of the world and tell myself that being apart was punishment for being extremely happy. When I boarded the plane to fly back to her, I was like a young child, full of excitement and longing.

Now, in a few unexpected words, it was possible that our idyllic world was going to be shattered.

Holding her close to me, the wetness of her tears on my cheek, I knew I was going to fail her. I knew that there was nothing I could say or do that was going to make the horrible realisation of what she had told me go away. I didn't want to know any more and yet wanted to know everything. I needed to be told that she was not going to leave me, she wasn't going to leave the world we had both built to house our love for each other and the love we had for the twins. I wanted her to tell me that it – and I had to think of it as *it* – had been caught early enough for her to be completely cured.

Something told me that she was not going to be able to give me that reassurance and that our time together was limited. I had to have the strength to face the truth and make what time we had left together as painless and as happy as circumstances would allow. Being selfish was not an option: she would not be thinking of herself, she would not be thinking of dying, she would be thinking of how I was going to manage without her.

Two years is all we had.

They were two years that sped by in what seemed like a quarter of the time. Belinda received the best treatment possible and that gave us longer than we could ever have hoped for. We spent the time crying and laughing together. The Managing Director of the company I worked for was marvellous and created a job for me which allowed me to work from home for most of the time. I had to go over to the States about once every couple of months but only for a few days.

On that fateful evening, once neither of us could cry any more, Belinda told me that she had put off going to see the doctor because she could not, and would not, accept that there was anything wrong with her. Even if there was, what the future held for her was too frightening to contemplate.

When I was away, she buried herself in her work, and spring-cleaned the house from top to bottom at every opportunity. She had felt a lot of discomfort in her lower back but she put it down to over-exertion.

Then the pain began to spread upwards. She told me nothing because she did not want to worry me but eventually, once she knew I was engrossed in my work in Nigeria, she went to our GP. He immediately sent her to a specialist in Leicester and it was his report she had received a couple of days before I came home. There was a malignant growth centred in her right lung; there were also signs that it had already begun to spread.

She had surgery followed by courses of radio and chemotherapy. At first, the prognosis was good but suddenly, after a year, she became quite ill. She fought and fought and there were days when she would smile and tell me it had all gone away, but then within twenty-four hours the smile would disappear.

She continued to work until the last couple of months and the doctor told me afterwards that her perseverance and stubbornness had kept her going. The treatment she received was secondary only to her own will power.

Early on she lost weight but it seemed to stabilise. Once the twins went back to school we discussed over and over again whether they should be told but decided that the longer we were able to hide the truth the better it would be for them. However, in March this year when Belinda became too ill to work, they had to know.

I went down to their school and told them. Their young minds fought against it initially but then almost overnight they seemed to mature. Isabelle automatically assumed the maternal role and during the early stages of the Easter holidays took over the cooking, washing and cleaning from me, and told me to spend as much time as I could with mummy. David, bless him, felt slightly marginalised which meant he took to cleaning the cars when they did not need it, mowing the lawn although the grass hadn't started growing after the winter, and generally doing manly things.

Belinda died a week before the end of the Easter holidays, only four weeks after I had told the twins how ill their mother was. She spent a few days in hospital, but when we were told that there was nothing more that could be done, she insisted on coming home.

Her parents came to stay for the final few days. They had aged dramatically, especially her mother, and although her father put on a brave face, the worry took its toll.

Each night I held Belinda as she slept.

Then early one morning, she was not able to hang on to life any longer. I felt her take her final breath and she was still, at last at rest

The peacefulness and relief showed in her beautiful face.

She had been an inspiration to us all and to the many friends who had helped.

At her funeral, the local village church was full to capacity. She had not wanted any flowers, other than from immediate family. Instead, she asked people to give to Cancer Relief.

It was her wish for her grave to be in the church cemetery

close to the old wooden bridge, which we, as a family, fondly called Pooh Bridge. Next to the bridge was the ford she loved, she always said it took her back to when times were simple.

Standing on the bridge once everybody had gone, I felt guilty as I recalled something I had thought when I suddenly accepted one day that I was going to lose Belinda.

From the day she pleaded with the hospital to let her go home, I knew that I would have to get away as soon after her death as was decent. I knew that the house, the garden, the surrounding countryside, even the shops we used to visit would hold too many memories of her presence and I did not want to share her passing with anyone.

I had to get away.

The time had now come and I wished I had never had the thought in the first place.

The twins went back to school three days after their mother's funeral and they assured me that they were all right.

"Mummy wouldn't have wanted our education to suffer," David told me in a quiet, catching voice, fighting back his tears.

They organised themselves for their return to school and refused any help from their grandparents or me. When I dropped them off at school, their housemaster, Mr Postance, was there to meet them. I had never come to terms with handing them over into the charge of another man.

I had already told the twins what I intended doing and they said they empathised but told me to be careful and I was to call them as soon as I got back. Taking Mr Postance to one side I told him I would be away for a couple of weeks.

He said he understood but his expression suggested the opposite.

His lack of understanding really did not matter to me.

Chapter Two

Shrugging off my backpack, I dropped to my knees next to the bedraggled figure lying in the shallow ditch in front of me. Her long hair partially covered her face but she appeared to be in her early twenties.

Her left arm was in full view but the other one was underneath her body, trapped as she fell. I looked around but all I could hear were the birds announcing the onset of dusk and the slight breeze-induced movement in the trees above me.

Other than the sounds of nature, there was nothing.

I could see in the dim light that the girl was fully clothed, which I found extraordinary. Victims of physical attack – that's what I assumed had happened – were rarely offered the courtesy of being covered up.

My mind was racing.

I knew I mustn't touch or move anything but there was something that wasn't right and, before starting back through the woods to notify the police, I needed to know what I was dealing with.

Flipping open the top of my backpack I reached inside for the torch and switched it on. The girl was wearing walking boots, jeans and a green anorak. There was no sign that her clothing had been disturbed. Directing the beam onto her face, I bent over and moved her hair to one side so I could see her better. Her closed eyes made her look as though she was sleeping; there was even a slight smile on her lips. Her features were Asian, although her colouring suggested that her mother or father, or even a grandparent, might have been Caucasian.

Placing the backs of my fingers against her cheek, I expected her skin to be cold and lifeless but it wasn't; her skin was warm under my touch.

It took me a few seconds to find an explanation for what I had discovered. I had automatically assumed that she was dead but now there was a possibility that she was still alive. I moved my fingers down to her neck and felt for a pulse.

It was there, strong and slow.

Again, I looked around, trying to work out what to do and what might have happened. A couple of minutes ago I couldn't move her because I might disturb some evidence but now I didn't want to cause her further injury.

Feeling round her neck there was no sign that it was broken and her posture suggested that there was no obvious break elsewhere either, except maybe her right arm.

Slowly I reached under her head. A rock obstructed any further movement, but the side of her head felt wet and, taking my hand away, I could see in the torch light the sticky redness of her blood.

Gently, I half lifted and half dragged her out of the ditch before using the torch again. Her hair was matted with blood but her injury didn't seem to be that serious. I knew that if I was going to help I had to move her further away. I needed to clean the wound as best I could. She was breathing normally and her pulse was still strong and even, but her eyes remained closed.

Other than the torch beam, the little natural light left was fading quickly. There was no way I was going to be able to get her through the woods and to a hospital without causing her more injury, and probably injuring myself as well. I took off my own anorak and covered her before looking for somewhere to erect my tent. About fifty yards away I found an even piece of ground among some small fir trees. Because of the light it took me a good ten minutes to put up the tent and lay out the sleeping mat and bag, but eventually, accompanied by a good deal of muffled swearing, I managed it.

Retracing my steps I went back to the girl, and as carefully as the ground and the light permitted, I carried her the short distance to the tent. With a lot of manoeuvring, I managed to get her lying on the sleeping bag.

After boiling some water and letting it cool slightly, I bathed the wound on the side of her head. The lesion wasn't deep but obviously she had given herself, or somebody had, such a thump that she had knocked herself out.

Searching in the small first aid box I carried with me, I put a pad over the wound and bandaged it in place. Again, I checked her pulse and concluded there was little more I could do for her other than hope she would regain consciousness soon. I needed to determine whether she was well enough to walk back to civilisation. There was no way of telling how long she had been lying in that ditch, but the blood in her hair suggested it hadn't been for long. After removing her boots, I covered her with the sleeping bag and propped her head on my rolled-up anorak. She looked peaceful. I noticed a small twitch at the corner of her eyebrow that may have suggested consciousness wasn't far away.

My diet since I set off on my period of solitude had been unbalanced to say the least. During the day while on the move I relied on chocolate bars and ready-cooked snacks I bought in any small shop I passed, but for the evenings, I carried an assortment of dry rations including a bag of rice. I always had a two-litre container of water that I topped up at every opportunity. It was heavy but I regarded it as essential. With the aid of the torch, I looked through the meagre choice for that evening and smiled as I wondered if I ought to cook for two.

Official campsites were off the agenda as far as possible and each evening I endeavoured to find a secluded spot well away from the beaten track. I spent my nights in out-of-the-way woods. I wanted to make sure that when I lit a small fire or my camping-stove it couldn't be seen unless somebody was passing close by.

To date, I hadn't been disturbed.

The county I was in was Derbyshire and about five miles northeast of Ashbourne, in a spot – according to my map – called Dove Dale. A river ran through the centre of the wooded valley but I hadn't had time since finding the girl to see if the water was clean.

I moved a few yards away from the tent and let my eyes get used to the darkness before unfolding the small spade I carried. After scraping a dip into the earth, I intended building a fire to heat some water for cooking. I had a camping gas stove but I tried not to use it too often, preferring to save it for emergencies – not that, until now, I'd had any.

When looking around for twigs and small dead branches for the fire, I realised the temperature had dropped and I rather wished I had kept my anorak on. My thoughts made me glance back towards the tent, and at that moment the flap was moved to one side: a head appeared, the white bandage quite prominent in the gloom. I switched off the torch and stayed where I was to see what my guest would do.

She came out of the tent a little further and looked about her. "Hello," she whispered.

I switched on the torch again and her head immediately shot round, which meant she was now looking in my direction. Her face told me how frightened she was and she withdrew a little into the tent like a tortoise retreating into its shell when startled.

Making sure I didn't shine the torch directly in her face, I took a couple of paces towards her. "Don't be frightened," I said as softly as I could. "You've had a nasty bang on the head."

She looked up at me as I got closer and I could see sheer terror in her eyes. I was afraid she was going to scream. I stopped a few feet away from her and hunkered down, shining the light on the ground between us.

"My name's Richard and I found you unconscious in a ditch about fifty yards away. How are you feeling?"

She screwed up her eyes and regarded me uncertainly before reaching up and touching the bandage. "You did this?" she asked.

"Yes," I replied, aware that she spoke with a slight but noticeable foreign accent. "I don't think you have done yourself any permanent damage but you were unconscious for quite a while. May I come a little closer?"

She didn't answer straight away, then she nodded but at the same time she withdrew a little further into the tent.

"I can appreciate how frightened you must feel but you have nothing to fear from me. I want to help," I told her.

She screwed up her eyes again but then she appeared to come to a decision about me. "Thank you." She came out of the tent and sat on the dry pine needles. Reaching into her anorak pocket, she extracted a packet of cigarettes and a lighter. I didn't accept her offer of one, although the temptation was strong.

"What happened?" I asked as she inhaled deeply and blew the smoke into the night, shaking slightly.

She took a few seconds to answer. "I am not sure. Please," she added, "is it possible I could have a drink of something?"

"I'm so sorry," I said, getting to my feet. "I was forgetting my manners." I reached for my backpack. "You have a choice – water, tea or coffee. The tea and coffee will take a little longer because I'll have to boil the water."

"Some cold water will do."

"You were going to tell me what happened," I said, passing her a plastic cup of water.

"Thank you." She shook her head. "I really am not sure but … but may I ask you a question?"

"Of course."

"Where am I and why am I with you?" She sipped the water.

"It's a long story, erm … I'm afraid I don't know your name."

"Ingrid, Ingrid Mesterom."

"Hello, Ingrid," I said reaching across the space between us. "My name is Richard, Richard Blythe."

She took my hand hesitantly. "Hello, Richard." There was the hint of a smile on her lips.

"In a nutshell, Ingrid, I'm on a walking holiday and I came into these woods to camp for the night and I found you. I didn't want to move you too far in case your injuries were worse than they seemed. I was waiting for you to regain consciousness before deciding what I should do next. I was going to light a fire and cook a simple meal when you woke up."

I watched her as she took in what I said. She was a pretty girl, with long black hair and her large eyes like jet lignite, a stone I sometimes came across during excavations. In the halo of light thrown out by the torch, she appeared quite mystifying. The bandage looked like a bandanna round her head but fortunately, there was no sign of blood seeping through it, I could assume the bleeding had stopped.

She drew deeply on her cigarette before stubbing it out. Looking around she asked, "Did I have a rucksack when you found me?" She seemed to have accepted my explanation.

"No, not that I saw, but from the way you're dressed I thought you'd been out walking as well."

"Yes … yes, I was and I did have a rucksack," she continued a little impatiently while looking around, although it was now quite dark under the trees and neither of us could see beyond a few feet from where we were sitting.

"Do you remember anything about what happened?"

Again she was silent for a few seconds, her eyes on mine, assessing me. "I am, like you, on a walking holiday and I wanted to reach a village called Mayfield tonight. There is a guesthouse there, where I intended staying the night. A man stopped his car and offered me a lift but I told him, no, I did not want one but then I realised I was not going to reach Mayfield before it was dark, so I changed my mind." She lit another cigarette. "The man seemed all right and talked to me in the car but then he stopped talking and seemed to be looking for somewhere." Ingrid was fiddling with her nails. "He parked his car in a car park by some woods and … and he put his hand on my leg. His attitude changed. The look in his eyes was frightening. I opened the door and ran. He got out also and chased me but he was not fit and when I ran into the woods, he seemed to give up. I carried on running but then I think I must have tripped and the next thing I remember is waking up in your tent." She took another sip of water.

"You did the right thing, and fortunately, other than a nasty crack to your head, nothing worse happened to you. Your rucksack - did you take it with you when you escaped from the car?"

"I remember now, it was on the back seat so I cannot have done." Ingrid's accent had become more prominent and her pronunciation more precise as she related what happened to her, and I guessed, supported by her name, that – regardless of my earlier belief that she was Asian – she was either German, Swiss or Austrian, though her nationality was irrelevant at that moment.

"What about your money and other valuables? Were they in it?"

She shook her head. "I carry my purse in my anorak." Ingrid reached into one of the inside pockets and extracted a brown purse which she showed to me. "I'm sorry, but it was one of the first things I checked when I woke up."

I shook my head. "I would have done exactly the same. Anything else?"

"There was a camera and a mobile phone in the rucksack, some food and extra clothing but nothing of any importance ... yes, there was," she added quickly, her hand darting to her mouth. "My passport was in it, in the bottom under my clothes."

I reached over for my map from my backpack and spreading it out between us, shone the torch on it. I pointed to the woods we were in. "Do you know where this car park is?"

Ingrid got onto her knees and took the torch from me. Peering at the map she traced her finger along one of the roads. "I think it would have been about there," she suggested, pointing at a white 'P' in a blue square. When she turned round to look at me her hair brushed against my face, but when she realised how close she was to me she moved away quickly.

I still wasn't trusted.

The car park she pointed to was one I'd passed through as I looked for the path that would take me into the woods. I didn't remember seeing any cars, neither had I seen anything resembling a rucksack but, then again, I wasn't looking for either.

"Right," I said, refolding the map. "We have a choice: it's nearly eight o'clock and we can either get you out of these woods and into Mayfield, that'll take about an hour or so to reach, or you can stay here and I'll see you safely to the nearest police station tomorrow ..."

"Police station!" Ingrid said abruptly. "Why would I go to the police station?"

Surprised by her reaction, I said, "To report what happened, of course!"

She curled her legs under her. "But there is nothing to report. He did not do anything to me."

"The next female he considers attacking might not be as fortunate. You can describe the man, surely?"

"Yes, but ... I think I feel safe here with you. I will decide what to do in the morning."

I took that as her answer to my earlier question and again I was a little surprised. "Well, all right ... would you like me to go to the car park to see if on the off-chance he discarded your rucksack? It's dark here, but there will still be some light to see by down there."

"And leave me here alone?"

"You'll be all right. One thing I've learnt over the last week is that woods such as these are lonely places at night. All I've ever heard and seen are wild animals. It'll only take me about twenty minutes to get to the car park and back." I stood up. "I'll leave you with this torch. I've got a spare in my backpack."

"Is there anything I can do while you are gone?" Ingrid stood up next to me and she swayed slightly.

I put a restraining hand on her arm. "Are you sure you're all right?"

She smiled. "I have a little headache but yes, I am all right. What can I do while you are away?"

I returned her smile. "Boil some water and make us a meal?"

"Of course," she replied, her expression serious.

I got the fire going and then, when I started to get other things together, Ingrid informed me that she was quite capable and almost ushered me away. When I walked back onto the track, I could see her busying herself with the packets of food and the single pot I carried with me.

The improbability of my situation only hit me as I began to climb and stumble up the track towards the car park. Surrealism had surrounded my existence since I set out on my self-induced solitary confinement, and finding Ingrid the way I did only added to my extraordinary experiences. I suppose a psychologist would have said that the decision to commence my selfish isolation would let me find myself again after losing Belinda. For me, though, it was simply the need to escape from reality, and Ingrid had certainly helped on that front. There was something nagging away at the back of my mind that suggested it hadn't been chance that had drawn me to that particular spot and at that particular moment, but other than being irritated by my own thoughts I couldn't find an explanation.

The path crossed the stream, courtesy of some rather slippery rocks, and as I climbed the bank on the other side and emerged from the wood, the rush of the water over the weir I had rested by earlier that evening reached my ears. It was also noticeably lighter and I was able to switch off the torch. The car park was deserted and there was no obvious sign of Ingrid's rucksack. I was about to give up when a splash of red in some bushes caught my attention.

On further investigation, what I'd seen turned out to be exactly what I was looking for. It couldn't a mere coincidence.

Picking up the rucksack by one of its handles I gave it a cursory inspection – none of the fasteners was undone, and other than being slightly damp there was no discernible damage.

There was a lightweight sleeping bag rolled up and retained by straps under the rucksack. Retracing my steps towards the track leading back into the woods, I felt that maybe I had done the right thing in coming to look for Ingrid's belongings.

After re-crossing the stream, I was suddenly aware that I was not alone, and looking up I saw a man standing by a small gate leading out of the car park and onto a by-road. He was leaning nonchalantly against one of the uprights and I smiled when even in the dim light I could see he was chewing on the stem of a piece of grass. I raised my hand in acknowledgement and he nodded in return – he looked as though he was in his mid-sixties and he had a rugged appearance.

After hesitating, I decided on impulse to approach him. I was aware that if I continued along the track he would see me disappear into the woods and he might be inquisitive enough to follow me.

He didn't change his stance as I walked up to him, but he did take the bit of grass from his mouth in anticipation of the need, perhaps, to speak.

"Good evening," I said, stopping a few feet from him.

"'Ullo there," he replied. He was wearing an old hacking-jacket under which there was a scruffy brown shirt, his trousers were baggy and fawn, and he had what appeared to be old hobnailed-boots on his feet. It looked as though I had guessed his age correctly.

"Nice evening," I offered.

"'Tis that," he agreed.

"Ideal for walking."

"'Tis that," he said again. He was watching me intently.

I put my hand on the gate as though I intended going through it and he stood to one side. "Thanks. Do you live locally?" I asked, swinging the gate open.

"Yep, do that."

"Is that a hotel over there?"

He looked in the direction I was pointing. "Yep, 'tis that."

"Good, maybe I'll be able to get a room, then."

"Possible." He was a man of few words but as I started to walk past him he added, "Saw you pick up the bag."

I stopped and turned to face him. He had narrowed his eyes in concentration. "I'm sorry?"

"Saw you pick up the bag," he repeated, indicating Ingrid's rucksack.

"Oh, right."

"Saw the man who put it there too," he added.

He had suddenly gained my interest. When I passed through the car park earlier, I was sure there was nobody there and I assumed, after Ingrid told me what had happened, that whoever her prospective attacker had been was long gone.

"What do you mean?" I asked him.

"What I said. Man in a car pulled in well o'er an hour back, waited a short while, dumped the bag and then drove arf. Was going to 'vestigate meself when I saw you comin' darn the track the first time." He stopped and waited for me to respond.

"The first time?" I said.

"Yep, afore you went into them woods," he said.

There was I thinking nobody was about. I wasn't sure what I should say. I held up the rucksack. "It belongs to a friend," I offered as an explanation.

His expression told me that he wasn't convinced, which was understandable because it was an inadequate explanation especially after he'd said he saw who dumped the rucksack.

"What sort of car was it?" I asked.

"Black, V Reg, big bugger."

"And the man?"

"Car was between 'im an' me. Couldn' really see." He shrugged. "Maybe thirty-odd, dark 'air, tall, probably a foreigner."

"What makes you think that?"

"Weren't local, looked foreign. Asian maybe."

I raised my eyebrows. "I see. Look, this probably seems a bit suspicious to you. Let me prove this rucksack does belong to a friend of mine." Lifting the rucksack off my back, I started to undo the straps.

"Na, no need," he said, shrugging again. "No business o' mine. You says it's a friend's, it's a friend's."

I frowned. "That's reasonable of you."

"Na," he said again, smiling for the first time. "You wouldn't believe what I sees in these parts – none so funny as folk."

"I bet," I said, returning his smile.

"Must be goin', wife'll have me tea ready, late as it is."

With that he turned, and without saying goodbye, started off down the road with a slow but determined stride, his hands thrust deep into his pockets.

I watched him until he disappeared round a corner. He didn't look back once. Another lonely man, I thought, but to him the rucksack incident was a mere drop in the ocean, which suggested there was a lot more to his world than he wished to communicate. What I didn't know then was that Ingrid's rucksack, although it may have been of only passing interest to him, was the precursor to changes in my life and the lives of others; changes that were going to have long term and serious consequences.

Chapter Three

The area around the tent was in total darkness.

I approached cautiously keeping the beam of my small torch pointing straight at the ground. The embers of the fire were smouldering and the saucepan was to one side, the top covered by a metal plate. I felt the saucepan and it was still warm. Standing up I looked around but I couldn't detect a sound that was out of the ordinary. I put Ingrid's rucksack next to my backpack inside the tent, and then stood still to discover if I could hear anything – there was nothing.

Where was she? Maybe she had gone somewhere to have a pee ... then again she may have decided I wasn't trustworthy after all. Her passport was in her rucksack or so she'd said. She wouldn't leave without that.

I didn't feel hungry but I did feel very worried. After crawling into the tent and I waited. If she approached, I would hear twigs breaking underfoot or the brush of her jacket against the undergrowth.

At some stage, I must have dozed off.

Throughout the night, I remember waking up every half hour or so because my concern as to Ingrid's whereabouts hit me straightaway. If I had not found her rucksack and the food had remained uncooked, I might have decided that the whole event was a dream but of course, it wasn't.

During one of my brief waking moments I realised Ingrid didn't know I'd found her rucksack – the man who left it must have been her assailant and was getting rid of evidence – which meant she didn't know I had her passport and other belongings. Maybe she had gone to look for the rucksack herself ... but where?

At something like six o'clock in the morning, I was suddenly fully awake. Ingrid had not returned. Light was beginning to filter through the trees. After crawling out of the tent I was tempted to look in her rucksack for any clues, but although I did reach for it, I decided that I would wait until it was properly light.

I threw away the congealed remnants of the meal Ingrid had half-prepared and then made a cup of tea. Why had she bothered to cook anything? If she had changed her mind about me, why didn't she leave as soon as I went off to look for her rucksack?

I wasn't a threat but I suppose she wasn't to know that. All I was to her was the bloke who had found her, bathed and bandaged her wound and then offered to try to find her rucksack. She knew nothing about me, only my name.

Ingrid Mesterom: was that her real name? She had sounded German, but if a German wanted to use a false name then she would use another German name – it wouldn't make any difference. I didn't even get a good look at her. You tend not to take too much notice of somebody's looks when you think they are dead, and then by the time she regained consciousness it was too dark. The closest I got to her was when I carried her from the ditch to the tent, but that told me nothing other than she wasn't overweight. I remembered a slight whiff of perfume that didn't blend to well with the aroma of the decaying leaves in the ditch where I had found her.

Discovering Ingrid was the first event - if that's what it can be called - that had happened to me since I started my quest for isolation. I had gone by train to Manchester and then caught the 'trundler' to Buxton, which I left on foot, heading east. I took four days to cover the ten miles to Bakewell, sticking as close to the River Wye as conditions allowed. I ambled, backtracked, stayed in one place for hours, took diversions and probably to cover ten miles I walked nearer sixty or seventy. I hadn't done a lot of walking before and had sought the guidance of a helpful shop assistant in Northampton, who seemed to know what he was talking about. In fact, the shop assistant was so good that he eventually talked me into parting with nearly five hundred pounds, but everything felt comfortable and he assured me that none of it would need any running in.

I had constantly questioned my motives for wanting the isolation in the first place. David and Isabelle had said they understood but I didn't share their understanding. During our travels, when Belinda was still alive, I often looked at the wooded areas we passed and wondered what it would be like to live off the land and not have access to modern conveniences and utilities. I had tried to analyse my thoughts but dismissed them as daydreaming when my analysis got me nowhere. However, now that I was actually putting the abstractions into practice, some of the answers were beginning to become apparent.

I hadn't done everything I'd previously imagined.

I still relied on supermarkets for sustenance. I might have been able to trap the odd furry creature but I would have then buried it with full military honours, thereby completely defeating the objective. Potatoes and other vegetables I saw growing in the fields were always a temptation but as far as wild mushrooms and other fungi were concerned, I would have poisoned myself before gaining any nourishment.

If close by, I bathed in the main river or one of its tributaries either after dark or very early in the morning in the most secluded spot I could find. The experience was always invigorating. I ought to have - but I hadn't - read up on the laws affecting living rough and guides to camping. I wanted isolation and the thought of joining others sitting round a campfire singing Ging-Gang-Goolie filled me with dismay!

Belinda, of course, was constantly on my mind. She was after all the reason why I was here. I had talked to her and asked her if she understood. I then smiled when I imagined her giving me one of her funny looks. She was happy, I told myself, and living on one of the clouds I watched floating across the blue sky as I took a rest in some sheltered spot. I had seen other ramblers but if I spotted them early enough, I would make a detour thereby avoiding contact. When that was impossible, they either got a cursory nod or, if they were lucky, I passed the time of day.

Finding that as the days went by, I was becoming more and more content with my own company, was quite heartening. I adopted a simple routine: went where I wanted, stopped when I wanted to, ate when I needed to and with the obvious restrictions, camped where I perhaps shouldn't have.

When pitching my tent I assumed that I was breaking some bylaw or other but I had never come across any marauding gamekeepers with twelve-bore shotguns, as a result I remained in one piece. The tent was small and I concealed its location as best I could.

However, two days before finding Ingrid, I did make one significant decision. I accepted that the weather had been kind and might have influenced my judgement. After returning to the real world, I may also question my motives, but I needed to either leave behind the world that Belinda and I had enjoyed, or learn to share it and our experiences with others. In other words, I had to move on and take my memories with me.

Once I started going abroad with my job, I had spent so little time with her I felt the need to make up for my selfishness now that she was gone.

Money, fortunately, wasn't a problem.

Although not yet forty, there was enough capital in the bank for me to live comfortably without the need to continue my globetrotting. I would have to get some sort of part-time job to keep me active – such a statement made me feel a good deal older than I was – but I didn't want anything that would generate the stresses that I had become accustomed to.

I could afford to see David and Isabelle through school and then on to university, should they do well enough and decide to go, but that was four years away. I seemed to gain momentous satisfaction from my decision, and after checking with Belinda's cloud that she agreed, I promised myself that regardless of others who would try to persuade me not to go, I wouldn't change my mind. I would be in charge of my life rather than my life being in charge of me. I was less than a year away from being forty years old and I was proud of the decision I had made.

Perhaps my need for isolation had paid off. Coming to a decision like that after only a week was certainly a step in the right direction.

Then some silly girl who had knocked herself out while trying to escape from a prospective rapist interrupted my relaxed new world.

I had done the honourable thing and helped her and, in return, she had half-cooked me a meal before disappearing into the night without even a thank you.

So why was I sipping my tea, thinking and worrying about her? I didn't know her or if her hurried explanation as to how she finished up lying in a ditch were true … or anything else about her if it came to that.

However, her rucksack was inside the tent and maybe … just maybe, it would reveal a little more about her.

Chapter Four

With more light slowly finding its way into the woods, I fumbled my way down to the river. The rising sun had managed to penetrate the canopy and at one point the temperature seemed degrees warmer as its rays hit the water.

I conducted my morning ablutions in the clear but cold water, feeling slightly guilty for disturbing the tranquillity as my feet sank into the muddy bottom and stirred up the sediment. Moving further out into the river I slid slowly beneath the surface, feeling the current trying to drag me downstream.

The sensation was invigorating.

Over another mug of tea and a marmalade sandwich, I reconsidered my intention of looking in Ingrid's rucksack. Wouldn't it be more sensible to hand it in to the nearest police station? She had already been the cause of my worst night's sleep since starting my isolation.

Why did I want to know more about her?

Leaving well alone was probably the right option.

But temptation got the better of me. After making another mug of tea I reached for the rucksack. The side-pockets revealed very little – underwear, socks, a map of the area, some string, a small penknife and torch, and the camera and mobile phone Ingrid had mentioned. Another pocket contained a half-eaten bag of crisps, some fruit juice and empty chocolate wrappings.

The contents of the main part of the rucksack were equally normal until I took out a spare pair of jeans. Underneath the jeans, I found Ingrid's passport and some letters. The address on the envelopes was to a place called Cochem in Germany, which I couldn't place but I thought I'd heard of it somewhere before, or maybe read about it for some reason.

Putting the rucksack to one side, I noticed the corner of what looked like a plastic bag sticking out from the rigid bottom. After fiddling with a zip, I found two plastic pouches: one contained a white powder and the other what looked like unrubbed pipe tobacco.

It didn't take a rocket scientist to work out what I was looking at – the white powder was almost certainly cocaine and the look-a-like tobacco, cannabis.

Moreover, there were significant amounts of each.

Like many others of her generation, little Ingrid had resorted to drugs for her kicks. I had glanced at, but hadn't been really interested in newspaper articles arguing the pros and cons for the legalisation of cannabis usage. It never even entered my head that the twins' school had a drugs problem among the more senior pupils. Why did I restrict my apathy to the senior pupils or even the pupils at all?

I picked up the pouch containing what I thought to be cocaine. Again, I didn't know much about it but its weight, maybe half a pound, seemed a lot for one person's personal use, but I didn't really know. The cannabis was in a solid block measuring about three inches by two inches and an inch thick, once more rather a lot more than, in my ignorance, would be needed by one person.

Putting the pouches back in the rucksack, I reached for the passport. It was issued in Germany six months earlier, and because of the lack of immigration stamps, it had either been used little or only within the European Union. Flicking to the back page, Ingrid's image stared at me. Her Asian features were more obvious in the photograph. Unlike most passport photographs, it was quite flattering, but having only seen her face in the dark or by torchlight, I had no idea how accurate the photograph might be. Her hair looked shorter. Her date of birth was given as 14th April 1978, which meant she had turned twenty-two only a month earlier, and her height was 1.66 metres or because I thought pre-metric, about five feet four inches.

Except for the passport and letters, I put everything back in the rucksack. I did however check the labels on her spare clothes and all were bought somewhere in Europe, except for her underwear and socks which looked brand new and, from the labels, pretty expensive – I knew this to be the case because, by coincidence, Belinda had bought her underwear from the same chain.

The next decision I had to make was what should I do with what I had found, and what it told me about Ingrid? If anything, the contents of her rucksack gave me some idea as to why she might have decided my involvement was not to her advantage.

I had intended to spend that day wending my way slowly northwards, back towards Buxton. Arriving on Tuesday of the following week by public transport, I then proposed testing my newfound hiking skills on the Lake District.

Why should my recent experiences make any difference?

All I had to do was drop the rucksack off at the nearest police station, provide them with an explanation and my personal details should they wish to contact me again, and then resume what I had planned. On the other hand, I could leave the rucksack in the woods and move off as though nothing had happened.

But something had happened.

If Ingrid's explanation as to why she had been there was credible, there was a man in the area who regarded lone females as fair game. The police should know about that. They should also know about the drugs I had found.

Could any of it wait?

Would a few days make any real difference?

It was another nice day and the woods were now alive with early morning noises. There was still nobody about.

I took down the tent and packed it and my other belongings

away. Rejoining the track that ran through the woods by the river, I had a decision to make. If I turned right, I would head back towards Ashbourne, five miles away but if I turned left, it was thirteen miles to Buxton, my intended destination.

I wasn't normally indecisive but it took the toss of a coin to help me make up my mind.

After turning left I found Ingrid's body less than one hundred yards from where I had camped.

There had been no attempt made to hide her.

She lay like a rag doll a few yards inside the tree line, and on this occasion there wasn't any doubt in my mind … she was dead. Her eyes were open and staring, and there was dried blood at the corners of her mouth. She was still wearing her anorak but her jeans, underwear and boots were missing, as was one of her socks.

The bandage with which I'd dressed her wound was also missing. She looked a lot smaller than her five feet four inches, and very vulnerable, although her vulnerability would no longer affect her. Her stomach was bloody and there was a dark red patch on her anorak in the middle of her chest.

An image of Belinda lying dead in bed flashed into my mind, but her death had been a release from the pain: she had ultimately wanted to die so she could be at peace. Ingrid had been scared and, as far as I knew, did not want to die.

Somebody had tracked her down and murdered her, but why? The uncomfortable and restless night I had spent worrying about her was in vain; her young life had already ended.

I put her rucksack next to her body and undid the pocket to locate her mobile phone. Fortunately, the phone was switched on but the battery was low.

I pressed number nine three times and asked for the police.

"I need to report a murder," I informed the female voice at the other end of the line. The reception wasn't good and she asked me to repeat what I'd said. "I'm phoning to report a murder."

"I see, sir," the voice said in a casual tone. I would have expected the same reaction if I had been reporting a lost dog or a stolen car. "May I ask where you're phoning from?"

"I'm in the middle of some woods in Derbyshire and I've found the body of a dead girl."

"Right, sir. Can you give me your exact location, please, sir?"

"Would you like a grid reference or directions?" I asked, looking around. There was every possibility the murderer was still in the vicinity and he might even be watching me. At that time in the morning it was unlikely there would be any other hikers about.

"If you can give a grid reference, sir, that would be most useful." After fumbling with the map, I gave her the ordnance survey map number and then the six-figure grid reference. "Thank you, sir. Can I have your mobile number, your name and address, please?"

"I don't have the number, it's somebody else's phone."

"That's all right, sir, I can see the number on my screen. Your name and address, please?"

I gave her both before asking: "Can you tell me how long it'll take for someone to get here?"

"I can't at the moment, sir. Is there a nearby road where you can wait to give further directions when the police do arrive?"

"Look I'm in the middle of a wood and I'd prefer not to leave the girl. She might be dead but –"

"I understand, sir," she said, interrupting me. "There'll be an ambulance as well. How close can a vehicle get to where you are?"

"If it's four-wheel drive about one hundred yards., but a normal vehicle probably three-quarters of a mile."

"Thank you, sir. You are sure the girl is dead?"

"Certain."

"The police will be with you as soon as possible and they may ring you once they're in the area."

"All right."

It was a few minutes before eight. I checked up and down the track that ran north-south through the woods; there was nothing and nobody.

Sitting down, I rested my back against the trunk of a tree and waited. Ingrid's lifeless hand was inches from me and without thinking, I picked it up and held it in mine. Her hand was cold. The fingers – the webs between them a waxy-yellowish colour – were already showing signs of rigor mortis. I wanted to close her eyelids but knew that I must leave her as I had found her. I reached into my backpack and took out my towel, which was still damp from my morning swim, and draped it over her hips and thighs. She deserved some dignity even in death.

I heard a plane fly over, the sound of a distant tractor starting up and the constant rush of the river running towards the second weir that was less than a hundred yards away. I turned Ingrid's small hand over in mine and looked at her nails. They were manicured and quite long, and were painted with a colourless gloss.

Why?

If what she told me were true, there was no logical explanation as to why she was murdered. I weighed up the facts but they all seemed incongruous now.

When trying to escape from a would-be attacker she knocked herself out. The bloke I had spoken to down by the car park had seen the driver of a large black car throw her rucksack into the undergrowth and then drive off. That had been shortly before I entered the woods for the first time, but I neither saw nor heard a car … nor did I realise somebody was watching me.

When I got back to the tent after finding her rucksack, Ingrid had disappeared. Her rucksack contained what I assumed were cocaine and cannabis and finally she was murdered some time after I'd left her and only a matter of yards from where I was trying to sleep.

I heard and suspected nothing.

If I'd taken her with me when I went to look for her rucksack, she would still be alive. Unknowingly, I had left her to die.

I must have nodded off. The mobile phone rang, jolting me back to consciousness.

Ingrid's hand was still in mine.

"Mr Blythe?" a male voice asked.

"Yes."

"I'm Sergeant Cotton from the Ashbourne Police. You reported that you'd found a body."

"Yes."

"Are you still there?"

"What, with the body?"

"Yes."

"Yes," I said.

"Can you give directions?"

"Where are you?"

"In the car park down from the Izaak Walton Hotel."

It was the hotel I'd pretended to go towards when talking to the local man.

"Leave the car park to the north, cross the field and then follow the track to the left of the river and you can't miss me. It's about three-quarters of a mile."

"Thank you, sir. We'll be with you shortly."

I ended the call and looked down at Ingrid. Picking up her hand again, I lifted her fingers to my lips.

"Goodbye," I said. "I don't know who you really are and why somebody wanted to kill you, but nobody deserves to die the way you did."

Lowering her hand to the ground, I reluctantly let go of it.

Chapter Five

There were five of them and I heard their progress along the track long before I saw the lead police officer. Two were in civilian clothes and the other three were in uniform, one a sergeant. They saw me waiting by the tree and slowed down, almost as though I was immediately on the suspect list, which meant I needed approaching with caution.

I had thought about what I was going to say and I suppose I'd concluded that if I were the police I certainly wouldn't take any account I proffered at face value, which explained why I understood their scepticism.

All I could do was tell them the truth and let the evidence confirm my version of events. I believed in the British legal system and although the media constantly thrust injustices down our throats – and those found guilty when they weren't had my utmost sympathy and support – for the vast majority of the time I believed the system got it right.

"Mr Blythe?" the uniformed sergeant asked as he approached.

"Yes," I answered, holding out my hand. He took it without hesitation. The others had spotted Ingrid's body and were ignoring me.

"Sergeant Cotton, sir. We spoke on the phone." The sergeant took me by the arm and started to lead me further up the track. "Would you mind coming over here, sir?"

"Sergeant, I have spent the last hour plus only a few feet from that poor girl. Taking me away from her now isn't going to make the slightest bit of difference." I did not resist the pressure on my arm but I remained reluctant to hand Ingrid over to these strangers. Apart from her murderer, I was probably the last person she saw on this earth and I felt I owed her something.

"I know, sir," he replied, "but we don't want to disturb any evidence."

I looked over my shoulder and the older of the two detectives was bending down over Ingrid's body. Seeing him move the towel I had placed over her made me squirm. She was no longer a human being who warranted respect The other detective was looking around the immediate vicinity. The uniformed constables were already beginning to mark off the area. They each had rolls of tape and various other bits and pieces, obviously believing that I really had found a body and that I wasn't some crank who enjoyed wasting police time.

"Now, sir," the sergeant said, moving in front of me, "can you tell me how you came across the victim?"

I gave him a digest of the previous sixteen hours and he listened without interrupting. More fluorescent jackets appeared on the scene after about five minutes. They were paramedics who went straight down towards Ingrid's body. An older man in civilian clothes carrying what could only have been a doctor's bag accompanied them.

"You were saying?" the sergeant asked, regaining my attention.

"Sorry. That's when I phoned for the police."

"I see, sir." The older of the two detectives came up the slope towards us. "This is Detective Sergeant Matthews, Mr Blythe." Although he was older, he couldn't have been more than thirty and he was well dressed in a suit, white shirt and a floral tie. He had donned a pair of rubber boots. "Mr Blythe, Brian, he reported the incident."

DS Matthews offered me his hand before smiling laconically. "Mr Blythe." He looked back over his shoulder. "So, you found her, did you?"

"Yes." The look in DS Matthews' eyes suggested it would be wise if I restricted what I said to answering his questions, and not volunteer anything further until asked.

"Would you mind repeating what you told me, Mr Blythe?" suggested Sergeant Cotton.

When I had finished, DS Matthews scrutinised the notes he had taken and then, pointing his pen at me, he asked, "You said you found her the first time at about six-thirty yesterday evening?"

"Yes."

"And where precisely was she?"

I pointed back down the track towards the car park. "About one and fifty hundred yards further along the track."

"And she told you she'd been trying to escape from some would-be attacker?" His eyes never left me when he spoke. It was obvious what conclusions he had already drawn. I had told him exactly what had happened but I couldn't offer any proof.

"Yes."

"Why didn't you report the incident straight away?"

"I was going to, but when I discovered she was still alive, my priority was to do what I could for her and leaving her alone didn't, at the time, seem the right thing to do."

"I see," DS Matthews said, exchanging a look with Sergeant Cotton.

The older man who had accompanied the paramedics down to Ingrid's body approached us. He too was wearing a suit, but he had an old-fashioned trilby-hat on his head framing a face that communicated years of experience but little hardship. He nodded at me and then looked at DS Matthews.

"Been dead approximately twelve hours, single stab wound, probably a narrow-bladed knife between her breasts and into the heart. I would estimate she took only a short while to die. Abdominal lacerations superficial by comparison, probability that she was sexually assaulted but, as usual, I'll be able to tell you more once I can get to work on her. She was a pretty girl and young too, such a waste."

His final words, directed towards me, made me aware the police officers were watching me. The pathologist, if that's what he was, nodded at me again, and without another word headed off back along the track towards the car park.

"I'll have to ask you to come to the station and make a statement, Mr Blythe," DS Matthews told me.

"I understand."

"As you are on foot I'm sure Sergeant Cotton will give you a lift." Then, with a wave of his hand, he turned and started down the slope. He stopped when he was a few yards away. "Oh, Mr Blythe, the mobile phone you used to call us, you said it wasn't yours. Do you still have it?"

I felt in my anorak pocket. "Yes, I'm sorry," I said handing the phone to him as he came back to me. "And the towel you found on the body, that's mine."

"We'll hang on to that if you don't mind," he said.

"No problem."

"There's nothing else?"

"No, not that I can think of," I told him.

I walked out of Ashbourne Police Station six hours later. A Detective Inspector Rowlands and DS Matthews had interviewed me and to say that I received a grilling would be an understatement. Initially it was simply a repeat of what I'd already told Matthews and Cotton but then I suddenly remembered that I still had Ingrid's passport and her letters in my anorak pocket. I had leafed through the passport but hadn't read the letters therefore I had no idea what they contained, but for some reason the address on the envelopes had ingrained itself on my mind. On realising my oversight, I handed the passport and letters over and the detectives' approach changed.

Their looks implied that I had deliberately withheld critical evidence, they then backtracked over everything and their tone became hostile rather than receptive.

Moreover, there were the drugs, or what I had assumed were cocaine and cannabis. Even though I explained how I had found the drugs in Ingrid's rucksack – as the police did later – I had no proof that the drugs weren't mine in the first place.

Rowlands suggested quite forcibly and often, that after calling the police I didn't want to be found in possession, so I had put the drugs in the rucksack to steer them away from the truth.

Not believing the way the interview was going, it appeared as though Rowlands, in particular, wanted to pin something on me, no matter how tenuous. Fortunately, as I had no proof that I hadn't put the drugs in Ingrid's rucksack, the police had no proof that I had. My fingerprints would be on the wrappings because I admitted I had handled them, but…

It was stalemate, but again fortunately and for the time being the law of the land was on my side.

I didn't know the rules that had to be applied to police interviews, but I'd seen sufficient pseudo-police dramas on television to know that I had to be offered a solicitor if they intended arresting me. There was no such offer, leading me to assume that, although their attitude changed, they had no evidence to support any charge they might try to bring against me.

A swab was taken from the inside of my mouth but they didn't actually accuse me of anything. However, they left me in little doubt as they brought the interview to a close that I should not leave the country.

On leaving the police station, my accompanying smile was tinged with irony. Maybe I had been lucky, if I had been the police and was presented with the 'facts' perhaps I would have been equally suspicious.

I was back where I started twenty-four hours earlier.

The weather, which had become overcast and drizzly, mirrored the way I felt – downright miserable.

When leaving Ashbourne the previous day, I was in high spirits, spurred on by my recent decisions I was looking forward to the northerly leg of my journey back to Buxton.

Now, at four o'clock in the afternoon, with the rain spattering on my face, the desire to spend another night in a cramped tent in a wet wood deserted me.

My statement to the police contained my home address and telephone number but I explained to Rowlands that it was unlikely I would be there for at least another two weeks. No, I wasn't going abroad but surely I could continue my 'holiday'. He tried to suggest that I couldn't but withdrew his objection when I asked for a justification. Understanding his concern, I did offer to phone him every couple of days to see if there was any further 'assistance' I could give with their enquiries.

That seemed to appease him.

I found a back-street hotel that turned out to be better than its position or its external décor suggested. After eating an early and wholesome, if not overly imaginative dinner, I bought a bottle of whisky from behind the bar and retired to my room. There was nothing on the television worth watching but I watched it anyway. It was a strange feeling … I didn't want company of any sort, but I didn't want to be alone with my thoughts either.

Lying on the bed with a tumbler of whisky within easy reach, I wished that I could relive the moments after first finding Ingrid – she would have been safe now, not lying in some refrigeration unit in the local morgue.

It was all so wrong, so very wrong and only added to the melancholy that had brought me to the area in the first place.

In my travels I had seen my share of death, squalor and

sickness but I had also had the privilege to see and recognise the incredible determination that some people show under the most gruelling of circumstances. I had, rather hypocritically, worked alongside people who were the subjects of oppressive governments that squandered millions of pounds on projects that would not benefit the vast majority, governments that used force to suppress people who were actually their greatest asset, and governments that ignored corruption because to do otherwise would sever their own lifelines.

I had seen, but fortunately not that frequently, corpses rotting by the roadside, their deaths caused by whatever the imagination conjured up. However, nothing I saw was personal. Belinda's passing was extremely personal, and now Ingrid's murder, was affecting me in the same way. I could do nothing about the horrific scenes I had witnessed but I could have done something about saving this young girl's life.

The more I thought about it the more whisky I drank, and the more I drank the more bizarre my thoughts became. I had come to Derbyshire to mourn the loss of a woman who had meant more to me than life itself: a woman for whom I would have died if it had meant she could have lived. Now I found myself grieving for a complete stranger: a stranger who entered my life in the most unusual – and dramatic – of circumstances, and a matter of hours later had left in the most ghastly of ways.

Half a bottle of whisky told me that I was responsible and that I really should have behaved in a totally different way. I may not have thrust the blade of the knife into Ingrid's heart, but I was now, in my addled mind, an accessory.

I retained sufficient self-control to know that my melancholy was alcohol induced. Not having touched a drop of alcohol for a week hadn't helped. All too often I decided, alcohol makes people say and do things that reveal their inner psyche – the real person behind the veneer we think we want others to see. Seeing a young girl murdered and mutilated, a girl with whom I had been speaking only hours earlier, a girl who had half-cooked me a meal before being dragged to her death, was too much.

She hadn't been a photograph in a paper, an unknown body lying by the road, she had been a real person and I felt guilty.

When the bus I was on passed the turning for the village of Tissington, I looked left towards Dove Dale but I could only see the tops of the trees in the valley. I had decided to leave the area and use public transport to get me back to Buxton before retracing my steps back to Medbourne and home.

The need for escapism had left me.

Having woken up that morning with a thumping headache and the expected hangover hadn't surprised me. I didn't need to look at the half empty bottle of whisky to find out why I felt awful.

Neither the weather nor my mood had improved and returning home seemed the only option that might introduce a semblance of normality back into my life. I called in to the police station and left a message for DS Matthews – he was out – which explained that there had been a change of plan and I would be contactable at the address I'd given him after all.

I was no longer sure how the police really felt about me.

The DNA from the swab they had taken would prove that if Ingrid had been raped I wasn't the man they were looking for, but I was sure I was still high up on their suspect list, if they had a list. Maybe I was the only one they suspected, but thus far they had no proof and nor, if my faith in the legal processes was to be substantiated, would they ever find any.

I didn't speak to anybody during my journey home.

The effects of my over-indulgence with the whisky bottle took a long while to wear off and my need for sleep was impossible due to grotesque images of Belinda, rather than Ingrid, lying dead and mutilated in Dove Dale.

The taxi driver from the station in Market Harborough tried to strike up a conversation but he was astute enough to appreciate that I wasn't in the mood. To make up for my rudeness I gave him an unnecessarily large tip when he dropped me off – he went away happy.

The sun was shining and there was a light breeze coming across the fields. I began to open the gate but hesitated as I remembered Belinda watching me put it in place. I had bought a five-bar gate from a local farmer when he had decided to make one field out of two. Although I was considered a leading expert on the design and construction of dams, Belinda's opinion – and I suppose mine also if I were being truthful – of my ability to complete simple DIY tasks was unenthusiastic to say the least. She had watched me from the house and then used the excuse of bringing me a mug of tea to assess, surreptitiously, my progress. We were both surprised when the gate had stayed in place, and even more surprised when it survived the rigours of gales, heavy rain and the odd minor collision with visiting cars.

That was three years ago and it was still standing, although it did need a damn good oiling.

The gravel crunched under my feet as I walked up the driveway. The lawn was in need of a mow but it would have to wait. The front flowerbeds, although colourful, required weeding – I didn't look too closely.

Charles and Elizabeth, Belinda's parents, had said they would check on the house while I was away but the mail on the floor inside the front door suggested they had yet to make their first visit. They, quite naturally, took their only daughter's death extremely badly – every parent wants to die before their offspring – but added to the pain was the fact that Belinda had idolised them and her parents reciprocated her feelings in every way.

In fact, they were so close that on occasions I felt a pang of envy, quickly followed by guilt. I had undergone a rigid but subtle vetting process before they accepted that Belinda and I were right for each other. Although I felt resentment at first I eventually came to understand their motives, even more so after the twins, and especially Isabelle, were born.

Before I embarked on my attempt at escapism, I met up with Charles in a local pub and he explained that they both needed time, time not to forget but to recover. Elizabeth had found it difficult to be in the house knowing that Belinda wasn't there. On the two occasions they had visited since Belinda died, Elizabeth wandered from room to room with tears in her eyes – I had done the same but only in the privacy of my own company. The value of the daughter, mother and wife we had lost was incalculable.

Shaking myself out of my reverie, I opened the front door.

The phone was bleeping to tell me there were some messages but I ignored it, taking the mail and local papers into the kitchen. Most of the letters were circulars that went straight into the bin unopened except for the ones addressed to Belinda. Even seeing her name on an impersonal piece of paper gave me something to hang onto. There were the usual bills and a credit card statement.

After making a mug of black coffee – there was no milk in the fridge and I hadn't thought of buying any – I toured the house, going into every room, opening the curtains and subconsciously making sure nothing had been disturbed. I would ring Charles to tell him I was home. I didn't want them driving past and wondering why the curtains were no longer drawn closed.

I talked to Belinda as I went from room to room, explaining how I felt. Her personality was there on every wall, in every carpet, in every cushion cover, in every pattern, in everything. Although she had included me in the decision making process and listened attentively to the suggestions I made, I knew I was useless at such things.

The house was *her* and therefore it was *us*.

We bought the house five years ago – was it really five years? – for a good price as it was in dire need of renovation. We kept its original name, Blue-Ridge, although David in particular thought it was naff – his word! Evidently, its name had changed in 1890 when one of the sons of the then owners moved to Virginia. We had a family discussion and finally decided to leave it as it was for the time being.

Built in the early 1800s, the only original features were the outer, and some of the inner, supporting walls, the inglenook fireplace in the living room, and the outhouses. We spent thousands on rewiring, new floorboards, central heating and decorating. The value of the house almost tripled but that was irrelevant. It stood in about half an acre, most of which was taken up by a reasonably productive orchard. From the front bedroom windows, we could see the rest of the village, but Blue-Ridge's isolation had also meant extra thousands being spent on the security system.

It was now a lovely house but its attractiveness, as with its market value, was worth nothing without the person who had laboured to make it that way.

The twins loved it.

Looking out of David's bedroom window, I could see him and Isabelle playing in the garden with some of their many friends from the village, and others they often brought home from school during exeat weekends and half terms. After Belinda died and the day before they went back to school, Isabelle had stood with me at the same window, her arm round my waist and mine round her shoulders, and let her heart out.

"You'll never sell Blue-Ridge, will you, Daddy?" she implored.

"One day I may have to," I replied, tightening my grip on her shoulder, knowing that it wasn't the answer either of us wanted. At thirteen, there were times when she could have the perspective of a twenty-year old: at other times she was still a little girl.

"You can't," she said quietly. "This house is mummy and if you sell it you'll sell all the memories that go with it." She looked up at me and there were tears in her eyes.

I tried to smile. "Don't worry, Bella. If the need ever arises I'll have it redecorated before selling it and then those memories will stay as ours."

I didn't want to make promises I couldn't keep but inwardly I knew that it would take a herd of wild horses to drag me away.

She frowned as tears rolled down her cheeks. "What do you mean?"

"Mummy wouldn't have wanted this house to become a mausoleum. She would want us to move on with our lives."

This time her eyes opened wide with shock. "You're not going to remarry are you?"

I managed a real smile and, shaking my head, I turned my daughter round until she was facing me. "Bella, your mother and I were devoted to each other and although I can't promise that there will never be another woman in my life, she will never replace what we had. Your mummy will always be your mummy. Wherever any of us might be, and whoever we might be with, in the future, she will always be with us."

Reaching up she placed her hands on either side of my face. "I understand, Daddy," she said but I hoped she didn't.

In the main bedroom, I lingered at the end of the bed as I pictured us together; together until the end. Her clothes were still in the wardrobes, her bottles and potions still on the dressing table with her photographs. This room, the whole house, told me that she was with me, alive in my mind and my heart: still alive in whatever I looked at.

Was I wrong to tell Isabelle that mummy wouldn't have wanted the house to become a mausoleum? Belinda had no control over what the house became.

Only I could do something about that.

From our bedroom window, the village had become less stark in appearance. The spring, and now early summer, had revitalised its winter isolation and the trees had become more rounded, green with energy and beauty. The trees also hid quite a lot of what was evident during the winter but the church still dominated the landscape, its spire pointing towards where Belinda was now at peace.

It seemed only yesterday when Belinda and I had stood by the same window when we had been viewing the house and, without saying a word, knew it was for us. Smoke was rising from a few of the cottage chimneys in the valley, a cockerel crowed and the church bell struck eleven o'clock – it was idyllic, as we had thought our lives were.

Now I looked down towards the village on my own. A young couple, maybe in their thirties, were walking hand in hand down the lane. They stopped at the gate to Blue-Ridge where they paused for a few seconds looking at the house before moving on. I saw the woman look back before making some comment to the man, and then they carried on with their afternoon stroll in the welcome sun.

I hadn't recognised them.

There wasn't a sound other than the grandfather clock ticking in the hall and the bleeping of the answer-machine, the latter snapping me out of my musing and bringing me back to the present.

Suddenly, an image of Ingrid lying dead and mutilated in

Dove Dale flashed through my mind. It was something I would never forget, maybe something I would never want to forget.

In the hall, I picked up the backpack I had dropped by the front door and took it into the utility room. After emptying it and putting the washing straight into the machine, I hung it in the cupboard wondering if it would ever have any further use. I had bought it, along with everything else, specifically for my short-lived escape. Taking my walking boots off, I realised that Belinda would have disapproved of my tramping round the house in them and, as for going upstairs wearing anything but socks or slippers on my feet, that would have guaranteed verbal if not physical abuse.

There were three messages on the answer-phone.

One was unintelligible, another was from my solicitor in Market Harborough asking me to pop in the next time I was in town to discuss the progress of probate on Belinda's will, and the third was from Peter Schuter III. Peter was my boss in America, and based in Denver, Colorado. He had accepted my resignation with great reluctance, arguing that I was far too young and talented to be giving up such a satisfying and lucrative career. I had thanked him for his unwarranted compliments but I had made up my mind.

I think if my main reason hadn't been losing Belinda he would have persisted, but he hadn't. Rather presumptuously, he did advise me that he would approach the Board with a recommendation that I should receive a significant golden handshake. His call was to tell me the Board had agreed his recommendation, but on one condition, and would I contact him about it when I got back from my trekking?

I checked my watch.

It was four o'clock and although still the morning in Denver I decided to leave it until the following day.

What I didn't know as I pressed the button on the answer-machine to delete the messages, was that the phone call I would make the next day was only going to add to the frightening episode in my new life that had started with the grim discovery in Dove Dale.

Chapter Six

The rectangular fields and long straight roads that made up the countryside on the approach to *Düsseldorf Flughafen* in Germany were visible at the time the aircraft started its descent

It was a clear day and the flight from Birmingham was short and uneventful. The aircraft was flying parallel to what I knew to be the *Düsseldorf* to *Roermond* autobahn, and at after five o'clock on a Tuesday, the roads were busy with commuters speeding home after a day's work.

The aircraft wasn't full by any means and I had enjoyed a reasonably comfortable flight. Being one of only two passengers in business class, the flight attendant – she told us her name was Mandy – was able to look after her charges extremely well and without being obtrusive.

Peter Schuter III hadn't said in so many words that my golden handshake was dependent on my attendance at this year's annual conference, but he implied that it could be beneficial. He wanted me to share my experiences from a project in Africa I had been involved with since the previous year's get-together. The project had been particularly difficult due to the location of the prospective dam and the over deposition of coarse materials from the surrounding hills could have caused problems.

I had reluctantly agreed.

Before leaving England, I had another session with DS Matthews, at his request. Informing him that I needed to go abroad for a conference seemed to generate unnecessary activity but I had reached the stage where I found it amusing rather than an inconvenience. DS Matthews came down to Market Harborough to see me and we spent a couple of hours together going over my version of events yet again. I got the distinct impression that either they didn't have any other leads or those they did have hadn't taken them anywhere and I remained, for perhaps the wrong reasons, on their suspect list.

Nothing Matthews said suggested that they had cause to speak to me again other than if they continued clutching at straws. With no evidence to support the alternative recommendation, he had to accept the fact that I was going to Germany and that I would get back in touch on my return. He did advise me that the Coroner's Inquest wouldn't sit for at least another two to three weeks but whenever it did sit I would, quite naturally, be required to attend as the main witness.

I spent the remainder of the two weeks before setting off for Germany sorting out the house and garden. I called in to see Charles and Elizabeth a couple of times and told them about my experiences in Derbyshire. After the mandatory two days of coverage, the media's interest in Ingrid's brutal murder waned, as was to be expected. My name, much to my relief, was kept out of all the papers and away from the press.

Charles was circumspect and Elizabeth was distraught.

After the worry and anguish brought on by Belinda's death, what had I done to deserve being thrown straight into a murder enquiry? Elizabeth's logic sometimes warranted time for reflection but on this occasion, I agreed with her and left it at that.

The weekend before I flew to Germany was an exeat weekend and we'd already planned that I should go down to the children's school and take them into London for a treat.

We did exactly that.

The cultural aspects of the weekend were interspersed with far too much junk food but we had a thoroughly enjoyable time walking, visiting museums and going to the cinema. A chorus of negativity greeted the suggestion of the theatre, so I reluctantly went and watched the new Star Wars movie. I didn't mention the murder to them. I saw little point. They may have read about it in the papers and, if they had raised the coincidence of my being in the same area, I was prepared to tell a little white lie to steer them away from the truth. It was the second time I had seen them back at school since their mother's death. I think we found it easier but there were still long silences during which it didn't need a mind reader to know what each of us was thinking.

I took every opportunity to look at them both. At thirteen, or nearer fourteen as David constantly reminded me, they were still alike and yet different. Similar to many others of her age, Isabelle was thirteen, going on seventeen or eighteen, or even twenty as I implied earlier.

Belinda and I hadn't allowed her to grow up too quickly and fortunately she didn't seem to resent our control. We wanted her to enjoy her childhood and again, fortunately, many of the other parents of daughters of a similar age in the village seemed to have the same attitude towards their offspring. Of course there were parents whose daughters were allowed to wear make-up, nail varnish and 'unsuitable' clothes, but they were in the minority.

The headmistress of the village school merely shrugged when we discussed the matter at a social in the village hall. "Thank God that's all it is," she had commented. "In this day and age I'm lucky I'm not being sued for looking at someone's little darling the wrong way!"

Since being at boarding school, Isabelle hadn't really changed, but she had developed. She was an attractive girl and she was going to break many hearts. She dressed sensibly – her mother's influence – but she was now growing her nails rather than biting them. She had begun to wear make-up but, again, she didn't overdo it. However, even her sensible clothes couldn't disguise the young, maturing figure underneath. I saw her receive a number of admiring glances from young men we passed, and some who weren't that young.

Isabelle couldn't hide the fact that she noticed the looks she was getting. She and Belinda had been very close. Sometimes, but not that often, my opinion was sought during their discussions but mostly I was told they were indulging in 'girls'' talk and therefore not only was it inappropriate for me to listen but also my views would be equally unacceptable.

It worried me that Isabelle no longer had Belinda to confide in and to help her through the more difficult teenage years. I hoped that she would eventually turn to me but it was too early. She was doing well academically in most subjects although she particularly liked music. According to Anthea Brookfield, her music teacher, Isabelle had taken to the piano like a duck to water and was showing exceptional promise for the future.

David, on the other hand, was already two to three years behind Isabelle in the maturity stakes. He was into sport and played all ball games well. He was a fanatical Manchester United supporter and as the school had a couple of teachers who were also supporters, every now and again spare tickets for a home game appeared out of the blue, resulting in David and some other boys going to Old Trafford.

In the classroom David gave me the impression that he attended because he had to, but he could equally well do without the boring bits. His achievements didn't exactly bear out his reluctance, but he put it down to luck.

Belinda and I had been simply relieved.

David was a couple of inches taller than Isabelle but shared her blonde hair and blue eyes. All the sport he played meant that he also weighed a good three stone heavier than she did, and I suppose he looked older than his years.

However, he was still at the stage where girls were to be tolerated. They giggled a lot and were generally boring, talking about things that didn't interest him or his friends in the slightest. I smiled when he related stories from school; Isabelle simply put out her tongue.

While roaming around London, we talked about my experiences in Derbyshire and I hated myself for lying to them when I explained I had cut short my expedition because I came to the conclusion pretty quickly that I wasn't really the camping type.

They didn't ask any searching questions.

Of course, I was proud of the twins: proud of what they were achieving and proud of the way they were coping with the loss of their mother. Isabelle was more understanding of my feelings. David tried to hide his feelings and I suppose he expected me to hide mine as well.

We were all clingy during our short trip to London. Whenever we walked along the crowded pavements, I had one on either side, their arms round my waist and mine round their shoulders, and created the sort of pedestrian obstruction we would normally have complained about. We had fun and it was with great reluctance that I took them back to school on the Sunday, yet again unprepared to hand them over to their proxy family.

After leaving the main building and as I was walking back towards the car, I heard the crunch of somebody coming across the gravel behind me.

It was Isabelle.

She came up to me, flung her arms round my neck, and rested her cheek against my chest.

"You're okay, Daddy, aren't you?" she asked, looking up at me, her pretty face covered with concern.

"Of course I am," I replied, kissing her forehead.

"But we've got the school and our friends. You haven't got anyone now." The frown remained on her face.

I smiled. "I've got the golf club and I'm not exactly shutting myself off from the world."

"But your job, you've given that up. What will you do?"

"You choose your moments, don't you?" I admonished her jokingly. We were standing next to my car and I could see across to the main entrance where parents were dropping off their children. "I'm not exactly on my last legs, you know. I'm still under forty ..."

"Just."

"All right just, but ... oh, I don't know, Bella, I'll look for a job locally and take whatever might be on offer. It'll all sort itself out, don't you worry."

She took hold of my hands. "Daddy, can you afford for David and me to stay at St Edward's? I didn't want to ask in front of David. You know he'd get the wrong end of the stick."

Isabelle's question surprised me because I had deliberately kept away from the subject of money as I didn't want either of them to even think they were a burden. Of course, I would have preferred to have them at home which would allow them to travel daily to the school in Market Harborough now that my globetrotting was over, but they really did seem to be happy at St Edward's. David was getting all the sport he wanted and Isabelle thrived in the boarding school environment. They wanted to stay and it would have been cruel of me to take them away. I had no other reason. We were well off and Belinda and I had taken out various insurance policies – Belinda's life policy alone covered school fees and, if all went well, the expense of two university places as well.

I squeezed Isabelle's cheek and smiled. "Yes, I can afford it, so don't you worry about that. If I fall on hard times, you'll be the first to know."

Isabelle, a little reluctantly, returned my smile. "You're sure?"

"I'm sure."

"And you won't be lonely?"

"I've told you, I fly to Germany on Tuesday and then, when I get back, I intend playing a lot of golf after which I might go down to the job centre."

"The job centre?" She looked quite shocked.

"I'm joking, but you never know, they might have what I want."

"Bella!" Somebody called and Isabelle looked over her shoulder.

"Coming!" she shouted to another girl I couldn't see. "Must go, Daddy." She reached up and kissed me on the cheek. "Take care of yourself."

"You too, Bella, and thank you for your concern."

I watched her run back towards the main entrance and stood by the car for a few seconds thinking about what she had said.

Over the preceding few days, I found the frequency with which I thought about Ingrid Mesterom becoming less and less. Belinda was constantly there, but I was learning to cope with the trauma of discovering a murder and the brutal images that went with it.

Seeing Isabelle disappear through the doors into the school and for some inexplicable reason, a perfect image of Ingrid's mutilated body forced its way into my mind, and I shuddered.

The clunk of the wheels lowering brought me back to the present and I looked out at the ground rushing past.

The flight attendants were already in their seats for landing and as I absentmindedly switched my gaze towards them over the seat in front of me, I thought how alike one of them was to Belinda: she sensed me looking at her, made eye contact and smiled. It was a professional smile and one that she would have offered to anybody who she thought was uneasy about the landing. I smiled in return and perhaps let my eyes rest on her a little too long.

Belinda would have been about four or five years older but the more I looked at the flight attendant the more the likeness was there. Her shoulder length blonde hair tied back in a ponytail in the same was Belinda used to wear hers when she was being practical. An oval face, with high cheekbones and large blue eyes, tapered to what I called, with Belinda, a cheeky chin. Her smile revealed the dimples ... the likeness really was uncanny. She hadn't been in business class during the flight which meant I hadn't noticed her before. Was I looking for something that really wasn't there? She held my eyes for a few seconds longer before she turned away to say something to the other flight attendant sitting next to her.

There was bump as the aircraft touched down, followed by the roar of the engines going into reverse. On the few occasions I had flown into *Düsseldorf*, I never regarded it as an attractive airport but then again, what constituted an attractive airport? The last time I flew to Germany was a couple of weeks after the awful fire in 1995 that cost an awful lot of lives. The airport authorities had reacted with typical German efficiency and erected alternative arrival and departure areas that appeared to operate as effectively as their purpose-built predecessors. The investigation into the cause of the fire suggested a welder doing some work in the roof cavity above the arrivals area, had looked away at the wrong time.

Poisonous fumes swept among the unsuspecting crowds waiting for passengers to emerge. The lucky ones reacted quickly, unlike the Japanese tourist who decided it was the time to take photographs of the drama unfolding in front of him.

He paid with his life.

When I left the aircraft, I nodded towards the female flight attendant on whom my eyes had lingered perhaps a little too long. I saw her name was Wendy. She held my gaze again and this time her smile seemed genuine rather than professional. She wished me a safe onward journey and then switched her attention to whoever was behind me.

Once in the gangway, I smiled as I imagined Belinda wagging her finger at me. When we were out, she used to point to females she thought were more than slightly attractive and wait for my reaction with a knowing expression on her face. She would then ask me what I found most attractive about the female she had pointed out. Her explanation for her behaviour was that if I noticed something she could replicate – a hairstyle or clothing maybe – then she would. I always thought she was testing me.

I collected the hire-car I had pre-booked and drove the forty miles south on the autobahn to *Bonn*. The Hilton Hotel overlooking the *Kennedybrücke* and the Rhine was the chosen location for the conference this year. I was fortunate that my room had a small balcony from which there was a splendid view of the river.

There was a Reception in one of the anterooms before the formal dinner and, as I stood on the balcony sipping a gin and tonic and watching the river traffic, for the first time I wished I could give both events a miss. The annual conference brought together the same main and sub-contractors every year, regardless of its location and we shared the experiences, problems and solutions that had come out of the preceding twelve months.

According to the programme I was handed on arrival, my sixty-minute session was programmed for the second and final day.

Surprisingly, I actually enjoyed the two days more than in previous years mainly because I knew at the end of the conference I was a free agent. None of the problems discussed were mine any more, and whereas previously I would leave with more work than when I arrived, it was good to know on this occasion it all belonged to somebody else.

It wasn't that I hadn't enjoyed my job because I had, but my enthusiasm for it had died with Belinda. I had made a few good friends and many acquaintances over the years, and I would be remaining in touch with a few of them.

My session seemed to go well. It generated an amazing number of questions, which suggested that maybe I hadn't put enough detail into my brief. I overran my time allowance by at least thirty minutes. Peter Schuter III said some nice words at the end of my presentation, accolades he then repeated during the final dinner. There was much handshaking, back slapping and promises of staying in touch. I was surprised as I drove away from the hotel on the Friday morning that I felt relieved to be free from the formality of such conferences. My conscience suggested there ought to be a smidgen of regret as well, but there was not.

I had hired the car, an Audi A3, for a full week, having already planned to see a bit more of Germany before returning to England. With this in mind I found myself heading south on the autobahn towards Koblenz without knowing what my destinations might be.

I crossed over the Trier to Weisbaden autobahn and decided to continue south towards Strasburg, letting the time of day determine my ultimate destination. Approaching the viaduct over the River Mosel, I changed my mind and took the next exit. Joining Route 49, which ran southwest along the left bank of the river, I asked myself why I had altered direction.

It was almost as though some unseen force was in control.

It was a gorgeous day. The sunshine reflecting off the water and the lack of traffic made me feel tranquil. I slowed down a little to enjoy the moment.

My thoughts were wandering again.

I had already put the conference behind me, relieved that it was all over. Belinda, as always, was either at the forefront of my mind or not far away from it. We had been to Germany together but not to the area I was now driving through. When the twins were young, Elizabeth and Charles kindly took them off our hands for a fortnight, which gave Belinda and me time to take a break together. We flew to Munich and then toured Bavaria before dropping down through Austria to the Italian lakes.

Belinda, although the most tolerant of people, couldn't for whatever reason stand the Germans. She found them arrogant in the extreme and her love for the countryside, and in particular the Bavarian Alps, failed to increase her enthusiasm sufficiently to want to return. Afterwards we settled on France or Spain, the former ironically generating similar feelings in me towards the French to those Belinda had for the Germans.

Following the road that ran parallel to and close to the river, I wished that she could have been with me. Exploring and sharing new places together had become a pastime for us and we hadn't let the twins reduce the adventures we had.

Now I was on my own but the past was still with me.

I described everything of any interest to Belinda, even pausing in my descriptions and pretending to hear her comments. I told her about the almost claustrophobic steep hills erupting towards the sky on either side of the narrow and fast flowing river, the terraced vineyards hanging on precariously as they flourished in the sunshine, and the strange looking contraptions used to access the grapes. Anybody watching might have thought that I wasn't alone: although I suppose I wasn't and never would be.

South of a village called Alken, I crossed over the river and saw a road-sign to a place called Cochem. I slowed the car and pulled into a lay-by. I sat and stared at the road ahead, not aware of the other vehicles drifting past in either direction.

Cochem? Why did I recognise that name?

Then it dawned on me.

Of course, the envelope I looked at after taking it out of Ingrid's rucksack.

Is that why I had subconsciously chosen the Mosel?

Was it really that simple and coincidental?

Ingrid.

The address I had seen on the envelopes that I'd eventually handed over to the police, was an address in Cochem, and now I was only a few miles away from it.

I didn't know whether I wanted to proceed: there was something ominous about what might lie in store. My life with Belinda and the brief but horrendous experience I had with Ingrid Mesterom, we now in the past. Ingrid was dead. I would have to relive my experiences when I returned to the UK but there was certainly no need to dwell on what had happened when I was supposed to be relaxing.

Why would I want to go to Cochem?

I got out of the car, crossed the road and walked down to the river's edge. I hadn't realised the strength of the current but now I was close to the water I could see how strong it really was. A couple of barges going upriver were battling against the flow whereas another barge coming in the opposite direction seemed to be skimming across the surface. Each barge was loaded to the gunnels with what looked like aggregate, which made me wonder why someone hadn't got their act together and reduced the river traffic by at least two barges. The barges were also low in the water but the crews appeared to be unaware that, in my opinion, their charges were on the point of sinking.

A couple of wagtails were flitting around the water's edge a few yards away, the sun was shining and there was a light fresh breeze coming off the water. Other than the infrequent noise of the traffic behind me up on the road, the rush of the river and the chugging of the barges, there wasn't a sound to spoil the tranquillity.

I asked myself why was I considering wrecking it all?

Why was I contemplating going to Cochem and possibly meeting with complete strangers just because I had the unfortunate experience of seeing someone they might have known, lying dead in an English wood?

However, there was more to it than that.

I had not only seen Ingrid when she was alive, I had also spoken to her. I had cared for her while she was unconscious, bathed her wound and bandaged it, and almost shared a meal.

I had then deserted her,

My neglect leading ultimately to her death.

Maybe my conscience was driving me forward. The police had listened to what I had to say but they were detached; they knew less about Ingrid than I did. At least I had seen her when she was alive. I had not had the opportunity to talk to anybody who could empathise with me about my experiences.

I hadn't told Elizabeth and Charles everything. I restricted the truth to the morning when I found the body. I didn't mention what had happened the previous evening.

A jet crossing the clear blue sky tried to disturb the tranquillity. I shaded my eyes with my hand and watched its slow vapour-trailed progress as I attempted to guess its destination. Regardless of where the aircraft might have been going, at that particular moment I rather wished I was on it.

I knew my heart was going to overrule my head

I also knew that my intended actions were misguided, but that didn't seem to make any difference.

Back in the woods of Dove Dale, and for no obvious reason other than it was my destiny, I'd memorised the address on Ingrid's letters. My thoughts at the time had bordered on being irrational but unbeknown to me, or anybody else, I had mounted the first step leading to tragedy.

By willing myself to go to the address I'd remembered, I was merely closing the gap to the heartbreaks that awaited me.

Therefore I only had myself to blame for what might happen.

Chapter Seven

From the moment I drove into Cochem it was obvious that it was a tourist trap.

Pedestrians packed the pavements and the traffic congestion brought almost everything else to a halt. Taking a turning to the right away from the river and the traffic, towards the railway station, I followed the flow and finished up re-crossing the river courtesy of the *Alte Moselbrücke*.

The cars on the bridge came to a halt, and as we sat nose-to-tail I noticed a hotel on the opposite side of the river and a couple of buildings down on the right. I didn't think I had any hope of getting a room, but more by luck than judgement I found my way to the back of the hotel where there was a small car park.

In my rather poor German I asked the receptionist whether there was a double room available – Belinda couldn't be with me in a single room – and, to my surprise, the receptionist said there was.

"Ant how many nights vill you being staying, sir?" she asked, her heavily accented English preferable to my attempts at her language.

I had always tried to learn enough of any language to get by on my travels. Like many others, my fluency improved when I had a few drinks. I found that the French tended to make you suffer and deliberately spoke more quickly to confuse matters, whereas the Germans, unless you spoke their language effortlessly, preferred to test their English. Their poor English was better than a foreigner's poor German – maybe Belinda had been right about German arrogance, at least the French were honest.

"*Ich denke, vielleicht zwei nachten,*" I replied trying to be clever and then I added, "*minimum.*"

Why I thought I'd be in Cochem for two nights let alone more than two nights, I didn't know.

"Thank you," the receptionist acknowledged looking up and handing me a card to fill in. "May I see your passport?" she asked, smiling, sticking to her choice of language.

"*Natürlich,*" I said, handing over my EEC passport.

She gave me a searching look before scanning various pages of my passport in confirmation of my identity.

In her mid-thirties, the receptionist wasn't unattractive. Her blonde hair was coiled on top of her head and her blue eyes suggested that her ancestors had almost certainly been Aryan. Automatically I glanced down at her right hand and saw that she was wearing a wedding ring. When she looked up again I was smiling but not because anything amusing had happened.

The room was comfortable, spacious and tastefully decorated. It was on the third of four floors, and the small balcony overlooked the Mosel River. I began to think I had perhaps underestimated rather than overestimated my length of stay. After unpacking and although it was only four o'clock, I helped myself from the complimentary bottle of Mosel wine I found in the fridge and went back onto the balcony.

The traffic was still heavy and there were tourists galore milling around the bridge I had crossed, boarding various riverboats that were moored on the opposite side of the river.

I spread out the local tourist map that was on the small chest of drawers in my room, and tried to relate what I found to what I could see in front of me. My eyes drifted across the map to the north of the town and, by chance, fell on *Landkern Strasse*, the address on Ingrid's letters:

Fraulein Ingrid Mesterom
Landkern Strasse *44*

58312 Cochem
Deutchland

I looked up almost believing that I was going to be able to see through the hundreds of buildings between the *Am Hafen* Hotel and *Landkern Strasse* and, although it was a warm afternoon, I felt a shiver run through me.

Glancing to my left, I could see an extremely picturesque and intimidating neo-gothic castle perched on a hill at least three hundred and fifty feet above the River Mosel. A brochure I picked up with the tourist map told me that I was looking at the *Reichsburg Cochem*. Built in the early eleventh century it had survived fire and pestilence, sale and resale. In 1689 and during the War of Succession, troops belonging to King Louis XI of the Palatinate, almost sealed its fate as they undermined, planted explosives and blew it up.

After years of rebuilding and maintenance, the castle, once again, dominated the town of Cochem. Now run as a business, it attracted hundreds of thousands of visitors every year.

I stopped reading and looked up at the castle.

It seemed to be beckoning me.

Standing on the opposite side of the road from No. 44 *Landkern Strasse*, I tried to look inconspicuous. I had left the hotel about an hour earlier and wandered around the town for a while before heading for the street in which I believed Ingrid had lived.

The number of tourists appeared to have thinned out a little but the narrow streets didn't help and they were still teeming with people of all ages, sizes and nationalities. I heard French, Dutch and English being spoken as well as German, and there were other tongues I didn't recognise. I contemplated eating early but the first restaurant I tried was full so I decided to leave it until after I'd located *Landkern Strasse*.

I suppose what I was looking at was a typical road that I would have expected to find in the outskirts of any German town. *Landkern Strasse* was straight but steep, leading from the river up into the hills and towards the village of, not surprisingly, *Landkern*.

A mixture of relatively modern houses adorned either side of the road, each built to a different design. No. 44 was on the left and setback a little further from the road than its neighbours. The front garden was immaculate. There were bushes, shrubs, rocks, gravel and patches of blazing colour divided by a path that led to a green front door. It was a double-fronted two-storey house and there were green shutters – the colour matching the front door – at each of the four windows that I could see. Elaborate lace curtains hung either side of the downstairs windows and potted plants covered the windowsills. A dark-blue BMW 3-Series parked by the house had its offside wheels up on the wide pavement.

Aware that I was staring at the house, I walked uphill passing it on the opposite side of the road before turning and walking back down the hill again. While contemplating what I should do next, the green front door opened and two people – a young man and a woman – walked out and started down the path. I couldn't really see what they looked like because both of them were wearing the ubiquitous baseball caps and their faces were in shadow. I guessed their ages to be in their mid to late twenties.

Another older woman remained at the door and watched their progress. I thought the man and younger woman were going to get into the car but he unlocked it, retrieved a lightweight coat and then jogged after the woman who was already a few yards down the road. The older woman at the door shouted something after them and they both acknowledged whatever she had said with a wave of their hands as they continued on their way. Realising that the older woman was looking at me, I smiled in her direction and then, with a slight nod, followed the other two, remaining on the opposite side of the road.

The couple walked down into the town and into the main square by what I knew to be the *Rathaus* or the town hall. They stopped in the middle of the square and exchanged a few words before the female reached up and kissed the man on the cheek. It was the first opportunity I had to see their faces and to my surprise they were both Asian. The man looked as though he had some Chinese or Japanese in him, but the woman, not unlike Ingrid to look at, was more Malaysian.

After saying their goodbyes they parted, the man headed towards the main bridge over the river and the woman turning right, went into the narrow streets of the shopping area.

I had achieved what I wanted.

Having seen where Ingrid had probably lived, I could have argued that I hadn't really followed this couple into town because in reality they had been going in the same direction. Now they had separated, and for whatever reason, I suddenly wanted to know more. It couldn't have been a coincidence that they were both Asian and had come out of the house I knew was connected to Ingrid.

On impulse, I decided to follow the woman.

There were still a lot of people about but it was relatively easy to keep up with her without being conspicuous. At one stage, when she was quite close, she turned her head to glance in a shop window and I was able to get a better look at her. I had already noticed that she had long jet-black hair fastened unceremoniously with a rubber band and the resultant ponytail fell to almost half way down her back. About five feet three inches tall, her jeans, trainers and a pink sleeveless top all looked new. The baseball cap seemed slightly out of place, it gave her a tomboyish appeal but nothing could disguise her figure.

She was walking quite determinedly but something in a fashion shop window obviously caught her attention. I stopped abruptly causing somebody to run into me from behind. A middle-aged woman uttered something guttural and I smiled an apology. When I looked back towards the woman and saw her face in profile, her likeness to Ingrid was very apparent. Her hair was different but the face in profile was similar – not to the point where they could be mistaken for each other, but the similarity was intriguing.

I was surprised that I was able to recall Ingrid's face in any detail but I had held her cold dead hand in mine and had looked down at her beautiful but bloodied face while I waited for the police to arrive.

The woman, who was now no more than ten feet in front of me, turned away from the shop window and, unaware of my close scrutiny, rejoined the column of people pushing their way down the narrow street. I paused and let her get about twenty yards in front of me before stepping out into the crowd.

Turning left into a pedestrian passageway, I had to slow down because there were fewer people about. The passageway led down to the river.

I stayed a safe distance behind her.

When she went into a small tobacco shop, I walked past the shop towards the river and waited. She came out of the shop a matter of minutes later and this time I saw her entire face. Stopping outside the doorway, she concentrated on opening a packet of cigarettes. Her skin colouring, the shape of her dark eyes and mouth, her nose and even her chin, were remarkably like Ingrid's.

Suddenly I was aware that she was looking at me, and for a moment our eyes met, but then, with a slight smile, she looked down, slipped the cigarette packet into her pocket and carried on down the passageway towards the river.

I wasn't sure what to do.

I hadn't intended any covert activities: all I had wanted was to find the house and then decide whether to go and knock on the door or not. I had followed this young woman on an impulse. Perhaps now was the time to walk away. I glanced quickly to my right and saw her turn right along by the river. She didn't look back ... I assumed that she accepted I was another man with an imagination. I jogged to the corner and was in time to see her disappear into a bar.

After deciding, again on an impulse, not to walk away, I selected a table by the window.

At first I didn't see her when I entered the bar but, after I had ordered a small beer from the waitress, she emerged from the ladies' toilet. Stopping by the counter she exchanged a few words with the waitress before the woman I had followed came across the room in my direction. I averted my eyes and pretended to be studying a beer mat but she moved back into view as she sat down opposite me.

"I understand you are British," she said in English.

I looked up and her jet black eyes were piercing. "My German is obviously not as good as your English."

"Why are you following me?" she asked, ignoring my attempt at humour.

The directness of her question threw me. I suppose she felt safe and confident. The waitress, although serving another customer on the opposite side of the bar, was watching us closely.

"What makes you think I was following you?" I said, my mind in a whirl. "I came in here for a drink."

"And so did I," she replied, smiling at the waitress as she deposited my beer and a red wine on the table. "*Vielen Danke*, Helga," she said, picking up her glass of wine while still looking at me. She sipped the liquid before she spoke. "When I came out

80

of the house in *Landkern Strasse*, you were standing on the opposite side of the road watching the house. You followed Michael and me down the hill and then, when we separated by the *Rathaus*, you stayed with me." She took another sip of her wine. "I stopped to look in a shop window and you also stopped." Her eyes never left mine as she pulled the cigarette packet from her pocket, extracted a cigarette and lit it. I couldn't help but notice that she smoked the same brand as Ingrid. "I stop for these," she said, holding up the packet, "and you are outside the shop when I come out. I deliberately come into this bar and you are also here." She paused, taking a long drag on her cigarette. "I ask you again, why are you following me?"

She was too calm, too collected. It wasn't normal for a young woman to manoeuvre a man she thought was following her into a corner to ask him who he was and why he was following her. She was too sure of herself and too sure that she had the advantage.

"Your English is excellent," I observed, smiling.

Her nostrils flared in anger. "Look," she said between clenched teeth, "all I have to do is nod at Helga and the police will be here within minutes. Who are you and why are you following me?"

For some reason the change in her mood suggested she wasn't feeling as confident as I originally thought. Not sure what I should say, I played for time. "Perhaps it's all a coincidence and maybe I ought to ask you the same question."

She looked across the bar towards Helga.

Other than Elizabeth and a few nameless females in *Bonn*, I was closer to the woman opposite me than any other female since Belinda had died. It suddenly hit me that I had withdrawn into myself and I hadn't really had what might be called a conversation with anybody. *Bonn* had been all small talk, so small that I couldn't really remember what had been said. I had distanced myself from what had been my life before I even got there.

It had all been a formality and perhaps a charade.

No, that was unfair, it wasn't their fault.

Some of the delegates had probably already conferred and decided that my rudeness was due to the stress caused by Belinda's death; why else would I have resigned from such a rewarding job? Although I had spent many years away from her – earning the income I believed I needed to give her what I thought she wanted – all the time she would have been happy and content if I had simply been with her and earned a modest salary. If the twins had gone to the local comprehensive then maybe they would have been happy too.

Perhaps I had misjudged an awful lot but by the time it dawned on me it was too late.

The woman in front of me stubbed out her cigarette in the ashtray.

"You don't seem to be the sort of man who might prey on single females. I don't think I am a bad judge of character and although I met you for the first time only minutes ago, I think perhaps you had a reason for being here. You did follow me, you can't deny it, but you followed me maybe to tell me something. If I felt threatened then I wouldn't be sitting here, I would probably already have telephoned the police."

She reached for another cigarette and I took the opportunity to signal to the waitress that I wanted her to bring fresh drinks to the table. Helga nodded, checking with the woman opposite me before turning away to go behind the bar.

"May I ask your name?"

She blew smoke towards the ceiling, her eyes telling me that although she didn't think I was a threat, telling me her name was becoming too intimate. She thought for a few more seconds and then decided in my favour.

"Marie," she said quietly.

I reached across the table. "Hello, Marie, my name is Richard Blythe," I said.

She took my proffered hand without any show of reluctance. Her hand was small, soft and fragile in mine, but her handshake was firm and genuine.

"Would I be right in saying that your full name is Marie Mesterom?" I asked.

Her expression didn't change. She withdrew her hand from mine and reached for the cigarette in the ashtray.

"No, my name is Marie Schmidt," she said almost casually. "Why did you think my name was Mesterom?"

I became a little restless.

I had made a terrible mistake: this woman was nothing to do with Ingrid. The similarities were, after all, nothing but a coincidence.

"I'm sorry," I said, hesitantly, "I may have misread something."

Marie frowned. "What is there to misread? Did you think I was somebody you knew?"

"No, no," I said quickly. "I don't, or should I say didn't know you. No, I thought you might be related to somebody I once …" I was going to say 'knew', but then I didn't *know* Ingrid, "… somebody I once met."

Helga arrived with the drinks and Marie said something to her quickly and in German. Helga nodded and gave me a guarded look before picking up my empty beer glass and withdrawing back to the bar.

The frown was still on Marie's face. "Are you in the habit of following people who resemble other people you have met?"

I smiled, feeling slightly embarrassed. "No, it's not like that."

"What is it like then?" She drained her wine glass, her eyes never leaving mine.

I owed her an explanation. "I met somebody in the UK who lived at the address you came out from in *Landkern Strasse*. Because I was in the area I thought I'd take a look – being nosey, I suppose."

Marie's expression changed as I was speaking. "This person back in the UK, was she Asian like me?"

"Very much like you, yes."

The tears were forming before I had even answered her question fully. "Where did you meet this person?"

"I don't think –"

"Mr Blythe, I would like to know, please."

"This is a little difficult, Marie. You see there was a crime involved and I don't –"

"My ... my sister was murdered in the UK about four weeks ago, Mr Blythe. Was it ... was it my sister you met?" The tears were quietly rolling down her cheeks. I reached for my handkerchief and gave it to her. She took it without hesitation and dabbed at her eyes. "Was it, Mr Blythe?"

"Was your sister's name Ingrid?"

She nodded.

"Yes, then I think it was your sister I met."

Marie lit another cigarette before saying, "Would you tell me how you came to meet her, please?"

I didn't give Marie all the details but I did explain the circumstances under which I had met her sister. She listened intently, smoking another two cigarettes as I did. It was a strange sensation because I felt deeply sorry for Marie. Although I held back on the more gruesome aspects of my experiences, I could not hide the fact that I had been with her sister a matter of minutes before she was murdered.

Marie reacted almost as though she had known nothing. She knew her sister was murdered but what I was telling her appeared to be new to her. On the other hand, I felt a wave of relief wash over me. Other than the police, I hadn't been able to discuss my feelings with anybody. The twins didn't know and nor did Charles and Elizabeth, the only people who did know were those in authority – and whoever had murdered Ingrid.

The simple act of sitting in a bar and talking about what I had experienced was acting as a safety valve; it was allowing me to release some of the pressure that had built up inside me. I realised that coming to Cochem had probably been for that very reason but by meeting Marie, it had let a lot more emotion flow. I was able for the first time to share the way I really felt with somebody who had been close to the victim, to Ingrid. Only God knew how Marie must have felt.

When I had finished, Marie sat for a few minutes looking into space, the smoke from her cigarette curling upwards. Helga passed the table a couple of times looking concerned but this time she looked to me for confirmation that Marie was all right.

After what must have been three or four minutes, Marie stubbed her cigarette out and looked at me.

"We have been here for nearly a week and I had given up hope of finding out about anything that might have happened." Her voice was almost a monotone and she was speaking quietly. "We were going to go back tomorrow or the day after. There was no point in staying any longer. We learnt nothing in England and nothing here. Nobody would tell us what really happened."

"I'm sorry to interrupt, but who is *we*?"

"What?" she asked absentmindedly.

"We, you said we. Are you referring to the man you were with?"

"Michael? Yes, Michael and I are here together. The house you saw us leave was where Ingrid lived – well lodged would be a better description." She screwed up her eyes. "You said *Mesterom*. You said she told you her name was Mesterom."

I nodded.

"Why would she tell you that?"

"I've no idea, Marie. Her passport gave the same name though."

"Did it?" she asked, her voice adopting a more resigned tone. "You see somebody could have told me that, but nobody did. They all looked at me as though I was some sort of foreign imbecile." She reached across the table and touched my hand with her fingers. "Thank you."

"There's nothing for you to thank me for."

"You've told me more in the last thirty minutes than anybody else has told me in nearly two weeks. In England, they simply confirmed that Ingrid was murdered and that they needed to keep her body for further forensic tests. It was while we were waiting that we decided to come over here to see where she lived, and in the hope that somebody, anybody could tell us what had been going on. Her landlady could tell us nothing, although I think she had her suspicions."

"Where are you from, Marie?"

She looked up. "Singapore. Michael and I are from Singapore. He is a police officer but he's here unofficially. He came with me as a friend."

"I see." I thought for a moment. "So you came to Europe when you heard the tragic news."

Marie nodded, her head dropping again. "Yes. They got my mum's number from Ingrid's mobile phone and called. After two weeks I couldn't just sit and wait for a letter, another phone call, something that would tell me what was happening. I had to come and find out for myself, but as I said, I haven't been successful. It's been a wasted journey until now." She glanced at her watch. "Look, Mr Blythe, I am due to meet Michael in about five minutes. I would prefer to tell him what has happened alone but would it be possible if we could both meet you later on?"

"Of course."

"Michael, being a policeman, might be a bit suspicious of you, especially as you have appeared out of the blue." She smiled an apology. "I'm sorry I was suspicious of you."

"You had every right and I understand," I said. "Where would you like to meet?"

"Where are you staying?"

"In the *Am Hafen* hotel, on the other side of the river."

"Can we contact you there?"

"Of course! What sort of time?"

"About eight o'clock. Perhaps we could go and eat somewhere,' she suggested, standing up. "Thank you again, Mr Blythe. Under the circumstances, it was difficult for you to tell me what happened, but you have made our journey worthwhile."

'I —"

"No, let us leave what else is to be said until later. I must go."

With a last look and a weak smile, Marie left the bar.

I ordered another drink and mulled over the coincidence of meeting Marie. If I hadn't chosen that particular moment to go to *Landkern Strasse*, I probably wouldn't have known that she existed, let alone meet her.

Playing with the condensation on the tall beer glass in front of me, my thoughts roamed around everything that had happened.

It was difficult to believe.

I regarded myself as a mature, sensible and rational man who wouldn't let the wool be pulled over his eyes that easily. I wasn't gullible or overly naïve, but there was something strange about the situation in which I now found myself. It was almost as though Marie had been expecting me and hadn't done a particularly good job at covering up her lack of surprise and, more importantly, concern.

The tears had been there but a good actor can conjure those

up at any time they want. I was the one who was now suspicious but I didn't know why.

There was something not quite right.

Neither of us had offered any proof to the other that we were who we said we were. We had taken each other at face value.

I thought I had confirmation of my suspicions with what happened next – I was right in one way but wrong in another.

As I was finishing my beer and contemplating what I should do next, two uniformed police officers came into the bar and went over to Helga.

She pointed in my direction.

Chapter Eight

Wearing the standard German police leather jackets, peaked caps and with prominent but holstered pistols on their hips the two men looked quite intimidating. They were both clean-shaven, the younger one dark and swarthy and in his twenties, the other one looked about forty and was blond.

Having reached the table the older of the two took charge. "*Sprechen-Sie Deutche?*" he asked, his voice gruff.

I smiled, not fully understanding the situation, but something told me to play the innocent foreigner abroad. "*Eine kleine bischen,*" I replied slowly. "*Aber veillecht Sie sprechen Englisch besser.*"

I hoped my deliberate poor attempt at German showed willing.

The police officers exchanged looks. "Your name, please?" the older one asked in English.

For obvious reasons, my table had now become the centre of attention. The other customers were getting some free entertainment.

"Richard Blythe," I said, trying to smile my innocence. "May I ask what this is all about?" My mind was working overtime attempting, again, to think of a reason why the German police were suddenly interested in me.

The younger police officer came a little closer to the table and put out his hand as though he wanted to help me get to my feet.

"Ve vud vant you to com viz uz," the younger one said. If the situation hadn't appeared serious, I would have found his accent quite amusing – it was what every tourist would have expected.

"Why?" I asked, looking at the officer whose hand was now on my arm encouraging me to stand.

"Ve sink you vill com." The pressure on my arm increased.

"Herr Blyze," said the older man, "please come vis us. Ve vant to ask you zum questions."

"Why can't you ask them here?" By now I was standing and moving out from behind the table. Both police officers were shorter than me but the older man took hold of my other arm and their grips were firm. I was frog-marched out of the bar then assisted into the back of their police car, which already contained a driver.

The two police officers got into the car, one on either side.

I attempted during the short drive to the police station to discover what was going on but they ignored my questions. After a short ride, the car stopped outside a rather austere building. I was 'assisted' up the front steps and swiftly guided into a room with bars at its window, a metal table and four metal chairs. The walls were a pale dirty yellow and a single light bulb hung from a long flex in the middle of the ceiling.

Police interview rooms were the same the world over.

My hosts told me to sit down and wait.

In the car and now, I hoped the immediate conclusion I had drawn was wrong, but everything pointed to Marie Schmidt being responsible for what was happening. There was no other explanation.

But why?

After about ten minutes of staring at the dirty walls and trying to see beyond the maelstrom of thoughts going round in my mind, I was joined by a man and a woman, the latter carrying a plastic cup of coffee that she put in front of me, before sitting opposite me and next to the man. There was something familiar about them but I had no idea why the thought should cross my mind. They were both casually dressed. He was wearing faded jeans, an open neck long-sleeved blue check shirt and black slip-on shoes. He was a big man, probably a little under six feet tall, about thirty with a dark rugged complexion and smiling brown eyes. The woman was a few years younger. She too was wearing jeans with a pinkish sleeveless T-shirt. Her hair was short, almost boyish, and she needed her roots dying. Standing about five and half feet tall, she had a nice figure, a pretty but lived-in face, and bluey-green eyes.

What was I doing taking all that in within the first few seconds?

"We have been told you do not speak any German," the woman said in English, fiddling with a pencil that had been lying on the table.

I picked up the plastic cup and took a sip of coffee. "Thank you for this," I said, smiling. "It's not that I don't speak *any* German, but I certainly don't speak it well enough to cope in a situation such as this, whatever it might be. It's rather fortunate that you speak English well." I took another sip of coffee, my eyes not leaving hers. "May I ask what is going on?"

Ignoring my question the man said, "We are being impolite as we have not introduced ourselves. My name is Karl Henke and my colleague here is Anna Schwartz." Neither of them suggested there was a need to shake hands. "We are with the *Nationale Kriminal Polizei.* The equivalent in England I think is called the NCS or National Crime Squad." He paused and then asked. "And your name is Richard Blythe?"

I felt like saying that if their names were Henke and Schwartz my middle name was Penelope. They were no more German than I was. Why the pretence? "Yes, it is, but –"

"Thank you, Herr Blythe." He glanced sideways towards the woman.

Anna Schwartz screwed up her eyes as she looked at me. "Herr Blythe, why are you here in Cochem?"

What was happening wasn't simply incredible and a little

scary, it was also bizarre. Being forcibly removed from the bar can't have been within the law .... On my travels I had come across some pretty corrupt police forces and I had paid my fair share of bribes which had hopefully ensured safe passage as far as the next corruptible police post. However, I had never been in trouble with the police, corruptible or not.

My recent experiences in Ashbourne couldn't be classed as *being in trouble*.

Although I had seen the inside of any number of police stations all over the world, my visits had always been on my terms. Now it looked as though I was in for a grilling about why I was in one of the most popular tourist attraction in middle Germany.

Nothing added up.

I placed the plastic cup carefully and deliberately on the table and looked at both detectives. "I doubt, even in Germany, it is the norm for a foreign tourist to be manhandled out of a bar and taken to a police station without explanation, simply to be asked why he was there in the first place. Even I know that under European law, if not under German law, what you've done is against my human rights. You can either give me a good reason as to why I should even consider answering your question or, alternatively, I will walk out and I might pretend this little charade ever took place. What do you say?"

The man's expression remained stern but interested, his cheeks colouring slightly. The woman, though, leant back in her chair, crossed her legs, and appeared amused.

"Herr Blythe," said the man, leaning forward, "we are only asking why you are here in Cochem."

"And I am only telling you that unless you can give me a good reason why you should want to know, you are abusing your authority. At the moment, I am more than willing to put your behaviour down to over-zealous policing. Shortly though, I may involve your superiors. Which is it to be?"

"You are not in the position to threaten us, Herr Blythe. I must warn you –"

I spread my hands. "What? What must you warn me about? And what position am I in? I repeat, give me a reason to help with whatever this is all about, and if I can I will, otherwise I'm leaving."

I began to get up.

Henke sighed and Schwartz sat forward again, the look of amusement still on her face. I resumed my seat.

"Herr Blythe," she said, "your reaction is as we would have expected ..."

"Now you're being patronising."

"No," she continued, "that is not our intention but it would help if you were to answer the question." She reached into her shoulder bag and extracted a packet of cigarettes. I declined her offer. "Maybe if I put the question in context, you would understand."

"Maybe," I said.

"All right what is your interest is in Marie Schmidt?"

Her question shouldn't have surprised me, but it made me hesitate which seemed to please Henke.

They waited, their eyes boring into mine.

"I'm sorry," I said, "but although I admit I did meet somebody by that name earlier, I can't see that it gives you a good reason to haul me in here."

"Herr Blythe," said Schwartz, "would it help if we told you that we know who you are?"

I smiled and shrugged. "What exactly does that mean?"

"We know that you were witness to a murder in England in April," Henke said. "We also know the connection between the girl that was murdered and Cochem."

Now I was genuinely surprised, and some of my confidence

left me. "If you know that much," I said, "you can tell me why I'm here." I held up my hand. "Before you do though, your description wasn't strictly accurate. I didn't witness the murder, I found the girl after she was murdered."

Henke bowed his head slightly. Schwartz just looked at me. "I accept my choice of words was poor," Henke said, "but you must admit that by coming here we cannot put it down to a simple coincidence. If your version of events in Derbyshire is to be believed, how did you connect the victim to Cochem?"

"You can put the reason I am here down to whatever you like," I said. "And the connection is quite easy to explain, I saw some letters addressed to Ingrid Mesterom and remembered the address." I paused. "But before I say anything else, this isn't right."

"What do you mean?" Schwartz asked.

"I mean ... you, your attitude and the obvious pretence –"

"Pretence?" It was Henke this time.

"Your English is far too good and I doubt whether you are anything to do with the German police. I'm not sure about the legality of masquerading as German police officers, but before I say anything else I would like to see some form of identification."

Schwartz glanced at her colleague and then held up her hands. "Okay, Mr Blythe," she said, "maybe we ought to have been a little more up front with you, and you're right, we aren't with the German police. It was a little naughty of us to even try that on."

"Naughty?" I said. "I would say downright stupid, illegal and ... anyway, I'm willing to listen."

Sitting back, I waited.

"We had to enlist the help of the local police," Henke said, "because we actually have no jurisdiction here or anywhere else in Germany. We can't tell you who we work for but all I can say is that the reason we wanted to speak to you is a matter of national security."

"By national, I presume you mean British?"

He nodded. "Yes."

"And you can't tell me who you are working for?"

"No, I'm sorry," Schwartz said, reaching for her cigarettes, "but it's unlikely that we would have been able to make use of this police station if we weren't who we say we are."

"Can I presume that Schwartz and Henke aren't your real names?"

"You can."

"But I'm not to know what they really are?"

"Sorry, no."

"All right, for the moment I'm willing to play your little game but can I also assume that I can walk out of here whenever I want to."

"Yes."

"All right … I am still listening."

They told me that Ingrid Mesterom – Mesterom was a false name and her real name was Schmidt, at least one question was answered – was part of an international criminal organisation. They were in Germany following up their investigations connected with her murder, but more directly, with what she had been doing in England.

When I walked up *Landkern Strasse* they had been sitting in a car – which I hadn't noticed – further up the road observing the comings and goings from No 44. Seeing me there was too much of a coincidence.

Their interest in Marie Schmidt and her companion, Michael Lim, originated in England, when the two of them visited the police station in Ashbourne asking questions about Ingrid. 'Henke' and 'Schwartz' were due to come to Cochem anyway, and seeing Marie and Michael visiting No 44 today was not a surprise, but seeing me was. Thinking their investigations in Cochem were going to come to nothing, when I appeared on the scene their interest was renewed.

Without telling me how or why, they recognised me straight away and immediately obtained authority from their superiors in the UK to question me.

My appearance generated equal interest in the UK, and that's when in only a matter of hours, it was arranged for me to be 'picked up' by the German police.

"Hopefully you understand we can't tell you more than we have," Henke said.

"I have little choice but to understand," I said. "And I also understand why seeing me generated some interest."

"It certainly did that," Schwartz said. "Are you now willing to tell us why you are really here?"

Telling them the truth – why would I feel the need to tell them anything else? – seemed to satisfy them, and after a couple of questions they sat back and sighed. After the excitement my presence caused, the truth must have been a disappointment.

Although I attempted to glean a little more information about Ingrid, my hosts remained tight-lipped, explaining that to reveal anything would jeopardise any future investigations.

"It would be best," Henke said, "if you remained in ignorance."

Throughout the session I had with them, I kept on asking myself, and on a couple of occasions them too, what was the point of it all? I had simply been in the wrong place at the wrong time, an innocent bystander. They had agreed, but equally they expected me to understand their logic: the need to question me resulted from the fact that I was there.

"If you were us –" Schwartz started to say.

"But I don't know who you are," I said, interrupting.

"All right, but if you were us and a witness to the murder

associated with our ongoing investigations turned up hundreds of miles from the scene of the crime, outside the house where the victim had stayed, wouldn't you be suspicious?" Schwartz asked.

"I've told you I understand and I've explained, and I hope you have accepted why I am here, but you have told me absolutely nothing in return. Who Ingrid really was? What crime she was supposed to be involved with? Why she was murdered? Whether …?"

"And we've explained why we can't tell you anymore," Henke said.

"No you haven't," I said accusingly. "You've told me absolutely nothing."

"That's the way it must be," Schwartz said.

"All right,' I said shrugging. 'Then I'm leaving. I've told you everything that Marie Schmidt told me and, like you, I think she is simply a grief-stricken sister who wants to know what the hell is going on."

"And so do we," Henke said as I stood up.

It was after nine in the evening when I got back to my room in the Hotel *Am Hafen*. A *Schnell-Imbiss* by the river was the eventual source of my evening meal. A *curry-wurst* and *pomfrites* wasn't my idea of sustenance but I really didn't feel like anything else. The sausage was rubbery and the chips tasted of anything but potato, but the meal filled a gap.

Sitting on a bench, I watched the evening river traffic returning from the various dinner-cruises and some youths nearby, worse the wear for drink, provided the entertainment. The experience I'd had was uppermost in my mind and it had an adverse effect on my appetite. Some of the late-night ducks on the river benefited more than I did from what I had bought.

Having thought Marie was the source of my encounter with

... with what? MI6 or 5 ... I had no idea, but I was pleased that she wasn't the reason I'd been questioned. But, I was disappointed there had been no contact from her.

I ambled back to the hotel deep in thought, but I did check twice to see whether there was anybody who looked as though they were interested in me, that was before it dawned I wouldn't know whether I was being followed or not.

I had watched too many in-flight movies.

After collecting a couple of bottles of local red wine from the bar, I went to my room to do some real drinking and real thinking. Because the evening was quite warm, I took a bottle and a glass out onto the small balcony. There were quite a lot of people about on the opposite side of the river and boats were still disgorging their clientèle. It was such a naturally relaxing scene it was hard to believe that the young woman I had talked to before she was murdered in the middle of the Derbyshire countryside, lived for whatever period a few hundred yards away from the river I was now looking at.

There were answers out there somewhere, but I wasn't sure I wanted to know them..

Marie hadn't left a message in Reception. I assumed she had spoken to her friend – I now knew his full name was Michael Lim – and he had decided that I should be given a wide berth. It was more than likely that they had returned to the bar where I had met Marie in the first place and been told of my *arrest* by the police.

The hours I had spent on planes were spent report writing, reading, sleeping or watching the in-flight movies. Generally, I didn't read a lot but I could tell whether I was going to enjoy a novel by the first paragraph on the first page. I didn't really care who the author was as long as he or she wrote in a language I understood – which meant using words I didn't subsequently have to look up in a dictionary – was entertaining and didn't become too implausible, I was happy.

My simple standards also applied to the films I attempted to watch. However, whereas the films and the books were mostly fictional, my recent experiences were not.

Being told by the two stooges – that's how I now felt about them – that almost from the day I had found Ingrid I had been followed was the biggest shock. Not only was I followed but everything about me was investigated: my parents, schooling, where we'd been on holiday, what groups I had been involved with at university, any sympathies I'd had, my career, the countries I had worked in, everything. The British authorities probably now knew more about me than I could remember myself.

However, once again, that's where they stopped. There was no explanation as to why there was a need to follow and investigate me in the first place.

The wine began to have the desired effect and my thoughts became disjointed but not too irrational ... there were a lot of questions and few answers.

A large river launch was manoeuvring against the wharf on the far side of the river and I could see that its passengers were dressed in dinner jackets and evening gowns. The music was still playing and two or three couples had decided not to lose out; they were still jigging away on the launch's top deck.

Then I think I heard a slight tap on the door of my room.

Looking at my watch I wasn't surprised to see that it was well after midnight. I left the balcony, expecting to hear the door being knocked again, but it wasn't. Lying on the carpet, one edge still under the door was a white envelope addressed to Herr Blythe, Room 40. Ripping the envelope open I took out a single sheet of paper. Both the address on the envelope and message were hand-written in blue ink:

Mr Blythe

Meet me tomorrow morning up at the Schloss. There is a café below the first set of steps.

Be there at ten-thirty.

Marie.

Chapter Nine

I woke to another glorious day after the expected fitful night's sleep. Images whirled round my mind to such an extent that I had been out on the balcony again at three o'clock in the morning. I stayed there until I was sure that if I went back to bed there was a good chance I would go back to sleep. However, what seemed like only minutes later the sun's rays were streaming in through the window and I could hear the early morning traffic bringing Cochem to life.

It was my first morning in the town, yet I felt as though I had been there for days.

After half enjoying a continental breakfast I decided to find the café below the *Schloss* Marie had mentioned and wait at a discreet distance to see if I could observe her arrival.

I hadn't been told that she was mixed up in anything other than her search for the truth, but I wanted to be a little more certain that she was genuine before meeting her. I had no idea what I thought waiting and observing the café would achieve. I can only assume I thought that by trying to play at being a tourist it would give me something positive to do under the circumstances.

A walk through the town following the signs to the *Schloss*, led me uphill towards the robust castle walls. The café was easy to find, and as I was there by nine o'clock I carried on up to the castle itself. The views from its ramparts were spectacular, not only of the town but also towards the far reaches of the river. I was quite early in the morning which meant I had most of the area to myself. I found somewhere to sit down and admire the view.

I must have dozed off because I was suddenly aware of movement near me. A small boy and girl standing hand in hand were watching me curiously. I smiled but didn't get a response. A woman – more than likely their mother – turned away from the wall and, on seeing what the children were doing, proceeded to chastise them with an apology to me. I wondered if she would have been as apologetic if I hadn't been dressed properly and had a bottle in a brown paper bag at my feet.

Perhaps such occurrences didn't happen in Germany.

Belinda would have been delighted if they had.

It was nearly ten-twenty, which meant I must have slept for over forty-five minutes and dashed my plans into the bargain.

I remembered dreaming of Belinda ... at least something hadn't changed. Walking down the hill against the flow of tourists, I spotted Marie straight away. She was sitting on the terrace with her back to me, obviously expecting me to appear from the opposite direction.

I stopped and watched for a few seconds.

She was wearing jeans and a loose top that was more like a vest. Her jet-black hair was in a ponytail and there was a large pair of sunglasses hiding her eyes. A shoulder bag hung from the back of the chair. She looked like any other sightseer who had stopped off for a break en route to the castle. The smoke from her cigarette curled upwards in the still air. There was a tall glass of what looked like lemonade in front of her.

Mounting the steps to the terrace, I moved towards her and she sensed my presence straightaway. She turned round and smiled a welcome, moving the sunglasses onto the top of her head.

She gestured to the metal garden chair opposite her and I obediently sat down. She watched me for a few seconds before speaking.

"I'm sorry about last night," she said, "leaving as quickly as I did but I had to meet Michael."

"It's me who should be apologising," I said. "I'm afraid I was detained elsewhere and wasn't back at the hotel until quite late."

"I must also admit that I did wait in the hotel until after nine o'clock," Marie said.

"I'm sorry."

"There's no need to apologise, Mr Blythe. I left a note for you and obviously you got it or you wouldn't be here."

"Yes, thank you. It was pushed under my door."

A waitress appeared and I ordered a coffee. Marie declined the offer of another drink with a slight shake of her head, at the same time lowering her sunglasses – I could no longer see her eyes.

"I expected your friend ... Michael did you say his name was?" She nodded. "I expected he would be with you."

"He may be here a little later. He's gone to see the local police to try and find out if they knew anything about what was going on." She picked up her glass and took a sip of lemonade.

I wondered if they would tell him about my temporary detention and questioning.

"I would have thought he would have made contact with the local police as soon as you arrived. You said he was in the Singapore police didn't you?"

The waitress put the coffee in front of me.

"Yes, he is but he's not here officially. I think I told you yesterday, he's with me as a close family friend."

I tasted the coffee. It was bitter but exactly what I needed. "Marie, can I ask what you have discovered about your sister? I appreciate you couldn't tell me anything yesterday evening because I had rather sprung myself on you, but I assume asking me to meet you this morning means that there is more to say." I placed the cup back in its saucer, trying to penetrate the darkness of her sunglasses. I needed to see her eyes.

She shook her head. "There is nothing really that I can add. Ingrid came to Europe about a year ago on the pretence of continuing her studies. She was doing modern languages but from the outset there was something not right. Her letters became infrequent after a couple of months and then stopped altogether about six months ago." Taking her sunglasses off and putting them on the table, she reached for her cigarettes and lit one before carrying on. "I was going to come looking for her anyway but then we got the tragic news that she had been murdered."

"You told me how the authorities found you, I think you said your mother's number was on her mobile phone. But from what you told me yesterday she was travelling on a false passport."

"I didn't say anything about that yesterday, so how do you know?" Marie said, her eyes narrowing.

"Well, I don't," I said in a hurry, "but your name is Schmidt and she was using the name Mesterom. I saw her passport when I found her and unless Mesterom was her married name then..." I was kicking myself, it was Henke or Schwartz who told me Ingrid had been using a false passport.

"I think I would like you to tell me everything, Mr Blythe, and not only what you suppose I want to hear." She looked at me and I sensed from her eyes that she had become suspicious.

"Please call me Richard," I suggested. "I'm sorry, but it's something I was told last night." I took a deep breath. "After ... after you left the bar a couple of policemen came in and I was, to put it politely, escorted to the police station where I was questioned by a couple of rather unlikely looking characters who wouldn't tell me who they were or where they were from."

Telling Marie the detail of my session in the police station seemed the right thing to do, and the little I had managed to put together as a result.

"I see, they thought you were here in Cochem because of Ingrid, is that right?" Marie asked.

"Well they were right weren't they? I was here because of

Ingrid but they thought I was a link, someone worth investigating," I said.

We discussed my time at the police station for a few minutes and then Marie asked, "Richard, was Ingrid mutilated in any way?"

"I'm not sure …"

"No, please, it is important. We have been able to get nothing out of the authorities in either England or here. Even when Michael told the police in England that he too was a police officer, it didn't make any difference. All I know is that my sister is in a mortuary in England, in Ashbourne. I had to identify her but there was nothing else. She … she looked peaceful." Marie hesitated. "We … we were told that her body would have to stay there for a little longer because the investigations were still ongoing. That is why we decided to come to Germany while we waited."

"Yes, you told me yesterday but I'm not sure there's a lot I can add either."

Attracting the waitress' attention I ordered a beer. Marie changed her mind and asked for lemonade.

"Anything will be more than we already have."

I thought for a moment. "All right," I said. "but there is only a little I can add to what I you already know."

I described exactly what had happened from the moment I first came across Ingrid.

"You had a chance to talk to her before she was murdered?" Marie asked, sitting forward in her chair.

"Yes I did, but I knew nothing about her so the relevance of some of what she said didn't mean anything to me."

"Please, what did she say?"

"If you are sure."

Marie nodded. "It's important."

The beer arrived and I took a sip before answering Marie's

question.

"She told me she was on a walking holiday and had accepted a lift from some man in a car. He got fresh with her but she'd managed to escape and ran into the woods where I found her. She said she must have tripped over and knocked herself out. She was still unconscious when I found her."

"Did she describe the man ... the one who molested her?"

"No, not really." I went on and told her about the old fellow I had met by the car park from where I had retrieved Ingrid's rucksack. "He saw the man who dumped the rucksack. Whether it was the same man who had given Ingrid a lift, I don't know, but it must have been. The old man told me the other man was thirtyish and Asian."

"That's all you know?"

"Yes. I'm sorry."

"Can you tell me again what happened after you found her?" The expression on her face was serious but it didn't detract from how attractive Marie was. She was a lovely looking girl in her mid-twenties with everything to live for, as her sister had been.

Once again, I told Marie everything: from the moment I entered the woods in Dove Dale to when I caught the train back to Market Harborough. She listened intently, smoking another three cigarettes and switching from lemonade to red wine. We sat and talked for well over an hour. I answered her questions as honestly as I could.

When I had finished Marie went back to the question she had asked over an hour earlier. "Richard, you said that when you found her in the morning, she had been stabbed and that some of her clothing was missing."

I nodded.

Marie was doing her best to speak without letting her emotions show, but as she asked her question, her eyes began to water. She quickly reached for her sunglasses.

"You also said that her abdomen had been slashed." I nodded again. "Can you say whether the cuts were," she hesitated, "were random cuts or whether they formed a picture?"

I frowned. "A picture? I'm sorry, Marie, I don't understand."

Marie dipped her finger in her wine and traced some lines on the Formica surface of the table.

"Did the cuts look anything like this?" she asked.

I twisted my head to see what she had drawn. It looked like a '9' and a 't' with a line across the top - 死. Seeing the marks made by the red wine on the white surface, my mind went back to the time when I sat next to Ingrid holding her hand while I waited for the police. All I had seen was the rather grotesque wounds left by the knife. The cuts had been quite deep. Looking again at what Marie had drawn, I couldn't say that there was any resemblance to the image I had of Ingrid's slashed stomach.

Shaking my head, I said, "No, Marie … I don't mean, no. I mean, I can't say definitely that this is what I saw. There was a lot of blood."

Marie winced and took a deep breath. "Are you sure?"

"I can't be sure either way, I'm sorry. Surely the police would have been able to tell you? There was a photographer there and he would have taken pictures of the wounds."

"I asked the police but they told me that what I described meant nothing to them." Marie looked down, obviously disappointed that I wasn't able to confirm either way what she had asked.

"What does it mean?" I asked pointing at the now fading lines on the table.

"It may have suggested who had killed her, that's all."

"Why?"

"It's a calling card left by one of the most vicious groups of drug-smugglers in the Far East. When they murder the opposition, they are not frightened of telling the world they were responsible. They are proud of their work. What I drew is the Chinese symbol for death."

Marie drained her wine after which she looked around for the waitress. If she had found out so little from the police in England, I wanted to ask her how she knew about drug-smugglers and their calling cards. But then it dawned on me that because Michael Lim was with the Singapore police, he would know such things and would have told Marie. When I found the drugs in Ingrid's rucksack, I concluded that they were more than she needed for personal use, but any conclusion I drew then and now was pure supposition because of my ignorance on such matters. On the other hand, Marie now seemed to be a lot more knowledgeable than she originally implied. My original suspicions were, to some extent, confirmed by Henke and Schwartz but now Marie seemed to know more than they did ... courtesy of her travelling companion.

"Are you telling me that Ingrid was mixed up in drug smuggling?" I asked, hoping I sounded genuinely surprised.

"I think so," she replied. "She became involved with the criminal world while she was at university in Singapore. I don't know any more than that but eventually it has to be the reason she was murdered."

'I thought such things couldn't happen in Singapore," I said, knowing my question was unnecessarily frivolous.

Fortunately, Marie didn't see it that way. "Even in Singapore with the threat of the death sentence hanging over the drug smugglers, it still happens."

I sighed. "I don't think there is anything else I can tell you, Marie. I'm so sorry about Ingrid and if I could go back –"

Marie reached across the table and placed her hand in mine. "There is nothing you could have done, Richard, believe me but thank you for trying to help Ingrid and thank you for telling me what you have." She drank the last of her wine. "Now, I must go and find Michael, if we were going to see him he would be here by now." She began to get up but then resumed her seat. "Richard, if you are in the habit of taking advice from people you hardly know, may I suggest that you put what you have experienced, and what you now know, behind you and get on with your life. I know nothing about you but I can only guess that sitting back in England you have a lovely wife and some equally adorable children. Go back to them and, although you will never forget what has happened, do not let it play any part in your life from now on." I started to interrupt but she carried on. "I can understand why you felt the need to come here but now you have done what you needed to do. Leave this place and leave with it what I have told you. You are not involved anymore."

She took her bag from the back of the chair and this time she did stand up. I stood with her.

"It is my turn to thank you," I said.

"There is no need. You are an intelligent man who inadvertently got mixed up in something that must now seem to you to be in a different world. Leave it there." She moved closer to me and reached up to kiss me on the cheek. Then with a final weak smile, she brushed past me to the top of the steps leading down from the café.

I turned and watched her go.

She walked quickly down the hill until she was out of sight and maybe, out of my life.

She was right.

I had become involved in something that, regardless of my experiences gleaned from around the world, put me well and truly out of my depth.

Although the lovely wife Marie referred to was no longer there for me to return to, Belinda was still with me in every other way. I still had the twins and I had a future to plan ...

whatever it might be. In the last a twenty-four hours, I had been in a world that was alien to me.

Did I still want any part of it?

No.

It was a few minutes before twelve o'clock and it was a lovely day. A group of Japanese tourists were hovering at the top of the steps, obviously wondering whether I was about to leave the table.

The waitress approached, and after writing on a pad she gave me the bill I had completely forgotten about. I paid her before following the same path Marie had taken down into the town of Cochem.

Leaving this lovely German riverside town within the hour would mean I could leave Ingrid and Marie's world behind.

I had my own life to lead now.

A couple of thirteen-year-old children needed me.

I also wanted to talk to Belinda about things that mattered.

Chapter Ten

True to my word, an hour after Marie disappeared from my life I had booked out of the *Am Hafen* hotel, and was on my way back to *Düsseldorf* for an unscheduled flight home.

During the drive, I gave a lot of thought to what had happened, its implausibility at times making me wonder whether any of it had actually occurred. Had I been dreaming from the moment I found Ingrid in Dove Dale? That possibility was even more incredible but it showed how my thought patterns were developing.

I opened the front door of Blue-Ridge late on the Saturday afternoon. It was an overcast day and there was quite a wind blowing, with grey clouds scudding across the sky. I immediately went to the phone, rang the twins' school and managed to speak to Isabelle. She sounded happy and was really looking forward to the following weekend, which was an unexpected exeat because normally there were only two per term. When I dropped the twins off before I flew to Germany, they said they would prefer to come home for their next exeat rather than go on another of my educational tours of museums.

While on the phone, Isabelle asked whether she could bring a friend home with her. "She'll be no bother, Daddy."

"Of course," I told her. "You're not going to let me do the cooking, are you?"

"Daddy, I wouldn't wish that on my enemies, let alone my best friend," she replied, laughing.

"I'll have you know, young lady, I'm quite a good cook."

"Who told you that?"

"Well ... erm ... nobody actually, but ..."

"I'll do the cooking, then."

"Yes, all right."

"How was Germany? Did your last conference go well? Do you miss it?" she asked in a rush.

"Whoa, whoa! Which question do you want answering first?"

"Sorry, Daddy," she said.

"Germany was fine. Your mother would have hated it." That got a snigger from Isabelle. "The conference was a success and I must admit I enjoyed it. And to answer your third question, no, I don't miss it …"

"Not yet," Isabelle said.

"I took a slight diversion on the way back and went down the River Mosel as far as a place called Cochem, spent a night there and then came home."

"Why?" Isabelle enquired in a typical teenage voice that expects a logical explanation for everything.

"Just for a breather before coming home, to unwind after my final break with Astek, I suppose."

"And?"

"And what?" I asked.

"What happened?"

"What do you mean, what happened?"

"You're dithering, Daddy."

I smiled at her choice of word. "No, I'm not, I'm having a conversation with my daughter and telling her what I've been up to for the last week, that's all."

"But what have you been up to?"

Her persistence began to worry me. It was almost as though she knew what had happened and was testing me.

"Isabelle," I said warily, "what exactly are you getting at? There's more to your question than daughterly interest."

"Oh nothing."

"Isabelle, come on, no secrets."

"It's something Carrie said when I told her you were away," she said quietly. "And stop calling me Isabelle. Your name for me is Bella," she added indignantly.

"Sorry, Bella, yes, I'm sorry. Who is Carrie and what did she say?" I reached up and adjusted the picture that was hanging above the phone table, smiling when I realised it was one of the few pictures I had never straightened before. Belinda liked pictures to be slightly crooked because of something she'd read in a *Feng Tsui* book. It used to infuriate her when I went round the house straightening them all.

"Carrie's a girl in my year. She's a troublemaker and likes winding people up," Isabelle said.

"And how has she been winding you up?" My mind relaxed. It was nothing to do my own experiences.

"She ... she asked me the other day how many women you'd been to bed with since mummy died. I ... I lost my temper and told her that you weren't like that, that you and mummy loved each other and that you still loved her." Isabelle paused momentarily and then said almost in a whisper, "Carrie said that I was being naïve and that men were all the same and that you would take every –"

"All right, Bella, I get the picture," I said unnecessarily forcibly.

In many ways, what Isabelle had said shook me more than if she had told me the police had been to the school and asked her and David questions about me. I didn't know quite what to say to her – would she believe me if I told her the truth? There was little point in telling her anything else.

I had no idea what Isabelle knew about the facts of life, but I had to assume at nearly fourteen she knew more than I gave her credit for. Belinda told me during one of her forward planning moments a few weeks before she died about the more intimate discussions she and Isabelle had. Of course, I knew that they used to go into a huddle every now and again but neither of them ever told me what they talked about, even when I asked. If it was anything serious then I knew that Belinda would have told me, but otherwise it remained strictly confidential between the *girls*, as Isabelle used to call the two of them.

Now my nearly fourteen-year-old daughter was asking me a straight question. Had I or had I not been to bed with another female since her mother died? It was obviously important to Isabelle and I suppose it should have been important to me but, up to that point, the opportunity had not been there and nor had the need.

"Ignore her, Bella. You're right, she obviously enjoys winding other girls up," I said.

"But have you, Daddy?"

"I think that's a rather personal question, don't you? And not really one a daughter should be asking her father, especially a daughter who is only thirteen."

"Nearly fourteen," she threw in absentmindedly. "I'm sorry, Daddy, but you did tell me to discuss anything with you, anything that might be worrying me. I just …"

"All right, I understand." But I probably didn't. "You can tell Carrie that all men aren't the same and for your ears only, no, I haven't."

There was an audible sigh on the other end of the phone. "I said you wouldn't have. You couldn't."

"Then there's nothing to worry about is there."

I didn't add that the opportunity hadn't arisen and if it had I would be able to give her the same answer. Although, perhaps Carrie was right, maybe all men were the same. If the opportunity had arisen … well. It was less than two months since Belinda died and I did not want to be with another woman. If I went with somebody else, it would mean Belinda wasn't the last …

I changed the subject. "Who will you be bringing with you next weekend?"

"Jane, she's my best friend now."

"Oh, I thought Sue was your best friend?"

"We had a row."

"I see." Isabelle had gone back to being the thirteen year-old and I thought it would be best if I didn't pry.

"I'm looking forward to meeting her. I'll be there a little before midday on Saturday."

"Don't be silly, Daddy, lessons will go on until at least four o'clock. We'll be ready minutes after we finish."

"You'd better be. Have you seen David?"

"I saw him at breakfast but the cricket team has an away fixture. They've gone over to Haileybury, I think."

Having promised I would get through for sports matches and other events as often as I could, perhaps I ought to have known. However, I couldn't remember David telling me what games were on. Somewhere in my study I had the school programme for the summer term. I made a mental note to find it. Things were going to have to change.

"All right, tell him I called and I'll see him next Saturday. Oh, and Bella, do you want Jane to share your room or shall I make up the spare bed?" I asked.

"No, she can use my bed. I'll sleep on the futon."

"Fine, see you on Saturday, then."

"Don't plan anything special, Daddy. I fancy a lazy weekend at home."

"I won't. 'Bye, Bella."

"'Bye, Daddy, and Daddy, I love you."

"And I love you. 'Bye."

There were tears in my eyes when I put the phone down. It only ever happened after Belinda died. The secure world I thought we lived had been shattered. Losing Belinda had made Isabelle and David more precious than life itself, and when I put the phone down it was as though I was severing more than a telephone connection. The Cochem incident should not have happened; I had put myself at risk.

After shaking my head and drying my eyes, I checked the mail, which was on the telephone table. I assumed Elisabeth and Charles had paid the house a visit during my short absence, unlike when I was in Derbyshire.

One of the letters advised me that the inquest into Ingrid's death would be held in Buxton the following Thursday and I was required to attend. It had taken an inordinate amount of time for the inquest to happen and now I had received only a few days' notice to be there. The post-mark told me the letter was a week old. I rang the number given in the letter and was surprised when somebody answered at that time on a Saturday. After advising the abrupt woman who called herself Ms Felton, she assured me it would take no more than one day. Even if it did, she told me, "It wouldn't continue over the weekend."

To be honest, I had forgotten about my attendance at the inquest in Ingrid's death. The letter and phone call annoyed me. I wanted to move on not be reminded that there was now a need to repeat everything in an open Coroner's court.

After unpacking, I went into the study to find the school programme. Belinda often referred to me as a methodical person rather than tidy. She wasn't being critical, simply observant. Everything on my desk had its place and I knew to within an inch where things should be.

The paperweight wasn't as I had left it, the miniature clock Belinda's mother gave me had been moved and the ornamental letter opener wasn't in the same compartment in the Georgian letter rack.

I frowned.

Since I flew to Germany somebody had been in my study and moved things on my desk. I looked around the room for any other signs but none was immediately apparent until I noticed a book slightly proud of the others in the tall bookcase. It was an atlas Belinda and I had bought the children when they first started school. I shrugged and put it back, this time lining it up with the other books.

My purpose in the study momentarily forgotten, I went from room to room to see what else there might be that had been interfered with. The living room and dining room produced nothing suspicious, neither did the conservatory ... but the kitchen did.

Some of the tins of food were not as I had left them and the cutlery drawer had definitely been disturbed. Upstairs there was further evidence that somebody had searched every room. I had left Belinda's clothes alone. She had her own space and that space remained important and personal to me.

Her underwear drawer wasn't fully closed. Her bras and pants weren't in the same order. She had always kept the whites and blacks at the front and the coloureds at the rear. Each bra should have had its matching pair of pants adjacent to it, but now there were unmatched pairs. The drawer below, where she kept her slips and what she always referred to as her 'yes please' apparel, had also been disturbed.

Somebody had rather unprofessionally rifled through Belinda's chest-of-drawers.

Her dressing table was the same.

One of my suits in my side of the wardrobe was in the wrong place. I went over to Belinda's bedside table and slowly opened the top drawer. It was where she kept many of her private possessions. The lower drawer contained birthday, anniversary and Christmas cards going back as many years as we had known each other. She hadn't kept them all, only those from immediate family and then from the twins when they had become old enough to write their own cards. The top drawer contained her more personal items and I had never looked inside it. I didn't know whether it had been opened and searched but the belief that some stranger had breached Belinda's secret life made me feel extremely angry.

While I was in Germany, and more specifically Cochem, and I was being approached by what I believed were representatives of a British security organisation, the house had been methodically – but none too professionally – searched from top to bottom.

But for what?

I could think of nothing that would be of any use to the security services. If burglary was the motive and items stolen then – ironically – I would have felt a little better than I did. Burglary and the invasion of privacy that goes with it, is bad enough but at least the intruder is there for personal gain and may only take items of value.

Having my life, and more importantly my memories of Belinda, invaded in the most underhand of ways, was totally unacceptable. Even if Elizabeth had been in to tidy, she would not have opened any drawers, let alone touch what was inside them.

The twins' rooms were their own private sanctuaries, and as long as they kept them reasonably tidy, Belinda and I had let them have them the way they wanted them. Isabelle was the more adventurous, making a good deal of effort for her room to reflect her young personality. David had settled for a few risqué posters and a Star Trek bedspread. Regardless, somebody had been in the house and, if it wasn't Elizabeth, then my expensive security system had been easily breached.

I left the house and drove the short distance to see Elizabeth and Charles. They were busy in their greenhouse tending their tomatoes, peppers and lettuces. I had sensed a slight distancing develop between us since Belinda died, so I was pleased when they were happy to see me. Of course they didn't blame me in any way and maybe I was being overly sensitive, but Elizabeth in particular gave me the impression that as a couple we were to be doted on; as the father of two of their grandchildren I still had her respect but not a lot else.

They stopped their chores and we went into the house for a cup of tea. I told them about my trip to Germany, leaving out what had happened in Cochem. I saw them exchange looks when I explained the continuing need for solitude.

Charles was an ex-Army officer who had reached the rank of Colonel before retiring early and becoming a management consultant. He always found it somewhat amazing that people in industry actually listened to him regardless of his lack of experience in the private sector. He had doubled his Army salary for twelve years before retiring for good. Their house on the outskirts of Market Harborough wasn't palatial but it suited them admirably. They were both keen gardeners, spending most of the late spring and summer months pottering. They took three months off every year and flew to Cyprus for what they called peace and relaxation. Charles was now sixty-seven; he still had his military bearing and he tended to converse in short, sharp sentences. Verbosity for him was a waste of energy.

Elizabeth, as I explained before, took Belinda's death very badly. She accepted that when the time came it was a release, and being deeply religious she also accepted that what Belinda would have found on the other side had to be better than the pain her daughter had suffered during the last few years of her life. An elegant lady, Elizabeth was the same age as Charles but she looked a good few years younger. Tall with beautifully styled grey hair, she had handed on her personality to Belinda. She always saw the best in everybody – except for the Germans in Belinda's case – and was at times unforgivably generous. She helped in many of the charity organisations in Market Harborough but was always worried sick that people would regard her as a *do-gooder*.

It was for this reason I felt guilty thinking that her attitude towards me had changed. It was more likely that it hadn't – maybe even the opposite applied – but perhaps I felt responsible to them for letting their daughter die so young.

"Did you go to Blue-Ridge while I was away?" I asked as Elizabeth poured me a second cup of tea.

We were sitting in their sunroom, and although it was overcast outside, the brightness of the flowers and plants lit up the room.

"Called in the day before yesterday, erm … Thursday," Charles offered.

"Why?" Elizabeth asked as she handed me my cup and saucer.

"Just wondered," I said. "The mail was on the telephone table, that's all."

"Wasn't going to leave it on the floor, old boy," said Charles, a smile on his face.

"Has something happened?" Elizabeth gave Charles a disapproving look. She always said he would cut himself on his sharpness one day.

"No, not at all," I responded, perhaps a little too quickly. "I wondered, that's all." I thought it was best to change the subject. "I spoke to Isabelle earlier today."

"Oh, how was she?"

"Fine thanks. David was away playing cricket at Haileybury. I'm going down to pick them up on Saturday for an unexpected exeat, something to do with being good boys and girls, and they want to spend what's left of the weekend at home. Would you both like to come over for Sunday lunch?" They exchanged looks. "Don't worry, Isabelle will be doing the cooking!"

"For all of us? Why don't you all come over here?" Elizabeth suggested. "It'll be lovely to see the children, especially as it's unexpected."

"Isabelle is bringing a friend for the weekend."

"One more won't make any difference, and anyway Charles would prefer it that way," Elizabeth said rather brusquely. Charles was a creature of habit and I knew his Sunday lunches at home were sacrosanct. He didn't mind how many were there to eat as long as they ate round his table.

I wasn't too sure Isabelle would be happy because she had specifically asked me not to plan anything. She loved her grandparents dearly but she could be quite stubborn when she wanted to be.

"That might be better, thank you," I said. "We won't be able to stay too long after lunch because I'll have to get them all back."

"We'll have an early lunch then, say twelve for twelve-thirty?"

"That's fine."

Charles followed me to the car leaving Elizabeth standing at the front door.

"Everything all right?" he asked, putting a friendly arm round my shoulders. We were about the same height and probably the same weight. He had lost most of his hair but his face was still handsome and tanned. Belinda had idolised him.

"I miss her, Charles," I said. "I feel incredibly empty without her."

"We all do, old boy. She left a gap in all our lives but none of us knows what you must be going through." It was quite a speech for him, especially one in which he shared emotions. "But is there anything else? Ever since you came back from Derbyshire you seem to be preoccupied. Is it the young girl you found?"

I smiled at him. "Did Elizabeth put you up to this?" I asked, ignoring his question.

"We have discussed you, yes. I would be lying if I said we hadn't."

"I'm all right. It's just that –" I couldn't finish the sentence.

I shook him by the hand and waved to Elizabeth as I got into the car. She raised her hand in response but her whole manner was one of concern. I hoped by saying what I had that they would accept that Belinda's loss was my only reason for being the way I was.

Indicating left to turn onto the main road, I felt Belinda beside me, already discussing how well her mother and father looked and how nice it was to have them living quite close.

Involuntarily I felt my eyes begin to water ... again.

I am not going to dwell on the Coroner's Inquest into Ingrid's death. Suffice to say that in my considered opinion, it was a farce and severely dented my previous faith in the British justice system. I appreciated that the job of a coroner was to establish the cause of death, and not to determine criminal liability but for me, this particular inquiry fell short of determining the truth..

It was obvious that orders had come down from above as to the conclusions the Coroner should draw, and any evidence that might contradict this order wouldn't be introduced in the Court. The probable involvement of Governmental departments wasn't even hinted at, and I could not introduce anything I gleaned from my experiences in Cochem. No wonder the inquiry was over in a day.

After giving my evidence, the Coroner looked at me over his reading glasses, and asked me whether, in retrospect, I would have left Ingrid Mesterom on her own while I went in search of her rucksack. I wanted to reply by saying that had I stayed, he could be sitting in judgement over two deaths, not one. I did explain, perhaps a little sarcastically, that like all other human beings, I didn't have the benefit of hindsight. If I had, then no, I would probably not have left her.

The Coroner glared at me but said nothing.

The short-lived inquiry concluded 'unlawful killing' in the case of the death of Ingrid Mesterom.

During the drive to Buxton, I wondered whether Marie and Michael would make an appearance but concluded that it was unlikely.

I was right.

The press were in Court but not in great numbers. The police from Ashbourne also gave their evidence and there were passing nods of recognition but little else. It was as though the authorities accepted that there had been a murder and the appropriate procedures had to be gone through, but other than that it was to be swept under the carpet as soon as possible.

At least I could now get on with my life.

Chapter Eleven

Although I hadn't decided what to do – if there was anything I could do – about Blue-Ridge being searched, I needed to put it to the back of my mind, Isabelle and David deserved an untroubled weekend. The last thing the twins needed was a distracted and paranoid father. Nevertheless, there were still so many unanswered questions. There was an obvious connection with what I had been told by the two stooges in Cochem, but my imagination didn't let me go any further. Then there was the farcical inquest in to Ingrid's murder.

What real proof did I have that anybody had been in the house in the first place? There was nothing stolen and, to the unknowing eye, nothing had been disturbed. It was probably too late for me to do anything official about the intrusion, plus the fact that it was unlikely the intruders had left any fingerprints or any other evidence. What I wanted to know was – *if* the trespassers were from some Government department – had they gone in before the meeting in Cochem or after? If it was after, then I believed I had real cause for concern.

Saturday was a bright but windy day. After passing through the school gates and negotiating the bend before driving up the long driveway to the main building of St Edward's School, my thoughts were at last on the weekend. Other than Sunday lunch with their grandparents and in accordance with Isabelle's wishes, there were no other plans.

Similar to other older boarding schools, St Edward's was an awesome building. I did hope though, that its splendour wasn't taken for granted – I wanted it to be inspirational for its students as well. The driveway opened out onto spacious lawns and a car park that fronted the junior school to the left, with the main school to the right. The recent extension – 1960s – to the junior school included some not so architecturally acceptable classrooms on two floors, but the old chapel and living accommodation dated back to the early nineteenth century. There had also been extensions to the senior school but four floors of classrooms, offices and accommodation that had been adapted from an even earlier late eighteenth century seminary, hid them from immediate view. The whole school seemed to convey a message of power, authority and influence from within, and relaxation and leisure outside.

David was already waiting with a small rucksack slung over his shoulder. He waved as he saw me coming and I steered the car towards him.

"Hi, Dad," he said climbing into the front of the car. We gave each other a hug and then he threw his rucksack on the back seat.

"Where are the others?"

"Others?" he asked.

"Bella said she was bringing a friend home for the weekend. She said her name was Jane." I turned off the ignition.

"She didn't tell me," he commented critically. "Who did you say it was?"

"Jane somebody or other."

I saw Isabelle come out of the main building and look around for the car … I flashed the lights before getting out and waving.

"Hi, Daddy," she said with a beaming smile on her face. "This is Jane." She indicated a tall, slim girl behind her who was eyeing me a little anxiously.

"Hello Jane." I held out my hand, smiling. "I'm Richard."

"Hello Mr Blythe." Her face went from looking anxious to exhibiting a radiating smile that uncovered a set of gleaming white teeth against her dark brown skin. "I'm Jane."

I let go of Jane's hand and looked at Isabelle who came forward, threw her arms round my neck and kissed me on the cheek. "Good to see you again, Daddy!" she said.

"And it's good to see you, all three of you," I said, stealing a glance at Jane to make her feel part of the family group. "Right, come on, the longer we stay here the less time you'll have at home."

There was little traffic on the roads, which allowed us to cover the sixty miles in about an hour and a half. There was constant chatter from the back seat as Isabelle and Jane recounted various events that had occurred at school since I had last seen Isabelle. David kept on giving me sideways looks and raising his eyebrows, but remained silent, watching the road ahead.

The latest gossip included the fact that Miss Jessop, their history teacher, was leaving to get married. According to the girls, she was far too old to marry and have children.

"She must be at least thirty-five," Isabelle said. "And do you remember Jessica, Daddy?"

I was negotiating the roundabout under the A1 (M). "I think so, she's in the year above you, isn't she?" I looked in the rear-view mirror; Isabelle and Jane were watching me intently. I wondered what was coming because they were both keen to see my reaction.

"Was," said Isabelle. "She's been expelled."

"No, she hasn't," snapped David. "She's been suspended while the situation is being investigated," he added in a tired, monotonous tone. It was the first time he had spoken since getting in the car but, in his defence, it hadn't been easy to get a word in edgeways.

"It's as good as being expelled," retorted Isabelle.

"What's she been up to?" I asked, slightly amused.

"She and Mr Langley were found together," Isabelle volunteered in a mischievous voice.

"Found together? What do you mean?" I asked, knowing

what was coming next.

"She and Langley were caught together in his rooms," David chipped in before Isabelle could say anything.

"David! I wanted to tell Daddy." There were times when there was a reversal of David's supposed immaturity next to Isabelle's. I knew he was looking at me. I smiled.

"But she can't be more than fifteen. What do you mean, they were caught together?"

"Well," Isabelle began, "she says she'd gone to see him to get some help with a maths assignment but that's not what Mrs Craig said."

Mrs Craig was the school nurse, and from previous reports she spent a lot of her time skulking round corridors and eavesdropping. She regarded it as part of her duties but the pupils thought she was strange, but obviously not so strange as to refrain from broadcasting her side of the story on this occasion.

"So what was Mrs Craig's version?"

"Well," Isabelle began again, "Mrs Craig said that she went to Mr Langley's rooms to discuss the open day that's planned for early July before we break up …"

"Get on with it," David pleaded next to me.

"Shut up, David." The twins rarely argued or were nasty to each other. I put the current exchange down to the fact that Jane was in the car. "Mrs Craig said that she admits she was at fault because she knocked on Mr Langley's door and then walked straight in without waiting for a reply, but she also says that it's a good job she did." Isabelle paused for breath and David kept quiet. "According to Mrs Craig, Jessica and Mr Langley were kissing and the front of Jessica's shirt was undone."

"I see," I said. Although I knew what had been coming I felt quite concerned. "And Mrs Craig told you all this, did she?"

I accelerated past a combine harvester that was taking up

more than its share of the road.

"Not exactly," Isabelle explained. "She didn't tell us face-to-face but that's what happened. We were told by one of the girls in Jessica's year."

"And what has happened to Mr Langley? I presume he has been suspended too."

"Yes, but he's still on the grounds because he's got one of the school houses."

"Do I know him? I can't recall the name."

"No, he only started this term. You haven't met him yet."

"It doesn't sound as though I'm likely to. He hasn't made an auspicious start."

"It will be Jessica's fault," Jane suddenly said. "She flirts with all the boys and it probably goes beyond flirting with some of them." I looked in the rear-view mirror and Jane was looking straight at me. "She will have led him on."

I felt uncomfortable under her gaze and I wondered, on initial impressions, whether she was necessarily the right sort of girl for Isabelle to have as a best friend. I had no grounds for thinking such a thing, it was only a feeling.

The subject was changed, and soon afterwards, we arrived at Blue-Ridge.

I felt sorry for David.

From the moment we entered the house Isabelle assumed the dominant role. She and Jane were in charge for twenty-four hours. I fully appreciated that I could have said something but I had enough on my mind without adding to it. David tried to be sociable but gave up after a while and looked forlornly at me. I suggested he went to his computer in his room, assuring him that somebody would give him a shout when there was either food on the table or something else worth coming down for.

We went shopping on the way home because I had done nothing about getting anything in for the evening meal. Isabelle playfully rebuked me but I let her get away with it because of Jane's presence. We settled on a pasta dish that the girls prepared between them. David made a comment about *Bella Pasta* but only I heard him … we exchanged smiles. I had to admit the food was very good and all three children looked grown up sitting at the table with glasses of white wine in their hands – a small token from me in recognition of their advancing years.

We talked generally.

I gleaned a thing or two about Jane. Her full name was Jane Michaeline Mdeke, she was fourteen and a half years old and she was from Zimbabwe. Her skin was a dark shade of brown, as were her eyes. She had a pretty, expressive face with full lips and gleaming white, even teeth.

Both girls had changed into jeans and baggy tops, whereas David had settled for joggers and a sweatshirt. Jane's parents were black Zimbabweans, her father holding a reasonably senior post in the Home Affairs Office in Mugabe's Government. It was a topic I didn't dwell on because of what I had seen in her country when I was working there about five years ago, but at least I was able to talk generally about Harare and the bush with some authority. Jane spoke about both with some enthusiasm too, enjoying being able to relive her experiences of home. I wanted to ask her who was paying for her schooling in England, but decided not to..

I changed the subject when I sensed Isabelle was beginning to feel a little left out and David was looking bored. I explained that we were going over to Market Harborough the following day for lunch and Isabelle began to whine, but she reacted to my glare, which warned her not to push her luck too far. I wondered how the twins' grandfather would react when he met Jane.

He was in Salisbury in the Embassy at the time when Mugabe seized power. I thought it might be an interesting luncheon and I made a mental note to help a little by ringing them and forewarning them about who Jane was and where she was from.

David drifted back to his computer and the girls insisted I put my feet up while they washed the dishes. Afterwards they went up to Isabelle's room and the peacefulness in the house was suddenly shattered with the regular, boring beat of some modern pop group I'd probably never heard of.

I smiled and could see Belinda sitting opposite telling me that I was young once.

At about ten-thirty Isabelle came into the living room looking a little worried. "Daddy?" she began, sitting on the side of my chair and putting her arm round my shoulders. "Has somebody been going through the things in my room?"

I had been asleep but her question brought me immediately to my senses. "By somebody I presume you're asking if I've been through your things?"

She shook her head. "No, that's not what I'm saying. It could just as easily have been Grandma."

"What makes you think anybody has, Bella?" I turned my head which allowed me to see her eyes.

She screwed up her face. "Nothing really, but some of my things aren't as I left them."

"Such as?"

"Well for a start, the clothes in my wardrobe aren't in the same order." Fortunately, or in this case unfortunately, Isabelle had inherited her mother's need for tidiness and mine for orderliness. "My shoes have been moved and things in my drawers aren't where I left them."

"Maybe it *was* your grandmother. Maybe on one of the occasions she came in when I was away she tidied all the rooms. Some of them did need it, didn't they?"

"David's did you mean. He says his room hasn't been

touched. I asked him. Not that he'd know even if a tornado had taken up residence!" She pursed her lips in thought. "If it was Grandma, why didn't she do David's room as well?"

I decided to laugh it off. "Perhaps it was too untidy even for Grandma and she thought she'd need to spend a full day on it later."

Isabelle didn't smile. She looked at me, a serious expression on her face. "Daddy, you won't get annoyed, will you?"

"That depends on what you're going to tell me?"

Her question suggested I might be more concerned than annoyed. Something told me that either I wasn't going to be able to provide an explanation or I wasn't going to like what I was being told.

Isabelle looked away, her embarrassment obvious. "When my periods started last year, they were quite heavy, so Mummy took me to the doctor and she thought the best thing I could do was go on the pill. I was on them for about a year but then I stopped, but I kept the ones I hadn't taken in my bedside table. Surely even Grandma wouldn't go in there, would she?"

"No, I wouldn't think she would but why did you think I would get annoyed? I knew about you going on the pill. Mummy told me."

She looked surprised that Belinda had broken what might have been a confidence. She thought for a few seconds. "I left them in the back of the drawer. When I opened it this evening they were in the front."

I shrugged. "Maybe you were mistaken."

Her expression told me that this was not a possibility. "My diary was in there too and that has been opened."

"How do you know?"

"It's not that I didn't trust anybody but I kept a rubber band round it that was always lined up with a couple of marks on the cover. That's the way I left it, but the band has been moved and therefore I know somebody has opened it."

"I see." I wanted to say that I could promise her that it wasn't me, but that would have been trite under the circumstances. "Even if I had known your diary was in that drawer you know how I feel about you and David having your privacy."

"I know, Daddy, but somebody has opened it. I'm not lying." She looked close to tears.

"I still can't see why you thought I would be annoyed."

Isabelle sniffed and looked up at the ceiling and this time there were definitely tears in her eyes. "I thought you might have seen what I had written."

"Come on Bella, love, what is it?" I pulled her towards me and she buried her face in my chest. I put my hand on her hair and smoothed it. "Anyway, as I haven't been in your diary there's no way I can know what you've written and there's no reason to tell me, is there?"

She sniffed again. "I would have told mummy."

"You and your mother had lots of girly conversations and secrets that I was never privy to. Why should this be any different?"

She slipped off the arm of the chair and wedged herself next to me. "Because if I had told mummy about it, she would definitely have told you."

"Bella, I'm sorry but I'm getting confused. What exactly are we talking about now?"

Picking up one of my hands in hers, she looked at me and the tears started rolling down her face. Between sobs she said, "A week before Mummy died I was exceedingly low. I knew she didn't have long to live and I couldn't bear the thought of being without her. Do you remember the weekend before was quite hot?" I nodded. "A group of us from the village went for a walk in Mulberry woods and one of the boys and I went off on our own." She lowered her eyes and looked at her hands holding mine. "I nearly did it, Daddy, and I wrote about it in my diary," she said in a rush, her head stayed bowed.

I assumed my thirteen-year-old daughter had told me that she had nearly had sex with a boy in Mulberry woods a week before her mother died.

I didn't know how to react.

How should a father react? I didn't know whether to be grateful because she was now being honest with me and she had used the word *nearly*, but then again was she only being honest with me because she thought I had read her diary?

How would her mother have reacted? And how would I have reacted when Belinda told me? Because Isabelle was right – her mother would have told me. I didn't know how intimate their discussions had become.

I hadn't even thought about discussing the facts of life with David.

Should I have done? He was only thirteen.

Embarrassed by my own indecisiveness and lack of understanding, I still couldn't say anything. The thought of my little girl being touched in that way, whether she had consented or not, was more than I could take on board.

She was still a child.

Isabelle was watching me closely, I had to say something. She was still crying quietly and I fully appreciated the next thing I said could affect our relationship for quite a while.

"Bella, what do you mean when you say you *nearly* did it?' I asked.

"I mean ... I mean," she said, "he touched me and I touched him but we didn't ... you know what I'm trying to say, Daddy.'

I smiled and nodded. "I know exactly what you're trying to say, Bella, and –"

"Daddy, I'm sorry. I was out of my mind with worry and I thought, rather stupidly, that maybe, just maybe it would help the way I felt. I thought it would take my mind off what was happening back at home."

"And did it?" I asked quietly.

She shook her head slowly, bowing her head again. "It wasn't too bad at the time but afterwards I felt awful. It made me feel even worse. I felt, and still do feel so guilty, with mummy as she was ..."

I took my hand from hers and cupped her face, brushing my thumbs against the tears. "Don't ask me to try and understand why you thought being with this boy would help, Bella, but at least you discovered it wasn't the answer. If it helps, the first time I touched a girl like that I was a little over a year older than you are now. And she –"

"How old was *she*, Daddy?"

"I was going to say ... she was fourteen as well."

"Then ... you are not annoyed?"

"Annoyed? No. But you are my daughter and, well, any father would feel as I do now. You are growing up, of course you are, but there are certain things that ought to wait. Thank you for telling me."

She looked at me for a few seconds, trying to weigh up what I had said to her. "I didn't tell you because I thought you had read my diary," she said, sniffing again and wiping her eyes with the back of her hand. "I told you because I would have told mummy."

"I know."

"And because the pills were in the same drawer, I thought you would think that I was ... "

I put a finger to her lips. "Stop it, Bella," I said gently. "There's no need."

She looked down at her hands again. "Do you want to know who he was?"

Without hesitation I said, "No, I don't, but I would like to know how old he was."

"Fifteen," she said.

For some reason hearing that the boy had also been underage, helped. They had been two young people experimenting who had the sense to stop before things went too far. I doubted whether the boy felt the way Isabelle obviously did, but that was one of the facts of life. If it had been David confessing he had done the same thing, he too would have got the same reaction, but maybe I would have understood a little more readily.

"I won't do it again, Daddy, I promise."

Her promise and the innocence that went with it brought a genuine smile to my face. "You will, Bella, many times, but make sure you're a good deal older and it's with the right man."

Her face lit up. "Thank you, Daddy. I do love you. I'm sorry I let you and mummy down."

"You didn't let us down, Bella. You stopped before you did something you really would have regretted. Now you need to look to the future not the past. You had better go back to Jane. She'll be wondering where you've got to."

She leant forward and kissed me on the cheek before running out of the room without another word.

I hadn't given Isabelle an explanation of who and why somebody had been rifling through her things. I did hope, though, that in the last ten minutes we had reached the start of a better and fuller relationship: a father and daughter who missed the one person who would have been able to deal with her confession properly.

I could do little about what Isabelle had told me, but knowing that somebody had searched her room, and therefore David's, regardless of the fact that he thought nobody had been anywhere near it, was different. Violating my children's privacy was maybe less important when compared with Isabelle's experience, but at least I could try to find out who had done it and why it had been done.

Sunday lunch didn't turn out to be the difficult occasion I thought it might be. My concern proved unfounded the moment we walked into the house, when Charles and Elizabeth took an immediate shine to Jane, and Jane lapped up the attention she got.

For Charles and Elizabeth it was an opportunity for a trip down memory lane and Jane was more than willing to join them. She was thoroughly charming and attentive, listening when spoken to and making some comments and observations that were way beyond her years.

I had occasion to be in the kitchen with Elizabeth directly after the meal as she was preparing the coffee.

"You both seem to like Jane," I said.

"What a lovely girl," Elizabeth replied without turning round. "She's an example of what modern day Rhodesia can do for their children." The choice of the word Rhodesia didn't surprise me. I don't think I had ever heard either of them refer to Zimbabwe as Zimbabwe, but I had thought Jane would object, but she didn't. She said she was from Zimbabwe and when Charles had called it Rhodesia in reply, Jane didn't bat an eyelid.

I had decided not to phone ahead in case it caused more concern than was actually needed. In retrospect, I was pleased I hadn't.

"I thought Charles might not approve," I suggested.

This time Elizabeth did turn round. "Why on earth would you think that? She's such a charming girl and it's not her fault they have got a thug, a murderer, a thief and a philanderer as a President."

"But her father works for the President."

"She didn't chose her father and he probably didn't expect

things to turn out the way they did. It's a bit like Hitler's enemies during the war. Many of them worked quite close to him. Maybe Jane's father is biding his time, waiting to pounce." She switched on the percolator.

"Is that wishful thinking, Elizabeth?"

"Even if it is, that doesn't stop Jane being a lovely girl and obviously a good friend to Isabelle." She busied herself getting cups and saucers from the cupboard.

Elizabeth mentioning Isabelle reminded me I wanted to ask her again about their visits to the house while I was away. "Changing the subject, Elizabeth, thanks for looking in on Blue-Ridge while I was away. I'm sorry it was bit of a mess."

Elizabeth turned away from me and rested her hands against the sink. I saw her head bow slightly. "That's all right, Richard. I must admit I didn't go upstairs and I only vacuumed and dusted downstairs." Elizabeth paused and I shook my head. Now there was no doubt about the intrusion. "I miss her so much, Richard, I can't go into Blue-Ridge without seeing her in every room. I can hear her laughing, scolding the children when they were younger. I can see her in the kitchen, I see her everywhere."

"That's what she would have wanted, Elizabeth."

She turned but not before I saw there were tears in her eyes. "Is it, Richard? Is it really? She wasn't even forty and here I am nearly in my seventies with, as far as I know, not a thing wrong with me. Why did God have to take her first? Why did He deprive the children of a fine mother, and Charles and me of our only child? Why, Richard, why?"

"There is no reason, Elizabeth. No-one would be able to answer your question."

Turning round she looked at me, her elegant face swamped with pain. I wanted to reach out to her and share her grief but we had never been close enough for me to think she would want me to.

Maybe now was the time to try to get a little closer.

I stepped towards her but she immediately turned and picked up the tray. "I'll take this through. It'll soon be time for you to take the children back to school," she observed in a bit of a dither.

In the dining room, Charles had the children in fits of laughter.

Children?

I now knew at least one of them who had tried to be an adult before she was grown up. Isabelle and David had been very good at the meal table. There had been no loud sighing as Charles prattled on and on about Rhodesia to Jane. Every now and again, I caught Isabelle giving me a furtive glance, and when I caught her eye she let a rueful smile cross her lips. On one occasion she mouthed 'I'm sorry, Daddy' but unfortunately David was watching her and raised his eyebrows wanting to know what was going on between us.

We had about an hour after we got home before we needed to set off for St Edward's. David dashed upstairs to finish off a computer game he had started that morning, and Isabelle and Jane went to have showers and change back into their uniforms. St Edward's was strict during term-time. For exeats, students left and returned to the school in uniform, but for half term and at the end of term the rules were relaxed.

I was in the conservatory sipping a mug of coffee and watching a couple of grey squirrels darting back and forth at the bottom of the garden when I heard a slight cough behind me. Jane was standing at the door with a towel wrapped round her, speckles of water still on her dark skin.

"I'm sorry to intrude, Mr Blythe, but I wanted to say thank you for a lovely exeat." She stepped down into the conservatory.

"That's all right, Jane, it was good to meet you. You must

come again." Her choice of attire was a little unconventional, but her reasoning was explained when she looked furtively over her shoulder and then back at me.

"Isabelle's in the shower and I won't get the chance to speak to you on your own again." Before I could say anything she carried on. "I hope you don't mind me being personal, but I wanted to thank you for reacting the way you did when Isabelle told you what she had done. She's been worried out of her mind, she felt so guilty."

The shocked look on my face must have been obvious. "I, erm, well ..."

Jane came closer to me. She smelt of soap and I had to remind myself quickly that I was looking at a fourteen-year old girl.

"She told me the first day back at school what had happened and she has been looking for an opportunity to tell you ever since. The business about her diary and the other things gave her that opportunity. She's very pleased that you now know and you're not too angry, especially after I told her that you'd probably only set out to tidy up her room in preparation for her coming home this weekend."

"Jane, I think there has been a misunderstanding." I put the mug on the table and moved closer to the window, needing to put a bigger gap between us.

"What Isabelle did, Mr Blythe, is not unusual. Many of the girls at school have lost their virginity by the age of fifteen. They are the lucky ones."

"What?" I almost shouted. "She told me –"

"No, no, Mr Blythe, I didn't mean Isabelle. I wanted you to know that ... that she is Little Miss Innocent compared to a lot of the girls."

"Jane, I think ... no, what did you mean when you said they are the lucky ones?"

Jane looked over her shoulder again. "I was twelve, Mr Blythe, and it wasn't because I wanted it that way. I was raped by my uncle."

"Jane, where are you?" We both heard Isabelle calling from upstairs. "Jane," Isabelle called again, and this time it sounded as though she was halfway down the stairs.

"I wanted to tell you to allow what Isabelle did to be kept in perspective," Jane went on in a rush, lowering her voice. "I know I'm from a troubled country and what I've told you doesn't make things right, but she was a young girl experimenting, that's all."

"Jane!" This time Isabelle's voice came from the kitchen. "Jane, Daddy, where are you?" Frustration was setting in.

"You may only be fourteen, Jane, but …"

Jane had already turned and was stepping up out of the conservatory. She stopped and said over her shoulder, again in a loud whisper, "In Zimbabwe, Mr Blythe, the less time you spend being a child the more chance you have of survival. In a way I was lucky to have reached twelve because the majority don't."

"There you are," Isabelle said coming across the living room. She gave Jane and me a funny look. "What have you two been talking about?"

"I came down to say thank you to your father," Jane commented innocently.

"What, dressed like that, you'll give him a heart attack. Come on."

Isabelle smiled at me and then grabbed Jane by the arm and steered her across the room. At the door, Jane paused and looked back at me. Her expression finished off what she had been saying and I knew that perhaps I had said the right thing to Isabelle after all.

Chapter Twelve

On the Monday morning, I spent over three hours on the phone trying to get through to somebody in any department in the Foreign or Home Offices who might be interested in what I had to say and recognise the names Schwartz and Henke, but I think I knew I was onto a fool's errand from the outset.

Using every tactic I could think of, from being a relative and wanting to pass on some important news, to needing to discuss an offer they had made, I got nowhere.

Everyone I spoke to blocked me. They were all polite and on one occasion, I thought I was making progress but finally, as with all other avenues I tried, the door was politely but firmly shut in my face.

I even contacted an old friend of mine, Steve Wainwright, who worked in London in the Civil Service, but he rang me back two hours later with a "Sorry, chum, but didn't get anywhere, I'm afraid." I couldn't tell him more than the names I had because I didn't want to get him into trouble, but even if I had, I doubt whether he would have got any further. After a promise to meet up for a drink the next time I was in London and an offer from him to try if there was anything else he could do, we said goodbye, probably both wanting to keep the promise we made but both knowing we wouldn't.

Eventually I put whatever I was trying to do down to male pride. I had always been in charge and in control, therefore nobody had any right to invade my space – or anybody else's space I was controlling – without my permission. The names Henke and Schwartz were false, why couldn't I accept that and move on?

I went to bed and tried to sleep with the frustration and annoyance still competing for a place in my mind, Belinda then

joined in with her wry smile – "Men!" she said.
"What about men?" I asked her image.
"You don't know when to leave well alone, do you?"

On Wednesday morning among the bills and junk mail there was a letter from a very dear friend I hadn't seen for nearly three years, although we did send each other cards on our respective religious occasions and birthdays,

His full name was quite a mouthful – Dato Haji Abdullah bin Basrah Ibrahim – or for me, and only a few others, his name was Abby!

He was a high-ranking official in the Negara Brunei Darussalam Government with whom I had worked closely when I went to Brunei on a project in the early 1990s. I had to go back on a number of occasions and, on each trip, Abby and I became closer until eventually we concluded we were firm friends, in other words we totally trusted each other and discussed matters that weren't for outsiders' ears. Two worlds had come together in a way some would not understand or want to know about – a Muslim and a Christian were sharing a close and open friendship.

The fact that it was three years since we had seen each other was not an indication that our friendship had waned at all. It was my fault. Until I left Astek, my globetrotting hadn't allowed me to fit in another trip to Brunei – if I had wanted to see my family that is – and Abby was somewhat tied down with his responsibilities to the Sultan. Indeed, the last time we had seen each other was when Abby came to London in 1997, the year before Belinda fell ill. With the cards we exchanged – Hari Raya and birthday for Abby, and Christmas and birthday for me – we always enclosed long letters bringing each other up to date with what had happened and was likely to happen.

To get a letter in June from Abby, especially when my

birthday fell in October, was therefore unusual. I took the letter into the conservatory where I had left my coffee when I heard the post arrive. I opened the envelope a little apprehensively, expecting bad news but hoping it was simply to tell me he was coming to London again.

It was neither.

My Dear Richard

It is with great sadness that I write. I understand that Belinda passed away recently and I wish to pass on our sincerest condolences. I heard this heartbreaking news from a colleague who in turn discovered from Colin Ingram, you may remember him.

Had I known then I would have contacted you earlier but I fully understand that you and the children will have been under a lot of strain and grief.

Although I only met Belinda once, I told Nazira on my return from England that she was a beautiful and caring lady, who obviously adored you and your children.

Her passing will have been unbearable for you and it is with those thoughts in mind that I pass on Nazira's utmost condolences with mine.

I felt awful.

It was an oversight that would be difficult to explain. Abby met Belinda when he was last in London and we had dinner together in an excellent halal restaurant in Chelsea. Abby was unable to bring his wife, Nazira, because of commitments with her job, but he and Belinda got on marvellously well and, of course, there was an open invitation for us both to visit Brunei on holiday whenever we could. It was one of the journeys Belinda had always wanted to take but when I had the time she wasn't well enough – I had many regrets and not taking Belinda to Brunei was one of them.

Nazira is still enjoying her job but I think she may have allowed some of her frustration to show through recently because Major General Dato Aziz asked me whether she was after his appointment as Supreme Commander, and was she dissatisfied with being only his personal assistant!

The children are growing up far too quickly, even little, but now not so little, Leisha.

It was typical of Abby to introduce delicate humour after relating or commenting on some bad news; it was one of the reasons I adored him. He and Nazira had three children: Nadima fifteen, Ibrahim thirteen and little Leisha five, an admitted mistake, but nonetheless deeply loved like the other two. Nazira worked with the Royal Brunei Armed Forces in their Headquarters in Tutong. She was the PA to Major General Dato Haji Aziz bin Abdullah, the Supreme Commander, and had been in the post for a little under two years. Although an Islamic country, Brunei Darussalam, which had embraced Islam in the fifteenth century, was religiously to the left of centre, and females both single and married could work, drive, and shop without restriction. Wearing a scarf that covered their hair was a necessity but the accompanying face veil was not mandatory and few felt the need.

Richard, I do hope you do not mind if I use this letter of condolence to speak of another matter. It is the most secure means of communication as telephone calls are open to interception and e-mails read without you knowing who is reading them.

It is a matter of National importance I need to discuss with you but what it involves must wait until we can be face-to-face. Even then, we must be well away from others. I fully appreciate that your schedule will be full at such a sad time, but if you are able to come and see me then I can discuss this urgent matter with you.

Although Abby had heard about Belinda from a third party – Colin Ingram worked for a Singapore-based firm that dealt with ships' maintenance and we had met three or four times – he obviously didn't know that I had left Astek. If necessary, I had the time to respond to his request immediately, probably putting my time to better use than my plan to invade the Foreign Office.

May I suggest, Richard, that you ring me at home after six p.m. my time – after ten a.m. UK time – to tell me whether you can make it, and if so, when. You have my assurance that I will make all the necessary arrangements.

Once again, my dear friend, I am so, so sorry that you lost your lovely wife at such a young age. Our religious beliefs may be different but ultimately it is the same God, and each time I go to the mosque, I say a prayer for her and for you and the children.

I do hope we can meet soon,

Your dearest of friends,

Abby

I rang him thirty minutes after I'd read his letter and I tried to make sure the concern his request had generated wasn't mentioned.

He sounded as though he was in the next room. I could hear little Leisha playing and chattering away in the background.

Expressing his sympathy again for my loss, his tone didn't even hint that I was in the wrong for not letting him know, but I was sure that would come later. He was surprised, but nonetheless pleased, that I could drop everything and leave for Brunei at his convenience. He thought a week's stay would suffice.

I quickly checked St Edward's forecast-of-events and saw that if I left almost immediately I could be back before the next planned exeat, quietly hoping that the headmaster didn't have another attack of altruism. Abby told me that he would ring back with the flight details, explaining that it was all at his expense, including the hotel bills. Although Abby had a large house with ample room to put up guests, he suggested the arrangement we had come to many years earlier should remain. I would be far happier, according to him, in a first-class hotel rather than having to fight for things with his three children. I would have been happy with either but there were times when even Abby and I had to accept that there were cultural differences.

Ironically, if he ever came to Leicestershire, he would stay with me at Blue-Ridge and we would pop down to The Nevill Arms in the village for a pint or three. Abby was quite adaptable.

I rang St Edward's immediately and let them know I would be out of the country again for a week to ten days, and gave

Charles and Elizabeth as their immediate contacts, who were my next port of call.

A phone call would have been insufficient.

I could guarantee I would meet with disapproval from Elizabeth. She had never been happy that I had spent weeks out of the country and away from Belinda and the twins. We had never actually discussed the matter but Elizabeth had the ability to communicate without saying anything. Belinda had told me to ignore her, but Elizabeth's opinion merely added to my already rabid conscience. I knew I shouldn't be thinking like that, especially after Elizabeth's confession to me in the kitchen the previous Sunday, but I suppose in a way I still resented her reluctant acceptance of me as the bridge between her and her grandchildren.

It was with apprehension therefore that I parked in front of their house and rang the bell. There was no reply. I checked my watch and saw it was nearly one o'clock. Sometimes they went out for lunch during the week but not normally on a Wednesday. I rang the bell again – nothing. The curtains were open at the front of the house but other than that there was no sign of life. I crunched across the gravel to the garage and peered in through the frosted glass. I could see the outline of a car. Their house was within walking distance of the town centre and sometimes, on a nice day, Charles chose to ignore his ever-painful hip which allowed them to take a slow stroll into town.

I tried the side-gate between the garage and the house, thinking they might be in the garden although I couldn't hear them, but it was locked. Elizabeth had never liked to leave a key anywhere meaning there was no way I could get into the house. I had a key but it was on Belinda's key ring that I kept in the hall table drawer but hadn't thought to pick it up, never having had to use it before.

I was worried.

They hadn't said they were going to be away and even if they were, the curtains would have been drawn. Their house couldn't be seen from the road, being protected by some rather tall but unobtrusive Leylandii. Anybody wanting to see the house would have had to pass through the gates. The gravel added further security.

I stood outside the house for a few more minutes in the hope that they would return but, when they didn't, I decided to go back to Blue-Ridge and pick up Belinda's keys. Turning left out of the drive, in the rear-view mirror I saw a car, which materialised into a taxi, turn into the drive from the other direction.

I pulled into the side to execute a tight three-point turn. Charles was paying the taxi driver as I parked next to it. He gave me a weak smile of acknowledgement, accompanied by a slight raising of his hand. He looked drawn and tired, and his shoulders were unusually slumped. I didn't need anything else to tell me that something had happened to Elizabeth.

The taxi reversed out of the drive and Charles indicated that I should follow him into the house. He went into the kitchen and flopped onto one of the farmhouse chairs.

He looked up at me with watery and tired eyes. Despondency had replaced his usual brusque military manner.

"Elizabeth has had a stroke," he said, his bottom lip quivering. "Yesterday afternoon, found her in the garden when I got back from the Golf Club."

I sat down opposite him at the kitchen table. "Charles, I'm so sorry."

"Me too. Sorry I didn't let you know. Didn't want to worry you unnecessarily until …" He lifted his hand to his face to cover his embarrassment as tears flowed down his cheeks. "Don't know … what to do," he said croakily. "She's always been there. She'd … she'd tell me what to do if she could."

I could hear in his words exactly the ones I had expressed to myself about Belinda. I reached across the table and covered his other hand. He didn't take it away. "Is it bad?"

"Don't ... know. Never can tell ... with strokes." He took his hand away from his face and looked imploringly at me. "What am I going to do? She's my life."

"She's a fighter, Charles, she's one strong lady." I squeezed his hand.

"Came home to get her some things. Went with her in the ambulance yesterday," he said in a more controlled voice.

"Didn't they give you any indications?"

He shook his head. "Time will tell, maybe in a day or two. It might take weeks, even months."

"I see."

"Can't talk, left-hand side gone: face, arm, leg, everything. Conscious, eyes very bright but scared. What am I going to do?"

"You are going to get together what she needs and then I'm going to drive you back to the hospital. While you're sorting her things out I'll make us a cup of tea. What do two Englishmen do at a time like this other than have a cup of tea?"

His smile was tinged with obvious sadness.

Elizabeth was in a private hospital on the outskirts of Leicester. She had her own comfortably decorated and furnished room. There was a lovely view over the fields from her window but that was of little use to her at present.

She was lying on her back, her head propped up on at least three pillows, and looked peaceful, or as peaceful as the tubes and monitors allowed her to be. She was either asleep or dozing when Charles and I entered the room, and she didn't seem to sense our presence. The ward sister wasn't able to add anything to what Charles had already been told.

We decided to let her rest and go in search of a coffee. The word *search* wasn't necessary because there seemed to be coffee available at every corner. It didn't take long before we were comfortably seated with cups and saucers in our hands.

Charles understandably seemed miles away. I thought it best to stay silent until he was ready to say something. My mind went back to Belinda's time in hospital before she insisted on coming home to die. She too had been in a private hospital, but one more local to us in Oakham. The medical staff were brilliant, understanding not only the needs of their patients but also their visitors. The nurses seemed able to switch from their chosen profession to being hosts, depending on whom they were dealing with. I found it a comfort and I am sure many of their patients found comfort in it also. Belinda used to sing their praises all the time and ask why you had to pay private medical insurance for such an excellent service.

We discussed her naivety at length!

"It was Belinda," Charles muttered beside me. "Never came to terms with Belinda leaving us. Changed her." He looked down at the cup and saucer in his hands. "Then with David and Isabelle away at school, she wondered what it had all been about."

"We all wonder that, Charles, but the kids wanted to stay at St Edward's after Belinda died. Primarily, it's what they wanted that mattered and they believed it's what their mother would have wanted."

Charles simply nodded and went back to staring into space.

Understandably, I wasn't too happy but not surprised that Belinda and the twins were to be blamed for Elizabeth's current state ... but blame was the wrong word. They weren't being blamed, it was a matter of circumstances. I would have changed everything if I thought it would have brought Belinda back. I had witnessed and overheard any number of heated discussions between her and her mother concerning the children's schooling.

Elizabeth was in favour of keeping them within easy reach even though she and Charles had sent Belinda away to school. Her logic was that both she and Charles travelled the world with his job and therefore there was nothing else they could have done if they had wanted Belinda to have the best, but with Belinda staying in England when I was travelling, she didn't have to do the same. The argument that it was what the twins wanted held no water whatsoever.

"How can children of that age know what they want?" I could hear Elizabeth saying now, but she did have sufficient sensitivity to let up once Belinda's fell ill

"Don't have to tell me, old boy." Charles suddenly said. He was looking towards a couple of nurses who were talking quietly by a water dispenser, but I doubted if he could see them. "To see your only child being consumed slowly by a killer disease and finally being taken from you would be too much for anybody. Elizabeth is strong, I agree, but even she –" He broke off, unable to finish the sentence.

I put my hand on his arm. "I know it's hard now but she'll …"

"Doesn't hold you responsible either," he said, not hearing me. "Gives that impression sometimes, I know, but there's no malice towards you."

There was a suitable comment to make but then wasn't the time and I hated myself for even thinking it. Regardless of recent exchanges, I still felt Elizabeth tolerated me.

I don't think she ever really came to terms with Belinda and me getting married in the first place. Whether it was my chosen career or me that put her off, I never really knew. I hoped it was the former. Belinda always told me that I was imagining it all and that I could be a very good martyr to the cause, because deep down her mother loved me like the son they always wished for but never had – but I continued to have my doubts.

When we moved to Medbourne to be nearer to Elizabeth and Charles, I thought it might improve my perception, but nothing seemed to change – I got the feeling that I was being tolerated more often, that's all. Belinda had a facial expression that said, "You're being a martyr again," and she used it whenever she saw me react to something her mother said that I thought was personal.

Now I was reacting in exactly the same way to something Charles had said.

In many ways, I suppose Belinda was right; I was overly sensitive at times. I held Elizabeth in high regard and I looked upon her and Charles as more than only Belinda's parents – in many ways they were mine too. My mother and father had divorced when I was twelve and my sister ten. My father came home one Tuesday in the summer of 1973 and Fran, my sister, and I were sent upstairs to our rooms to do our homework but we actually sat at the top of the stairs and listened, cuddling next to each other for security, each knowing what was happening, neither wanting to admit it.

There was one almighty row.

For a long time I had sensed something wasn't right between my parents. Being still young, I put it down to adult behaviour. Adults had strange ways a twelve-year-old didn't understand. Fran would never discuss it. She loved her mummy and daddy and they loved each other, a simple but effective means of escape from the truth.

There was a lot of swearing and screaming downstairs but neither of them, thank God, resorted to violence. For some inexplicable reason, I respected them both for that. I still do today. From what Fran and I could hear, I gathered that Dad had been having an affair for some time with a woman where he worked and they had decided they wanted to be together.

Later mum told us he went off with the ubiquitous secretary.

He wanted, and got, access to us, but the weekends when we were with him were never a success. Fran and Melissa, his secretary and soon to be his new wife, never got on together to the extent that after only six months, Fran refused to go and stay with them. I only lasted another three months. I was old enough and wise enough, even at thirteen, to realise that they were trying to buy my loyalty and prise me away from my mother.

It didn't work.

Melissa was a good few years younger than dad and, from some of the looks she gave him when his back was turned, I wondered what her real motives were for taking him away from my mother.

In 1981, while I was at university, my mother got a letter from a solicitor in Edinburgh explaining my father was dead. He was one of two victims in a fatal car crash and that she was a beneficiary in his will.

My mother had remarried in 1979, and when she heard of my father's death, she and her husband were living in Australia and Fran with them. They lived in Perth and I saw them once every two or three years.

Fran is married now and has quite a brood, five at the latest count - three girls and two boys. I still communicate regularly with my mother, and with Fran, but after my father left her, she and Fran appeared to grow closer and closer together creating a sort of anti-male bond. I wasn't excluded, far from it, but there was a definite distancing. When my mother realised that not all men were *fornicating bastards* – a description I heard regularly coming from the bathroom when she was in there crying her eyes out – and remarried, I was coming to the end of my first year at university.

By this time I had already met Belinda and, although we were still discovering each other, we were secretly, but not always knowingly, planning our future together. We both had designs on the other but didn't speak about our feelings too loudly in case it scared the other one off. When I decided after finishing my degree not to join my mother and Fran in Australia, they took it badly and I never really regained the closeness we once had.

Belinda's family, small though it was, therefore became my family. Maybe because deep down I wanted Elizabeth to be a surrogate mother, I had become overly sensitive towards her. I knew I shouldn't take what she said quite so literally, but we never got close enough to break down all the barriers between us, perceived or not.

"Shall we go back to Elizabeth?" I asked Charles, taking his cup and saucer from him.

Nothing previously said or alluded to, none of the looks, the misinterpretations and the rancour were worth thinking about or worth remembering. Conscience can be a devil when we think we are about to lose someone close.

That evening, and after plying Charles with a couple of whiskies, I explained that I would probably have to go abroad for a week but that I was more than willing to postpone my trip if he thought I could help. My words were underhand. I was putting the responsibility on his shoulders to say whether I should go or not.

He looked at me over his whisky glass, his eyes strained from tiredness, worry and probably the alcohol. "Course you must go, old boy," he chirruped, his voice appearing enthusiastic but very much in contrast to how he must have really felt. "Needs must."

"What about you, though. You've never had to look after yourself before?"

"And you're going to do that are you? You're going to come and cook for me, do my washing and ironing, are you?" His tone was still jovial but I detected an underlying sarcasm that was unusual for him.

"That's not what I meant. It's that at times like this you need faces you know about you, not strangers." I reached for the whisky bottle and added a finger to my glass.

When Belinda was ill I had the twins and they were both marvellous, especially Isabelle. I also had Charles, Elizabeth and a few close friends.

Charles was a member of the local golf club and, like me, he'd made some good friends among fellow members. However, Charles was a private person. He didn't believe in communicating personal grief too widely. When Belinda died, he became even quieter than normal. I had managed to play a few rounds of golf – I suddenly had the time and my playing partners were sympathetic towards my loss but equally enthusiastic that I should look for pastures new because it was what Belinda would have wanted.

How they knew that I don't know because most of them had never met her.

I wasn't sure that Charles was capable of looking after Elizabeth at home if she were to be confined to a wheelchair; and if, at the other extreme, she were to go into a nursing home, I doubted if he would last five minutes on his own.

He could learn to care for himself but nobody could replace the companionship Elizabeth provided. Belinda used to watch them together and smile knowingly. Afterwards she would say, as though reminding herself, "They are absolutely devoted to each other. They might not say a lot but each knows where the other is and what they are doing. When I'm in the garden with mother, she's constantly looking over her shoulder and checking where he is. When he goes off to the golf club she worries; when he goes to the local shops she worries, and he's exactly the same with her. God knows what will happen to the other when it's time for one of them to go."

Now the time had come.

"Where are you going, anyway?" Charles asked, his words sounding slurred.

"The Far East," I replied casually, as though it was no more than round the corner.

"Like saying Africa," he said. "Where in the Far East?"

"Brunei."

"Brunei? Used to have an arrangement with the Sultan there, still do as far as I know. Had a couple of hundred British servicemen on loan. Damn good posting. Never got it myself. Almost went out for the Borneo Confrontation in the early 60s, but never made it. Can't remember why not. Didn't you go there a few years back?"

"Yes, Charles, I did."

"So why are you going? Thought you'd resigned from Aspect?"

"Astek, Charles," I pointed out, smiling. "I have, but an old chum has asked me to pop over to see him."

"Pop over? One doesn't pop over to the Far East. When are you going?"

"Probably Friday or Saturday, but I'll be back by the end of next week. There are school commitments and now, of course, Elizabeth."

Charles began to get up from his chair. "Don't you worry about me. Didn't spend all those years in the army without learning to look after myself. Can boil an egg and switch the vacuum on, you know. Slept in some most peculiar places in my time."

"Of course, Charles, but –"

"No buts, old boy. You bugger off to Brunei and hopefully when you get back there'll be some improvement."

Chapter Thirteen

The aircraft banked and I could see the Borneo coastline under the wisps of cloud. In most places a thin strip of white and yellow sand separated the grey-blue sea from the jungle's green canopy, in others the jungle seemed to be growing directly out of the water. There were no obvious hills or cliffs.

During our descent from over thirty thousand feet, the aircraft pitched and yawed and mine wasn't the only anxious face. The Captain informed us the aftermath of a tropical storm named Cimaron, was the cause of our discomfort.

We were flying in a Royal Brunei Airlines Boeing 757. Although I knew quite a lot about structural stress factors, and had flown all over the world, I had never experienced anything quite like the last twenty minutes.

Taking off from Changi Airport, Singapore, into a clear blue sky, the clouds built up quickly, obliterating the sparkling South China Sea. Fortunately, for most of the flight, the aircraft was above the storm but the strange swirling cloud eruptions below didn't auger well unless conditions improved dramatically and quickly. Once we started to descend and entered the cauldron, I have no idea how the aircraft stayed in one piece. At one point, we must have hit an air pocket of two or three hundred feet because the aircraft seemed to plummet and the passengers were too scared to scream. I was sitting in business class surrounded by mostly local Bruneian business executives who were openly praying to Allah. They believed that whatever happened was God's will, but their expressions suggested that His will on this occasion should be that they would see another day. I rather hoped that God would grant their prayers, and my silent ones.

There were three other European passengers in business class – two men and a woman – all sitting individually. One of the men had thick grey hair, the other, on the opposite side of the cabin, was thin on top and his liver-spotted bald patch was glistening with perspiration in spite of the air-conditioning.

The female, who was also on the other side of the cabin but level with me, was probably in her early to mid-thirties, with shoulder-length auburn hair. She had a pretty face that was now set in deep concentration as she tried to read a book, attempting to ignore the sudden jolts and descents. We had exchanged pleasantries when she boarded the aircraft in Singapore. The flight attendants, dressed in their attractive light blue and gold uniforms, were firmly strapped into their seats in front of us and the reassuring smile given to me by Wendy when I had flown into *Düsseldorf* prior to my fateful trip to Germany wasn't replicated. The Bruneian flight attendants were as terrified as the rest of us.

The last time I had been in Negara Brunei Darussalam in the mid-1990s, Europeans undertook the maintenance of the Sultan's National Airline on contract, and many of the pilots and co-pilots were European also. However, and as part of the *Bruneianisation* programme, Bruneian citizens were now trained in the maintenance of the aircraft and some of the Bruneian co-pilots were captains.

Whoever was at the controls of this particular aircraft was experienced, he had to be. The captain's voice had sounded European but that meant nothing if the plane hadn't been checked recently or properly, for airworthiness. In this instance, I hoped the captain was Bruneian, because it would be emblematic for the future of the country. I believed that The Royal Brunei Airlines did have an excellent safety record, unlike some of its South East Asian competitors.

"Cabin crew prepare for landing," the captain announced. The flight attendants looked at each other as much as to say: "We are prepared for landing. Any fool who's not strapped in deserves all they get."

Reluctantly, one member of the cabin crew did undo her seatbelt. She stood up and then carefully, clutching onto the sides of the seats as she moved down the aisle, checked that we were as we should be. I assumed other brave souls were doing the same elsewhere in the aircraft.

"Ladies and Gentlemen, this is your Captain. Sorry about the bumpy ride but we'll be on the ground soon. The tail end of the tropical storm we have just flown over and through, dictates the current weather in Bandar Seri Begawan, and it's awful. It was touch and go whether we landed at Bandar or elsewhere, but fortunately, the wind has dropped sufficiently for us to have a go. Kota Kinabalu is the nearest alternative, however I doubt if conditions are any better there. The temperature on the ground is 32°C and the humidity is at about 90%, the winds are strong and variable, and it's raining, pouring in fact. Welcome to Negara Brunei Darussalam!"

I looked at the woman sitting across the aisle and she turned her head towards me. She smiled and said over the roar of the aircraft's engines, "I have every faith in the fact that by 'have a go' he meant he had every intention of being successful."

"I hope so too." I said, smiling.

The aircraft suddenly lurched heavily to the right and there was a surge of power from the engines drowning any further chance of conversation. The flight attendant had fortunately already returned to her seat.

I looked out of the window and guessed we were about four hundred feet above the ground. We were flying over the coast and I could see heavy breakers doing their damndest to reach the jungle only a few yards from the shoreline. The aircraft lurched again and I stole another look at the woman. She looked terrified and I hoped another smile gave her some reassurance.

There was a sudden thump. Looking out of the window and

to my surprise, we were on the ground. The engines went into reverse, and the surge of power was comforting. From the rear of the aircraft there was loud applause and cheering. Those of us in business class joined in a split second later, delighted to be on terra firma.

"Ladies and Gentlemen …" It was the Captain again "… that, to say the least, was interesting but now we are down safely. Welcome again to Negara Brunei Darrusalam, where the local time is fourteen-fifty hours. Please keep your seatbelts fastened until we have docked and the cabin crew have opened the exit door. May I remind you that there is no smoking permitted until you are inside the terminal, although after our recent experiences you might feel like one now. I certainly do, but I must also refrain. Thank you for flying Royal Brunei Airlines and we look forward to you flying with us again."

A female voice translated the captain's announcement into Malay but I doubted whether his nicely timed witticisms would be included.

"Every faith," the woman repeated.

"Attention-grabbing wasn't it?"

"An understatement," she said.

"Richard Blythe," I said smiling.

"Sophie Mackintosh." We attempted to reach across the aisle and shake hands, but as we both had window seats, our belts wouldn't let us.

We both laughed.

There was much clicking of seat belts throughout the aircraft. People wouldn't believe they were really safe until they had their feet on the ground. It looked as though the airport had been significantly modernised since I was last in Brunei and it had been up to the best of Western standards even then.

"I'm not sure you heard me the first time, but my name's Sophie Mackintosh," she said, having shuffled into the aisle.

"Richard Blythe," I replied. We shook hands this time.

She was about five feet eight inches tall, and from the front she was even more attractive than in profile. She was wearing a pale green linen business suit that enhanced her slim but well proportioned figure. Under the suit she wore a yellow silk blouse which made me wonder whether she had been to Brunei before – yellow was the Royal colour and people were discouraged from wearing it. There was a string of pearls round her throat, but I noticed there were no rings on her fingers. I decided I had guessed her age about right - thirty to thirty-five. Her blue-green eyes were smiling at me and her tanned skin gave her a healthy sheen. Considering what we had been through, she looked remarkably cool and calm. I wondered why she was in Brunei and concluded, with no evidence whatsoever, that she probably had something to do with the British High Commission, in which case she should have known about not wearing yellow.

I reached into the overhead locker and extracted what could only be her hand luggage.

"Thank-you,' she said. "It was good to meet you, Mr Blythe, and I'm sorry we didn't have the opportunity to have a longer chat."

"Maybe we'll bump into each other again. It's not a big country."

She smiled at me and her eyes sparkled. Just before saying, "Possibly," she let the tip of her tongue touch her upper lip. She then moved down the aisle and exited through the front door.

I didn't see Sophie Mackintosh again.

Whether she was more important than I had thought I don't know, but I looked out for her at passport control, in the baggage reclaim area and then in customs, but didn't catch sight of her.

The airport had changed considerably and, fortunately, with it the efficiency. I remembered Brunei as a country that existed in the 1990s but still lived in the 1950s. It had inherited British bureaucracy from that period and had never managed to update it.

Everything was now well organized even to the extent that the bags were waiting for us when we got to the baggage reclaim area. I was impressed. The airport with its marble floors and pillars was fully air-conditioned and everywhere was spotlessly clean. Through the enormous floor to ceiling windows, I could now see the extent of the storm we'd flown through. The sky was grey, the visibility was very poor and it was lashing with rain.

I passed through the arrivals exit pushing a trolley and looked at a sea of local faces, and some European. I couldn't see Abby anywhere but then I heard my name being called..

"Richard!"

He was wearing a high-necked batik shirt, a black *songkok*, black linen trousers and black shiny shoes. It was three years since I had seen him but he hadn't changed at all. At five feet seven he was six inches under my height. He had well-cut short jet-black hair, a black well-trimmed moustache, a happy round face, bright brown eyes and a slim physique. He looked a lot younger than his forty-five years.

"Richard, Richard," he repeated as he reached me, "how marvellous to see you again, my friend."

We embraced like the good friends we were but I noticed over his shoulder that it generated a few, and not necessarily approving, looks from other Bruneians in the vicinity.

"Abby," I said, smiling and holding him at arm's length, "you haven't changed at all. If anything, you're looking even younger."

He winked, tapped his nose, and at the same time allowed a mischievous grin to cross his face. "Nazira, Richard, she keeps me young and active."

"Don't know what she sees in you," I commented, putting a hand on his shoulder.

He smiled. "And you, Richard, how are you?" His face became serious. His question wasn't only the polite thing to say, it was from the heart.

"I'm fine, Abby, thanks."

He didn't believe me, because although he smiled again, it was a smile of concern. "Perhaps we will discuss that later." He reached for the handle on my luggage trolley. "Come on, let's go to the car."

We began walking across the concourse.

"Good of you to dress up for me, Abby!" I said.

He shook his head but his *songkok* stayed in place. "Your memory must be going, Richard. It's Friday and for us Friday in the mosque is like your Sunday at church, we dress up for the occasion. We must respect He who controls our destinies," he added, still smiling.

"Ah! Of course, sorry, I forgot," I said.

Regardless of the number of times I had been to the Far East, and in particular to Brunei, I had never prepared myself sufficiently for the wall of gelatinous heat that hit me every time I left the airport building. It was like walking into a brick wall: stifling, airless and muggy. After being relatively dry courtesy of the air-conditioning first at Changi Airport, then on the aircraft and in the terminal, after only seconds the sweat was pouring off me. By the time we had walked the short distance – which fortunately was undercover – to Abby's car, I was awash, whereas Abby appeared to remain relatively cool. The rain was still falling therefore adding to the humidity.

Relief came as we drove away from the airport in Abby's air-conditioned four-wheel drive Range Rover, the road bedecked on either side with Brunei's National flag and many others I didn't recognise. We went under an ornate yellow, white and black arch with the Sultan of Brunei's picture prominent. He was smiling down on his subjects and those visiting his country. The elaborate flower and shrubbery beds were interspersed with trimmed plantain grass at the kerbside and everything looked orderly.

Abby saw me looking all about me. "Has it changed much?"

I peered through the windscreen. "The weather certainly hasn't."

Abby screwed up his face as he too looked up into the grey sky, the windscreen wipers doing their best to give him a clear view.

"This has been with us for nearly a week now but it's coming to an end. Hopefully tomorrow you will see the sunshine you are able to enjoy constantly back in England," he said.

He stole a mischievous look at me and smiled. Abby's sense of humour wasn't unique among his fellow Bruneians but where his was different was that he would tell a joke against himself before he told one against somebody else.

Certain circles would not have allowed his earlier and open suggestion that Nazira kept him fit and active – a man's sexual activities were for the privacy of his home and nowhere else. On the other hand, his remark was not one I would have made about Belinda, or any of my close friends would have made about their wives to anybody else.

"The airport is looking fantastic," I commented.

He gave me another sideways glance as he negotiated a roundabout under what looked like a motorway. "May I ask whether you thought there was anything wrong with it the last time you were in Brunei?"

"Well, other than the efficiency of the people running it, I must admit, no. It was modern then, but it's even more so now."

He nodded his head. "Exactly! I accept the people are more

efficient but wasting millions of dollars on continuously updating the airport is not my idea of progress. It's all to impress those from outside, when the money would be better spent elsewhere. Look at this motorway we are about to join – it wasn't here the last time you visited Brunei, was it?"

"No," I said.

"It's unnecessary and another waste of money."

"Still the rebel, I see," I said.

He shook his head this time. "It makes me very angry, Richard. You wait until you see Jerudong. You will think you are in Disneyland, but why do we need it?"

Abby's comments were a little worrying. He had been open with me in the past but he always added the caveat that he remained totally loyal to the Sultan and to the State. I detected no such caveat in his tone on this occasion and wondered whether this was the reason for me to travel ten thousand miles to see him. It would have been impolite for me to ask – it was for him to introduce whatever it was when he was ready.

We pulled up outside the Sheraton Utama hotel, which Abby thought I would prefer for old time's sake. A young uniformed baggage handler appeared, swung open the rear door of the Range Rover and offloaded my suitcases before I got out of the car. Abby had already cleared the way at Reception and registration was swift. My en-suite room was on the top floor at the front of the five-storey building, which meant it overlooked the Churchill Museum and the main Mosque. I could see many new buildings to the left, changing what I remembered of Bandar Seri Begawan's skyline. The window had tinted glass to reduce the glare from the sun but, even so, there was no evidence that Abby's forecasted weather improvements were on the way. I shivered slightly and made a note to adjust the air-conditioning once Abby had gone.

"Richard," he said, "I will leave you to settle in. I have to be at the Mosque in thirty minutes to show willing."

I frowned, another unusual remark. "Come off it, Abby, you'd be a fundamentalist if you could."

He didn't smile. "No, I don't think so, Richard."

Looking over my shoulder, I saw his eyes settle on the Mosque opposite.

"I believe in everything Islam stands for and what the Koran tells us, but when I see my religion and Holy Book being used wrongly, deliberately misinterpreted to defend an unjust decision or action, I get very angry. There is evil out there with crimes being committed in the name of Allah."

"I think I understand," I said.

"Do you, Richard? I'm afraid I don't." He was silent for a few seconds and then he switched back to the jovial Abby again. "If you want a drink, Richard, I'm afraid we're going through one of those holier than thou phases again, more hypocrisy. You can consume alcohol in your room as long as you sign a chitty to say it is for personal consumption and needed for medical reasons. I am afraid the bars downstairs are for non-alcoholic drinks only. The swimming pool is where you remember it to be. We still allow non-Muslim females to use it." He winked. "Other than that I will collect you at about seven o'clock, we would like you to have dinner with us and meet the family. They are all looking forward to seeing you again."

"Thanks, Abby," I said, holding out my hand. "Your hospitality knows no bounds, it's as though time has stood still."

He clasped my hand with both of his and smiled. "It hasn't, Richard, but you, like me, probably wish it had." He bowed slightly and left the room.

His final remark left me standing in the middle of the room frowning and looking at the closed door. There was something troubling him and it had to be the reason why I was there. I shook my head thinking maybe he had misinterpreted what I'd said.

Time would tell.

Going back over to the window, I could hear the Muslim call to prayer and I wished I could gain some strength from it. I remembered the second line from the *Adhan* (call to prayer) and it always had an impact on me – 'I bear witness that there is no god except the One God' – if that were the case and all religions believed it to be the case, the world would be a far better and safer place.

Chapter Fourteen

Nazira looked stunning and the children thoroughly scrubbed. They all greeted me at the front door of Abby's house, although *house* is a loose description.

Wealthy Bruneians and high-ranking officials owned colourful and over-elaborate houses with ornate marble pillars supporting equally elaborate entrances. Abby's house was no exception. Situated on the Tutong road out of Bandar Seri Begawan – Brunei's capital city – it was on the same road as the Sultan's palace, which signified Abby's importance. On a slight rise, it was possible to stand at the front door and see the golden dome of the palace itself.

The walls of the house comprised a white mottled ornate brick with grey mortar. The front door was blue with gold fitments and the blue roof and porch tiles matched the door. There were two flights of scrupulously clean marble front steps leading to the entrance. Supported on eight legs, the underside of the house created an open car park cum basement for their three cars and Abby's Range Rover. Also under the house was a well-kitted play area for their children.

At the rear of the house, more steps led down to staff quarters. They had three fulltime locals working for them: a cook, a cleaner and a gardener. Abby preferred to drive himself but whenever Nazira wanted to go out she had access to a Government car and driver if she wished.

Nazira looked striking. She had converted to Islam from Christianity before marrying Abby. They had met when he was a junior member of Brunei's embassy in Kuala Lumpar. Islamic, and therefore Bruneian law did not approve of physical relationships between Muslims and non-Muslims, it was therefore easier for Nazira to convert from Christianity than it was for Abby to give up what wasn't a religion alone but a lifestyle.

Seeing her for the first time in many years made it seem as though time had stood still, for her at least. Not unexpectedly, looking at her also made me think of Marie and Ingrid; there were many similarities. Nazira – her Christian name had been Angeline before converting to Islam – was the product of a mixed race marriage. Her father was Indian and her mother Malaysian and Nazira had inherited the best of both cultures.

Although she had embraced Islam out of her love for Abby, she retained independence of thought. When moving with Abby in the higher circles of Bruneian life she adopted the traditional modes of dress and behaved accordingly. However, when at home and mixing with non-Islamic cultures she dressed casually or informally. Abby, when it was appropriate, loved her belief in temporary non-alignment, explaining that he was getting the best of both worlds: a compliant and orthodox wife when the needs warranted them but a freethinking and sometimes quite dominant partner on other occasions. Over what was an illicit beer for him, he once told me he particularly liked sexual subjugation and Nazira willingly obliged his fantasy.

His choice of words had made me smile and his lack of embarrassment had caused the reverse in me.

This evening Nazira was wearing light-blue silk trousers and a white silk top. Her black hair shone with health and she had applied her make-up to perfection. There was a simple gold necklace at her throat, gold rings hanging from her ears and gold bangles on her wrists. She was a little taller than Abby but equally slim. When she smiled, there was a twinkle in her eyes and she literally glowed with vitality. She gave me a peck on the cheek as she welcomed me back to their house. I took off my shoes and stepped into another world.

The children were standing in a height-ordered line inside the door. Nadima and Ibrahim looked quite grown-up in traditional clothes. They smiled politely and proffered their hands as a welcome. However, little Leisha, although equally smart, didn't know me and I doubted whether the other two remembered me either. The little one clutched her sister's leg and tried her best to disappear into the folds of Nadima's clothing. When I bent down to say hello, she turned her face away in embarrassment.

The entire house was air-conditioned and the coolness was very welcome. It had stopped raining but it was still humid. Even the short walk from Abby's Range Rover to the front door had made me perspire. A maid, who looked as though she was a Filipino, came forward with a tray on which were numerous tall glasses containing a variety of cold drinks.

"We will have a proper drink later on, Richard," Abby told me with a knowing smile, his eyes indicating the children.

I nodded, returning his smile while selecting a glass of orange juice from the tray. "This will do nicely, thank you," I replied. From one source or another Abby would have obtained a few cans of Tiger or Anchor beer, not to mention a bottle of excellent malt whisky. They would all be secreted away somewhere.

We chatted but after only a few minutes, the meal was ready. Nazira suggested that the children might like to go to their rooms, and they obediently disappeared with respectful 'goodnights'. I guessed that each had their moments of disagreeableness or even disobedience – what child doesn't? – but from an outsider's perspective, they were children to be proud of.

The living and dining areas were one big room in the centre of the house. There was a bedroom at each corner – three of which had en suite bathrooms – and the kitchen was through swing doors to the rear of the house. The rosewood table and chairs could seat at least ten people. The three of us sat at one end, with Nazira at the head of the table – deference to her being in her non-Muslim mode!

The meal, a mixture of Malaysian and Chinese dishes, was delicious and its aroma even better, but it wasn't until we were served with an exotic fresh fruit salad that Nazira delicately introduced Belinda's death into the conversation. They had both offered me their commiserations on arrival but I guessed for the children's sake, the subject was quickly changed.

"You should have let us know about Belinda," Nazira scolded, while carefully balancing a piece of a star fruit on her fruit-fork.

"I'm sorry." I stole a look at Abby and he raised his eyebrows. He and I had discussed Belinda during the short journey from the hotel and he had warned me that I would have to face the music from Nazira. "I should have let you know, both when she fell seriously ill and when she died. But to be quite honest with you … well, you know what I'm trying to say."

"Off course we do," Nazira said. "How are you coping?"

I shrugged, finding it difficult to think of the right words. "She was my life, Nazira and I…"

She put a hand on my arm and gave me an understanding smile. "It is me who should apologise, Richard."

"No, not at all. We had both prepared ourselves for what we knew was going to happen but that didn't make it any easier when the time came."

"What about the children? They must be nearly fourteen now."

"Yes, their birthday is in August but of course you know that. They will be on their summer holidays as usual. When their mother died, they were marvellous and in many ways they coped better than I did. Isabelle in particular was a pillar of strength and still is." I took a deep breath. "It's Belinda's mother who is now giving us reason to worry."

Abby stopped eating and looked at me. "Why, Richard?"

I put my spoon down. "She had a stroke on Tuesday and when I left England she was still in hospital."

They both said, "I'm sorry," together.

"Understandably she took Belinda's loss badly. She became introspective overnight, absorbed by her grief. I suppose something like this was likely to happen. Belinda's father is there though, and he was the one who insisted I accept your invitation, Abby." He gave a slight shake of his head and looked sideways at Nazira, who frowned.

"Invitation?" she repeated, looking confused. "I thought you were here on business, Richard."

Abby's closed his eyes and I realised from his guilty look that Nazira knew nothing about the real reason why I was in Brunei and, at that particular moment, neither did I. I thought quickly. "Well I am," I said unconvincingly, "but the dates were flexible and I rang Abby to see which dates were most convenient to him. When I say he invited me, after speaking to him we came up with dates that suited us both."

"I presumed that you were here to do something about the damming project in Bangar," Nazira said, still confused.

This time Abby nodded slightly. I hated lying but I had little choice. "Yes, that's right but I'm not here officially. I have resigned from Astek but because I know more about the project than anybody else, well, the planning was incomplete the last time I was here and there are a few loose ends to tie up."

"Why did you resign, Richard?" Nazira asked.

"I need to be in England for the children," I said.

"I understand," Nazira said, her smile sympathetic. "But you are here unofficially?"

"Yes," I said. "The project was shelved but now …"

"… it's being dusted off, is it?" Nazira remained

unconvinced.

It was Abby's turn to tell a white lie. "In a way," he offered. "There are some technical questions that need answering and that is why Richard is here."

Nazira used her little finger to scoop up a small piece of mango that had fallen onto the table. "When you decide between you to tell me the truth, do let me know," she said quietly and then, "Coffee, Richard?"

"Please," I said a little too sheepishly.

The maid cleared the table and the three of us moved across to the living area.

On the way back to the hotel, and after apologising profusely for the umpteenth time for any embarrassment he had caused me, Abby eventually got round to the real reason for my visit.

"It's nothing to do with Bangar, Richard."

"I had deduced that," I said, smiling. Abby was westernised in many ways but the embarrassment of losing face was still part of his nature. I did find it quite incredible, though, that he hadn't told me what Nazira knew and what she didn't know. Arriving for dinner after travelling ten thousand miles was bound to generate the question of why I was here in the first place. If there was something to cover up then we could have at least agreed a simple and acceptable story.

"But now is not the time to discuss it," Abby volunteered. "We need complete privacy and the only place I can guarantee that is if we go out in the boat tomorrow."

"By boat I presume you mean that rather luxurious launch you keep in the Muara marina?"

He nodded. "I have replaced the one you saw last time." We were approaching the hotel and there was little traffic about but Abby was driving as though we were navigating Hyde Park corner. "But, yes," he said seriously, "we will go out on my launch. If I collect you from here at about ten in the morning we'll go offshore for a few hours and then I promise you I will tell you why I asked you to come."

"Can't you give me an inkling now?"

He pulled up outside the hotel and turned to face me. "Richard, I can't." He looked furtively about him. "We have to be alone. When I tell you what is going on I am sure you will understand why I am being evasive now. I ask you to be patient until then."

"Abby, my friend, I will probably spend all night trying to work out what is worrying you, but I have too much respect for you to pressure you any more now." I held out my hand and Abby took it.

I smiled.

"Thank you for a most enjoyable evening. Nazira is as gorgeous as ever and the children are a credit to you."

"Thank you, Richard, and thank you for your friendship. I know we come from different worlds but we must never let that interfere with what we have."

The expression on his face was full of sadness.

After the expected restless night, I crawled out of bed a few minutes before seven and decided to go and have an early morning swim. Everything had gone through my mind during the night.

From the moment I saw Abby at the airport I realised something serious was troubling him. There had been nothing during my time with him and Nazira that alluded to what the problem might be. At least it didn't seem to be marital.

During the night, the possibilities leapt in and out of my mind but I simply couldn't come up with an obvious explanation. Eventually I must have fallen asleep with the belief that tomorrow would reveal the truth.

It was a small pool – no more than fifteen metres long – but the coolness of the water was invigorating. The hotel terrace, with a about a dozen white tables, chairs and umbrellas advertising Marlboro cigarettes, was to one side, and on the other side were changing cubicles clearly designated for male and female usage. At one end a small bar, its shutters down, would serve snacks and non-alcoholic drinks, and at the other end a number of large bougainvilleas provided privacy from prying eyes.

At that time in the morning, I was alone and swam four brisk lengths before resting in one corner. Closing my eyes I let the many thoughts I had conjured up during the night float back into my mind, trying desperately to make sense of them. At one stage I concluded that if Abby's problem were personal he wouldn't have wanted me to fly all the way to Brunei to offer help. In fact, I believed the opposite might have applied – he would have come to me.

"Good morning."

My eyes opened and initially I couldn't locate where the greeting had come from, but then she spoke again.

"Good morning, I hope I didn't wake you."

She was at the other end of the pool, her arms, like mine, spread either side on the edge of the pool. Her chin was above the surface of the water and there was an impish smile on her lips.

"Good morning," I replied automatically, recognising her but not immediately able to recall her name.

"Sophie Mackintosh," she said helpfully. "We met on the plane yesterday."

"Of course," I said feeling embarrassed. "I'm sorry. I was miles away. Richard Blythe."

The smile stayed. "Yes, I remember," she said admonishingly. She looked up at the clear blue sky. "At least the weather has improved and the air has cleared. It's going to be a hot one."

I hadn't noticed what the weather was doing other than it was no longer raining …looking up I nodded. "We're fortunate to have arrived when we did."

"We could have shared a taxi." She was swimming across the pool towards me.

"Sorry?"

"I said, we could have shared a taxi, yesterday, from the airport, we could have shared a taxi." She was a few feet away now, the pool shallow enough at that point for her to stand.

"I didn't see you once you'd left the aircraft. I was met by a friend anyway."

"I know. I saw you with him."

I found her comment strange but decided not to pursue it any further. "I was out to dinner last night, otherwise we may have bumped into each other earlier."

"Out to dinner with your friend?"

I got the distinct impression she was playing with me for some reason. "Yes, that's right. We've known each other for years and I went and had dinner with him and his wife."

Sophie Mackintosh looked at me before dipping her head below the surface of the water. After resurfacing, her hair was like a skullcap and her face sparkled as the water drained from it. She was wearing, from what I could see under the water, a black one-piece swimming costume. Although non-Muslim female guests of the hotel could use the pool, bikinis were not an appropriate form of dress.

"Have you had breakfast?" she asked.

"No, not yet," I replied. "I came down here first to wake myself up."

"Me, too," she said. "Would you like to share a table or are you the type who doesn't like conversation before ten o'clock?"

I smiled. "Not at all, I would love to."

"I'll see you in the dining room in about half-an-hour then. I'm going to swim a few lengths first, so don't laugh."

She didn't wait for a reply.

For somebody so slim she had a powerful stroke, and the way she turned at the end of the pool suggested that swimming hadn't perhaps always been just a social activity. When she had finished, she got out at the other end, picked up her towel from a sun-bed and dripped her way towards the changing rooms without saying another word. I noticed out of the corner of my eye a couple of the male Bruneian waiters watching from behind one of the windows. Judging by the expression on their faces and their gestures, they approved of what they saw.

The hotel dining room was spotless – everything sparkled with cleanliness. The room was air-conditioned and the windows, on the same side of the hotel as my bedroom, provided a view of the main road into Bandar Seri Begawan and the Churchill Museum, an ornate single-storey building built on the orders of the current Sultan's father to demonstrate his sheer adoration of Winston. The traffic was light and there certainly wasn't the frenetic activity that could have been found at this time of the morning in most capital cities.

After sitting down at a table for two in the far corner of the room, the waiter asked whether I wanted tea or coffee. I had already passed the buffet breakfast table that provided hot and cold dishes as well as the usual exotic fruits, cereals and juices. The waiter held out a chair for me, informing me in perfect English that Miss Mackintosh would be joining me shortly. Miss Mackintosh had been either extremely presumptuous or highly efficient. I smiled to myself when I realised I didn't really care which it was.

I was rather looking forward to her company.

She arrived about five minutes later dressed in another

lightweight linen business suit, the skirt resting just below her knees. Looking round, the other diners were mostly men of all nationalities and as they became aware of her presence, each followed her progress approvingly. I felt quite pleased that she was heading for my table, knowing that they would look at me and think whatever they wanted to think.

At that moment, I thought of Belinda.

I stood up as the same waiter pulled back Sophie's chair. She smiled at him and said, "Thank you". The waiter looked at her as though she had given him a million dollars.

"So," Sophie said to me, helping herself to coffee from the pot brought for me, "are you wide awake now?"

Why, I don't know, but I wanted to tell her that I was still dreaming, but fortunately for both of us I managed a reply we both would have expected.

In the time between leaving the pool and now her hair looked as though she had come straight out of a salon. The small pearl studs in her ears matched her necklace, and her make-up was simple but effective, the colour on her lids enhancing the greenness in her more blue than green eyes. She had high cheekbones, a small straight nose and slightly glossed full lips.

Absorbing the loveliness of the woman sitting opposite me, I again thought of Belinda and a feeling of guilt washed over me. I remembered Isabelle's concern about my selling Blue-Ridge, quickly followed by even greater concern that one day I might remarry.

Sophie Mackintosh was everything Belinda had been: beautiful to look at and sophisticated in everything she did and said. However, I sensed Sophie was more aware of what was going on around her than Belinda had ever been. Whenever I pointed out the admiring and salacious looks Belinda was getting, she always told me not to be so stupid.

I wondered whether the person I was looking at was genuine

or whether it was a veneer – a cover for a not so beautiful person underneath. Perhaps it was my defence mechanism kicking in but I hoped I was wrong. When she lifted her coffee cup to her lips, I checked again to see what rings she was wearing, but other than what appeared to be a sapphire on her right index finger, there was nothing.

She must have followed my eyes, because as she replaced the cup in the saucer she said, "No, I'm not. I was once but now I'm not. Are you?"

I tried to look puzzled. "Am I what?"

"Married?" she replied, tilting her head slightly to one side, the impish smile back on her lips and in her eyes.

"Like you, I was once but now I'm not. Shall we get some breakfast?" I said.

Sophie, to my surprise, helped herself to a cooked breakfast and fruit juice. There were, for obvious reasons, no bacon rashers or pork sausages, but there was plenty of choice and she walked away from the buffet with a full plate.

"So, Richard, what brings you to Brunei?" she asked spearing a mushroom and delicately popping it in her mouth. "Is it work?"

"Very indirectly," I said. "I've been here a few times in the past in connection with my work but on this occasion I'm here because I was invited back by the friend you saw me with." I felt free to tell Sophie the truth.

"You're on holiday? Brunei isn't known for its tourist attractions."

I forked some kedgeree into my mouth. "No, I know, but I've already seen what there is to see, except for the Theme Park in Jerudong. That wasn't built the last time I was here, but I gather it's quite a sight."

"You don't strike me as the sort of person who would be attracted by a theme park." Sophie didn't wait for me to agree or disagree before she asked, "And what line of work are you in?"

"Was in," I told her. She stopped chewing and gave me a surprised look. "I'm a Marine Engineer by profession and I was working for an American firm that designs and builds dams, until recently that is."

"Why did you part company?"

"I needed a change."

"And now?"

"Between jobs I think is the way it's described."

She smiled, putting her knife and fork down on an almost empty plate. "In your line of work I doubt whether you'll have any difficulty in finding something else."

"But for me a change is a change and, to date, I haven't decided what that change is to be. What about you? Why are you in Brunei?"

"Foreign Office," she said, picking up her fruit juice and looking at me over the top of the glass. "I work for the Foreign Office and every now and again I have to do my rounds. This month it's here, Singapore, Kuala Lumpur, Jakarta and, if all goes well, Hong Kong. I suppose I'm a sort of auditor," she added when I didn't comment.

I had spent hours trying to speak to somebody in the Foreign Office and was turned away, albeit politely, before I succeeded in talking to anybody who could help. Now, ten thousand miles away from England, I was having breakfast with one of the *unobtainables*, and yet I knew I couldn't broach the subject of harassment in Germany, nor, and more importantly, could I mention my house being searched. I had no idea which department Sophie Mackintosh was from but there was still something about her that suggested there was more to her than met the eye. She may have told me she was an auditor but her demeanour and my image of what an auditor should be like simply did not compute.

"What sort of auditor?" I asked, deciding to play along with her deception, if that is what it was.

She thought for a moment and then shrugged, the slight movement accentuating her slim shoulders. "Ensuring that procedures are following policy, I suppose would be the best way of describing what I do."

I think I understood what she was saying. "How long are you in Brunei for?"

She checked her watch. "I'm here until Tuesday of next week. I've done KL and Singapore, next stop Jakarta."

"And you're working on a Saturday?"

"Got to in my line of work but I do get tomorrow to relax." She hesitated, wanting to add something, but then looked at me expectantly.

"What are you doing for dinner this evening?" I hoped I had guessed right.

"I've got to go to an official lunch tomorrow at The High Commission but this evening I'm free." I had guessed right.

"In the foyer about seven o'clock?" I suggested.

She shrugged. "Yes, that's fine. Where are you going to take me?"

"You'll see but dress casually."

"Sounds intriguing," she said.

"Not a description I would use, but you'll have to wait and see."

Chapter Fifteen

Although Abby had told me he had changed his boat since I was last in Brunei, the new one certainly wasn't what I expected. He informed me with great pride that it was a 50ft Ocean Alexander Motor Yacht.

It was fully air conditioned with two spacious double ensuite staterooms plus a three berth forward cabin, also with ensuite. There was a large saloon and fully equipped galley, a huge upper deck fly-bridge area and a walk-in engine room with stand-up headroom. Although nearly twenty-years-old, Abby said he fell for the launch the moment he saw it, and I could understand why – it was unadulterated luxury.

I didn't dare ask how much the launch had cost him.

We roared away from the Muara naval dockyard and I could see in his eyes that he got a tremendous kick out of the powerful throbbing from the two in-board engines, and was equally delighted to be able to show off to me his relatively new acquisition.

Muara was home to the Royal Brunei Armed Forces Naval Squadron as well as The Sultan's rather splendid Royal yacht. Looking back towards the port, there were three fast-torpedo boats in view – one of which was in dry dock – and a minesweeper. There were also a few smaller naval vessels, but none could match the splendour of the Royal yacht that was alongside the main quay, its vast white hull gleaming in the sunshine, and a thin trail of smoke coming from its single funnel.

"Quite a launch," I shouted, clinging onto the rail in front of me against the buffeting each time we hit a wave. "It must be your pride and joy."

He smiled. "Second only to Nazira and the children," he

shouted back, the wind making his shirt billow out behind him. He was wearing the baseball cap he had always wore when we played golf together, a plain pale blue short-sleeved shirt, dark blue shorts and open-toed sandals. I had managed to pack suitable clothing in anticipation of what Abby and I might be doing.

During the short drive from Bandar to Muara, Abby and I had exchanged pleasantries only. He wanted to wait until we were alone and out at sea before saying anymore about why I was there. The secrecy was becoming more intriguing by the minute.

Passing the turning to the Panti Menteri Golf Club he commented that we must have a game before I went back, which suggested that his problem might not be as serious as I originally thought. If he was contemplating a round of golf then perhaps my imagination had been working overtime.

During our intermittent periods of silence, my mind wandered back to the breakfast I had shared with Sophie Mackintosh. She was very pleasant company and none of the hardness I had suspected was there. I anticipated enjoyable evening with her, although there was a distinct possibility that what Abby had to tell me might put the dampers on it.

I hoped not.

We powered our way out to about four miles offshore and anchored a hundred yards from the yellow sands of a secluded, uninhabited and idyllic small island. Abby suggested that we went for a swim first, which we did, and afterwards we took ice-cold drinks up to the top deck and sat in the shade of a side awning.

Abby looked at me for a good few seconds before he spoke. "Richard, I am afraid something is going on and unfortunately, but hopefully for the right reasons, I am limited in what I can tell you about it. However, I would trust you with my life and it is on that basis that I have persuaded the Government, and by that I mean His Majesty the Sultan, that I should seek your help in a matter that could affect the stability of my country and ultimately its future. You are the only personal link I have with the UK that I can trust to the extent that is needed. Do you understand?" Abby took off his glasses. I had never seen such a serious look in his eyes before.

"Abby, I count you as one of my closest and dearest friends and yes, you could trust me with your life.." I smiled. "It's a pity we live so far apart – I'd love to be able to thrash you at golf every weekend."

Although he looked serious, Abby accepted the need for a touch of light-heartedness as it underpinned our relationship. "Richard, I am much improved, as you will find out."

I smiled ruefully but then respected Abby's need to be serious. "If I'm able to help you, I will, you know that. I admire and respect you and your country too much not to offer help if I can. But from what you've said already, and that's very little, the situation has to be political, so are you sure I'm the right person you should be telling whatever it is?"

He shook his head a little as he looked at the now empty glass in his hands. "Richard, before I do tell you a little more I am afraid I must ask you what you might consider to be a strange and personal question."

I shrugged. "No change there then," I said, "ask away."

He slowly raised his head. "What is your relationship with the lady called Sophie Mackintosh?"

"Sophie Mackintosh?" I repeated, taken aback by his question. "That is a strange question,' I added.

"Yes, I know but I will explain. So how well do you know her?"

"Well ... well, I don't think I can really I do *know* her. We came in on the same aircraft yesterday, met in the swimming pool this morning and then had breakfast together, and that is the extent of our ... relationship as you put it. We've literally only known each other for a few hours."

"So you did not know her, nor did you know of her, before yesterday?" Abby asked, his face still serious.

I shook my head and spread my hands. "Honestly, Abby, I really don't know her."

He nodded. "I thought that would be the case."

I drained the now warm orange from my glass. "I think you'd better start at the beginning, Abby, but before you do, I'm having dinner with Sophie Mackintosh this evening. Does that in any way change what you're able to tell me?"

Abby nodded and did let his expression lighten a little. "As long as you promise me that you only wish to see her again to find out if her figure is as good out of a swimming costume as it is in it."

I smiled. "I wish ... but have you been spying on me, Abby?"

"Not me, Richard, but yes, you are being watched but it is for your own safety."

"My own safety? Since when have I ever been in danger in Brunei?"

He smiled and inclined his head. "Never before," he said.

"Are telling me I am this time? Why?"

The sudden noise of jet-engine aircraft distracted both of us.

Abby turned away from me and looked in the direction the noise was coming from. I didn't see the planes at first because I was looking up, not straight ahead. It wasn't until they were almost on top of us that I saw them. There were three fighter aircraft flying in close formation, they weren't more than forty feet above the sea and they were heading straight for us. Abby and I automatically crouched down, trying to make ourselves as small as possible, but I remained fascinated by what was coming towards us. When they were about four hundred yards from the boat, all three aircraft suddenly went into a steep climb. The noise and heat from back-blast left by their engines was horrendous.

Looking up I saw the planes levelling out from their climb at about five thousand feet and then, almost in slow motion they headed back in the direction from which they had come.

"What the hell was that all about?" I asked, helping Abby to his feet.

He was also watching the retreating aircraft. "I do not know for sure, Richard, but I think I can hazard a good guess." Sitting down, Abby looked quite shaken as he replaced his sunglasses that had fallen off as the planes forced us to lie flat on the deck. "Did you see their markings, Richard?"

"Not really." I said. "I was more intent wondering what they were trying to do. They were so close I could see the pilots and the heat from their afterburners could have killed us. Were they Sukhoi Su-27s."

Abby nodded and said, "They were Chinese Air Force jets."

The noise from the aircraft was now faint. "Chinese? You sound as though you aren't surprised to see them."

Abby smiled ruefully. "I am not, Richard." He looked over his shoulder.

"They were probably having a bit of fun but they were a long way from home. If they were Chinese, they must have come from a carrier."

"You are right, Richard." He looked out to see again before taking a deep breath. "Shall we have some lunch and another drink, and then perhaps I can disclose a few things to you without further interruption?"

We went down into the air-conditioned saloon where he produced various tasty morsels from the fridge and as we sat and ate, he told me why he thought we had been buzzed by the jets.

"Those jets will have been from a carrier off the Spratley Islands," he said, "I think we talked about them the last time you were here."

I nodded. "Yes, we did. You told me there were disputed territories, not only because of their strategic value but also because of off-shore oil and gas resources."

"That's right, Richard, but the region is still largely unexplored and there are no reliable estimates of potential reserves. Over the years, the Spratley Islands have been claimed in whole or in part by all the main oil and gas producers in the region, all of which, except Brunei, now have a military presence on the islands. Although there have been minor skirmishes, the main antagonists being China and Vietnam, all claimant countries have declared their intention to resolve any claims peacefully."

I frowned. "So, can I presume that isn't the reason why I am here?"

Abby dipped his head. "You can, Richard, but not completely, please bear with me for a little longer. What I have told you is probably why the Chinese Air Force has playfully strafed us. Brunei may be hundreds of miles from the Spratley Islands, and we may be the only nation in the area not to have a military presence there, but we still have as much right to claim an interest as any other nation. The Chinese are becoming increasingly confrontational and testing the defences of peripheral countries. We are now outside Brunei territorial waters and therefore if I were to initiate a diplomatic protest, the Chinese would simply apologise and say that their planes had as much right to be in the area as anyone else. When they saw my boat, they immediately climbed to avoid an accident."

"And in reality, Abby, what's the truth?"

"In reality, Richard, it might sound a little fantastic but I would not be surprised if our, or maybe just my presence out here had not been reported and what we experienced was a deliberate act of intimidation towards a senior minister in the

Brunei Government."

I spread my hands, appreciating what he had told me about the Spratley Islands but they were a delaying tactic. The real reason I was there had yet to be revealed, but I felt I needed to humour him for a little longer. "It's obviously happened before," I said.

"Yes, but not to me." He hesitated for a moment. "Can we go back up on deck, please, Richard? I would prefer to be able to see what is around us."

"Of course," I replied, hiding my unwarranted amusement from Abby. I followed him up the steps to the top deck.

Abby rested his hands on the rail and looked in the direction from which the aircraft had approached earlier. "Richard, I am sorry for what I am about to say, but it is your government that is the cause for the concern within my own administration."

"My government?" I said. Abby's statement in its own right was surprising but, more importantly I couldn't immediately understand why it was me who was being told Brunei's problems. A close friend or not, inter-Governmental disagreements were way out of my league and I didn't want to become involved.

However, the intrigue maintained my interest.

Abby turned from the rail. We were in the open. The sun had passed its zenith and was beating down onto my head. I shaded my eyes with my hand.

"My country relishes the special relationship it has with Britain. We go back many years. Before our independence, and since, we have been taught many good things." He let a slight smile creep on to his lips. "You might think that in certain areas we have not progressed at any speed but that is our way." He paused. "Britain has retained many loyal friends in the Commonwealth and I become annoyed when I read about the criticisms laid at Britain's doorstep especially when such criticisms include exploitation. Of course Britain took advantage of the natural resources they found, but at least they made the indigenous people aware of what was available to them in the future. My country is a prime example. We are small and ruled by what others call a benevolent dictator, but we are prosperous and without the early British influence we would not be where we are today." Abby refilled our glasses from the jug he had brought with him. "When loyalty is suddenly brought into question, though, it makes the faithful wary of what is being done. It makes them look beyond maybe the obvious political reasons behind the change in attitude."

He paused once again to draw breath and it gave me the opportunity to interrupt. "Abby, I agree with what you're saying but can you put it into context? What I'm hearing you say is that Britain has in some way reneged on the special friendship it has with Brunei."

He narrowed his eyes. "Breaking a promise, Richard, is not something we Muslims take lightly. A promise is a commitment that cannot be broken. Britain always promised to be here for us if we were threatened."

"I'm sorry, Abby, but you have lost me." I wanted to add 'again' but at least now we were getting somewhere.

"Do you remember the last time you were here and when we were playing golf, we discussed the December 1962 rebellion in Brunei?"

"Yes," I said, "and if I remember correctly, you said it was something that could have meant everything but finished up meaning nothing. Am I right?"

Abby nodded. "It lasted only days, although it was May of the following year before it was certain that all subversive elements had been dealt with. Fortunately, the subversives' planning was bad and the support expected from neighbouring sympathetic elements, did not materialise, but British troops from Singapore and Malaya were mainly responsible for the failure of the rebellion."

What we had discussed over four years ago came back to me. "Didn't you say that although it was insignificant as rebellions go, it was the prelude to the Borneo confrontation?"

"That's correct, Richard. The Indonesians didn't want Malaysia to grow stronger by taking Sarawak and what was then British North Borneo, into what is now the Malaysian Federation, and we were drawn into the conflict." Abby looked at me and paused before saying, "I think history is going to repeat itself, Richard."

"What?" I said, "the Indonesians are –?"

"No, no, this is nothing to do with the Indonesians. When I say history is repeating itself, I mean the Brunei Rebellion. We believe there are now more seditious elements here in Brunei and in Sarawak and Sabah who are planning to overthrow His Majesty the Sultan and his loyal supporters. Their aim is to make Brunei part of The Federation, but we wish to retain our independence. We think –"

"I'm sorry to interrupt, Abby, but if I understand you correctly, are you saying that the Malaysian government is behind what you believe is going on?"

Abby turned and looked towards the horizon. "There is no proof, but it could be more serious than that, Richard. We think there are elements within the British government that might be involved and supporting the radicals."

I shook my head. "The British government is behind a plot to overthrow the Sultan of Brunei? No, Abby, I can't believe that. Why would –?"

"Resources, Richard. That is why I told you so much about the Spratley Islands. With what is going on in the Middle East, Western governments need to look elsewhere for secure oil and gas supplies in case they can no longer import from the Middle

East. In addition, with a good percentage of the gas being imported by the West from Russia, that link could easily be broken. Although resources in South East Asia are currently small by comparison with the Middle East, what might be found of the Spratley Islands and elsewhere, could tip the balance."

"But why would Britain want to make an enemy of Brunei, we have always been on such good terms. Surely, we would want to –?"

"Malaysia, Vietnam, The Philippines and of course China all have designs on these untapped resources," Abby said, interrupting. "Although Brunei is a rich country we are considered insignificant militarily and strategically. Some feel that our resources ought to be managed by a larger concern, not by an unimportant little country ruled by a single sultan who spends freely without any thought for his country's neighbours."

"I see." I said, but I didn't see at all. "I'm almost lost for words, I had no idea … but …" I shook my head again, I needed to bring what Abby was saying back down to my level, and there was only one way of doing that, "… what is Sophie Mackintosh's connection with all of this … and how did you know –?"

"If you were going to ask how I knew you would be on the same flight, I didn't know, Richard. I invited you over here because I thought with your connections with the Americans and maybe your contacts in the UK, you could perhaps discover the truth."

I was beginning to feel the effects of the sun and although I had put on plenty of high-factor sun cream, the afternoon sun was merciless. However, the sun's heat was a minor irritation in comparison with what Abby was telling me.

"Can we go below deck, Abby?" I looked up. "The sun is …"

"Yes, of course Richard, I was forgetting my manners and I am sorry."

He surveyed the water around us before leading the way down the ladder to the deck below.

"I think we should be starting for home soon," Abby said twiddling a few of the knobs on the display in front of him. "The sky is getting a bit dark in the west. I think there might be a squall coming in."

I moved in front of Abby.

He was still concentrating on getting the launch under way. I wondered if he was having second thoughts about what he had told me.

"So you think Sophie Mackintosh is connected in some way to what you believe is going on, is that right?" There was little point in beating round the bush. What Abby had described really was out of my league but I was still intrigued as to why he had asked me to come and see him.

He turned the key in the ignition and there was a spluttering as the powerful engines coughed into life. He looked at me, locking his eyes with mine.

"I think maybe it is too much to ask of you, Richard."

"If you don't ask in the first place, you'll never know will you?" I smiled understandingly.

Closing his eyes, his head dipping slightly, Abby pursed his lips before saying, "When I discovered you and this Mackintosh woman were on the same flight, and that you had met and had breakfast together ... I changed what I was going to ask of you. Although she has no direct contact with His Majesty the Sultan, we believe she holds the key as to what your government's intentions really are. I might be wrong but I would like you to find out whether our concerns are justified or whether we have misjudged what is happening."

"Wow!" was all I could think of saying, followed by another inadequate, "I see. By saying, I see, I am only referring to what you've said and not the enormity of your request."

"It was wrong of me to even think of it in the first place, Richard. Whatever we try to find out diplomatically, we receive the same answer. We have made representations to the High Commissioner here, and our Ambassador in London has been in talks with your government, but we always get the same reply. Very flowery political terminology is used but the message is quite simple – nobody is aware of any revolutionary activity in my country. We have not made any direct accusations because we are not certain, but we do need to know."

"And you think I have the ability and the contacts, including Sophie Mackintosh, to achieve what you are asking?"

Abby looked up. "I don't know, Richard, but I am asking you as a dear and close friend to do what you can. We need to know whether we should be worried. If what we believe is true, then we may have to consider other alliances – maybe with Indonesia – that previously we would have thought impossible and ones that certainly would not have received Britain's approval. Brunei may be small and, in the eyes of some nations, insignificant but we are still a proud people and we would not give in to any aggressor, internal or external, without putting up the best fight possible. We would be fighting for the very survival … the very survival of Negara Brunei Darussalam." His voice broke and there were tears his eyes.

I reached across the space between us and put my hand on his arm. "Abby, I really don't see what I can do. I understand your concerns but I am no more than an out-of-work marine engineer. I have no contacts in the British Foreign Office –"

"Except Sophie Mackintosh," Abby reminded me.

"All right, except Sophie, but other than her I wouldn't know where to start and, even if I did, I wouldn't know who and what to ask."

"But you now have a starting point and I think you have a saying what you call 'pillow talk'" Abby said.

He pushed the gear lever in front of him and the boat moved forward slowly, turning the wheel we were running parallel to the island we had anchored near. Once settled on his course, he made eye contact but the expression on his face told me that I really had little choice but to do as he asked.

"I can't promise anything Abby, but if I can I'll try to find out what she may or may not know."

"I cannot ask more of you than that, Richard, and you never know, you might enjoy finding out."

Chapter Sixteen

Having put on a pair of reasonably presentable lightweight cotton chinos and a cream short-sleeved shirt, I went down to the foyer to wait for Sophie. I had been waiting in the small anteroom opposite Reception for about five minutes when the lift pinged as it reached the ground floor. Sophie stepped out and immediately had the attention of the two male receptionists and a group of European businessmen at the table next to me.

Abby had dropped me off at the hotel a few minutes after three o'clock this afternoon, and after a refreshing swim, I fell onto my bed in an attempt to get a few hours' sleep, which didn't happen. My time with Abby whirled round in my mind as I endeavoured, once again, to make sense of everything. The previous night it had been because I didn't know, now it was because I did … or I thought I did.

Belinda, Blue-Ridge, the twins, Charles and Elizabeth, they all seemed to be part of a different world. When I couldn't sleep and in an effort to bring the others all closer to me I tried to ring Charles to ask after Elizabeth but there was no reply and the answer machine hadn't been switched on. I had only been away for forty-eight hours but it seemed like a lifetime. I assumed that Charles was with Elizabeth in the hospital because I didn't want to assume anything else. He had the telephone and fax numbers for the hotel – email addresses would have meant nothing to him. If there was a change in Elizabeth's condition he had promised to let me know. No news was good news – I hoped.

Belinda was there, as ever, in my mind. I needed to talk to her because I wanted to ask her what I was now involved with. I was really having great difficulty in taking on board exactly what Abby had told me and, more importantly, what he had asked me to do.

Since discovering the unconscious Ingrid Mesterom in Dove Dale, my life had become one big surreal cauldron. I had expected my invited escape to Brunei and Abby to introduce a touch of familiarity. It had, at first, but then Abby had merely added to the unreality. There was obviously no connection between events in England, Germany and now Brunei but even so, I wondered what was going to happen next.

The Chinese fighters were real. The look in Abby's eyes was real. His request was real but the circumstances were bizarre. If Abby were simply a friend with an ordinary job, then I might have been able to understand his concern and his request may have been more realistic. The result would be the same though, because I didn't have the knowledge or the contacts to know where to start. However, at least everything would have been at a level with which I could relate and it wouldn't have been a senior minister in the Brunei government asking me, an amateur, for help. Although I didn't want to think of him like this, his behaviour and his appeal bordered on the unprofessional.

Nevertheless, watching Sophie walk across the foyer of the Sheraton Utama Hotel towards me took my mind away from what had happened today and in the preceding few weeks. What was going to happen in the next few hours suddenly became more important.

When I stood up to greet Sophie, Belinda flashed back into my mind and her expression suggested that I ought to enter into whatever might happen with great caution. Women are good judges of other women and their intentions. Belinda was telling me to tread warily and play Sophie Mackintosh at her own game. I wasn't sure what Belinda meant, but I would do as she asked.

I stood up, smiling and Sophie leant across the space between us to give me a peck on the cheek. She smelt of CK perfume, the same as Belinda sometimes used to wear. The connection wasn't lost on me.

"I hope I'm not overdressed?" she asked taking the seat next to mine. She was wearing a light-blue long-sleeved silk blouse with its collar turned up. Her white cotton trousers finished an inch above her ankles, the blue belt was the same colour as her blouse and her white open-toed sandals, showing off her delicately small feet, were a shade or two darker than her trousers. Everything looked expensive. The gold bracelets on her wrists matched the necklace at her throat.

"Perfect," I replied, doubting whether she had a pair of scruffy jeans to her name. "Would you like a drink before we go?"

"I would love a gin and tonic but will stick to a grapefruit juice," she said.

A waiter was hovering by the bar door, I called him over and ordered the drinks. "They go through phases," I said. "Sometimes you can get a drink and sometimes you can't. I wish they would simply do one or the other."

"Yes," she said absent-mindedly, taking in the foyer decorations and the people in it. "As one of its main hotels, I always think they could do better than this. It's not exactly the Ritz, is it?"

"I suppose if tourists, in the strict sense of the word, were encouraged, they would do something about it, but they need neither the money nor the tourism. It's clean, air-conditioned and the food is good." I shrugged. "I suppose it could be worse."

"It could certainly be worse," she commented as the waiter arrived with our drinks and a small plate of hors d'oeuvres. "Where are you taking me tonight?" She picked up a smoked salmon creation and popped it into her mouth.

"If I told you, I think you probably wouldn't want to go."

She held my eyes and there was a slight smile on her lips. "It sounds intriguing." She didn't seem as animated as she had been at breakfast. I wondered whether she had simply had a hard day or whether something else was troubling her. I was also asking myself whether what Abby had suspected was true: was she what she purported to be or was she something little more sinister? Belinda's warning was in the back of my mind as I watched Sophie sip her grapefruit juice and screw up her face in disgust.

"Did you have a hard day?" I asked.

She took the glass from her lips a little too quickly, looking at me. "I'm sorry, does it show?" she asked, inclining her head. "I love Robert Cruickshank to bits but he doesn't run the most efficient of High Commissions. He's an absolute sweetie but an administrative nightmare, which resulted in a difficult day to say the least. Sorry."

"No need to apologise," I said. "I thought you might join me in a minute or two." The sarcasm was unlike me but, for some reason, it seemed appropriate.

Sophie, without appearing to be offended, put her hand on my arm. "I really am sorry. If only I could have had that gin and tonic."

"Be patient for another twenty minutes or so," I said.

It was actually nearer thirty minutes.

The taxi I booked earlier was waiting for us outside the hotel and the driver knew exactly where I wanted to go. Sophie took one look at the outside of the restaurant – a loose description – another look at me and then at the taxi as it retreated back towards Bandar Seri Begawan.

"It's a shack," she observed accurately.

I nodded, smiling. "I think Mama Wong would prefer to call it a lean-to or an add-on."

"Mama who?" she asked as I held the door open for her.

"Mama Wong."

"Sounds like the proprietor of a brothel rather than a ... a café," Sophie informed me, looking for a table.

I took her arm and guided her towards a table for two by the wall. "Give it a chance," I told her, pulling out her chair for her.

She regarded the plastic tablecloth and cheap cutlery with disgust, which made me smile. There were no candles on the table, the room was too brightly lit and the off-white walls were decorated with a mixture of prints and frames that most people would not hang in their garden shed. It wasn't the setting for a cosy evening but Mama Wong's always held a few surprises that I hoped even Sophie would be pleased with.

There were about twenty other people at scattered tables, who were mostly European but there was a Chinese family at one of the tables in the far corner. Sophie and I had been given the once over as we walked through the door but each table had gone back to its private conversation by the time we sat down, although Sophie, as would be expected, was getting a few furtive glances.

A young Chinese girl came from behind the counter at the far end of the room and thrust pieces of cardboard into our hands.

"You want drink?" she asked.

"Please." I glanced at Sophie. "Two special tonics, please."

"Two speshall tonics," the girl repeated, writing something down on a scruffy piece of paper.

"I think I can guess what special tonics are, am I right?" Sophie asked, holding the piece of card between her fingertips as though it was a dirty rag. "Don't forget I work quite a lot in Muslim countries."

"You'll see. I recommend the fish and chips, and the mushy peas. They're the best this side of Harry Ramsden's."

"It's almost the only thing on the menu, are you serious?"

"Completely," I said.

The girl arrived back at the table with two plastic beakers

containing ice and a sliver of lemon. Next to the beakers, she placed, quite noisily, two open cans of Schweppes tonic water. After pouring the contents of one of the cans into Sophie's beaker, I handed it to her.

"Cheers!" I said picking up my beaker and tapping it against Sophie's.

Looking a little apprehensively at the edge of the beaker, Sophie took a sip and her eyes shot open. "Wow! And yes, cheers!"

I smiled. "Worth waiting for?"

"This is a tonic and gin not a gin and tonic," she told me, taking an enthusiastic further sip. "That's powerful. I've been in some places but these *special* tonics surpass anything I've had before."

"If you think that's good, wait until you get the fish and chips."

The girl approached the table and I ordered without asking Sophie if she actually liked fish. "And," Sophie added, "another two of your special tonics." After draining her beaker, she poured the remainder of her can into it. "I've been coming to Brunei for five years and I didn't know this place existed."

"In many ways it doesn't, for obvious reasons. What do you fancy with your fish, a Muscadet or a Chablis?"

"A Chablis, I think."

"A Chablis it is."

"Does this place ever get raided?" The girl had already returned with our second special tonics and Sophie poured them.

"Mama Wong has been running this place for well over fifteen years and I've been told in that time the police haven't set foot through that door." The gin was coursing its way through my bloodstream and was having the desired effect. "There's nothing illegal about fish and chips and tonic water."

"Obviously there's all the alcohol you want in the

Commission and I have been to a couple of restaurants in Bandar that sell special tea, but that turns out to be only beer. This," she indicated the beaker in her hand, "is like nectar."

"Pleased you like it."

"You certainly know how to treat a girl," she said, a mischievous smile on her lips.

"I do my best."

"I'm sure you do," Sophie said, peering at me over the rim of her beaker.

The fish and chips arrived and I asked the girl for some French lemonade. The chances of Sophie getting the Chablis she wanted were extremely remote but after two of Mama Wong's special tonics, who cared? *Vin Blanc de Table* would be as palatable as the best Chablis available in Singapore.

Sophie ate in silence for a good five minutes, looking up every now and again. The expression on her face suggested that she was enjoying the products of Mama Wong's kitchen. If we had gone through to thank the chef, we would probably worry about food poisoning for the next twenty-four hours. I had eaten there probably a dozen times – not with Abby though, he was too well known – over the years but there had never been any side effects.

Mid-way through a large plate of battered fish and chips cooked in beef dripping, and a generous helping of mushy peas, Sophie put her knife and fork down on the side of her plate, picked up her French lemonade and took a healthy gulp.

"I've been on some weird dates in my life but you're right, if you had told me where we were going before we left the Sheraton Utama, I would have refused to budge. Now I'm here, all I can say is I wouldn't have missed the experience for the world. Thank you." Her smile was genuine and the fingers she placed on the back of my hand warm.

The fans whirled – Mama Wong's didn't extend to air-conditioning – and the disconnect between the resultant humidity and eating fish and chips became totally irrelevant. Two of Mama Wong's special tonics combined with a bottle of her French lemonade seemed to create an atmosphere that I hadn't experienced for a long time. When Sophie picked up the last chip from her plate with her fingers and delicately placed it between her lips, her knife and fork lying on an empty plate, I didn't see her as somebody I had only met the day before but somebody who was desirable and, rightly or wrongly, available.

I closed my eyes.

Belinda's warning, my conscience, Isabelle's concerns, Abby's beliefs and my early misgivings weren't there anymore. I was with a very attractive female who had accepted my invitation to have dinner with me.

"Richard?" I felt the coolness of her fingers on my arm again. "Richard, are you all right?"

I heard Sophie's voice but for a few seconds I was still lost in my thoughts. I was fooling myself. Of course everything was still there, they had all still happened. Being with Sophie was only a temporary respite from the real world.

"Richard?" she asked again. "Are you all right?"

This time I opened my eyes and shook my head. "I think so," I said. "It's a long time since I downed two strong gin and tonics in a matter of a few minutes. I think the sun may have got to me today as well. Abby and I went out on his boat."

She smiled, her fingers softly moving on the back of my hand. "I'm glad it's not only me the special tonics have affected." She looked down at my plate. "You haven't finished your chips."

"I couldn't, I'm fit to burst."

"The black coffees aren't special too, are they?" Her fingers were still on my hand and she was watching them as she stroked me gently.

Her touch seemed totally natural and I was enjoying it.

"The coffees can be special if you want them to be but I think I might forego the experience for the moment. Maybe before we leave?"

We both started to speak at the same time. "Sorry, you first," I suggested.

"I was going to ask how long you had been divorced," she said. "A personal question, I know, but I want to know a little more about you. Do you mind if I have a cigarette? I don't smoke a lot but I always carry a packet for special occasions."

"Go ahead." She offered me the packet but I refused.

"So, how long?" she asked again, exhaling towards the ceiling.

"Belinda and I weren't divorced ..."

"Oh!" Sophie said, taking her hand from mine.

I smiled, and this time I put my hand on hers. "I didn't say aren't, I said weren't. She died in April this year."

There were a few seconds silence as Sophie sat and looked at me. She stubbed out the half-smoked cigarette in the foil ashtray.

"I'm sorry, Richard. I wouldn't have asked if I had known."

"If you'd known you wouldn't have had to ask. You didn't know and, under the circumstances, it was probably an appropriate question." I drank the rest of my coffee and looked around for the Chinese girl. She was seeing to another couple who had arrived about five minutes earlier. "Belinda died of cancer in April after a brave fight."

"I'm so sorry, Richard, but for the right reason this time. Do you have any children?"

I nodded. "I have thirteen-year old twins, Isabelle and David. And you?"

It wasn't that I didn't want to talk about Belinda, I did, but such situations can be awkward and I had found that people felt they ought to ask further questions but didn't quite know what to ask. I decided to save Sophie any embarrassment.

"I have a daughter, Emma. She's the same age as Isabelle and David." When I didn't say anything she added, "I've been on my own now for about nearly six years … not that I'm counting."

"On your own?"

"Well, I mean without my husband. We divorced in ninety-four and since then I suppose I can say I have been on my own. Emma's away at school which means we see each other at exeats, half-terms and holidays. She goes to her father sometimes but his wife seems to want to sever all connections and isn't keen on Emma going there. I feel so sorry for Emma, she loves her father but he dotes on the latest model. Poor Emma is paying the price."

I managed to attract the waitress's attention as she passed the table. "More coffee and a brandy?" I asked Sophie.

She nodded.

I remembered that the brandy was a special Coca Cola. "I find such situations very sad," I said, wondering why any sane man would want someone like Sophie out of his life.

"I'm thirty-seven years old and at thirty-one I was replaced by someone younger. It's as simple as that but still a little humiliating." She reached for her cigarettes. There was the expected bitterness in her voice. "Let's say that my ego was severely dented." After lighting her cigarette she added, "No, don't let's say that, let's say what I mean. The bastard was tired of me, some little tart opened her legs for him and that was it for me, cast aside as though I didn't matter at the ripe old age of thirty-one." Her eyes began to water, and I wondered whether the alcohol had taken longer to work on her than it had on me. "She didn't last long either. He is now a couple of months short of forty and two years ago he married a twenty-one year old.

Why are men such bastards?"

I was slightly amused by her question but didn't show it. Sophie was opening her heart, albeit her openness was alcohol induced, but she was still saying what she wanted to say. I wondered when she had last felt able to do that. I wasn't flattering myself but I got the impression, as I had before, that the Sophie on the surface was different to the real Sophie. I doubted whether many people got to see the latter.

I didn't actually know what to say. She had been hurt, and as far as I could tell, she was still hurting.

A genuine compliment, though it was due would be misplaced, but silence wasn't appropriate either. I wondered why I was even bothering to think like that. Why did it matter? I wasn't sure that I wanted this outwardly strong-willed woman to start crying on my shoulder. I could cope quite easily with her confidence, even dominance, but feminine weakness wasn't in her character, or so I believed, and it threw me.

I settled for, "Not all men are bastards."

She looked at me with slightly glazed eyes, a definite frown on her forehead. "I didn't mean to imply they were, Richard." This time her fingers didn't reach for the back of my hand but rested against my arm. "Mama Wong's was an experience, and one I wouldn't have missed for the world but I'm ready to leave now."

Fortunately, when we got outside a taxi was about to move off, having deposited a rather rowdy group of Europeans at the door. He beamed when he realised he had a return fare. The heat was oppressive and, rather like Mama Wong's, the taxi wasn't air-conditioned. The short trip back to the hotel didn't generate any further conversation, the only noise came from the engine of the rather clapped-out Mercedes. Either the tappets needed adjusting or his little ends were on the blink. Our driver appeared unperturbed.

Sophie stared at the floor indicator in the lift as we rose swiftly to the top floor in the Sheraton Utama. A simple shake of her head told me she didn't want another coffee before retiring. She stood a couple of feet away from me, her arms hanging loosely by her side. The change in her mood since she had introduced her wayward ex-husband into the conversation still confused me.

For some reason I had expected to be grilled about my day at sea with Abby, and conversely I had expected to have the opportunity to find out a little more about what she actually did. Neither expectation was realised. The evening was normal. We met on the plane yesterday, again in the pool this morning, had breakfast together and then went for a fish and chip supper. We were behaving as though we'd known each other a good deal longer than we had.

The lift doors opened and Sophie stepped out into the wall-to-wall carpeted corridor and waited with her back to me.

"I've got some decent brandy in my room courtesy of Robert Cruickshank. Would you like a nightcap?" she asked without turning round.

Before I could answer, she reached for my hand led me down the corridor towards her room. My mind was screaming, telling me to stop now. But my brain and my legs seemed to be disconnected, and rather like a lapdog I allowed myself to be guided away from sensibility into what had to be fantasy. I tried to call upon Belinda, I wanted to hear her telling me not to be stupid but I had temporarily lost contact.

After going into her room, Sophie said, "God, it's nice to get back into the air-conditioning. I don't know how these people survive day-in day-out in these conditions. The brandy's in the bedside table and I'll have a large one," she added before disappearing into the bathroom.

I went over to the window. Although it was only a few

minutes after nine-thirty, there was little traffic on the road below me. Each car passed in silence forty feet below. If the cars were sparse, the pedestrians were non-existent. It could have been four o'clock in the morning anywhere else: in Brunei it was only mid-evening.

"Sorry, the glasses were on the bathroom shelf," Sophie said, coming out of the bathroom.

After her invitation and remark about the air-conditioning, I thought perhaps her motive for going into the bathroom was to slip into something cooler, but I was wrong.

She came over to the window and handed me the cut-glass tooth-mugs.

"I'll have a large one," she said again.

I had misjudged her and the situation, and allowed my own expectations to cloud my judgment. Standing next to her as we sipped our brandies, the lights of Bandar Seri Begawan flickering in front of us, I felt confused.

Sophie's presence was obviously the main source of my confusion, but there was also Belinda and Isabelle to consider. I didn't know what was expected of me and I felt like a teenager on his first date. Belinda and I had been lovers and soul mates for over twenty years, I didn't want to break what we had … in my mind that bond still existed.

Nevertheless, as I watched Sophie when we were in Mama Wong's I wanted to kiss her and I wanted to see if my imagination was telling the truth about her. I accepted the chemistry was there – for me anyway – and therefore my feelings were those of any heterosexual man but it was because of this bond I still had with Belinda … and promise I'd made to Isabelle … that how I felt then and now was wrong.

I loved Belinda with all my heart.

I was still in love with her and nobody could ever replace her, nobody had any right to try to replace her. What I felt towards

Sophie might have been normal but it was too basic to replace what Belinda and I had. Our love for each other was spiritual. If I ever touched another woman, then she would be the last female I was intimate with, and not Belinda.

She had been and still was my life, but although I accepted she was now dead and buried in the graveyard in Medbourne, for me she would always exist. She was there in my mind the way she had been in my life.

It was all happening too soon.

Chapter Seventeen

I did not see Sophie again until after she had been to The High Commission for her official lunch. For me another troubled night's sleep followed our evening out but by the time I crawled out of bed and rang her room she had already left.

This time and in theory, I could control what kept me awake but it was to no avail. Feelings and emotions were perhaps something less controllable than I thought because they had a way of manifesting themselves into images in the mind. I woke up feeling as though I hadn't slept at all.

Ringing Abby at home I used the excuse that I had probably had too much sun the previous day and did he mind if we didn't meet up again until the following day. We hadn't actually agreed to meet but I thought it would be best to touch base with him, especially as he would be waiting to hear if Sophie had said anything. I kept my report simple – there was actually nothing to report – to satisfy his obvious concern over the security of the passage of any information.

Nazira had answered the phone.

"Good morning, Richard." Her voice suggested that she was having a silent chuckle to herself. I doubted whether Abby would have told her anything about the Chinese jets, nor what we actually discussed. However, as the PA to the Supreme Commander of the Royal Brunei Armed Forces, she probably knew more than she would tell either of us.

"Thanks again for a lovely meal, Nazira. Your hospitality was as outstanding as ever," I said.

"My pleasure, Richard. I hope we will see you again before you go back to England."

"Of course you will." If she had known the real reason for my being in Brunei she may have asked why we weren't seeing each other every day. "I don't know how much longer I'll be in Bandar but maybe you and Abby could come to the Sheraton Utama for a meal." Before Nazira had even answered my suggestion I realised it was a little silly.

"I can entertain whom I like in my own house, Richard, but unfortunately eating in public, and especially with infidels such as you," she said laughingly, "is still frowned upon, and with Abby's position we have to be careful."

"Yes, I'm sorry. That was stupid of me. I forgot I was an infidel."

Nazira laughed. "Of the worst kind, Richard, and don't you forget it. I'll call him. I presume it's him you want to speak to."

"Yes, please."

Her voice dropped slightly. "Take care, Richard and don't put yourself in danger."

Abby and I spoke for only a couple of minutes. I told him that my conversation with Sophie had been about our respective children and other innocent subjects that two people discuss when they are getting to know each other. His tone indicated his disappointment but we agreed that he would ring me the following morning and we would arrange to meet.

Cooling off as best I could in the hotel pool after a late breakfast, Nazira's coded warning was on my mind. It was a strange thing for her to say, and yet I couldn't ask for an explanation.

After a few hours by the pool and a light lunch I went for a walk into the centre of Bandar Seri Begawan and took a water taxi to Kampong Ayer, the Water Village. The sheer engineering brilliance of being able to build a small town on stilts strong enough to withstand the fast current of the River Brunei had always fascinated me.

Nearly ten thousand people lived in the village, complete with shops and a wooden mosque. By going to the village, as well as to admire the engineering, I also I hoped I would spot anyone from whatever faction that thought I was important enough to follow.

Was I being overly mistrustful?

After thoroughly enjoying my walk and forgetting that I ought to be looking over my shoulder, I went back to the hotel and resumed my position on the pool terrace with a cold orange and lemonade and a two-day old copy of *The Times,*

Sophie appeared minutes later.

She walked slowly across the terrace, the heels of her slingbacks clacking on the tiles. She was wearing a floral dress, a sun-hat and sunglasses. I stood up and she sat in the chair opposite mine, taking the hat off once she was under the umbrella.

"God," she said, "that was hard work. I'll have a quick drink and then get changed for a swim. How's your day been?"

"Lazy," I commented, signalling to the waiter who was hovering by the doors.

While she was quenching her thirst, Sophie told me about the lunch and having to be polite to people she wasn't particularly keen on. They were all European, mainly British, and boring. It was supposed to be a relatively informal curry-lunch that the High Commissioner held every month, but it struck her that the men and their wives all felt they needed to impress, to score some brownie points.

Evidently, there was one exception. He was an Army Colonel who was the senior British Loan Service Officer on detachment to the Sultan's Armed Forces. Sophie told me that she found him intriguing: he was about forty-five, tall, slim and handsome with close-cropped blond hair and the lightest blue eyes she had ever seen. She thought she recognised him from somewhere but, when they got chatting, they couldn't discover where it might have been.

"He was like a coiled snake," Sophie said. "He was sociable and attentive but I could see him watching what everybody else was doing, He wasn't rude, but he was aware. His wife was reptilian as well, but she resembled a toad rather than a snake." Sophie looked at me over her glasses to see how I was reacting to her observation, a smile on her lips. "I had obviously spent too long with her husband and they left early but not before he told me he'd been in the Special Forces at some stage in his career."

After finishing her drink, Sophie went to get changed, had a swim, and then rejoined me at the table.

"That's better," she said, towelling herself dry before applying copious quantities of sun-cream. She had a slight tan, probably picked up from Singapore and the other places she had already been to. The cut of her red swimming costume complimented her slim figure and I could see out of the corner of my eye that the waiter was back on station.

"Time for tea," I suggested, lifting my hand and calling the waiter over.

"So," she said once the waiter had begrudgingly left. "What are your plans for the rest of the day?"

Sophie had said that she was in Brunei until Tuesday and I assumed she would be at The High Commission for most of that time. If I was going to find anything out for Abby I would have to make use of every opportunity.

I looked at my watch. "It's just gone four and it'll be dark by six-thirty, seven o'clock. We could always go down to the beach for a couple of hours, if I can find a taxi that is."

"There's no need. I brought back one of the cars from the pool at the Commission. This beach, are we likely to be surrounded by locals?"

"I doubt it, not at this time on a Sunday."

"I've got a bottle of red wine in my room. We can sit and

watch the sun go down."

While Sophie disappeared to get changed, I cancelled our order for tea and managed to get a cool box from the hotel kitchen into which they kindly put some leftovers from the cold buffet lunch: a couple of bags of ice would keep the food fresh.

We drove out on the Muara road, turning off onto the track that would take us to Cave beach. I was pleased when I managed to find the turning straight away because it certainly wasn't that easy to spot from the main road. I had only been there twice before with a couple of friends I had made among the British civilians who worked for the Sultan on contract.

They had left Brunei in 1997 and we had since lost touch.

The beach was a couple of hundred yards from the road and we could only get the car about half way down the track. It was bumpy and needed a bit of skilful driving but Sophie seemed to enjoy the experience. Leaving the car, the jungle's humidity and the cackling of some birds brought the scene to life. I didn't know how often Sophie had been off the beaten track in Brunei, or anywhere else if it came to that, but if her furtive looks into the undergrowth were anything to go by, not often. I gave her a reassuring smile as I took the cool box and towels from the boot of the car.

"Peace and tranquillity,' I said.

She reached into the car for her bag. "If you say so, but I reserve judgement," she said, still looking about her.

"If we stay on the track the snakes and spiders will leave us alone," I said, smiling at her.

"Don't joke about such things," she replied. "I hate spiders ... and snakes ... and centipedes ... and cockroaches ... and ..."

A single cave – eaten away by the elements in a prominent rock structure – gave the beach its name. The beach wasn't easy to find, which made it attractive for those who wanted some privacy. It was about fifty yards deep at high tide and about a hundred yards long, forming a half moon of white sand. The jungle provided a backdrop and scattered along the beach were some smaller rocky areas. A fresh water stream divided the beach and, because of the recent storms, it was flowing quite quickly, stirring up the silt as it reached the sea. The cave was to the left of the beach.

I thought the beach's isolation might provide an ideal opportunity to move on with Sophie and perhaps ask a few questions to see if there was anything in Abby's suspicions about her. I was a complete amateur at passive interrogation – judging when the time was right was important. Anything I might glean and could report to Abby would at least show that I had tried.

During the night, as well as thinking about the effect Sophie was having on me, I had also decided that a dear friend or not, I was going to have to disappoint Abby. If Sophie wasn't able to throw any light on the matter then that would be that; I wasn't going to take it any further. It wasn't that I was worried, but I didn't know what I was doing and a fumbling amateur can only guarantee one outcome, and anyway, the thought of quizzing Sophie didn't sit easily with me for other reasons.

Putting the hotel beach towels down in the shade of some small rocks a short distance back from the water, I surveyed the scene while Sophie shrugged off her dress. Underneath she was wearing the black swimming costume she had worn the first time I saw her in the pool at the Sheraton. It was a perfect early evening: the sky was a clear blue, the sea calm, the humidity not as bad due to proximity of the sea, and the sun was well over an hour away from dipping below the horizon. The only sounds were the lapping of the waves and a birdcall every now and again from the jungle behind us.

"Aren't you going to strip off?" Sophie asked, settling down onto her towel.

"I'm going to get some driftwood for a fire. It'll keep the bugs away because they get a bit tiresome at this time of day."

"Do you want a hand?" The offer was made absent-mindedly, because, as she made it, Sophie lay back to soak up what was left in the sun's heat.

"No thanks."

I wandered away in search of the wood. Because of the recent storm a lot of the wood was still damp which meant I had to go closer to the jungle to find anything suitable. I collected a small bundle of reasonably dry driftwood before heading back along the deserted beach to Sophie.

"I'll go and have a look the other way. There wasn't much over there," I told her dropping the bundle by the rocks.

"Before you go, will you put some cream on my back, please?" She rolled over onto her front and then peeled the top of her costume down, handing me the cream. Squirting some of the cream from the tube onto her back and working it into her skin was a lovely sensation ... hopefully for both of us.

"That was kind of you," Sophie commented, lifting her head, her eyes on mine.

"How much do you want on?" I asked, hoping my unease didn't show too much.

"That's fine," she said, twisting a little towards me. Her breast was almost exposed. "Can you do the tops of my legs as well?"

I put some cream onto the backs of her thighs and rubbed it in as quickly as possible. Sophie settled back down on the towel.

"That's great, thank you," she said.

Without saying anything else, I headed off along the beach in the other direction. Sophie's request had been innocent enough, but my reaction concerned me. She was still a stranger and the simple act of putting sun cream on her back and legs was sensual. I had misjudged the previous evening, and now I was perhaps misjudging Sophie's intent once again. I was acting like an immature teenager.

Belinda had been dead less than three months and yet I was allowing a controllable situation to get the better of me ... was that a silly thing to think?

I bent down and picked up a piece of driftwood.

I was thirty-nine years old with two teenage children, I had recently lost my wife, and my mother-in-law was, as far as I knew, critically ill in hospital. Nevertheless, I was allowing a woman I had known for forty-eight hours to take over my mind because, whether I liked it or not, she was featuring more and more in my thoughts, and not because of the mystery that surrounded her.

Even when Abby told me that she might be the source of at least some information on an extremely important political situation, her image had appeared but for the wrong reasons. I saw her with me not as an acquaintance but as a friend, a close friend. We were exploring together, finding out about each other, discovering what was important and what was unimportant.

Once again my thoughts were muddled, and all because Sophie had asked me to put some sun cream on her back and legs.

The screams reached into my mind and mingled with my irrational thoughts but quickly assumed precedence over anything else on my mind.

Then the screaming masked out all other thoughts.

The screams were real.

Somebody was in agonising pain. The screaming made my blood run cold. I had never heard anything like it before. I stood still, trying to work out where they were coming from.

I turned round.

Having walked beyond the Cave, I no longer had a view of

where I had left Sophie. I dropped the wood onto the sand and began running. The screams were still piercing every nerve in my body. The soft sand slowed me down. I lost balance and fell over, scrambled to my feet and tried desperately to run faster.

I rounded the corner past the cave and looked to where I had left Sophie.

She wasn't there.

I stopped, searching the beach for her.

Running a few more paces, I fell over again, got up and scrambled forward. The screaming was coming from the water. I changed direction.

Then I saw her.

She was in the shallows clawing at the water. Throwing her head back she screamed again but it was cut off as her body slumped and her head fell backwards into the water.

I reached her seconds later.

Taking hold of her hands, I dragged her from the water and as I did I saw what had caused her agony.

It was almost transparent with a tinge of blue.

What the hell was it?

A shimmering translucent mass of what looked like jelly.

I dragged Sophie out of the water and the thing moved with her. Its tentacles wrapped round Sophie's thighs shone in the fading sun. The jellyfish was pulling her away. I grabbed a rock and smashed down as hard as I could on the slimy fingers of hell enveloping her legs. I felt useless but I acted instinctively. I threw the rock at the main body of the jellyfish and then dragged Sophie further onto the beach.

She was quiet, perhaps unconscious.

The screaming had stopped.

Not even a whimper.

Her head was to one side, her eyes closed.

I assumed she had gone into the sea where the freshwater

stream joined it to cool off and this thing had been waiting for her. This thing had wrapped its slippery arms of death around her.

I tried to think.

What should I do?

I had heard about using vinegar or even urine on jellyfish stings. For her to collapse like that it must ... was she still alive? I ran up the beach, grabbed a towel and attempted to wipe away the bits of slime that were still on her legs. The red welts were like furrows across her thighs and calves. Christ!

I had never seen anything like it before and I was panicking.

She hadn't pulled up her costume before going into the water. Lowering my head, I put my ear between her breasts, praying that I would hear her heartbeat. The lapping water masked any sound ... I couldn't hear anything. I lifted her arm hoping I would find a pulse in her wrist ... if it was there it was so faint I couldn't detect it.

I looked up into the fading blue sky and shouted, "Not again, please God, not again!"

How many more?

Squeezing her nose, I prised open her lips, checking her airway before blowing into her mouth. After a few breaths I stopped. How many should I do? I couldn't remember. Putting the palm of one hand onto her chest between her breasts I pressed, lifted, pressed, lifted, pressed. One, two, three, four, five, six, seven, eight.

Back to her mouth, deep breath – blow in, deep breath – blow in. I remembered there was enough oxygen in exhaled breath to give life to somebody. Deep breath – blow in, deep breath – blow in.

Heart, back to her heart. Hands can give life. Press hard – release, press hard – release. God, please don't let her die.

Don't let another one die.

All of a sudden, she began to shake. Her hands, arms, legs and feet began to tremble. Her entire body convulsed. She was alive, thank God!

But, it wouldn't be enough.

I had to get her to hospital. How could I drive and try to keep her alive? I looked around, praying that somebody else would be on the beach having heard Sophie's screams, but there was nobody.

I left the first towel where I had thrown it: there may still have been jellyfish spores on it. I looked down at the murderous mound of jelly in the water and then it came to me.

Box jellyfish!

Sea Wasp!

What had I read other than the fact that the sting could be fatal? Sometimes found lying in the shallows where fresh water meets seawater. There was a chance in a million of seeing one, but if they made contact with anything, they wrapped their tentacles round it.

Its tentacles had found Sophie's thighs, Sophie's legs.

Hospital, I had to get her to hospital.

The shaking had become uncontrollable. She was in shock, but she was alive. The shock could kill her. It nearly had, so it could again.

I ran up the beach and grabbed the other towel. On seeing the red wine Sophie had brought from her room, I wondered. Vinegar, urine, red wine – maybe it would work. I smashed the neck of the bottle against a rock and then poured the wine over her twitching legs. I tried to pour some on all of the welts but there were too many. Then I thought of the ice. Should I put the bags of ice on her legs? Was I doing the right thing? I threw open the cool-box. Not all the ice had melted. I tried to cover the areas that were badly stung, sliding the ice gently up and down the wounds.

I pulled up her swimsuit to cover her breasts and slipped the straps over her arms and shoulders. Why I was thinking of her dignity at a time like this? I was wasting time. Was I expecting her to die? Holding her in a sitting position and wrapping the towel round her shoulders, I lifted her. She was as light as a feather. Her head lolled against my shoulder.

Was she still alive?

The shaking had subsided but was that wasn't necessarily a good sign.

I carried her up the track to the car. The ice was melting too quickly in the bags. Shit! I realised I didn't have the keys. They must be in her bag that was down by the rocks. After lowering her gently onto the track I raced back down to the beach, grabbed her bag, her dress and sandals. The rest would have to wait.

The rest could go to hell.

I probably broke every traffic law in the book: speed limits, traffic lights, give-ways, and all the laws of the road. Oblivious to what was going on around me, I concentrated on what was going on in front of me. For once, I was thankful that there was little traffic on the Brunei roads, and what was there tended to ignore what other drivers were doing. I was another incompetent; I needed avoiding, and ignoring.

Where was the hospital? Shit, I didn't know where the hospital was. I had automatically headed for Bandar but I hadn't the faintest idea where to go. There were no signs that I could see. Was I looking for a Red Cross? No, you idiot, it would be the Red Crescent!

Were Muslim hospitals signposted with the Red Crescent?

Sophie was on the back seat which meant there wasn't anything I could do for her while I was driving. Every now and again, I looked over my shoulder but I didn't know whether I was looking at her dead body or whether she was hanging on to life. I thought I saw her twitch but it may have been the car hitting a bump. She was still in her swimming costume with a towel draped over her, the bags of little more than cold water splayed across her thighs.

Then I saw it – a sign!

The Raja Isteri Pengiran Anak Saleha Hospital – of course, the RIPAS – I remembered going there once with another employee of Astek. A simple cut was infected and I took him to the RIPAS to get it treated. How could I have forgotten? How could I be so stupid? It was on a hilltop about half a mile from the centre of Bandar. I was on a dual carriageway and I accelerated as I saw the sign.

Screeching to a halt outside what I assumed was Accident and Emergency, I lifted Sophie off the back seat and rushed in through the automatic doors. I stopped. There wasn't anybody who resembled a nurse, a doctor, anybody. I was frantic: so close and yet … there had to be somebody. I was in a hospital for God's sake.

A door swung open and a nurse came through. She walked across the foyer of the hospital and she had quite a few files in her hands. The other people in the area stared at me as I rushed towards her.

"Nurse, nurse," I shouted. I prayed she spoke good enough English to understand what I was about to say.

The nurse stopped and looked at me, a worried expression on her face that vanished as soon as she realised the bundle I was carrying was a human being. She came over to me and said in perfect English, "Can I help you, sir?"

"Thank God!" I shouted. "I think she's been stung by a box jellyfish. Help her please."

The nurse placed her fingers against Sophie's neck, without taking her eyes from mine. She was assessing me. "A box jellyfish?" she repeated.

"I think so – a box jellyfish, a sea wasp."

"Come with me," the nurse ordered.

"Is she still alive?" I pleaded, following the nurse through a swing door and down a corridor.

"Yes, but only just."

We turned a corner and we seemed to be in a small reception area. The nurse leant across the counter and said something to another nurse who immediately picked up the phone. A wheeled stretcher appeared from nowhere and another nurse lifted Sophie out of my arms and placed gently on to it.

Turning the trolley round the nurse disappeared back through swing doors.

The nurse who I had seen first came over to me. "Wait here, sir, and somebody will come and see you shortly."

"Will she be all right?"

"How long ago did it happen?" the nurse asked.

"I really … I really don't know … maybe twenty, thirty minutes."

The nurse frowned. She had a pretty face and I guessed from the way she was dressed that she wasn't Bruneian; she was probably on contract from Singapore or Malaysia.

"If it was a box jellyfish then only time will tell but the fact that she has survived the first bout of shock is a positive sign. She's in good hands."

"Thank you," I said. "You've been most kind."

She smiled again. "It's my job."

"What people like you do is never simply a job," I told her, meaning every word.

"I hope she pulls through, Mr … Mr …?"

"Blythe, nurse, my name is Blythe."

"If she's strong, she will survive, Mr Blythe." She pointed towards the reception desk. "The nurse over there will want some details."

"Thank you again."

"My pleasure," the nurse said before she went back down the corridor.

I looked over towards the reception desk. The nurse behind the counter had a pen poised.

After giving the nurse the few details I knew, I sat in a very uncomfortable plastic chair and waited. All I knew was Sophie's name, her age and that she worked for the British Foreign Office. I didn't know her address or anything else about her. The nurse behind the reception desk had given me an inquisitive look when I couldn't answer what she no doubt thought were the simplest of questions. I suggested she ring the British High Commission and ask for a representative to come to the hospital.

It was nearly six o'clock.

I assumed the High Commissioner lived on the Commission premises. He could be alerted and order one of his minions to come and assume responsibility for Sophie. I wasn't going anywhere but Sophie was in Brunei on official business.

Watching the inactivity in A&E, I wondered what the hell was going to happen next. One minute I was being asked to cross-examine a visiting member of the Foreign Office, the next minute I'm dragging the person I'm supposed to interrogate from the clutches of what I believe to be one of the most dangerous creatures to roam the South China Sea. I knew little about box jellyfish other than the fact that they could kill and invariably did. During my first visit to Brunei, I remembered being warned about the various undesirables that waited in the shallows around the waters, but, in the same breath, I was also told that the chance of encountering a dangerous creature was remote.

Sophie was unlucky.

The red welts on her legs had looked awful. I hoped that what I had done was right, or at least helpful.

I found it difficult to believe that it was no more than a couple of days since Sophie and I had shared the frightening experience of flying through a tropical storm and less than twenty-four hours since we sampled Mama Wong's fish and chips accompanied by her *specials*.

The door next to me opened and a small man in a white coat went over to the desk. The nurse was pointing at me. A man I assumed to be a doctor, turned round and faced me, pausing for a few seconds before crossing the short distance between us.

I stood up.

"Your name is Bly?" asked the doctor as he approached me holding out his hand. "I am Doctor Pengiran Haji Momin bin Pengiran Abdullah Wahab."

"Blythe," I said, shaking his hand, "Richard Blythe."

"Please sit down Mr Bly," he suggested, indicating the chairs. He sat down next to me and half-turned to face me. He was a small man, probably about five foot six tall, jet-black hair and a similar neatly trimmed moustache to Abby's. His glasses were gold-rimmed and the suit under his white coat expensive.

He watched me for a few seconds and then asked, "You brought the lady with the jellyfish stings to the hospital, Mr Bly?"

I nodded. "I did."

Smiling apologetically he spread his hands. "Mr Bly, may I ask whether you were the only person with Mrs Mackin … Mackin …"

"Mackintosh," I said, helpfully.

"Yes, Mrs Mackintosh, I am so sorry. Were you the only person with Mrs Mackintosh when the accident happened?"

"Yes, I was."

"May I ask what you did?"

"What, after she was stung you mean?" He nodded. "She was already in a state of shock when I reached her and I think she'd lost consciousness. I ... I checked her airway, gave her mouth-to-mouth and tried to keep her heart going. I'm not sure any of it was necessary."

The doctor's eyes opened wider. "They would have been necessary Mr Bly. Did you treat her legs where they had been stung?" There was a slight smile on his lips.

"Erm, well yes." I was becoming a little concerned in case I had done something that may have made matters worse. "I wiped as much of the jelly from her legs as I could with a towel, but then I used ice ... I put ice on what seemed to be the most badly stung areas when I was driving here." I closed my eyes, praying that I wasn't going to be told that Sophie was on the point of dying or had had already died. "And ... and red wine, I poured some red wine on the welts before using the ice."

The smile stayed on the doctor's lips. "Mr Bly, I think Mrs Mackintosh owes you her life." When I didn't react he carried on. "I will not go into a lot of detail but Mrs Mackintosh should be dead. She was stung badly and you were right to tell the nurse that it was a box jellyfish. The effect of having the sizeable area of her legs stung was potentially fatal. She could have died from heart or respiratory failure. The rapid first aid you gave her almost certainly saved her life. I would not recommend you use red wine again, Mr Bly, alcohol is not good for such stings, but the acid in the wine helped and then the ice definitely a good decision."

I sat back in the chair. "Thank God! And thank you, Doctor."

"Fortunately we do have anti-venom here. Although the stings are rare, they do happen and all the year round. Mrs Mackintosh is on a drip and there may be some reaction to the anti-venom, but I can say that she is out of danger."

"May I see her?"

"She has been sedated, Mr Bly. Maybe you can see her in a couple of hours." The doctor looked round as three men and a woman literally burst through the doors. They made a beeline for us. The doctor and I stood up together.

The men were all European, as was the woman. Two of the men looked to be in their late twenties, early thirties, tall and well built. The third man was a good deal older and shorter. The woman could have been anything from twenty-five to thirty-five, stocky, short hair and black-framed glasses. They were all casually dressed.

They ignored the doctor. "Are you Richard Blythe?" asked one of the younger men.

"Yes."

"Would you come with us, please?" The man who had asked the question moved to one side of me and the other, rather rudely elbowed the doctor out of the way, he then stood close to me on my other side. They both gripped my arms.

"Gentlemen," the doctor said, "May I ask what is happening?"

The older European stood in front of me but turned his attention to the doctor. "We will be taking Mr Blythe with us. Are the doctor looking after Mrs Mackintosh?" Doctor Momin simply nodded, somewhat overawed by what was happening. "This lady will be staying," the man said. The female stepped forward, took hold of the doctor's arm, and guided him away from the group.

He went obediently.

The older man turned back to me. "You will now come with us."

The grips on my arms tightened and I felt myself propelled forwards. I resisted.

"I'm sorry to disappoint you, whoever you are, but I would prefer to be asked and then I will make up my own mind whether I go with you or not."

The older man who had started to move ahead of us stopped

and turned round. "Mr Blythe, I think you are in enough trouble without generating any more for yourself."

I frowned. "Trouble? What trouble?"

"Mr Blythe, we don't want a scene here. You will come with us."

The woman and Doctor Momin had moved through the doors. The two nurses behind the reception desk were doing nothing other than staring in our direction, as was everyone else in the area, their eyes wide open with disbelief.

"A scene is what you'll have unless you tell me who you are and what you want." The goons – that's all they appeared to be – on either side of me exerted more pressure and I could feel myself being lifted.

"I am from the security section of the British High Commission and as you are a British citizen I am authorised to place you under arrest, Mr Blythe. I am therefore arresting you and you will now come with us."

"Arresting me for wha ..."

A pad covered my nose and mouth and my arms were locked to my sides. The immediate sensation was one of smell – it took me back to my early childhood when my mother used to use a little glass bottle of what she called Dab-it-off.

The smell was extremely strong.

My head began to spin.

My feet dragged along the ground as I was propelled forward. I tried to resist but then ...

Chapter Eighteen

I didn't seem to have any control over my eyelids but the brightness of the light coming from somewhere made them translucent. It was the strangest of sensations, I felt as though I was floating and yet my body was as heavy as lead. My head thumped, my mouth was dry and I was nauseous.

But I wasn't alone.

Not being able to open my eyes made me agitated but … maybe it would be better not to try. By feigning continued unconsciousness, I might learn a little more than I already knew … which was next to nothing. I didn't know who else was in the room with me but I certainly wasn't alone.

Lying perfectly still, I waited.

Whatever drug they used had knocked me out almost immediately, the smell of cleaning fluid was still in my nostrils. My brain was trying to tell me what the drug could have been … chloroform? It must have been chloroform. There was no way of knowing how long I had been unconscious. My legs and arms felt cold … I guessed I was still wearing the same clothes I had worn to the beach with Sophie.

I wondered how she was … and now … *what* she was.

Abby had implied there was more to Mrs Sophie Mackintosh than she wanted others – including me – to know about. One minute I am told that I probably saved her life, the next I'm abducted by three men from the British High Commission. Well, they said that's where they were from although they hadn't actually provided any identification. I hadn't asked for any either. They looked respectable enough but that didn't tell me anything – looks can easily deceive.

My nose began to itch and instinctively I moved my hand to scratch it, but I discovered my wrists were tied to something by what felt like some sort of soft material.

I heard a door open.

"How is he?" a gruff male voice asked.

"Coming round I think," a female replied. "His right hand twitched and his fingers moved. How much did you give him? He's been out for hours."

"Enough," the man replied. "I had better get Mr Bailey. It was good of you to sit with him. Will you be all right for a couple more minutes?"

"He can't do much, can he? Anyway, he doesn't look the violent type," the woman said.

"They never do," the man said before I heard the door close.

Other than the fact that I had actually been unconscious for hours, I learnt little from the exchange. I had no idea how long it would take for this Mr Bailey to appear and, as the woman appeared to think I was harmless, I tried to open my eyes ... I wasn't going to learn anything else with them closed.

It seemed to take ages and was quite painful, but eventually I succeeded. The woman I had heard speaking a few minutes earlier was sitting in a straight-backed chair by the door. She was leafing slowly through a magazine, unaware that I was watching her. There was a suggestion of recognition; something about her made me think I had seen her before.

Sensing my scrutiny, she lifted her head.

Recognition was immediate.

Her hair was still short but her roots no longer needing treating. It was the woman who had masqueraded as a German police officer and who had questioned me in Cochem.

"You ..." My mouth was still dry and my throat tickled. The nausea had receded a little. I coughed. "You ... you get around a bit, Frau Schwartz. One minute you are pretending to be a police officer in Cochem and now here you are in Brunei. What are you doing here?"

She continued to stare at me.

"Do you have any water?" I asked. "And why am I trussed up like a chicken?"

The woman allowed a weak smile to play across her lips. She stood up and crossed the room to a small sink. After filling a plastic cup with water, she held my head off the bed while I drank rather awkwardly. Some of the water dribbled down my chin but she didn't seem to notice ... or perhaps care.

"Are these really necessary?" I tried again to lift up my hand.

She ignored me and went back to her chair. Placing the cup on the table next to her, she watched me with the same knowing smile on her lips. She was wearing a plain green cotton dress and sandals. Her face seemed free of make-up and she wasn't wearing any jewellery.

"Not allowed to talk to me, is that it?" This time she simply raised her eyebrows. "Look, can't you even tell me what the bloody hell is going on?" I lifted my head off the bed as best I could but it was still thumping. "You were allowed to question me in Cochem. You were allowed to use false identities, but now you can't talk to me."

I shook my head and the thumping increased.

"Others will be here in a moment," she suddenly said in a soft voice

"And what's Mr Bailey going to do?" A frown joined her smile as I let slip that I had been conscious for a little longer than she realised. "Apologise? Tell me it's all been a horrible mistake, and then tell me exactly why I'm restrained after being drugged and kidnapped?" I tried to smile. "I don't think so, Frau Schwartz, or whatever your real name is."

She remained silent, the amused expression still on her face, the frown gone.

"At least you can tell me one thing, is Sophie Mackintosh still all right? Just before The High Commission snatch squad arrived, the doctor was telling me she wasn't going to die."

The smile disappeared from her face. "I've been told that she will recover."

I closed my eyes as a feeling of relief and sudden tiredness wafted over me.

"I'm pleased to hear that," I said, closing my eyes.

A matter of minutes later the door opened again. One of two men who entered the room I had last seen in the RIPAS hospital. I assumed the other one was Mr Bailey. They nodded at the woman, who stood up, looked at me and then left the room. The two men went either side of the bed and undid my restraints.

Swinging my legs off the bed, I immediately felt the room begin to rotate. The men stood to one side watching me. Waiting for my head to clear, I rubbed some life back into my wrists. The two men seemed unperturbed that I was now free, but on the other hand, they had no reason to be wary. I wasn't considering any form of violence and, even if I were, they looked quite capable of taking care of themselves ... and me.

"Can you stand?" the younger man asked.

"I think so," I said, and stood up. Although a little unsteady I didn't feel too bad.

Without another word, they led me slowly down a poorly lit corridor. Although I was wobbly on my feet, they didn't offer any help. Wherever we were, the air-conditioning was efficient. I obediently followed the men through another door and into a room that could have been mistaken for a large study in an English manor house. The walls were book-lined, the carpets soft under foot, the curtains at two large windows were velvet, and behind a large ornate writing desk sat a man smoking what looked like a Havana cigar.

Another man stood behind him, slightly to his left.

The men looked to be in their fifties. They were clean-shaven, both had greying hair, and rather incongruously, or so I thought, they were wearing dinner jackets.

The man behind the desk, who was overweight, indicated a chair in front of it. "Sit down, Mr Blythe," he ordered in a superior manner.

I thought about telling him where he could shove his chair but decided that if I was going to learn anything I thought it best not to upset him, and especially not in the presence of the other two men who were still standing behind me. Sitting down, I felt, for some inexplicable reason, particularly under-dressed in my shorts and sports shirt. Strangely, and perhaps again inexplicably, I didn't feel threatened. The method used to get me to the Commission was unorthodox but I didn't feel in any kind of danger.

I hadn't done anything wrong so my naivety and gullibility were probably my biggest enemies. Seeing the Schwartz woman had completely thrown me – Cochem and now Brunei. I really didn't see the connection ... perhaps I was about to told one.

After putting his cigar in the ashtray, the man behind the desk steepled his fingers, leant forward and stared at me for a few seconds.

"Mr Blythe," he said, "my name is Robert Cruickshank and I am Her Majesty's High Commissioner here in Brunei. I apologise for the way in which you were brought here but under the circumstances I am sure you will appreciate the need." I was going to interrupt and ask what these supposed circumstances were, but he carried on without a pause. At least he had apologised. "No doubt you are a little curious to know why you are here and why various things have happened to you over recent past, but maybe you have already put two and two together." I was going to interrupt again but this time he took one hand from the steeple and held it up to stop me. "Then again, Mr Blythe, perhaps I too am a little curious about what is going on and why you are here. Where do you suggest we start?" he said, steepling his fingers again.

"Why not with your explanation as to why I'm here?" I said.

"My question was rhetorical, Mr Blythe," he said pompously. "On this occasion I and Mr Bailey here," he continued, indicating the man behind him – I was wrong, he wasn't one of the men who came to collect me –"can't spend too long with you, we have to be somewhere else shortly. However, despite the methods used to bring you here, I thought it would be rather rude if we didn't meet and exchange some initial information, which would mean the next time we meet we can move on a little."

Without taking his eyes off me, he picked up his cigar, rolled it between his fingers, lit it again and exhaled a stream of smoke towards the ceiling. His greying hair was wavy and neatly cut. The dim light threw a shadow across his face but his features were angular and for some reason the shape of his nose suggested to me that he was from an aristocratic background – a strange observation. He commanded respect and, being the High Commissioner in Brunei, I was more than willing to give it to him, but I did object to the circumstances under which we were meeting.

He had given me the opportunity to respond. I had to try to put him off balance.

"Mr Cruickshank," I said, "your name is not new to me. Sophie Mackintosh has mentioned you once or twice."

There wasn't any response to what could be regarded under other circumstances as my impertinence. Cruickshank simply took another puff of his cigar before slowly replacing it in the ashtray, his eyes never leaving me.

"The methods used to bring me here do warrant an explanation ... and an apology. I agree, certain things bordering on the unusual have happened to me over the last few weeks and now I'm beginning to make connections. Having Frau Schwartz as my guard" – the two men looked at each other and frowned – "when I regained consciousness, and being drugged was certainly a surprise, but in retrospect probably it shouldn't have been unexpected."

Once again, Cruickshank's expression didn't change although I did detect a slight uneasiness from the man behind him.

"Mr Blythe, why are you in Brunei?" Cruickshank asked.

I looked from Cruickshank to Bailey before I spoke. I had nothing to hide … the truth, as is often the case, was probably the better option.

"I was invited by a friend," I said.

"And this friend is Dato Haji Abdullah bin Basrah Ibrahim, the Brunei Minister of Development?" His steepled fingers tapping together emphasised each exaggerated syllable. He had large pale and particularly hairy hands.

"There doesn't appear to be a need for me to answer, but I can't see why being friendly with a Brunei minister should cause … what it has."

Bailey appeared uneasy again. He looked the sort who might prefer slightly more grisly methods of extracting information. The enormity of what had happened wasn't suddenly lost on me, but I was still feeling quite light-headed and I wondered whether the drug they had used had some form of secondary effect. My thought processes added credence to this conclusion.

Cruickshank waved his hand and the two men who had been standing guard over me left the room.

"Mr Blythe, may I suggest we start being honest with each other?" he said.

"I couldn't agree more but I think you ought to be aware that I have been nothing but honest with you. I was invited over here by Abdullah and as far as I knew it, for purely social reasons." I adjusted my position in the chair. I was feeling thirsty but at least the light-headedness seemed to be stabilising. Although I was now closer to the Foreign Office than I'd ever been, I was not going to complicate matters this early on by repeating what Abby had told me, not yet, because I didn't know what I was dealing with.

Bailey came round the corner of the desk and spoke for the first time. "You went out with the minister on his launch yesterday. Why?" I had expected Bailey's voice to be as clipped and refined as Cruickshank's, I was surprised when he spoke in an educated Geordie accent.

Bailey rested against Cruickshank's desk. He was tall and slim whereas the High Commissioner appeared to be average height and overweight.

"Why does anybody go out in a boat?" I said. "Abdullah and I have known each other for years and he was doing no more than showing off his latest acquisition. What harm is there in that? We are probably going to have a round of golf together. Would you find that suspicious too?"

"No, if that's all it is," Bailey sneered at me. "It's a long way to come to go for a ride in a launch and play a round of golf," he said.

Cruickshank sat and watched me.

"Gentlemen," I said, beginning to lose my patience. "I assumed from the moment I was told that I was being arrested to the point when I woke up having been drugged by your thugs, that unbeknown to me I hasten to add, I had actually done something pretty awful. After meeting you, I still believed that you were going tell me that I had committed some heinous crime. But all I can gather from what has happened is that you are basing whatever it is you think I've done on some pretty flimsy evidence that I can neither confirm nor dispute because I haven't the faintest idea what you're alluding to." I moved forward on the chair and Bailey moved off the desk. "A fellow

Foreign Office employee of yours is, as far as I know, still lying critically ill in hospital after being attacked by one of the most deadly creatures in the South China Sea but you haven't mentioned her. The incident occurred when she and I went for an innocent couple of hours on a beach to watch the sun go down." I let my hands flop onto my bare knees. "Will one of you please tell me what the bloody hell is going on?"

Something didn't make sense.

Abby's reason for asking me to come to Brunei was unknown to me until earlier today. It certainly had nothing to do with my discovery in Dove Dale and happenings since. Therefore seeing the Schwartz woman again was the biggest surprise and made me rethink why I was in The High Commission. Cruickshank and Bailey were trying to connect my 'arrest' with Abby, which, if what Abby had told me were true, was understandable. If elements of the British government – and where better placed than in Brunei itself – were undermining the Sultan and his administration, my association with a senior minister was bound to have their interest. On the other hand, if Abby were wrong, why did they use such drastic methods to talk to me, in reality they only had to ask.

Perhaps there was some truth in what Abby told me.

Then, of course, there was Sophie Mackintosh. Because her 'accident' seemed to trigger everything that was now happening, she had to be the link, but that still did not explain why the Schwartz woman was in The High Commission.

"Mr Blythe." It was Cruickshank's turn to speak again and his tone had become slightly conciliatory. "Perhaps we have over-reacted," he said, leaning back in his chair. "It appears that maybe things aren't as we thought they were." He stood up and joined Bailey at the front of his desk. "We checked your background earlier – while you were sleeping that is – and what you have told us in this brief exchange, seems to support the facts as they have been presented. Yes, what happened to Mrs Mackintosh — and I'm pleased to say she will make a full recovery — did alert us to your presence with her, but from what you have said perhaps it is we who have not fully understood the situation." He looked at his watch. "Now we must go. I wish you good evening and I apologise for what happened to you."

Mr Bailey, I was pleased to note, was looking as confused as I felt.

"Are you telling me that that's it?" I said. "I can go?"

"Yes, Mr Blythe, that is precisely what I am saying. When Mrs Mackintosh is able, we will be talking to her and apprising her of what has happened. If there is a need to talk to you again, we will be in contact." Cruickshank tried to smile but it looked more like a scowl. He didn't appear to be in the slightest bit embarrassed by his sudden change of direction. If anything, I was getting the impression that he was actually quite relieved.

I stood up. "Are you really saying that I can walk out of here?"

He nodded while seeming to take no notice of Bailey's sideways look at him. "Yes, of course, and to add to my personal apology one of my drivers will run you back to your hotel."

"I'm not sure what you did to me would be legal in our own country let alone in a foreign one. I will be seeking advice and you will more than likely be hearing from me or my solicitor." I stood up as the door behind me opened.

Neither Cruickshank nor Bailey said anything further. Their expressions were sombre to say the least. I turned and with as much dignity as I could muster, left the room.

My escort wasn't quick enough closing the door behind me and I heard Cruickshank say rather loudly, "He wanted to know what the fucking hell is going on - how about you telling me first?"

Chapter Nineteen

Back in the Sheraton Utama Hotel I sat on the bed holding a glass that was half-full of whisky. Earlier I ordered a bottle via room service and signed a chitty to confirm its consumption was for medicinal reasons ... and it was.

I was physically shaking from the aftershock of what had happened, in many ways it was far worse than anything I had experienced in some of the most deprived countries in the world. Being drugged and abducted from the hospital was bad enough but what had happened in The High Commission seemed like fantasy ... it was though I was an actor in some third rate mystery thriller, with the emphasis on third rate. To try to clear my head I took another gulp of whisky and screwed my eyes shut – neither helped. I wondered what I should do next. Not even Belinda could help me on this occasion because there was nothing logical to discuss with her ... the explanation I could try to offer her was previously unsubstantiated but now it was farcical.

I downed the rest of the whisky and then reached for the phone. On arrival back at the hotel, I checked with Reception if there were any messages for me: there was one and it introduced a modicum of reality into the surrealism of what had happened.

The short message was from Charles.

He wanted to let me know that Elizabeth had made such good progress that she was at home and I wasn't to worry. I felt awful because I should have tried again to get in touch with him to ask how she was.

It shouldn't have been necessary for him to ring me.

After picking up the phone and on an impulse, I decided to ring Abby. It was late and the phone rang half a dozen times before it was picked up and then, unfortunately, by one of the maids. We had an unintelligible conversation and established little other than 'Master' and 'Missy' were out. I couldn't understand her English and she didn't understand my Malay. Finding both Abby and Nazira out at nearly ten o'clock in the evening was unusual. I did hopefully get the maid to understand that I wanted Abby to ring me as soon as it was convenient.

The phone rang again as soon as I put down the receiver. It was the hotel reception informing me I had a visitor; he was in the foyer and he wanted to see me. Feeling a little annoyed, I suggested that whoever it was could come up to my room but I gathered from the muffled exchange that followed this wasn't an option.

I said I would be down in fifteen minutes.

After a quick shower and much deliberation about who my mysterious visitor might be – and whether it was another twist to what had already happened – I took the lift to the ground floor, albeit somewhat apprehensively after my earlier experiences. The receptionist, who looked rather uncomfortable himself, indicated the far end of the foyer. The lights were dimmed and I couldn't see anybody at first, the foyer appearing to be deserted. I walked slowly across the marble floor, my rubber-soled shoes squeaking with each step.

There was a man seated at the far end of the foyer, his upper body hidden behind a copy of the Singapore newspaper, *The Straits Times*. When he became aware that I was there, he lowered the paper and a youngish local man folded it neatly before placing it on the table in front of him on which there was glass containing a fizzy drink.

The man stood up and proffered a hand. "Mr Bly?" he enquired, his mouth breaking into a polite smile, while the rest of his face remained passive. Abby had always been proud of the fact that he was one of the few Bruneians who was able to pronounce my name correctly. The doctor in the hospital and now this man had proved his point.

My visitor was about five feet six inches tall, slim with longer than normal jet-black hair. His lower jaw protruded slightly crookedly and his smile was lopsided as a result. I took his hand and looked at him inquisitively.

"You do not know me, Mr Bly," he said quite deliberately. "My name is Haji Ismail Bin Jarrarudhin and I am an Inspector with the Brunei Darussalam Internal Security Police." He gestured to the seat next to him. "Please sit down."

Sitting down as he asked, I realised the extra twist I had forecast was about to be revealed.

"May I get you a drink?" the Inspector asked, already raising his hand and beckoning a waiter who I hadn't noticed was standing by the door into the bar.

"Yes," I replied a little anxiously, "thank you. The same as you, please." The whisky I had consumed rather too quickly up in my room was still making me feel quite light-headed.

The Inspector held up his drink in one hand, showing two fingers with the other. The waiter nodded and disappeared into the bar.

"Now, Mr Bly, I must apologise for asking you to see me at this late hour, but it is important."

"How can I help, Inspector?" I asked, trying to remain calm on the outside but feeling my stomach churning. Although I had anticipated another twist, my mind was now trying to second guess what was going to happen ... and it was failing. A visit from the notorious Internal Security Police was perhaps more serious than anything that had already happened.

"Mr Bly, can you tell me why you were forcibly removed from the RIPAS Hospital this afternoon?"

His question was direct and the expression on his face suggested that he genuinely didn't know the answer and there was some concern in his eyes. If this was an official enquiry then I doubted whether the foyer of the Sheraton Utama Hotel would be the chosen place to conduct it. A stupid thought went through my mind: after being drugged and abducted by my own side, should I now be wary of somebody from the other side who seemed to be genuinely interested in my welfare?

Moreover, why was I regarding them as being on different sides?

I fully intended taking what had happened in The High Commission further but not with the local authorities – along with my solicitor, the Foreign Office was destined for another visit, but this time a successful one.

"I can understand what it might have appeared to be from an outsider's point of view," I said, "but if they'd known the circumstances, they may have understood."

The corners of the Inspector's mouth turned down as he took on board what I had said. "In Brunei we have a saying for someone who is confusing his listener. We say they are talking like an orang-utan. If I remember correctly, in England you say somebody is talking double-Dutch." He let the lop-sided smile return to his lips but his eyes weren't smiling. "What you have said is what I would expect a Dutch orang-utan to say." The smile became an accusatory grin. "Mr Bly, I am not an idiot. I know what I mean by *forcibly removed*, and so do you."

I nodded. "You are right, Inspector, and I'm sorry." I took a sip of my drink. "It was all a misunderstanding. I had been to the beach with a woman from The High Commission and she had an accident. I took her to the RIPAS. I think the people who came from the Commission misunderstood the situation and didn't bother to find out the facts. I went with them to explain."

"Mr Bly," the Inspector said patiently, "we now have a whole gathering of Dutch orang-utans." He inclined his head before carrying on. "Brunei is a rich country and His Majesty the Sultan uses its wealth to give his people a good standard of living, and one which is much higher than its neighbours in Sabah and Sarawak. He is a generous man, and therefore idolised by most of his people. Nevertheless, there are those who believe that benevolence does not excuse dictatorship and they generate rumours of wide corruption to stir up trouble in their pursuit of political change. Brunei's Internal Security Police come from the most loyal supporters of His Majesty for obvious reasons. We must protect His Majesty the Sultan and ensure his government remains stable at all times. To this end, investigations into disruptive behaviour are immediate and thorough. Dato Haji Abdullah, our Minister of Development, asked my department to keep a special watch on you." He smiled again when he saw my surprise. Abby had told me I was being watched but he hadn't told me it was by the Internal Security Police. Putting his hand near my arm, the Inspector continued, "But we were to watch you for your own protection, not because we thought you might be a subversive!"

"I'm pleased to hear that, Inspector, and again I must apologise," I said.

"I understand the situation with which you are faced. I would suggest that perhaps you do not know what is going on but you do feel you are in the middle of something. Am I right?"

"Totally, Inspector, but what I told you about the beach was the truth." My mouth was suddenly very dry, I picked up my glass and drained it.

"I know you went to the beach and also what happened while you were there. My team could not follow you to the beach because they would have been too obvious, but we were also watching Mrs Mackintosh from the moment she arrived at the airport, but for different reasons." I frowned and the Inspector leaned a little closer. "I have been told you that you coped extremely well with what happened and Mrs Mackintosh owes you her life."

Ignoring the compliment, my frown stayed. "May I ask why you were or are watching Mrs Mackintosh?"

"She is not what she seems, Mr Bly. She is something more than she purports to be. I am not sure you can trust her," the Inspector said solicitously.

"Dato Haji Abdullah implied the same but told me no more than that. Can you?"

A couple of European men in business suits came in through the front doors and went over to the reception desk. The Inspector didn't speak again until they had collected their keys and the lift doors had closed.

"Unfortunately, that is one of the reasons why we are watching her, to try and find out ourselves. I cannot tell you anything more than that because ... well, I am sure you understand there are certain things we must keep to ourselves."

"Can't you ask her or the High Commissioner? It's your country, surely you have a right to know."

The Inspector allowed yet another smile to cross his lips. "It does not work like that, Mr Bly. She has done nothing wrong as far as we know and diplomatic immunity operates in every country. Brunei is no different. We must find out by our own methods and, by telling you that, I have told you too much."

"Inspector, I presume you're aware that I was out on Dato Haji Abdullah's launch yesterday?"

"Yes, Mr Bly, of course I am aware."

"Once we were anchored offshore, we were buzzed by a couple of Chinese air force jets. Could they have had something to do with what is going on?"

"It is unlikely, Mr Bly," he said without hesitation. "The Chinese are always trying to show how big and brave they are. It happens quite often."

Abby had said the connection between the Spratley Island, the Chinese and the possible seditious elements, was unsubstantiated, at least he'd told me the truth about that. "So, the Chinese aren't currently considered to be a direct threat to Brunei's stability?"

"Being internal security it is not really my area, Mr Bly. However, there are many Chinese in Brunei and I also have many reliable information sources among them. I have heard nothing that suggests we, or any other South East Asian Nation, are under any greater threat than normal." The waiter was hovering again, out of earshot but hovering. The Inspector looked at his watch. "It is late, Mr Bly, but I would like a few more minutes of your time. Would you like another drink?"

"Yes, please."

I felt hungry as well as thirsty, but decided to order some food from room service later. I watched the Inspector as he waited for the waiter to go back into the bar.

Before the Inspector could speak again, I asked my next question. "I tried to speak with Dato Haji Abdullah before I was called down to see you, Inspector, but he was out. Do you know when he'll be at home again?"

"I would not usually be able to tell you, Mr Bly, but tonight I can. His Majesty The Sultan called an emergency meeting of his Ministers this afternoon and, as is normal, the Ministers' wives also meet with Her Majesty Pengiran Isteri Hajjah Miriam."

"I see, that explains it. Are you able to tell me ... no, that would be a silly question ..."

"If you were going to ask what His Majesty's meeting was about then yes, it would be a question I could not answer. If I may return to what happened at the RIPAS, Mr Bly, I would like to ask you again for the reason you were forcibly taken to The High Commission."

Spreading my hands I sighed. "Inspector, I apologise once more for trying earlier to make light of what happened but I really can't help you. One minute I was sitting with a doctor being told that Mrs Mackintosh was going to be all right, the next these three men arrive, tell me I have been arrested, drug me and a couple of hours later I wake up in what I believed to be The British High Commission. They start to question me, give nothing away in their questioning, and then suddenly it all stops and they drive me back to this hotel as though nothing had happened." I took a sip of my drink. "I really don't know why I was abducted. The only connection I made was that it happened after I took Mrs Mackintosh to the hospital, and after listening to what you have said, perhaps she was the real reason I was abducted."

"It is my turn to say, I see, Mr Bly." The Inspector had been staring at his fingernails as he spoke but he looked up at me suddenly. "You have spent a number of hours with Mrs Mackintosh. May I ask if she has said anything that you think might be of interest to me?"

"No, Inspector, I can't. Once again I must be negative, I'm afraid." I thought it best if I didn't mention what Abby had asked me to do. He believed he had good reason to go four miles offshore before discussing his concerns and I didn't want to break that confidence, but I would be speaking with him again, and soon, and when I did I would be asking him a few direct questions. "On Saturday Mrs Mackintosh and I went out for a meal ... but of course you'll know that." He nodded. "We talked about everything and nothing, our respective families and life back in England, that sort of thing. Then on the beach, the accident occurred before we'd really had the chance to talk about anything at all."

"I see," he said again. His eyes dropped back to his hands and he seemed to become uncomfortable, almost embarrassed. "Mr Bly, I am aware that you are a special friend of Dato Haji Abdullah. For him to ask for you to be protected from a woman as beautiful as Mrs Mackintosh suggests that she is perhaps quite dangerous." He paused before adding, "Maybe now is the time for you to leave Brunei and come back to see your friend again when it is all over."

"When what is all over?" I asked, knowing I wouldn't get an answer.

He spread his hands. "I most certainly cannot tell you that, Mr Bly."

"I understand, but does Dato Haji Abdullah know you are suggesting this to me?"

He shook his head.

"Yes, of course," he said quietly. "If he were here he too would ask you to consider my suggestion seriously."

"I will, Inspector."

"I will leave now, Mr Bly, and once again I am sorry for disturbing your evening." He stood up and offered his hand. "There are times when you must look beyond beauty and friendship to find the real person, Mr Bly, at other times the wise turn their backs and do not look for anything other than what they see."

I felt like being flippant and mentioning Dutch orang-utans, but instead I said, "I understand, Inspector."

"Good night, Mr Bly."

"Good night, Inspector."

Chapter Twenty

The following morning, after yet another awful night's sleep exacerbated by the hotel air-conditioning system making some most peculiar noises, I went to the RIPAS determined to get some answers.

At midnight, I had put a call through to Charles to tell him how delighted I was with his news. By the time we spoke it was after five o'clock in the afternoon in the UK and he answered the phone within a couple of rings. He was overjoyed when he told me Elizabeth was in the conservatory and he was preparing their breakfast. He described the way Elizabeth was as *remarkable*. She needed to take things slowly at first but the hospital believed she would make a full recovery. He was unbelievably chatty for Charles and I found his high spirits boosted my own, but only temporarily. Once off the phone my own world returned in abundance; each time I closed my eyes the images returned. I wasn't able to resolve anything and sleep was impossible.

I waited for the morning to come.

By the time I arrived at the hospital I had heard nothing from Abby either, which only added to my worries. After the visit from the Internal Security Police I wondered why I decided to go and see Sophie at all. She knew where I was, if there was anything she wanted me to know she could contact me. Before leaving the hotel, I had established that visiting times at the hospital were reasonably flexible but I had no idea what my reception would be like.

I assumed that the woman resembling Rosa Klebb would still be guarding Sophie, but I was wrong.

Sophie was in a side ward that was impeccably clean, lightly furnished, beautifully air-conditioned and welcoming. I was surprised that I was able to gain access to her without going through any checks, but the nurse showed me to the door without asking any questions and then after a friendly smile and nod of her head she departed to attend to her other duties.

Propped up on a multitude of pillows, Sophie was wearing a white cotton top, and a single sheet, raised slightly by a frame underneath, covered her from the waist down. There didn't appear to be any drips or the pinging of any monitors. She was reading a magazine. I had bought her a small bag of mixed fruit from the shop in the main foyer.

"Good morning," I said, standing inside the door looking at her.

She lowered the magazine and beamed at me. "My saviour!" she said.

"I wouldn't go that far," I suggested, crossing the space between us.

She held out her hand. "At least let me say thank you."

Her hand was soft in mine and suggested there was nothing ulterior in our meeting, but I still didn't know what I was really dealing with.

"It's good to see you looking so well," I said.

She kept hold of my hand. "Only because of what you did," she said.

She wasn't wearing any make-up, but if anything she looked younger without it. She seemed less businesslike and more vulnerable, more feminine. I wanted to put my arm round her and tell her that I would protect her, but from what? Maybe I was the one who needed protecting.

Only she could tell me that.

Sitting on the side of her bed, I reluctantly let go of her hand. She didn't attempt to take it fully away, leaving it within inches of mine almost as though she was saying it was there, if I needed to hold it again. I couldn't look at her. It was nothing to do with what I knew or didn't know, or to do with the bizarre events that had taken place since she was admitted, and nothing to do with what she might be. It was simply that I found her incredibly attractive and appealing. I can't think of any other way of describing the way I felt; there was something about her that made me want to ignore everything else. The urge to hug her, to comfort her, and to express how I was feeling was enormously strong. I closed my eyes hoping she wouldn't notice.

Inspector Haji Ismail words came back to me, "There are times when you must look beyond beauty and friendship to find the real person, Mr Bly, at other times the wise turn their backs and do not look for anything other than what they see."

Was I being wise? I wanted to call on Belinda, I needed to be told what was happening.

"Where are you?" Sophie asked softly, her fingers moving onto my hand again. I shuddered, opening my eyes. "I thought I had lost you," she added, smiling but a look of concern accompanied her smile.

Feeling flustered I looked around the small ward. "Where's your minder?" I didn't know how much Sophie would know, and at that particular moment I really didn't want to know what she knew, but I had asked the question.

"Minder?" she asked, appearing to be genuinely confused. "Who is supposed to be minding me?"

I wanted to say 'Rosa Klebb' but instead I shrugged and said, "Oh, before I left the hospital last night a woman from The High Commission was with you."

Her frown became more acute. "A woman was sent to be with me?"

Sophie seemed to know nothing about the previous night's happenings. I shrugged. "The High Commission sent somebody from the Commission to see how you were."

"Whoever it was left before I woke up this morning." Her fingers tightened on my arm. "No doubt somebody will be in later, but seriously, Richard, I owe you my life."

I was embarrassed. Suddenly the tiles on the floor became more appealing than the look in her eyes. Shaking my head I said, "Sophie, I acted on instinct. If I did save your life then it was more by luck than judgement."

This time she really squeezed my arm. "Look at me!" I lifted my head and saw that her eyes were watering. "Why are some men so self-effacing? If you hadn't done what you did, my body could well have been flown home in a box on the next available plane."

"I thought all men were bastards," I reminded her.

"No, not all, only those who decide to replace me with somebody else."

Not wanting her to feel indebted to me, I had to move on. We didn't have a future, therefore there should be nothing that meant either had a reason to contact the other after ... after what? After I discovered who she really was? Was that it? Was I scared that the person who was inexorably drawing me closer to her was going to become untouchable?

"How do you feel?" The question sounded trite but I should have asked it the moment I saw her.

She looked upset. "My legs are tingling now more than hurting. Like when you brush your hand against a nettle, the sting is irritating rather than painful. They told me the anti-venom would take a couple of hours to work but afterwards the relief would be magnificent. And they were right." She was watching me as she spoke, an inquisitiveness replacing the possibility that she had taken offence. When I didn't say anything, she continued. "And the scarring is going to be minimal, which is a relief."

"I'm so pleased," I managed to say.

The pressure of where I was, what had happened and who I was with was building up in me like the bloody water against one of the dams I built. Unlike my dams, though, I felt I could not open a sluice gate to let some of the pressure out. The relief would have been like the anti-venom Sophie had experienced. I wanted everything to go away, to wake up and be normal.

I wanted to be back with Isabelle and David, with Charles and Elizabeth and share with them the reprieve they were experiencing. I wanted to be with Belinda and feel her with me, next to me, guiding me. I needed to hear her voice, smell her perfume. The half of me that was missing had to return, I wanted to be complete again. These people and their world, and I included Sophie, were alien to me, they were strangers. They were confusing me and I didn't like them or what they were doing to me.

Their world wasn't my real world, my world was uncomplicated and easy to control.

Despite the air-conditioning there was perspiration on my forehead, and I could feel beads of sweat trickling down my back. I suddenly felt dizzy, and reached for the side of Sophie's bed.

"Richard ... Richard!" Her voice was an echo. I knew who was speaking but she was in a time warp. I was dreaming. I was asleep. That had to be the answer. I would wake up in a minute.

"Richard ... Richard ..." It was a different voice. I shook my head. Her voice was calling me. It was Belinda's voice. "Richard ... Richard." She had come back to me.

It felt as though I was sliding towards her.

Chapter Twenty-One

There was something cool on my forehead and it felt good.

I wondered if I was back in The High Commission. If I were, at least their hospitality had improved. My head was thumping again and I felt more woozy than nauseous. Deciding, once again, to pretend that I was still unconscious, I lay perfectly still. Perhaps they would reveal a little more than they had on the previous occasion.

Something was different, though.

The lights were softer – less penetrating.

There were also voices – distant voices. No, they were coming closer, speaking in a foreign language.

What was it?

Malay?

Why were they talking in Malay in The British High Commission?

The voices were closer, one either side of me.

Somebody picked up my right hand, and I felt fingers on my wrist.

"His pulse is still weak and slow but better than it was," a man said in English.

"Good," another man, said.

"He's a little feverish but his temperature has dropped."

"What caused it?"

There was a moment's pause. "Probably too much sun," the first man said. "He was dehydrated. We pumped a lot of fluid into him. It's not unusual, they come out here and don't bother to acclimatise then expect to be able to sit in the sun for hours without any adverse effect. He's not the first and he certainly won't be the last."

"Who is he?"

"His name is Blythe, Richard Blythe." The man talking to my left had managed to say my name correctly and he didn't speak English with the usual Malay accent. "He was visiting the woman who was brought in with the sea wasp stings, when he collapsed."

Collapsed? What did they mean I had collapsed? A stupid question – there's only one meaning that could be associated the word 'collapsed'.

I was still in hospital. I was nowhere near The High Commission; there was little point in carrying on the subterfuge. I slowly opened my eyes. The lights were softer but still bright enough for me to lift a hand to shield my eyes.

"Welcome back to the land of the living," the man on my left said.

I turned my head slightly. He was a European: his white coat, white shirt and blue tie were immaculate. He was tanned, had blond hair and he was tall but the most acceptable observation was that he was smiling. I tried to smile back at him but I have no idea whether I succeeded. Moving my head to the right I saw the other man. He was an equally immaculately turned out Malay, taller than average and he too was smiling.

"What … what on earth happened?" I asked through dry lips.

The Malay doctor spoke. "We don't really know, Mr Bly, but we think you may have had heatstroke."

Shaking my head, I said, "I don't understand. I was out on a boat on Saturday, and then on the beach for less than an hour on Sunday. Surely that wouldn't have been enough to …?"

The European lifted his hand to his mouth and coughed. "I am Doctor Fitzgerald, Mr Blythe," he said, putting his hands in his coat pockets. "I agree with Doctor Haji Suleiman, we don't really know. You had all the symptoms of heatstroke but people don't normally pass out as you did. We are waiting for the results of some blood tests then we'll know more."

"So what happens now?" I asked.

"Now you're back with us, we'll move you to a side ward. Once we've got the results we'll be able to assess what we should do next." Both doctors started to move away.

"What time is it?"

Doctor Fitzgerald checked his watch. "A little after midday," he said. "Your personal belongings are held securely, Mr Blythe. We'll have them sent to you once you are in the side ward."

"Thank you. Can I go and see Mrs Mackintosh?"

The doctors exchanged looks. "She's been moved, Mr Blythe. People from The High Commission came for her about half an hour ago. They have a small medical set up there with a trained nurse, she'll be well taken care of."

"I see. Thank you." I closed my eyes and Sophie's face floated into my mind.

Suddenly I felt alone.

I didn't expect to be kept in overnight for further observation but that is what happened ... or what was supposed to happen. Although I wasn't given all the details, evidently the blood tests showed that their initial diagnosis was correct. However, they had detected traces of opiates and alcohol in my blood and they asked whether I was on any medication. Evidently having opiates in my system when coupled with alcohol and too much sun, merely made what happened to me a foregone conclusion.

Shaking my head and saying, no, I wasn't on any medication, generated some confusion. I would have thought they would have know about my abduction, but ... the presence of opiates in my blood made me wonder if after the chloroform attack I was injected with something to keep me under. I remembered Schwartz asking how much I'd been given, and the answer from the nameless man was, 'enough'. Nothing would surprise me now.

   Staying overnight seemed the only option and if I were all right in the morning, I would be released by about ten o'clock after the doctor had done his rounds.

During my forced stay in hospital, I had two visitors, one of whom created a bit of a stir, but both gave me increased cause for concern.

I could see the looks of bewilderment caused by Dato Haji Abdullah bin Basrah Ibrahim, The Minister for Development, visiting this unimportant European who had spent too long in the sun. There was much bowing and scraping but eventually Abby managed to usher what appeared to be the entire hospital staff out of my side ward.

After closing the door, he removed his *songkok*, pulled up a chair and straddled it. With his arms resting on the back of the chair he looked at me and shook his head.

"I feel rather guilty, Richard," he said. "We spent too long out on the water on Saturday."

"Abby, my friend, I'm a grown man. I should have realised." I noticed that Abby was having difficulty in maintaining eye contact but I put it down to the fact that he was genuinely embarrassed. "How on earth did you find out? I was going to give you a ring when I got out tomorrow."

He gave a little shrug. "I rang the Sheraton to return your call and they told me you were in hospital but I didn't know why until I got here."

"Of course," I said, "when they decided to keep me in they said they'd ring the hotel to tell them. It could only happen in Brunei. Everybody knows everybody." I tried to make light of Abby's continued discomfort.

"I am sorry I didn't get back to your earlier, Richard, but after the meeting on Sunday we have been busy."

"Was it to do with what we discussed?"

He shook his head. "No, no, nothing like that. We have a number of foreign dignitaries visiting in the next few months and His Majesty the Sultan didn't think the preparations were going according to plan." He smiled for the first time since entering the ward. "And when His Majesty wants something to happen, it happens the way he wants it."

"Of course," I said.

I hadn't expected any visitors and therefore I hadn't planned any strategies, but I was surprised Abby hadn't mentioned my abduction form the hospital. It was only a matter of hours after he dropped me off at the Sheraton. If he had arranged for me to be 'watched' then he must know.

"By coincidence, Abby, when I was taken ill I was already in the hospital. Yesterday, I went to a beach with Sophie Mackintosh. There was an accident; well 'accident' is probably the wrong word, because she almost got herself killed. A box jellyfish stung her when she went in the water. Fortunately, I got her here fast enough for the anti-venom to be effective and she survived. I came to visit her this morning when I was taken ill."

Abby seemed surprised by what I'd told him. I was quickly coming to the conclusion that he knew nothing about what had happened to me since leaving me at the hotel. His behaviour and lack of knowledge were adding to my own confusion.

"Yesterday, you say?" was all he said.

"Yes, Abby, it was yesterday, after you dropped me at the hotel. After she was attacked I brought her straight here and luckily she is going to be back to normal soon." I lifted my hands and let them fall into my lap. "But I'm afraid this means that my chances of finding anything out from her are almost zero. She's been taken to The High Commission to recuperate and that could take days."

Even when I mentioned The High Commission, there was no reaction. Either there was a damn good reason why he was pleading ignorance or he genuinely didn't know what had happened.

"I see," he said, his head slumping into his shoulders.

"Abby, are you all right? You seem down, and your mind is obviously somewhere else."

His head shot up allowing me to see a look in his eyes that I had not seen before. It was almost accusatory, challenging.

"What do you mean?"

"Nothing, Abby, I don't mean anything but you seem totally preoccupied ..."

His eyes narrowed. "I'm sorry, Richard. The meeting with His Majesty was not what I expected, I thought all the right plans were in the right place. He gave me quite a dressing down in front of the others."

"I'm sorry to hear that, Abby," I said.

His eyes remained narrowed, almost as though he was challenging me to contradict what he had said. Why would I? I had never seen him like this before and it really worried me.

He wasn't the Abby I knew.

"It will all sort itself out," he said.

"Because of what happened, I'm afraid the chances of getting any information from Sophie Mackintosh ..."

Abby was rubbing his hands together. "His Majesty needs some good news and I want to be the one who gives it to him. I need to be back in favour. These visits were not the cause of the tension at the meeting, and his attitude towards me, it was this underlying threat that only those closest to His Majesty know about."

"I'm sorry if you feel I've let you down," I said.

"No, Richard, it is not you who has let me down. It is me who should be apologising. I should never have involved you in the first place. It was a ... what do you call it? Yes, a long shot. I suppose deep down I always knew that I was abusing our friendship. I am the one who is sorry." Abby bent forward, his hand reaching for mine.

"There was no abuse of friendship. If there had been anything I could have done, then you know I'd have been more than willing."

We shook hands, which seemed to be a signal for Abby to stand up and prepare to leave

"If Sophie hadn't had the accident, you never know, she may have told me something useful," I said.

"Unfortunately you are right, we will never know." He looked at his watch. "I am sorry but I must go. I have a meeting … but before I go, Richard, I would ask you to forget what we spoke about on the boat. It was silly of me to think … no, I must say no more. It was even sillier of me to involve you and it is now something I much regret. Do not think badly of me, Richard, our friendship is something I will always treasure, please believe me."

We shook hands again and I was about to ask him what was really going on, when the door to the ward opened, and Abby's exit committee either trooped in or were waiting in the corridor. Somebody had been watching us but not for any reason other than protocol. Abby looked over his shoulder and then back at me.

Something in his expression told me that we would not be meeting as close friends again.

He left without another word.

The ward door closed behind him and I felt it had also closed on another chapter in my life.

I did not have long to give much thought to and worry about Abby's visit before my next visitor arrived.

Having got out of bed, I was looking through the window towards Bandar Seri Begawan, watching the boats skimming across the water between Kampong Ayer and the town. The contrast between old Brunei, including Kampong Ayer, and the new Brunei was quite disturbing. Similar to many other cities and towns across the world, the starkness and often-grotesque modern architecture overshadowed the beauty of what was and what still could be. The sky was cloudless and I could see the heat shimmering in every direction I looked, but it still didn't make the concrete monstrosities appear any better.

My mind was still reeling after Abby's visit.

"Mr Bly?"

I turned round and Inspector Haji Ismail Bin Jarrarudhin was standing by the door.

"Inspector!" I said, not able to hide my surprise.

He stepped into the ward and closed the door before leaning against it. There was a serious expression on his face.

"Mr Bly," he said, clasping his hands in front of him. "I have come to give you a piece of advice, which if you choose to ignore might cause some unnecessary delays to your return to England."

"I'm sorry –"

"No, Mr Bly," he said, holding up his hand, "I am not here to discuss what I am about to say, I am only here to say it." He paused. "My advice to you is that you leave Brunei as soon as possible. To assist in your decision I have checked with the airport and there is a seat on a scheduled flight leaving at seven this evening. I understand you had an open business class booking for your return flight originally but I have now transferred this to the flight I have mentioned. Your ticket will be waiting for you at the airport."

"But I've been told that I –"

"You will be discharged from hospital after I leave, Mr Bly. You only need to pack and then proceed to the airport. The hotel told me that your bill has been taken care of, which means there is nothing to delay you." He felt behind him and opened the door. "Mr Bly," he said finally, "as I told you, what I am saying is advice. You do not have to listen but might I restate that should you choose to ignore what I have said then …" He shrugged. "I am afraid I will not then be responsible for what might happen."

With his final words ringing in my ears, the Inspector left, leaving the door to the ward open.

More intrigue, more confusion and more worry.

When was it all going to stop?

Chapter Twenty-Two

The Singapore Airlines 747 landed at London Heathrow shortly after seven on Tuesday morning. I had been away less than a week.

It was an unpleasant return flight, not that the weather or any other natural phenomenon played a part … unlike the flight from Singapore to Brunei when I first met Sophie.

I slept very little.

The ability to concentrate on anything escaped me. I couldn't watch and be distracted by an in-flight movie or read a book. The only respite came when it was time for a meal. At least then, I was able to focus on something else.

I didn't care whether my reaction to the Inspector's 'threat' was spineless or not. If I had stayed in Brunei and whatever he had predicted had come true, there would have been only one loser.

I was lost for an explanation.

There didn't seem to be a connection between Abby's request when out on his launch and what he said during his visit to the hospital. If anything, the two events contradicted each other. Even when applying a vivid imagination, it was all beyond explanation. Something was going on – something that was serious – but I had no idea what.

And … I no longer wanted to know what it was.

I wanted out.

The Inspector had given me good reason to get out.

Nevertheless, what was it about Sophie Mackintosh? Who was she? If what Abby told me was his reason for inviting me to Brunei was a lie, then what was his real connection with Sophie? The expression on his face when he left the hospital said it all.

There was no doubt he had lied to me, but why?

We had said goodbye and there was no 'until next time' even hinted at. He wasn't only telling me that our friendship was over, he was conveying something very final.

Why had Inspector Haji Ismail ordered me out of Brunei? Was there a connection?

There had to be.

My thoughts became as disconnected as the events I'd experienced. To slow down my whirling mind I even tried a couple of double gin and tonics but all they did was make me more morose.

There had to be another Sophie Mackintosh, I wasn't that easy to fool.

The alcohol at least allowed me to concentrate on the more acceptable aspects of her for a while. The way she had affected me was for real. I hadn't looked at, nor had I wanted to look at, another female when Belinda was alive. In fact, despite Isabelle's misgivings I hadn't looked at another woman in that way since Belinda died ... until Sophie Mackintosh walked into my life and affected me in the way she had.

I felt from the beginning that I had known her forever.

There was an intimacy within our minds, or so I thought, that precluded the need for any build up to a relationship. The images of her climbing out of the hotel swimming pool, crossing the restaurant to join me for breakfast, sitting on the opposite side of the table in Mama Wong's, were vivid.

When I went to see her in hospital after she was attacked by the sea wasp and was told that she would be all right ... nothing else mattered: her screams, the look of sheer agony on her face, the whimpering as I drove her to the hospital would never be forgotten but she had survived.

Perhaps deep down I hadn't wanted to know her secrets, maybe I was happy with the person she was and not what she did. I didn't want anything to colour how I felt about her. The Inspector's hypothesis about not looking too deeply if you were happy with what was on the surface, came back to me.

Although my mind was going round in circles, whenever there was a pause, a gap in the thinking process, she would leap in and fill it. Belinda had always been there to do that but now this stranger, who had had such an effect on me, had become an intrusion. She was interfering with the irreplaceable relationship I had with Belinda. I felt guilty but an indefinable ache took over and masked the guilt.

Anyway, there was little point in crucifying myself now because the moment had passed. Two lives that had been thrown together under the strangest of circumstances had just as easily been pulled apart by, what was to me, the unknown. It was something I would never forget but it was also something that was now at an end.

After drinking the second gin and deciding that another wasn't the answer, I tried to bring Belinda to the forefront of my mind but without success. Bailey, Cruickshank and their goons were there instead and with them came a multitude of questions that were unanswerable. From the moment I had entered Dove Dale, my life took a macabre twist that was destined to remain a total mystery. I was going to leave it all behind me, and concentrate on a future about which I could have some say. I had been living in a dangerous fantasy world. The world I needed was real and contained people who were dear to me.

There were also memories.

After collecting my car from the long-stay car park, I headed towards the M25 intending to stop off at St Edward's on the way home. Phoning Isabelle and David while in Brunei wouldn't have served a purpose, but I felt relieved to be back that I needed to return to my real life as soon as possible and they were the nearest source of what I had left behind.

I reached the school gates at midday. Having turned off the main road I hesitated but only for a few seconds. It was a lovely day and everywhere was colourful and peaceful. There was a cricket match taking place on the bottom square but from the size of the young boy doing a good impression of an off-spin bowler, I doubted whether it was David's year. Other *inmates*, as Isabelle always called them, were lolling round the boundary.

Further up the driveway I could see a few of the older boys making their way round the nine-hole par-three golf course hewn out of the landscaped lawns and copses to the front of the school. Mr Winstanley, the headmaster, had only been in the post for a couple of years but he had made some tremendous changes. His policy was to make education as enjoyable as possible, but woe betide any pupil, or member of staff or parent, who took advantage of his outlook on school life.

I parked a few yards from the main entrance to the senior school building and sat for a while taking in the activities going on around me. Brunei seemed as far away in time as it was in miles. I wound down the window and let the light breeze drift into the car, bringing with it the smells of early summer. Closing my eyes, the peacefulness washed over me. It gave me a feeling of total security, something I hadn't felt for far too long. Sophie drifted into my mind; her laughter, her smile, the look in her eye as she tentatively lifted the plastic beaker containing the best gin and tonic she had ever tasted. I shook my head slightly trying to rid my mind of the past I wanted to forget.

But she wouldn't go away.

She would remember me fainting in front of her. I had expected a note, a message from one of the nurses, something to tell me that she was thinking of me but there had been nothing.

What had I really expected?

She had thanked me for what I did so should I have expected

anything else? To her, I was no more than a casual acquaintance she had met on a boring trip to Brunei – ignoring her encounter with the jellyfish.

I felt a cool, soft hand pressing on my arm and I imagined it was Sophie's. "Daddy! What on earth are you doing here?"

I must have dropped off. The touch and the voice brought me a little drowsily to my senses and to Isabelle's beaming smile. "Daddy," she said again, "what are you doing out here asleep in the car park?"

I opened the car door and got out, giving Isabelle a kiss on her forehead. "Hello, Bella, and sorry if I surprised you but I flew in this morning and thought I would try to see you before driving home. I was going to come and find you but I must have dozed off. Put it down to jet lag."

Isabelle stepped back a pace or two. "God, Daddy, you were only away a week, less than a week in fact, but you've got quite a tan."

"Thanks but I can't think why, I didn't spend that long in the sun." I wanted to add that it had been long enough to hospitalise me, but the drugs pumped into me had probably been the real cause.

Isabelle came forward again and took hold of my hands. "It's a lovely surprise, Daddy. I happened to look over here from my room and thought I recognised the car."

"Have you finished lessons?" I asked hopefully.

"Not at this time, Daddy!" she replied.

I looked over my shoulder at the golfers and cricketers. "They look as though they have."

"Really, Daddy, if we all did the same thing at the same time, the school programme would be unmanageable. It's Mr Winstanley's idea." Isabelle left her explanation at that, almost as though the mention of the headmaster was all the clarification that was needed.

"When will you be free?" I began to think my impromptu visit was a bad idea.

Isabelle shrugged and screwed up her face. "Not until a lot later, and David's the same, I'm afraid. I don't know where he is at the moment but he's with me for history after lunch. Sorry, Daddy."

"That's all right, Bella, I should have thought." I smiled at her. "If I had come back from a longer trip then I might have tried to get you off this afternoon, but I'll go home. Your next exeat is when, the weekend after next?"

Isabelle nodded. "Yes, Daddy."

"All right, I'll be off." I put my hands on Isabelle's shoulders and pulled her towards me, holding her tightly against my chest. Automatically her arms slid round my waist as she returned the show of affection.

I kissed the top of her head. "Look after yourself, Bella." I could feel myself filling up. The guilt was washing over me again and I didn't seem to be able to control it.

When I finally let her go, Isabelle looked up at me, her forehead creased with concern.

"Has something happened, Daddy?"

I shook my head and closed my eyes. "No, Bella, nothing has happened. I'm tired after the journey. Can't a father show his daughter how much he loves her without something needing to have happened." I opened my eyes and beamed at her. "Come on, you go back to your friends and I'll see you again the weekend after next."

She looked up into my face, her eyes watering as she narrowed them slightly. My dismissal had not convinced her. She reached for my hands again. "Did everything go all right in Brunei? There's something you're not telling me."

"Bella, my love, everything is fine." What I was actually thinking was that she was as perceptive as her mother. Belinda had always known, regardless of how well I tried to hide it, when I had something on my mind. "Seriously, I'm very tired. I'm going to go home and, as you and David are constantly telling me to do, I'm going to chill out. Now off you go."

Isabelle lifted herself onto her toes and kissed me on the cheek. "Love you, Daddy. See you a week on Saturday." She turned to go but then stopped. "Can I bring Jane with me again?"

"Of course."

"Thanks."

She blew me a kiss, turned on her heels and skipped back into the school, whatever she thought had been wrong with me forgotten as she returned to her own world.

I hadn't told the twins about their grandmother: I didn't see the need until I knew how serious the situation really was.

And as far as Sophie Mackintosh was concerned … she would never be mentioned.

Chapter Twenty-Three

Blue-Ridge looked lonely but welcoming as I opened the gate and manoeuvred the car through it. The grass really did need cutting but I smiled to myself when I realised that I would have little else to do other than cut the grass for at least a week or two.

I was in a bit of a daze. In all the time I'd spent in some of the most lawless countries in the world – and where corruption and murder was a way of life – I had never been ordered (advised) to leave a country before. Brunei Darussalam was the last place I would have expected something like that to happen – but it had.

During the drive from St Edward's to Medbourne, and largely brought on by Isabelle and her intuition, I had made a number of promises to myself. The return flight from Brunei had brought me back to the real world but I hadn't made any plans about what I was going to do with it.

When Belinda's heart stopped beating, I had gone into a vacuum. My attempt at escapism into Derbyshire ended in disaster. When trying to relive the past by going to Brunei that also ended in disaster. Neither attempt at escaping had been rational. One was my way of burying my conscience as well as Belinda, and the other had actually been true escapism … geographically.

In a somewhat roundabout way the latter had at least told me that I did have a future – not that I doubted life going on but I could easily have found myself in a deep rut. If I could feel the way I did about Sophie then perhaps the loneliness I had envisaged was a product of the loss rather than a commitment. I had convinced myself that Belinda would not have wanted me to mourn her forever because she would have insisted that I move on – not necessarily go looking, but at least recognise the fact that somewhere out there I did have a future and perhaps that future might involve somebody else.

The cross-roads, roundabouts, inconsiderate drivers, and on one occasion a rather beleaguered decision whether to turn left or right, had only briefly interrupted my thought processes that culminated in the promises.

Promise one: Belinda would never mean less to me than she had when she was alive, but I had to look to the future and not spend the rest of my life in mourning.

Promise two: I would start, not look for but start a new career when Isabelle and David went back to school after their summer break … I thought I might try teaching.

Promise three: as well as finding that new job, I would redecorate Blue-Ridge exactly as I knew Belinda would have wanted it, with perhaps one or two minor adjustments.

Promise four: I would dismiss all thoughts of trying to discover an explanation for what had happened since Dove Dale.

Promise five: I would try to become a son to Elizabeth and Charles rather than the husband of their dead daughter.

And finally …

Promise six: David and Isabelle would have the best possible chance in life without stifling their own needs and aspirations.

With these promises firmly embedded in my mind, I crossed Blue-Ridge's threshold whistling for the first time in many months. Something good had come out of a traumatic period and whatever came my way me next I was ready for it.

Leaving my suitcase in the hall, I went through to the kitchen and made a black coffee before phoning Charles. My promises were not in any particular order of priority but Charles and Elizabeth were the first people who came to mind as I unlocked the front door.

"Seven seven five, one one six," Charles said, a little apprehensively.

"Charles, it's Richard."

"Hello, my boy," he said, his voice lifting. "Sounds as though you're next door."

"I suppose in comparison with Brunei, I am. I'm at Blue-Ridge."

"You're home?"

"Yes, Charles, I'm home. How's Elizabeth?"

"Fine, fine," he said. "Must come and see for yourself."

"Have you had tea yet?"

"Putting water in the kettle as we speak."

"I'll be there before the tea has brewed."

"Right, my boy," he said enthusiastically but he was also surprised. "I'll get another cup and saucer out."

"Be with you shortly, Charles."

I wasn't surprised that Charles had sounded surprised.

I had called during Belinda's illness and after her death but I had never phoned simply to invite myself round. Belinda always did the organising for the family; all I'd needed to know was where to be and when to be there, and on occasions what to wear. Only time would tell me whether I was embarking on trying to keep one of my promises too soon, but what I didn't know then was that one of my other promises was already in the process of being broken.

Elizabeth was in the conservatory and she looked a lot better than I expected. There seemed to be a slight debility in the left side of her face, but other than that, she appeared perfectly normal. She greeted me with a lopsided smile but actually put her arm round my shoulders as I bent down to kiss her on the cheek.

"Welcome home, Richard," she said.

"I've only been away a week, Elizabeth, and I'm sorry I

wasn't here when you came out of hospital." I sat down in the wicker chair next to her. I could hear Charles chinking the cups in the kitchen.

"Don't be silly. You were here when Charles needed you. There was nothing you could do after that." She looked concerned as we both heard Charles utter an expletive from the kitchen but then she shrugged and let a wicked smile cross her lips. "He loves looking after me. I feel a bit of a fraud."

"You deserve it."

With a slight bluster, Charles stepped into the conservatory, carefully carrying a tray in front of him. "Sorry, took a little longer than expected," he explained putting the tray on the coffee table.

"Did I hear something break?" Elizabeth asked him, at the same time stealing a mischievous look at me.

"No, no, nothing broken. Dropped the sugar, all cleared up now," Charles said, putting the cups on the saucers.

"Tell me about Brunei," Elizabeth suggested as she watched Charles being mother.

"Not a lot to report actually," I lied. "Nothing has changed very much. Money is still being spent as though it's going out of fashion but when there is so much of it, who can blame them?" When Charles passed me a cup of tea, I noticed that his hand was shaking slightly. "Thank you, Charles."

"Cake?" he asked, holding a plate of irregularly sliced pieces of fruitcake in front of me.

"You haven't given Richard a tea plate, Charles," Elizabeth commented from behind him.

"It's all right." I took a piece of cake and smiled at Charles who was looking serious and businesslike.

"You were telling us about Brunei, Richard," Elizabeth said once Charles had sat down.

The cake was lovely ... moist and crumbly. "When I say it

hasn't changed, the airport is now quite modern, there's a motorway and a theme park."

"Why did your friend – Abby, I think you said – why did he want you there that urgently?" Charles asked, looking slightly relieved now that tea was served.

I took a sip of tea. I needed to delay replying until I had thought of an answer. I decided to use what Abby had told Nazira. At the mention of his name, the expression on Abby's face as he left the ward flashed into my mind.

"Advice," I said, looking from Charles to Elizabeth, "but advice that needed to be given on the ground, if you see what I mean. Last time I was there, we had to leave a project I was involved with up in the air. There were political issues that we hadn't foreseen." I shrugged and picked up another piece of cake. I didn't like lying to them but the alternative wasn't an option. "Anyway, changes of heart and the need to move on as quickly as possible necessitated a visit, albeit quite a short one."

"Thought you'd finished with Aspect?" Charles said.

"Astek," corrected Elizabeth.

"I have," I said, "but there were bound to be a few loose ends. This was one of them."

"Hope you set your fee as high as possible." Charles said.

"I did," I lied again. A change of subject was necessary. "Anyway, Elizabeth, I'm delighted to see you looking so well. Charles told me that the prognosis is good."

Elizabeth's smile disappeared for a second or two but Charles was looking out of the window at a couple of doves that had landed uncomfortably close to his vegetable patch ... he didn't notice.

"I've been lucky," she said. "It's not everyone who gets a warning." The smile returned. "How else could I get Charles to do everything?"

Charles snorted. "You only had to ask, didn't have to get

yourself taken into hospital."

We talked for almost an hour.

I sensed a change in Elizabeth that suggested I wasn't going to have to work too hard on one of my promises. She had mellowed. Her stroke may have been only over a week ago but her recovery was remarkable. She hadn't moved out of her chair since I arrived which meant I didn't know whether her mobility was impaired. It was obvious from her dismissal, though, that she didn't want to talk about her experience other than to reassure Charles through me that she was fine.

Moving on to talk about Belinda was inevitable, but even then I sensed a change in attitude. When Elizabeth reminisced about happier times, I was included: I was part of the family group. At one stage when Charles, having turned down my offer to help, went into the kitchen to refill the teapot, Elizabeth looked at me for a few moments before asking a question she had never asked before.

"Do you miss her terribly, Richard?" she asked, leaning forward slightly.

I nodded and looked down at my hands. "More than I could find the words to describe. She was my life, Elizabeth. When she left, half of me went with her."

Her next remark suggested that she too had been aware of the perceived gap between us, but she couldn't have chosen a better time to bring it into the open.

"I haven't been fair to you since she died. I suppose I needed somebody to blame and as you had spent a lot of time with her when she was ill, you were the unfortunate choice." I looked up and could see the sincerity in her eyes. "You have always meant a lot to us both and yet I could never bring myself to tell you. We couldn't have asked for a better son-in-law. I am afraid I for one took you for granted. You know what Charles is like. If he stubs his toe, he thinks twice about swearing. You were there for him when he needed you and in his own way he has told me how grateful he is."

"There's no need to say thank you in a situation like this, Elizabeth. And, anyway, I was on the other side of the world when you came out of hospital."

Her smile accompanied a slight shaking of her head. "Male pride would have intervened. Charles would have wanted to prove he could cope."

"Yes, but –"

"No buts, Richard. Charles is a man of few words but when he does speak, I listen. I wanted to say that we are here for you if you ever need us for more than just a cup of tea."

Charles reappeared with the fresh pot, and other than a few knowing looks in my direction, Belinda wasn't discussed again.

That would have been for Charles' sake.

He wouldn't have been able to stand the embarrassment of discussing emotions with another man present. What Elizabeth had said, though, was music to my ears.

On leaving the house, I felt as though something quite momentous had happened and I wished that Belinda could have been there.

I could hear her now, "You see, Mummy thinks the world of you. I told you all your misgivings were in your head."

Chapter Twenty-Four

The following three weeks seemed to pass quickly.

I set about redecorating Blue-Ridge. To my surprise, I found that I was whistling to myself and painting to the highs and lows of the music that blared out from the radio, mainly Classic FM.

The kitchen, study and living room were finished before I collected the twins and Jane for the next exeat. We had a lovely thirty-six hours together. Although the improvement was maintained, Elizabeth wasn't up to producing one of her memorable Sunday lunches so Charles had to bow to pressure and he brought her to Blue-Ridge instead. I left Isabelle and Jane to do most of the preparation and cooking, the results of which were excellent. Even David, and Charles during a quiet moment, had to admit that they had done a superb job. Charles, Elizabeth and Jane reminisced about Zimbabwe once again but still without any reference to the political situation.

The weather was also exceptional, meaning that we were able to spend a lot of time outside. We had a barbecue on the Saturday evening and my competence to cook the sausages, burgers and chicken was accepted. Isabelle and Jane appeared to be on a constant high. David, probably sensing that he would be missing out, spent time with us rather than playing games on his computer. During the drive back to school, the three of them were chattering away about their recent experiences. Isabelle's admission from the previous exeat was not mentioned. It was in all our pasts; now we had nothing but our futures to look forward to.

The decorating proceeded with similar enthusiasm after the children had gone back to school. The house seemed horribly quiet but I knew that Belinda was with me and was watching over me. Anybody listening in would have wondered to whom I was talking.

Standing back to admire another piece of handy-work, I was unaware that I was days away from having not just one, but two of the promises I had made turned upside down.

It started with nothing more innocent than an early morning cup of coffee and the daily paper. I was sitting in the conservatory. The good spell of weather was temporarily broken and the rain was, aided by strong winds, was lashing down. The garden looked grey and dismal, the colours of the flowers masked by a perpetual gloom.

Out of habit I flipped through the paper initially to see if any headlines caught my eye, then I went back to the front page trying to take in what the editor had decided I ought to be briefed on that day.

There was the usual political analysis and because I had the same paper delivered each day, I tended to agree with the criticism, diagnosis and prognosis. I was constantly told that the ruling Labour party's manifesto was proving to be a pack of lies: what had been promised hadn't been delivered, and the non-deliverers were blaming their predecessors for not sowing the seeds of their success prior to handing over power.

Therefore, nothing had changed.

I was smiling at a particular editorial I could have written when, glancing at the opposite page, I saw a headline I had missed earlier, but now it had my total attention, the article I had been reading suddenly forgotten.

I didn't have to read beyond the headline to know that the minister being referred to in the article was Abby. He had told me it was goodbye but nothing could have prepared me for discovering the truth in the fourth column on page twelve of a *The Daily Telegraph*. I forced my eyes to drop below the bold print of the headline to discover the horrible facts of what had happened.

Brunei Minister Commits Suicide

It was announced yesterday by the Minister of Internal Affairs for Negara Brunei Darussalam that Dato Haji Abdullah bin Basrah Ibrahim, the Minister of Development, was found dead in his office. A spokesperson did suggest that, although internal investigations were ongoing, the Minister had taken his own life.

Dato Haji Abdullah had held one of the most senior ministerial appointments for over five years and was considered to be one of His Majesty The Sultan's closest advisors and allies. The spokesperson gave no indication why the Minister should take his own life. Married with three young children, he had risen quickly from a junior post in the civil service to a very senior position. There was no information immediately available that suggested there was anything in his past that would have been the cause of him taking his own life.

His Majesty The Sultan, who is currently on a low-key visit to the United Kingdom, was not available for comment last night nor was any member of the Royal party. Mr Robert Cruickshank, the British High Commissioner to Brunei, was also unavailable for comment.

Speculation that the Minister had become involved with some questionable aspects of an import/export business was denied.

Brunei Darussalam was once ...

Staring at the article, the words, the lines became a blur as I tried to take on board what was in the article.

Abby dead?

I couldn't believe it. He had no reason to kill himself, and his involvement with dubious import/export activities was equally unlikely. Nevertheless, I had to admit that when I saw him it was obvious that something was troubling him deeply. I had dismissed anything to do with the Chinese, but in so doing, I was no closer to the truth.

While decorating and during the odd unguarded moment some of the detail of my experiences had crept into my mind, but keeping my promise, I did my best to dismiss it quickly as it had sneaked up on me.

Now I couldn't stop it all flooding back.

I didn't get any more decorating finished, in fact little got done for the rest of the week. Each time I picked up the roller or brush, the enthusiasm for decorating had deserted me. I could see Nazira and the children, their faces covered in confusion as they tried to come to terms with what had happened.

That first night I seriously contemplated getting on the next available flight to Brunei, but what could I do? Even if allowed back into the country, which was unlikely, Abby's burial would already have taken place. At one stage early in the morning, the phone was in my hand and I started to dial Abby's home number but then I stopped and replaced the receiver – a few words of comfort was all I had to offer. Is it possible to comfort somebody having had a shock of that magnitude? Is the comforter not trying to find an excuse for his own inadequacies?

I woke up on the Friday morning feeling no better than I had on the preceding few mornings. I still didn't have the energy or enthusiasm to carry on with the house, so I decided to go shopping, not a task that I enjoyed but one that was necessary because stocks were running low. Not having played since Belinda died, I also decided to ring a few chums to see if they were available to play golf that afternoon. Having a round of golf would take my mind off things, if only temporarily.

I hoped Abby wouldn't object.

The previous evening I started a letter to Nazira – a coward's way out? – before driving into town I finished it off as best I could. Words had failed me. The letter took me over two hours to put together and I still wasn't happy with it, but there was nothing more I could say.

After clicking into answering machines for the first two calls, I gave up ringing my chums for a game of golf. It wasn't a good idea anyway – I wouldn't be good company, which might generate questions I wouldn't want to answer.

Having chosen a supermarket that Belinda and I rarely used, I wandered round in a daze knowing that when I got home I wouldn't want half of what I bought and I would have forgotten many other items I needed. Adding to my disquiet was the fact that I didn't know where anything was on the shelves. I hadn't used 'our' supermarket since April.

Dumping the plethora of carrier bags in the car, I went in search of a condolence card I could put in with the letter to Nazira. I saw a few people I recognised and hoped they accepted a polite 'Good morning' and a smile. I didn't want to get into a conversation with anybody.

I passed the old stilted Market Harborough Grammar School and headed for a small card shop tucked away in one of the side streets. Crossing the road beyond the school, I had a feeling I was being watched. I stopped and looked around me but there was nobody I recognised, or anyone who was obviously looking at me. I shook my head and carried on walking.

After Blue-Ridge was searched and then in Cochem when Henke and Schwartz told me I had been followed/observed – whatever they wanted to call it – I was acutely aware that it might all still be going on. I had no idea why it should be but my ignorance of events stretched way beyond those two facts.

Checking again, and shrugging off my suspicions, I headed for the card shop.

I was pleased when I found exactly the right card. Feeling satisfied that something had gone right for a change I called in at a small teashop for an unsociable cup of coffee. When closing the door, the same sensation was there. Looking through the glass door, I couldn't see anybody who might be interested in me, but I still selected a table that allowed me to observe as much of the street outside as possible.

The coffee was good.

An earlier customer had left a copy of *The Times* on the opposite table, I reached across to retrieve it and at the same time I happened to glance out of the end window. On the opposite side of the road, checking the traffic before crossing, was Sophie Mackintosh. I sat back without taking hold of the paper and watched Sophie. Although she was wearing sunglasses, there was no doubt in my mind that I was looking at the woman I had last seen in a hospital bed in Brunei. Automatically I reached into my pocket for some loose change, putting what I hoped would cover the cost of the coffee and a small tip on the table.

Sophie had crossed the road and disappeared out of view. Rushing out of the teashop, nearly colliding with a little old lady who was innocently passing by, I dashed round the corner ready to call Sophie's name but I couldn't see her. I ran to the next corner and looked up and down the High Street, but again it was as though she had been spirited away. Not knowing which way to go didn't lessen my determination to find her.

I was sure I hadn't imagined it – she had really been there.

I spent a good twenty minutes walking up and down the High Street, looking in every shop, checking every side road, every alleyway, glancing behind me, and praying that she was suddenly going to appear before me.

It couldn't be sheer coincidence that she was in Market Harborough; she had to be looking for me. What other explanation was there? I went back to the pedestrian precinct and again searched every shop but with no success. Unaware of who or what was around me, I carried on through the precinct to the supermarket car park. There was no point in searching anywhere else; it would be like looking for a needle in a haystack.

I sat in the car staring at the other shoppers.

Although I was sure there was no mistake, if the woman wasn't Sophie why wasn't she there for me to see when I left the teashop. Perhaps my suspicions were now confirmed, I was still under scrutiny, but why Sophie? It was too much of a coincidence that only a few minutes after having the feeling I should see her. Her hair seemed shorter, she was wearing a summer's dress that fell below her knees, and her sandals were a light tan, open-toed and fastened above her ankles. I had taken in all this detail in a matter of seconds so why would I make a mistake about her identity?

Why was Sophie Mackintosh in Market Harborough when I was in the same town? There was only one answer.

Eventually I drove home, unpacked the car and then took a rather generous whisky into the conservatory. Drinking at lunchtime wasn't a habit of mine but on this occasion I thought I might make an exception. My thoughts were all over the place again.

The weather had improved, meaning the garden regained

some of its beauty in the sunshine. The dahlias in the only flowerbed Belinda had allowed towards the end were in full bloom, with the bordering fuchsias and geraniums complementing the small but magnificent display. The garden had always been Belinda's pride and joy but as she became less able to tend it, we reduced it down to what I was now looking at. The previous summer she had sat in the conservatory for hours, a smile on her face as she enjoyed the products of her own talent, her modesty taking over only when somebody else admired her achievements.

Opening the side door, I wandered out into the 'her' garden. The grass, long enough to retain some of the morning dew, was once again in need of a cut, but a bit like the decorating, the energy and enthusiasm were simply not there.

At least seeing Sophie had temporarily taken my mind away from Abby's suicide. I scoured the papers for more information without success. Although he had been an important man in Brunei, his death had only warranted a few paragraphs on page twelve – an explanation probably didn't justify any coverage at all. When there was nothing in the previous day's paper, I had considered ringing the Brunei High Commission in London; however, it was unlikely they would have told me anything even though I was prepared to tell them of our friendship.

I turned round and looked at the house.

Things had changed significantly in only a few short months. I had lost the woman who gave me everything yet had expected so little in return. I had resigned from Astek, the company that had allowed us to enjoy a very acceptable standard of living, and the company whose severance package meant that I didn't have to work for years, if at all – but I had to remember that I did promise myself I would begin a new career after the summer school recess.

My mother-in-law had had a stroke from which, mercifully,

she seemed to be recovering, and it appeared it could be the catalyst to an improvement in our relationship. Although my relationship with Annabelle didn't need improving, it had moved up a notch or two because she thought I had ventured into her private space. We had shared her secret and now I regarded that as a positive move.

Outside the family, I had been a suspect in a brutal murder and then witnessed the legal system covering up what might have really happened. With my involvement in the murder investigation possibly over – not forgetting the interrogation in Cochem – and hoping a visit to an old friend in Brunei would bring a little well-earned respite, its Internal Security Police orders me out of country without explanation, and that was after being abducted and questioned by the British High Commissioner.

Not wishing to relegate Elizabeth's condition to being less important than any of the other occurrences, everything else happened because all I wanted to do was mourn the loss of my wife on my own and without any outside interference. In the end, the outside had done more than interfere.

I shook my head in disbelief and then wondered why I had left one final episode to last. In the midst of everything else that was going on, I met someone who had an undeniable effect on my emotions. Sophie Mackintosh took over my life for a short while to the exclusion of Belinda. I didn't like what was happening but there was nothing I could do about it. Therefore, seeing her, or seeing someone I thought was her, in Market Harborough had set my pulse racing, and it wasn't because I wanted an explanation for what had happened in Brunei, or why she was possibly following me.

My fascination with Sophie Mackintosh wasn't because she could be the source of enlightenment: it was because, regardless of the promises I had made, I couldn't get her out of my mind.

Perhaps, after all, she was the source of an explanation but not about Brunei. She could explain why she had come into my life so soon after I had lost Belinda; she could explain why I was having this constant battle with my conscience.

I was also rambling to myself, yet again. Going back into the conservatory and locking the door behind me, I decided I would go to the golf club after all. I needed a diversion and perhaps something to stimulate me other than the past and what might have been.

On a Friday afternoon, the Golf Club was invariably busier than on other weekday afternoons. Fortunate to find a recently vacated slot in the members' car park, I took out my clubs from the boot of the car before heading for the clubhouse.

Located between Great Oxenden and Market Harborough the club was neither ostentatious nor overly modest; it fitted nicely between the two descriptions. The course was nearly one hundred years old and the original clubhouse tastefully extended, allowing its five hundred members (and visitors) to enjoy excellent bar and restaurant facilities. The course was relatively short but demanding and normally a thoroughly enjoyable eighteen holes of golf.

Charles was a also member and we had played a few games together over the years, but he belonged to a close-knit group of over sixty-year olds who protected their right to play to their own standard, and sometimes to their own rules, with alacrity.

After dumping my shoes and clubs in the changing rooms, I went into the bar in search of a possible playing partner. It was two o'clock on a Friday afternoon, the car park was full but the bar was almost empty. I assumed that the sunshine had encouraged players rather than escapists to the club that afternoon.

I was about to leave the bar and have a round as a singleton when I heard my name called: "Mr Blythe!"

I turned round and saw Roland Crook the barman-cum-steward grinning at me from behind the bar. He had obviously been in the stockroom when I first went into the bar.

"Hello, Rollo," I said, walking a few paces back into the room. "How are you?"

"I'm fine thanks, Mr Blythe, but long time no see."

I shrugged. "A couple of months, Rollo, a couple of months." I didn't know how much he knew. I wasn't exactly a regular at the club. When Belinda was well enough to fend for herself, she had insisted on me going to play when I was back in the UK. Rollo and I had shared a few jokes and stories at the bar over the years and I suppose we had struck up more than a passing acquaintance.

"I was very sorry to hear about your wife, Mr Blythe." Trying to cover his embarrassment, he looked down at the glass he had picked up and was vigorously polishing.

"Thank you, Rollo. You're busy today."

"There are a couple of societies in and lunch was murder."

I leant on the bar. "I guess a round is not recommended?"

He glanced out of the window towards the first tee. "Probably not, looking at some of them I doubt whether they'll be back in under four or five hours. You could try going to the 10th, but you'll be in the middle of them then."

"Thanks for the warning," I said, beginning to move away from the bar.

"Did the lady get hold of you, Mr Blythe?"

"Lady, what lady?"

"Eh, Wednesday, about ten o'clock, this lady came into the bar and asked whether you were on the course."

Rollo suddenly had my undivided attention. "What did she look like?"

He thought for a moment. "She caused a bit of a stir, actually.

Not many ladies walk in here dressed for the city. Most of them are players, if you see what I mean," he added with a wry smile. "She certainly got the attention of most of the gentlemen."

"What did she look like, Rollo?" I asked patiently.

"Over five six, maybe five eight or nine, quite tall, actually. Sandra's five seven and she was taller than her." He saw my look. "Erm … early to mid-thirties, attractive, blue eyes, well a bluey-green actually, slim but, you know, well proportioned in the right places without being too personal. Shortish light brownish-blondish hair and a lovely smile."

"You were quite observant, Rollo."

He shrugged. "Learn to be in this job, Mr Blythe. But, as I said, she was unusual for ten o'clock in the morning and she wasn't the sort you forget easily."

"What did she say?"

"She came into the bar, had a good look round and then came over." He shrugged again. "I was doing some tidying. She asked if you were out on the course."

"And you were able to tell her that I wasn't." On Wednesday morning when I became frustrated with not being able to get on with the decorating, I had gone for a drive. I couldn't remember where I went in detail but at one stage I did drive past the entrance to the club.

"From here I can see most people starting a round, and that morning I'd been clearing up after a late-do the night before. I was able to tell the lady that I definitely hadn't seen you."

"I see. What did she do then?"

"She didn't seem too worried, said it wasn't urgent and that she'd probably find you at your house."

"Did she give her name?"

"No and I'm sorry, Mr Blythe, I didn't ask. Suppose I ought to have done really. But she gave the impression that she knew you well."

"That's all right, Rollo. I know who she was."

I drove straight back to Blue-Ridge. The doubts I had about seeing Sophie that morning had now disappeared. This time it could have been no one else but her; the description Rollo had given me fitted her perfectly.

She had been in the club on Wednesday and now it was Friday. If she was looking for me, why hadn't she come to the house? And how did she know I was a member of that golf club … of course, over Mama Wong's fish and chips I'd told her where I lived and I must have mentioned it then.

Nevertheless, if she were spying on me she wouldn't have been that open about looking for me. She would have known the next time I was in the club Rollo would tell me about her visit.

Where was she and what was she actually up to?

Chapter Twenty-Five

I did not have to wait long to find out.

I was not familiar with the car parked to the right of the garage but I certainly recognised who got out of it. Her presence explained why the gate was open.

The only occupant of the metallic-silver Audi was Sophie Mackintosh.

Watching my car crunch its way up the driveway, she stood with her elbow against the her car's roof and with her sunglasses dangling in the other hand.

"Hello Richard," she said as I slowly climbed out of my car, trying to think of something, anything I could say that would be sensible.

"Sophie! I suppose I ought to say this is a surprise but seeing you isn't unexpected."

"Why, was I really that obvious?"

"I'm not sure what you mean," I said, "but I've come from the golf club and yes, I do know you were there two days ago asking after me."

I closed the door of the car. Sophie was about ten feet away looking at me, she appeared cool and calm, and the opposite of the way I was feeling. Seeing the person who had been on my mind almost constantly since the sighting in Market Harborough was unsettling.

"There is an explanation," she said, tapping her lip with one of the arms of her sunglasses.

"You'd better come in," I said.

"Thanks." She reached into her car to pick up her shoulder bag. The car beeped as she activated the alarm.

I waited for her to walk past me, her expensive perfume bringing back the short-lived memories of Brunei. There were so many questions bursting to come out but I was determined to maintain my composure.

I didn't know why she had come to see me and I wasn't too sure I wanted to know.

She walked ahead of me along the hall towards the kitchen and dining room. Looking over her shoulder, she said, "Where shall we go?".

"Depends whether we are being formal or not," I said. "Kitchen to the left, living room is back here."

She smiled that smile again and reached for the handle to the kitchen door. "Have you decorated recently? I can smell paint."

"Yes, started a couple of weeks ago but I haven't finished yet." She walked over to the kitchen window and peered into the garden. She nodded. "I like what I see."

"Thank you. Would you like something to drink? I asked, opening the cupboard. I was pleased that I had been shopping, but she probably knew not only where I had been but also what I had bought.

She turned round and leant against the Belfast sink, the smile still on her lips. "Do you have any green tea?"

"Yes, Bella drinks it all the time."

"That would be lovely."

I needed to fill the kettle but Sophie was standing in front of the taps. I felt uncomfortable about crossing the kitchen because it would mean I would be too close to her: I would be invading her space and she mine, and it was too soon.

She must have sensed my hesitation. "Here, let me," she said, coming over and taking the kettle from me. Her hand touched mine and I felt a shock run through me.

Why was this woman still affecting me?

Plugging in the kettle and to hide my confusion, I got the mugs and tea from the cupboard. Over the years I had been in the company of hundreds of attractive women, some of whom, much to my amusement and to a certain extent my enjoyment, had flirted with me, and I with them, but none of them had affected me for more than a fleeting moment. I had always told Belinda about where I had been, and who had said and done what. She used to joke about the descriptions I gave her but there was always that look in her eye that warned me never to take the flirtations any further.

I didn't need to be warned.

Would I have told Belinda about Sophie? Having breakfast and an evening meal with another woman had never happened before. Our disastrous outing to cave Beach had been a little more intimate but … but if Belinda had still been alive then none of that would have happened.

"I was so sorry to hear about Dato Haji Abdullah," Sophie said behind me. She used his formal names but she knew I called him Abby.

I rested my hands on the work surface and closed my eyes. Did her condolences mean anything more than I was hearing? I wasn't surprised she knew about his suicide but I did find it a little suspicious that she mentioned it this early. Had she offered her condolences because she meant them, or were they a precursor to her revealing more than I wanted to hear? Perhaps she was testing me, finding out if I knew about it.

Then again, she was here and the ice needed breaking, we had to talk about something.

Turning round, I said, "Thank you. His death, especially as it is believed it was suicide, was a tremendous shock."

I gave her the mug of green tea, which she cupped in both hands before lifting it to her nose, her eyes closing as she savoured the aroma. "I love the smell of green tea," she said.

"Why are you here, Sophie?" The question was direct but it needed asking straight away. Our relationship had been unusual to say the least. We weren't like a couple of old friends catching up on what we'd been doing for the last month.

Lowering the mug, her smile disappeared. She stared at me for a few seconds before saying anything. "There are three reasons why I am here, Richard. Two of my reasons are connected but the third is not related with the other two, well, not directly." She took a sip of her tea, her eyes never leaving mine. "Can we go and sit down somewhere?"

I led the way through to the conservatory. Sophie again went to the windows and looked out over the garden. "I really do like it," she said before sitting down in what was still and always would be, Belinda's wicker chair. She kicked off her sandals and lifted her feet up onto the chair, smoothing her dress down over her knees.

If this was an official visit then I found her body language too casual. Perhaps it was more like the meeting of two old friends, both of whom had news the other needed to hear, but neither knowing where to start. We were establishing boundaries because I hadn't the faintest idea what was coming, I didn't really know where to start and what defences I might need.

Or maybe I should go on the attack?

I sat down in the chair – my chair – opposite her. "Where are you going to begin?"

She lifted her head, a sadness appearing in her eyes. "After what has happened, finding a place to start isn't that easy. I thought our friendship, if that's what it was, had come to end when you were spirited away from the hospital in Brunei."

"By spirited I presume you mean drugged and abducted?"

I hadn't seen her pout before, and for some reason it was an emotion I thought she wasn't capable of displaying in that way. It made her look very feminine, and incredibly vulnerable. She had been so in charge, so dominant, so in control, but now she seemed rather defenceless. If she stayed like this, how was I going to protect myself from my own feelings?

"I can understand how that must have seemed, Richard, and I'm going to try and explain but, before I do, can I thank you?" She put her mug on the small table next to her chair and began to get up. "Can I show you the real evidence of what you did for me." She lifted the hem of her dress to the top of her thighs and looked down. "That's what you did for me." She wasn't wearing any tights and her legs were pale, but across the front of both her thighs there were four faint pinkish lines. "My tummy's the same." She lowered her dress and sat down. "The doctors said that after a few more months there should be no sign of the attack. They have all said that I owed my life, and the lack of scarring, to you." She clasped her hands in her lap. "Thank you, I owe you more than I owe anybody else in the world."

I was embarrassed. "I told you in the hospital, I did no more than anybody else could have done. If by doing what I did I helped in your recovery, then of course I'm pleased, but …"

"Richard, will you stop being so bloody modest! You didn't *help in my recovery*, as you put it, you saved my life."

I looked up and it was obvious that I had upset her. Her eyes were watering, her hands clasped tightly in her lap in exasperation.

"Sophie, I reacted on impulse," I said.

I wanted to react on impulse again and cross the few feet between us. I wanted to show her how pleased I was that she had recovered, let alone that I had played a part in that recovery. Although I needed to put the past behind me and I had thought I would never see her again, I was actually more than pleased she was here. Deep down and despite my promises, I wanted nothing more.

"Richard, this isn't going the way I planned," she said solemnly. I was seeking solace in my mug of tea. I couldn't look at her. "Perhaps I ought to leave … it's not what I want, but –"

I shook my head slowly. "It's not your fault, Sophie. I

suppose everything has built up inside me, and when I thought I was beginning to resume a reasonably normal life again, the first reminder I have – you – puts me back to square one."

I managed to lift my head. Sophie was sitting forward, her hands resting on her knees. "I think you should be told what has been going on. You have every right to be suspicious of me …"

"I'm not suspicious of you, Sophie," I lied, "but I'm not sure I want to know what's been going on."

Sophie looked down at her hands as she pondered what she should say next. "I've been on sick leave since I came home and I've got another couple of weeks to go. My bosses want me to be fully fit before I return."

I tried to smile. "You've been through quite a traumatic experience. You deserve the break and as much sick leave as it takes."

She was still inspecting her hands. "But my bosses aren't who you think they are, Richard. I told you I was an auditor with the Foreign Office, but I'm not." She lifted her head slowly. "I work for Customs and Excise. I'm a senior investigator."

I felt my heartbeat quicken, and I closed my eyes.

Abby had been right in one way, but he was so far off the mark in another. Customs and Excise? An investigator? The possibility had never crossed my mind.

"And who in Brunei were you investigating?" I asked, lifting my head. I didn't expect an answer, but the one I got sent shivers down my spine.

"You, Richard, I was investigating you."

I stared at her, my eyes unblinking, disbelieving.

"Me? What do you mean, me? Why on earth were you investigating me? I –"

"That's one of the reasons why I'm here, Richard – to explain."

"And explanations are going to make me feel better, are

they?"

"Not necessarily." A note of resignation crept into her voice. "But I think after what has happened to you, you do warrant something." She paused for a few seconds. "Look, can we go for a walk? It's a lovely day and I would prefer to tell you what I have to tell you in the open."

Abby had wanted the privacy of the open seas to inform me of his concerns and now Sophie wanted to go for a walk. The reason behind Abby committing suicide had never been revealed in the papers and I hadn't bothered trying to find out. It was possible that what Sophie wanted to tell me would allow me to close the door on that aspect of Brunei if nothing else. It was for that reason only that I decided to agree to Sophie's request.

We were well beyond the Blue-Ridge's front gate and heading down the hill towards the village before Sophie started to give me her account of what had been going on.

The road was quiet.

If we had turned right out of the gate and gone uphill instead, we would have, after about three-quarters of a mile, come to the entrance to Nevill Manor, which stood beyond the junction for Drayton to the right and Uppingham to the left.

Blue-Ridge was the last but one house leading away from the village, and the security provided by the narrow and rarely used road was one of the attractions. Our neighbours kept very much to themselves. I smiled having used the word security; I now realised the woman walking with me may well have been responsible for unlawfully breaking into Blue-Ridge.

Sophie was looking out over the rooftops of the village, taking in the magnificent view Wignell Hill had to offer. I was walking on the other side of the road, my hands in my pockets, wondering what she was going to tell me, when she crossed the road and linked arms with me. I thought it an intimate thing to do, especially under the circumstances. Her hand was resting against my arm and I felt the same thrill as I had when our hands had touched earlier.

I wanted to object, but I couldn't. Her closeness was what I really needed and wanted.

"We became interested in you when we heard that you'd found Ingrid Mesterom's body," she said, her voice soft and not at all businesslike. "We had been aware that she was in the country but she had given us the slip. What she was doing in Derbyshire we don't know, but we assumed that she was taken there to be murdered."

I stopped and Sophie didn't have any choice but to stop next to me. "Are you telling me that Ingrid Mesterom was some sort of international criminal?" I looked down into Sophie eyes. Her face was so close to mine, all I had to do was lean forward and I could kiss her.

"That's what we were trying to prove," she said, and the moment passed. "She was a courier, or we thought she was a courier, but we'd got nothing on her at all. Over the previous six months, she had been in and out of the UK four or five times. She was even searched, and I mean a full body search, once but nothing was found."

"What were you looking for?"

Sophie looked at me as though I ought to have known the answer to my question, and I obviously did. "Class 'A' drugs," she said.

"Why do you think Ingrid was murdered?"

We resumed our walk. Having reached the first corner, we were passing the houses which indicated the start of the village.

"Another mystery but again we had to make assumptions. The description you gave the Ashbourne police of the man in the car park suggested he might have been from a rival cartel, but we really don't know."

"It wasn't my description. I merely passed on what somebody

else had seen."

"Yes, I know. We interviewed the man concerned but he wasn't able to add any more." Sophie was looking all around her as she spoke. Some of the houses we were passing were especially attractive.

"So why did I come under suspicion?"

It was Sophie's turn to stop. "The Ashbourne police thought your version of what happened stank," she said, bluntly.

"I told them exactly what did happen." I thought for a moment. "If they thought I was lying, why didn't they arrest me?"

"Initially there was no proof, well none that a defence lawyer couldn't have easily shot down. The forensic evidence didn't add up, but it was mainly because they did a trace on their computer and saw that Ingrid Mesterom was under surveillance. They got in touch with us and we asked them to back off because we thought you might be a new contact. They obliged."

"Are you telling me it *was* your lot that searched my house?"

"Yes, I'm sorry about that."

"Are you allowed to go around searching houses without the owner's permission?"

"No."

"At least you're honest."

We were standing to the left of the road with Sophie's arm linked with mine as a car was approaching, I didn't recognise it at first. There was sufficient room for it to pass.

But it didn't.

The car stopped about twenty yards away. I glanced in its direction again and that is when recognition hit me like a sledgehammer.

It was Charles and Elizabeth.

Sophie also looked towards the car and then back at me. "Who are they?"

"My mother and father-in-law."

Sophie immediately took her arm from mine, which actually made the situation Charles and Elizabeth were now staring at look a lot worse. I began to walk towards the car, leaving Sophie where she was.

I approached Charles's side of the car but I could see that Elizabeth was still staring straight at Sophie. "Hello, you two," I greeted them as light-heartedly as I could.

"Afternoon, Richard," Charles replied, but he too was taking sly looks towards Sophie.

I squatted down and asked a stupid question. "What brings you out here?"

With Elizabeth improving slowly, Charles took her out on more and more drives in the countryside to give her as much fresh air as possible. They had called in at least once or twice a week. I hadn't told them about Abby and neither of them, even if they had read about it in the paper, had made the connection.

"Thought we'd pop over for an afternoon cuppa –"

"But we won't bother," Elizabeth added, interrupting, her voice filled with suspicion. "We can see that you're already entertaining."

I looked over my shoulder towards Sophie. She was slowly walking towards us. "It's not what it seems," I said, looking back into the car and feeling there was a need for me to be uncomfortable. How many times do you hear people say *it's not what it seems* only to discover later it was exactly as it seemed.

"I'm sure it's not," Elizabeth replied.

"Now, now, Elizabeth, we don't know all Richard's friends."

"Maybe not," Elizabeth said.

Sophie joined me at the car and an introduction was only polite. "Sophie, can I introduce Charles and Elizabeth Norton."

Sophie reached into the car to shake hands and said, "Sophie Mackintosh."

Charles became a bit flustered. He would have been aware that he was sitting down and introductions don't happen when you're sitting down, especially not with a lady. However, he took Sophie's proffered hand and muttered something. She then reached further into the car, across Charles.

"Pleased to meet you Mrs Norton," she said politely.

"We were Belinda's parents," Elizabeth informed Sophie coldly. "Belinda was Richard's wife."

"Yes, I know," Sophie said sympathetically. "I was so sorry to hear about your tragic loss."

There were a few seconds of embarrassing silence but then Charles coughed and said, "Well, we won't keep you, my boy. Just thought we'd call in on the off chance. You could have been anywhere."

Sophie and I moved closer to Charles's car to let another one pass. "Well, you can still have some tea if you'd like. Sophie and I were only going for a short walk."

"No, no, wouldn't dream of it, my boy. I –"

Elizabeth interrupted him again. "We've been to tend Belinda's grave," she said, "and thought we'd come and keep you company. But as you already have some, we'll go home."

I thought Elizabeth's remark was a little unnecessary. They may have caught me arm-in-arm with another woman but there was no need to jump to the wrong conclusions, or was there?

I wasn't going to give Elizabeth the satisfaction – if that's how she felt – of allowing her to draw the only conclusion possible. We had been on far better terms since her stroke and my return from Brunei and I didn't want to spoil it. I couldn't tell them the truth and I didn't see why I had to start lying. I actually had little choice in the end but to leave them with whatever conclusions they had drawn, and would no doubt discuss, and then perhaps when I next saw them alone I would tell them some of the background and the truth.

Saving somebody's life was probably a good enough reason for them to pay you a visit.

We stood back as Charles selected first gear and watched as he continued up the road and turned in a gateway at the first corner. Coming back down the hill quite slowly, Charles tooted the horn and gave a small wave.

Elizabeth looked like thunder.

"That was my fault," Sophie said as we carried on walking towards the T-junction in the village. She linked her arm in mine again, not in the slightest bit upset by Elizabeth's obvious disapproval.

"Not at all, they simply jumped to the wrong conclusions. I'll speak to them later."

"You didn't tell me your wife's name was Belinda."

We had almost reached the junction with the main road through the village. Belinda's grave was in the churchyard that was coming into view ... I slowed down.

"We didn't really have long enough together in Brunei to go into much detail." I pointed towards the church. "That's where she's buried. Do you mind if we make a slight detour?"

"I wouldn't know it was a detour. I came from that way," she added, indicating the road to Uppingham.

We went through the small lych-gate into the churchyard. Passing the church to our right, I took Sophie to Belinda's grave. There were fresh flowers by the headstone. Elizabeth had asked me if I minded if she took responsibility for tending Belinda's grave and it would have been churlish of me to refuse. I had buried a few close memories of our relationship with Belinda in her coffin. I knew that in her hands she had the locket she had worn containing our photographs, and lying next to her was a framed photograph of the twins. On her other side there was a photograph of Charles and Elizabeth.

Sophie took her arm from mine once we passed through the

lych-gate, guessing that I would want this short visit to be very personal. Since seeing Charles and Elizabeth I hadn't thought about what she had told me so far, but now, as she stood a few paces behind me looking down at Belinda's headstone, I realised that regardless of my promise I wanted to know more.

"What was she like?" Sophie asked.

"Beautiful, beautiful in every way," I replied.

Had I brought Sophie to Belinda's grave for approval? Was I looking for consent? Why did I think that Sophie and I had any sort of future? I had told myself a thousand times that it was too soon, and anyway I was forgetting that for there to be a future both of us would have to agree to it. Elizabeth had already signalled her displeasure and that was before anything existed for her not to understand.

I must have stayed looking down at Belinda's headstone for longer than I realised. I became aware that Sophie was no longer behind me, and when I looked over my shoulder, she was standing on the old wooden Packhorse Bridge that spanned the stream – known as the Medbourne Brook – running through the middle of the village. She was looking down at the ford below the level of the bridge that allowed vehicular access to the villages of Hallaton and Slawston. The water in the brook was quite high and there were a few inches of water flowing over the road.

After joining her on the bridge, I rested my forearms next to hers on the railings.

"Were you very much in love?" she asked quietly.

"She meant everything to me," I replied, remembering how time and time again Belinda and I had stood on exactly the same spot, throwing sticks into the water and then running past the cottages by the side of the stream to the bridge by the pub to see who had won. The twins joined in ... sometimes, when allowed. Playing Pooh sticks had become a family tradition whenever I was at home. For us all, the bridge, only a few feet from Belinda's grave, had been the only Pooh Bridge in the country.

"Have I intruded?"

I turned my head, the impulse to kiss Sophie was strong, and this time I didn't stop to think of the consequences. Her lips weren't Belinda's lips and Sophie's taste was different, but her lips were soft and cool, and the feeling they generated in me was exquisite. I hadn't kissed a woman other than Belinda on the lips for over twenty years. We parted momentarily but only to put our arms round each other. I felt like a teenager again, a teenager who was experiencing his first intimate kiss. She pushed her body against mind and ...

I sensed rather than saw that we were not alone.

Opening my eyes I saw a couple of women walking their dogs. They had reached the Hallaton side of the ford below us. The dogs, three of them, were eager to get wet but their owners, bedecked in jodhpurs, Wellington boots and short-sleeved shirts, had stopped and were eyeing Sophie and me with derision.

I pulled away slightly but kept my hands on Sophie's waist. "We have an audience," I told her, indicating the two women with my eyes.

Sophie turned her head and looked down at them. "It's such a lovely spot," she told them, "so romantic and personal."

The women, covered in confusion, looked away. The younger of the two, probably in her mid-thirties, allowed an embarrassed grin to creep onto her face. The older woman – who could have been her mother because facially they were similar – jerked forward as the two Golden Retrievers, having become impatient with the water so close, decided to go for a paddle.

"Lovely afternoon," Sophie added, lifting her hand to her mouth to stop herself from laughing.

The women scurried through the water, pulling the dogs

behind them once they reached the other side. Sophie and I watched them until they disappeared behind the large oak trees that bordered the churchyard. I was surprised I hadn't recognised either of them because, if their dress was anything to go by, I could guess which end of the village they lived in.

"Your reputation has been blown sky high if the expressions on their faces were for real," Sophie told me as we carried on over the bridge.

I shrugged. "What reputation?" We moved down the slope to the road. "But I am sorry …"

Sophie moved round in front of me and stopped.

She put her hands either side of my face before saying, "Don't you dare say you are sorry ever again. The only thing you have to be sorry about is that you didn't kiss me earlier. If I hadn't wanted you to kiss me, it would not have happened." She reached up and those strange lips were on mine again.

"Come on," she added still on tiptoe and after what seemed like an eternity, "I've got lots more to tell you and there will be enough time for other things later when perhaps we'll be able to have a little privacy without bumping into your in-laws or upper-class voyeurs."

We walked the four-mile circuit from Medbourne to Slawston and then back to Medbourne. Sophie did most of the talking and I only interrupted when I wanted her to elaborate on, or clarify something she had said. She went over again what she had already told me and then resumed telling me about what were probably routine occurrences for her but, for me, she had slipped back into the world of fantasy I had first been told about in Cochem, a world that I had promised I would leave behind.

Soon after we left the village, Sophie's hand slid into mine and we walked the rest of the way hand in hand, our fingers entwined, the ensuing but short-lived silence necessary only for us to accept the intimacy of such a simple act.

Chapter Twenty-Six

"Before you start telling me what you think I ought to know," I said, "can you explain to me why you are able to be this open? I would have thought what you do and what you did would be terribly hush-hush."

I felt Sophie's fingers tighten on mine. "I will but would you mind if we left my explanation for a little longer, it is the second reason why I'm here."

I shook my head. "If you want it that way and as long as telling me won't get you into trouble."

"I'm a big girl now, Richard, and no, if my ... my masters discovered that I had given you some of the detail they wouldn't be surprised. With one exception, nothing I'm going to tell you will be a surprise to you, because you know most of it already, but it does need putting into context."

"You've surprised me already," I said, smiling.

"That's as maybe ... where shall I start?"

"What about at the beginning," I said.

"Dove Dale?"

I stopped and looked at her. "You know about Dove Dale?"

"Richard, I know more about you than ... well, let's say there's not a lot I don't know about you."

"All right," I said. "I'm listening."

"The police in Ashbourne didn't believe your story about what happened to Ingrid Mesterom. They –"

"I gathered that," I said, interrupting.

"Will you let me tell you this in my own way, please, Richard?"

"Yes, of course, sorry."

"You came close to being arrested and charged with Ingrid Mesterom's murder. If it hadn't been for an inquisitive detective constable you probably would have been charged."

We moved into the side of the road to let a couple of cars pass us.

"But I'll come back to that," Sophie said resuming her account. "Finding Ingrid knocked out in a ditch was one thing, pitching your tent, administering first aid, and then leaving her while you tried to find her rucksack, was, for the police in Ashbourne, so unbelievably contrived it had to be a cover story."

"But it was the truth," I said.

"I know, but when I put it in context, you'll understand why they were suspicious. Thinking back, Richard, would you have done the same things again?"

Shaking my head, I felt a little stupid. "No, I wouldn't. When I got back to the tent with her rucksack and discovered Ingrid had disappeared, I spent all night punishing myself and wishing I could relive the last few hours all over again."

"Then, as I said, you'll understand why the police were suspicious of you. You see even spending the night in the tent added to their suspicions. Knowing Ingrid was hurt, why didn't you go to the police that evening?"

I shrugged. "In retrospect, I should have done, I know, but …"

"The police had every reason to arrest you, didn't they?"

"Yes," I admitted, "and believe me, I understood at the time why it was pretty obvious they were leading up to my arrest," I said. "Nobody was more surprised than me when they suddenly let me go."

"That was because we had got involved," Sophie said. "The detective constable I mentioned earlier, did a computer search and Ingrid Mesterom's name cropped up on our confidential list of names that were of interest to us. We were contacted and that's when we asked for you to be released without charge."

"You can do that?" She nodded. "Why?" I asked.

"We had been tracking Ingrid's movements for nearly a year. Based in Germany, our European counterparts and we believed she was a courier for an international drugs cartel. She had been in an out of Heathrow, Gatwick and Stansted numerous times, and although subjected to a full body search on occasions, she escaped arrest. She remained high profile but when you found her, we had no idea she was in the country. She had slipped in somehow undetected."

I stopped again and faced Sophie, her hand still in mine. "But what was she doing in Dove Dale and why was she murdered?"

"I can't answer either of those questions truthfully," Sophie said. "The police passed on their suspicions about you. We found the man you spoke to in the car park when you found Ingrid's rucksack, and he corroborated that part of your story. However, that didn't reduce their or our belief that you were involved in her murder. We decided that maybe she had done something that riled your organisation, tried to go it alone, sell drugs rather than passing them on … a little contrived I know but when clutching at straws it's amazing what will be believed. Anyway, her untrustworthiness became her death warrant. "

"But she was raped and I wasn't the rapist," I said, perhaps a little too indignantly.

"She wasn't raped," Sophie said.

"What?"

"It was fabrication, Richard. When the police released you without charge, something needed saying that would make you think they suddenly believed your story of what happened, hence the rape, and the invented proof that you couldn't have been the rapist due the lack of DNA evidence."

"This is incredible and a little unbelievable." I said.

"It gets worse," Sophie said. "Come on let's resume our walk. It is rather lovely, regardless of what we are talking about and who knows what might happen when we get back to Medbourne."

Chapter Twenty-Seven

Sophie went on to tell me that when they started investigating me more thoroughly, my background generated even greater interest. Evidently, a number of the countries I had worked in were on their radar in connection with smuggling routes and in some cases, actual drug production.

"But something always nagged at me from the outset," Sophie said. "Why if you, or you and someone else, were responsible for Ingrid's murder, did you stay behind to involve yourself in any investigation. If you had upped and disappeared then no-one would have been any the wiser."

I nodded. "Good point, why didn't I think of that?" I said sarcastically. "And the answer is?"

Sophie took a deep breath. "Over confidence," she said.

"What? I'm sorry if I'm saying 'what' too often, but this is becoming increasingly ridiculous, not just incredible. After I found Ingrid's body, I sat with her and held her hand until the police arrived and then I did everything I could to help them with their investigation. My background, the reason I was in Dove Dale, surely all that was checked out."

"Yes it was, and for some it weighted the evidence against you even further, but I felt the opposite and that's when I decided you weren't what we thought you were. I was about to persuade my boss that everything was circumstantial and to some extent coincidental, then recommend that I should call off the hounds when you went to Cochem and met with Marie Schmidt."

"I was followed, I know that – Schwartz and Henke told me," I said.

"Do you want their real names?" Sophie asked.

"If you think it'll help me understand," I said.

"Angela Branson and Peter Donaldson," she said. "They were part of my team of investigators; hence their presence in Cochem and Angela Branson's in Brunei."

"Are you really sure you ought to be telling me this?"

"Richard, you have every right to bring charges of harassment against my own department and the foreign office. You were treated abominably, you deserve –"

I smiled. "I've already decided nothing like that is going to happen, deserved or not. The only reason I'm listening to you now is because you kissed me."

Moving closer to the grass verge, and after checking the road in both directions, Sophie kissed me again. "And will that make you listen some more?" she asked, looking deeply into my eyes.

Still smiling I said, "It might." I wanted to add that I could listen forever, but something at the back of my mind told me that I needed to resume control of my senses.

"You might change your mind when you hear what else I have to say."

"We'll see … I presume having decided I was not what you thought I was, my trip to Cochem put me back on your suspect list as well as your superior's, correct?"

"In a nutshell, yes, but reluctantly," Sophie said. "Then when you met with Marie Schmidt the following day, Angela Branson and Peter Donaldson reported back and recommended strongly that we should keep you on the suspect list for at least a month when you returned to the UK. However, they did accept that if you didn't do anything suspicious in that period, perhaps we could let you off the hook."

"I can't think what grounds Branson and Donaldson had for making that recommendation," I said, "but having my house searched and finding nothing incriminating, I don't understand why I was still under suspicion. What did I do to …" I shook my head "… let me guess, Brunei?"

Sophie nodded. "Yes," she said, "Brunei."

"I went to Brunei because a dear friend asked me to. I didn't know why before I went and I still don't know why."

"I do," Sophie said. "Or I think I do."

Sophie was on the same flight as me from Heathrow to Singapore but had travelled in economy rather than business class. The Customs and Excise budget had only run to business class from Singapore to Brunei. Between Heathrow and Changi, Sophie said she had walked the length of the aircraft on numerous occasions to make sure I hadn't parachuted to safety since her previous check!

When relating this part of the investigation, she stopped once again and turned to face me. I was on the road and she stepped up onto the grass verge.

"Richard, I want you to know that from the moment I located you at Heathrow, I saw something in you that simply didn't compute with the image I'd already formed of you as a result of other people's reports and recommendations. Yes, I'd been shown some photographs and read the reports, but pictures and the written word can be rather inadequate." She took both my hands in hers. "You have to see the person: you have to watch the way they move, the way they react when among other people. I watched you closely and even before we boarded the aircraft I knew that you had nothing to do with what we thought we were investigating."

I smiled at her. She looked very serious.

"And what pray was there about me that told you I was only Mr Joe Public?"

"You're mocking me but I'll tell you anyway," she said, with only a slight smile on her lips. "It was the way you moved around other people. What you looked at when you were waiting for the aircraft. People who are in the illegal drugs business don't pick up fluffy toys that have been thrown out of pushchairs."

"And how far away from me were you when I did that?" I couldn't remember the incident but Sophie's logic intrigued me.

She cocked her head to one side, trying to make out whether I was still indulging her. "I was about twenty feet from you actually, peering over the top of a magazine."

"I see, and by picking up this child's toy I was suddenly not guilty of being part of an international drug-smuggling ring? Is that right?"

"It helped," she replied. "And if you mock me much more I won't tell you what else happened."

"You haven't told me yet why my trip to Brunei renewed your interest in me," I said.

"It wasn't really me, it was my boss. He thought you were being extraordinarily clever. Being a marine engineer and travelling all over the world, but mainly to third world countries and in particular certain countries, gave you exactly the cover you needed to be the brains behind the organisation. He thought it was all too much of a coincidence. I knew Brunei because I'd been there three, no four times before during ongoing investigations."

"You realise this should have all stopped after Dove Dale, don't you? In fact it should never have started."

"I realised that when I saw you in Heathrow airport," Sophie said.

"But your boss thought otherwise …" she nodded. "All right, Brunei. That's not a third world country, why did my going there arouse further suspicion?"

"It wasn't Brunei on its own, it was Singapore because of the Mesterom and Schmidt connection, and then Brunei's neighbours, Sabah, Sarawak and Kalimantan. We knew one of the international smuggling routes passed through at least two of those countries …"

"And because I was going to Brunei …?"

"Yes."

"God, you have to have a vivid imagination to work in your lot, don't you?" I said.

"Sometimes, vivid imaginations are all we have to go on."

"That's quite frightening and now I'm speaking from personal experience. You were telling me that picking up toys wasn't conducive with drug-smuggling," I said, as we started walking again. A couple of cars had passed us, and I did keep my eye out for anybody who might recognise me but I didn't see any cars or occupants I recognised.

"Yes, I was, wasn't I? Well, other than the times I checked on you and when you went upstairs in the aircraft – I presumed you were going to the bar – I didn't really see you again until Changi."

"Wasn't it a bit dangerous sitting close to me on the flight from Singapore?"

"I didn't really have any choice and anyway getting closer to you was all part of the investigation process. There were only nine rows in business class, so it was easy." She interlinked her fingers with mine again. "What was more dangerous was the horrible weather we flew through."

"I think everyone else would agree with you there."

"No," she retorted quickly, "not because of the danger to the aircraft but because it gave us reason to communicate."

"You call that communication? We only exchanged a few words."

"It was enough for plans to be changed once we were on the ground."

I frowned. "Why?"

"I was due to stay at The High Commission but I rang my boss from the airport and persuaded him that I was more likely to find out what they wanted to know about you if I stayed in the same hotel. We'd met on the aircraft, so recognition when we met again in the hotel would be perfectly normal."

"But you said getting close was part of the process."

"Yes, but not that close."

"I agree. If I had been what your boss thought I was, he was placing you in quite a lot of danger … and," I said, "don't you think I might have become a little suspicious with somebody I believed to be from the Foreign Office, coming on to me?"

"Coming on to you? I wasn't and you weren't," Sophie said.

"What?"

"You weren't suspicious because you hadn't done anything and I wasn't in danger for the same reason."

"So, your early morning swim wasn't deliberate, is that what you are saying?" I looked at her sideways.

She nudged me with her elbow. "Indirectly, no, I admit … maybe … yes, it was."

"And there was I thinking dinner in Mama Wong's and the horrific trip to the beach were all because …"

"It was in part …" she started to say.

I glanced sideways and there were tears forming in Sophie's eyes. I squeezed her hand and said, "What you have told me has bordered, most of the time, on the unbelievable in so many ways. Harassment as you put it, is not what I would call it because I would prefer professional bungling and a total waste of resources."

Seeing her tears I guessed she was reliving the agony she suffered when attacked by the sea wasp.

After a few seconds silence, she said,. "And you're right, I deserved that. Those idiots in Brunei spend all their time living it up and then they make a complete cock-up of the first bit of real excitement."

"I'm pleased I was the source of their entertainment."

"I wasn't talking about you, I was talking about me."

Once again, we both stepped onto the grass verge to let a wide-wheeled tractor go by. The driver, a young lad in his teens, lifted his hand to his well-worn peaked cap and smiled. There was a cigarette dangling from his lips.

"What do you mean?" I asked as we stepped down onto the road.

"The High Commission knew why I was in the country this time, and they knew it was you I was investigating, but obviously they didn't know the whole story. When the jellyfish incident occurred, they panicked. They knew enough to be rather worried when they heard that you were with me when I was stung. How were they going to explain that away when I wasn't around to do the explaining for them?"

"But Angela Branson was, she was the first person I saw when I regained consciousness after being drugged. Was she on our flight as well?"

"No, she travelled out two days before, to pave the way for my ... and your arrival. Yes, she was there, but she was as worried as Cruickshank ... well, you know the rest. When I found out what had happened ... well, what I said wasn't particularly ladylike ... it might be best if I keep it to myself. I very rarely use the 'F' word. He tried to explain his actions away by saying that he thought he would be arranging for my dead body to shipped home in a box. There would be questions asked and he thought you had the answers."

"If you'd died there would have only been one cause," I said.

"Yes, but he didn't know that at the time."

"You haven't mentioned Abby and the Internal Security Police yet," I said. "You implied you knew why Abby committed suicide."

Sophie left the road and went towards a five-bar gate that led into a wheat field. The view covered much of the Welland valley and we could see Medbourne and the road leading up on the opposite side of the valley to Blue-Ridge. The house was visible and I pointed it out to Sophie. Resting her head against my shoulder, she slipped her arm round my waist.

"It's lovely here isn't it?" she said.

"This part of the county is beautiful. Belinda and I came up here and stopped at this same gate the first time we came to view Blue-Ridge. She used almost identical words to yours."

"I'm sorry, I didn't mean to …"

"You didn't … Sophie, I feel you're wavering for some reason but please tell me what you know about Abby. I can take whatever it is."

She took her arm away and walked a few feet away before turning to look at me. Although quite tall, she seemed too delicate to be in such a physical business. She couldn't have weighed more than eight stone. Her hands and feet were tiny, her frame slim, but under that slight external appearance there was obviously a woman with direction.

"The reason I'm hesitating, Richard, is because what I was told hasn't been confirmed and probably never will be." Sophie stepped back onto the road. "Can we carry on walking?"

I joined her and she took my arm. "Confirmed or not, I would like to know," I said.

"Unbeknown to me, you, The High Commission and God knows who else, Brunei's Internal Security Police were investigating your friend Abby. This is hearsay, Richard, but it is believed Abby was mixed up in or even the leader of a plot against The Sultan."

I stopped suddenly, not believing what Sophie had said. She moved in front of me and took my hands in hers.

"Richard, I –"

"I can't …" I started to say.

"I'm sorry, Richard, but that is what I was told."

"And … and I … God, I've been bloody naïve. When Abby and I went out on his launch, it was to tell me about a supposed plot against The Sultan, and he believed the British Foreign Office was in league with the subversives … it was all to do with oil and gas, and Britain looking for alternative supplies … God, I believed every word he told me."

"So, perhaps what –"

"He also believed you were part of the plot against The Sultan …"

"He what?"

"He wanted me to grill you about why you were in Brunei."

"But as far as I know, Britain's relationship with Brunei and therefore The Sultan, has never been stronger," Sophie said.

"That's exactly what I told him … now I understand what he was really saying to me. If you had been who he thought you were … it was all reverse psychology and I fell for it."

"His involvement is not confirmed but if it's true, it's unlikely it ever will be broadcast. It's not the sort of thing a country like Brunei would want the rest of the world to know about."

"And what you told me about being an auditor …"

"Obviously I had to lie to you about what I did,' she said. "Regardless of what I thought, you were still on the suspect list because my boss still thought differently to me."

We had entered the village of Slawston and the church was on our left. Sophie pulled me towards a bench in the churchyard and sat down.

I felt numb.

Shaking my head in disbelief, I said, "I don't understand why if you had been to Brunei a number of times before last month, he didn't know you were not with the Foreign Office."

"That's easy, Richard,' she said, leaning back against the bench. "Nobody other than The High Commission knew I was with Customs and Excise."

"You've also explained why the Internal Security Police were interested in me, eventually ordering me out of the country. I was friends with Abby ... and you. I think if I had been them I might have hauled me in for an explanation, rather than having a cosy chat and drink in the hotel."

Sophie nodded. "It all makes sense, doesn't it? The final pieces of the jigsaw puzzle have come together," she said.

I nodded. "It certainly ... I suppose, as you said, we will never know the truth. Did you know Abby's wife, Nazira, is the PA to The Supreme Commander?"

"Yes, I did know. But you're right, we will never know the truth, and perhaps it is best if we don't."

I took a deep breath. "For the children's sake I hope she was not involved in any way."

"I don't know, Richard. At least what I've told you has gone some to explaining why I am here."

"I agree with the *some way*," I said. "You said there were three reasons why you came to see me. I've only heard the first one."

"That's true," she said, a mischievous smile appearing on her lips.

Chapter Twenty-Eight

After getting up from the bench, we carried on through the village. We saw a few people who in the inimitable way of villagers all passed the time of day, and I assumed Sophie's silence meant she was reconsidering what extra she wanted to tell me. In the space of a couple of hours, our relationship had moved on at quite a pace.

Belinda was watching over me, and I knew she would understand, even encourage me, but I didn't understand. I didn't understand my feelings in Brunei and they were still confusing me. My confusion hadn't stopped me kissing Sophie, and we'd spent nearly an hour walking in the open holding hands. Although I'd been wary of the cars and people that were about, my behaviour suggested my caution was perfunctory – because deep down I didn't really care.

We were back on the road to Medbourne before either of us spoke again. Sophie would tell me her other reasons when she was ready, but there was something else I wanted to ask first.

"Why did Abby commit suicide if he was involved in this plot against the Sultan, surely he –"

"It's possible he didn't," Sophie said, interrupting.

Frowning, I said, "Are you saying he was murdered?"

She nodded then shook her head, a mannerism that endeared me to her even more. "No, I'm saying that it's a possibility. It would explain why no reason for his suicide has ever been given."

Shaking my head, my thoughts immediately shifted to Nazira and the children. If what Sophie was suggesting were true, Nazira would also know the truth. How could she be the PA to the Supreme Commander when at the same her husband was plotting to overthrow The Sultan? It didn't add up. There had to be another reason. Strangely I would have preferred to know that Abby had committed suicide for some personal reason, being diagnosed with a terminal illness for example, but to put Nazira and the children at risk was inconceivable.

Walking down the hill towards Medbourne, I felt as though Sophie had in the space of a little more than an hour, explained everything that had happened in my life since Belinda died and I had taken myself off to the supposed solitude of Derbyshire.

On reaching Pooh Bridge, we paused in the middle of the bridge and watched the water flow underneath, over the ford and down towards the pub. I smiled ruefully. We had no control over the swirls and eddies in the water below us in the same way we had no control over the whirlpools in our lives. We thought we did; we thought we had a choice, but more often than not, we didn't – the last few months had proved that to me.

"So," Sophie said finally, "there you have it."

"There I have it," I said. "I can't say it was the way I expected today to go when I went for a game of golf, but I'm pleased it did." I turned slightly and faced her. "Is it time to tell me what reasons two and three are?"

Sophie, her hands in front of her, suddenly looked vulnerable. "I've lied to you," she said quietly.

"About what?" I should have been concerned but I wasn't.

"You asked me earlier whether I was authorised to tell you what I have: I suppose the honest answer to your question is, no." She raised her eyebrows at the look of surprise on my face. "But I've told you now so it's too late."

"If you weren't authorised, then surely –"

"I'm not on sick leave," she said, looking down at the stream. "I've resigned. I handed my letter of resignation in last week and told them that they weren't to expect me to work my notice."

"But surely you'd be on sick leave anyway after what

happened."

She looked up and the expression on her face suggested that I was being rather stupid. "There was no point. I had made up my mind to resign the night before I walked into the water at Cave beach."

"Why?"

"Because, Richard, I had fallen in love."

Dorothy Stephens, the licensee's wife, looked quite surprised as we walked in. She was a squat woman who always looked extremely healthy, her rosy cheeks and tanned arms resulting from a varied outdoor life but none more so than being a member of a local walking club. She was always smiling, regardless of the time of day or what the weather. Although The Nevill Arms could be classed as our *local*, I couldn't say that Belinda and I had been regulars but we had been in often enough for me still to be recognised.

Belinda had accompanied me under duress – using her terminology not mine – because I regarded that supporting the *local* was part of village life but she thought that it should never become an obligation.

It was a warm early evening, and the tables outside by the Medbourne Brook were filled with all sorts; couples of all ages, cyclists and ramblers. Inside the pub the temperature dropped a few degrees and it was less busy.

"Hello, Richard," Dorothy said, looking up from drying glasses. Her greeting was for me but her eyes were on Sophie.

"Hi Dorothy, it's a lovely evening. It's good to see all those customers at this time of day."

"It certainly is, we've been busy all day. Saw you both standing on the bridge by the church when I took Dotty for a walk. I wondered if you were going to come in later."

Dorothy was still looking at Sophie ... an introduction was in order.

"Dorothy, this is Sophie Mackintosh and Sophie, this is Dorothy Stephens." The two women shook hands across the bar.

"Pleased to meet you, Sophie," Dorothy said pleasantly, first names being the order of the day in The Nevill Arms. "Now what can I get you both?" she continued, not waiting for Sophie to return her greeting.

I stole a sideways glance and the twinkle in Sophie's eyes suggested Dorothy's informal approach had amused her.

Dorothy had the reputation for being the source of any information required about anything or anybody in Medbourne. This was probably one of the reasons why Belinda, being a private person, hadn't always been a willing companion. I knew that going into the pub with a female Dorothy didn't recognise would be playing on her mind, but she certainly wasn't forward enough to ask outright who Sophie was and what she was doing with me. I was still reeling from what Sophie had told me earlier. I wasn't stupid enough not to have concluded that I was the source of her feelings and, understandably from my behaviour before and during our walk of confession, she had assumed that her feelings were reciprocated.

I remained confused by my feelings, actions and expectations … my conscience played its inexorable part as usual.

"Erm, a gin and tonic, and a pint of lager, please, Dorothy." Before going into the pub I had already asked Sophie what she would like to drink.

While Dorothy was pouring the drinks, I felt Sophie's hand slip into mine and she squeezed my fingers. Other than acknowledging my introduction with a nod and a smile, she hadn't said a word since we walked through the front door. Perhaps going into the pub wasn't the best of moves when Sophie had declared how she felt about me, but although it was a longish walk back up the hill to Blue-Ridge, I needed more time to think.

We took our drinks and sat in the corner by the unlit fire. Glancing out of the window I could see the small car park was almost full. The ducks and geese were all lying on the grass next to the brook and footbridge, enjoying the warmth from the early evening sun. All the customers at the outside tables seemed to be enjoying themselves.

"Was I too direct?" Sophie asked, breaking the silence.

I turned and looked at her. The expression on her face and in her eyes spoke a thousand words.

I had hurt her by not responding straight away.

She had been direct with me and expected me to be the same with her, even if it were to say I didn't reciprocate her love.

But I did feel the same, why couldn't I tell her? Since sitting down to breakfast in the Sheraton Utama Hotel in Brunei, and regardless of what else was going on, my conscience had been playing havoc with my feelings and vice versa.

Sophie had travelled up from London to see me and I had been rather naïve to assume that her reasons were to relate what I had been unknowingly involved with, and to tell me she had resigned. Kissing and holding hands were good indicators without the need for words. Had my conscience been telling me it would all go away … again?

I needed to say something.

"We haven't known each other very long but I have become accustomed to your directness," I said. Under the circumstances, I was trying to be amusing but my choice of words must have sounded silly. Her knee was touching mine, and as she sipped her drink, I wanted to tell her how I really felt. But I didn't want to confuse her as much as I was confusing myself. "I suppose I'm still trying to come to terms with what you said."

"Is it that difficult?"

"Not difficult, but rather unexpected."

She shrugged. "Unexpected? It wasn't me who kissed you on the bridge," she said. "Not the first time, anyway."

"Pooh Bridge," I told her.

"Is that what it's called?"

"Not by anyone other than the Blythe family, or not as far as I know. It's actually called the Packhorse Bridge," I said.

Sophie put her hand on top of mine, her fingers stroking slowly. "Richard, I'm not some mixed-up teenager with a crush. You said you're now used to my directness, I haven't let you down, then, have I? Since Jeremy and I split up, I haven't felt like this about anybody else, in fact I have never felt like this about anybody else full stop."

I watched her fingers moving, not wanting the sensation to ever end. "I'm extremely flat –"

"Don't you *dare* tell me you're flattered," she said, her eyes flashing. "If you want to tell me you don't share my feelings, then tell me straight. Don't pussyfoot around with gentle let-downs. I like my directness to be met with directness."

"I wasn't attempting to pussyfoot around," I said slowly. "It's not a question of whether I share your feelings or not, it's whether I ought to feel the way I do." I looked at my drink, moving the glass slowly, the amber liquid swirled round the inside of the glass. "Whether you want me to say it or not, I am flattered but ... but perhaps privileged would be a better word. You are a beautiful woman and I'm sure if I were to get to know you better, what I don't know about you would be equally attractive."

"There's a 'but' coming."

I looked at her and nodded. "There has to be a 'but', Sophie." I wanted to tell her that I was still mourning my loss. I wanted to tell her that in a year's time, two years', five years' even ten years' time, I would still be in mourning. Although other men might find it difficult to believe – I said it to myself often enough – since the day I fell in love with Belinda I hadn't looked at, nor imagined that there would ever be another woman in my life. She meant everything to me and was everything for me. There was never any deception, nor the need for lies. We often lay awake at night after making love and marvelled at how lucky we were. If anything, I was the only one who had introduced the circumstances that could have caused friction. My absences were necessary for the job I was in, but not essential. I could have just as easily got a job in England and even within commuting distance of Blue-Ridge. However, without my job with Astek we wouldn't have been living in Blue-Ridge.

Did that matter? It mattered to me … at the time.

I sometimes thought that Elizabeth's feelings towards me came about partially because she saw how devoted Belinda and I were to each other. I suppose every parent wants to see his or her offspring happy, but Belinda and I had been more than happy, our relationship was blissful, utterly idyllic. We didn't need anybody else and perhaps that is what had showed and was translated in Elizabeth's mind as a threat. Belinda and I had discussed my unsupported beliefs, but although she agreed that what we had was fantastic, her mother would never be resentful.

"What is the 'but'?" Sophie asked, breaking into my thoughts.

I shook my head. "I would have thought that was obvious."

"Belinda?"

"Of course, and I promise you there is n o other reason."

"I wouldn't have expected anything else, and by saying that I'm not being deliberately patronising." Sophie took her hand from mine and picked up her glass. "Richard, I'm not asking for a commitment, but from my point of view the situation is quite simple. I have fallen in love with you and I needed to tell you how I felt."

"Thank you," I said.

"That's a strange thing to say." Her eyes sparkled as she added impishly, "and what would you say if I suggest we finish our drinks and go back to the house?"

"I thought maybe we could get something to eat here or maybe pop into town," I suggested.

"It's a bit early," she pointed out, looking at her watch, "and I don't want to be within listening distance of anybody else. This is too important. Have you got anything in we could have to eat?"

"There's some fresh pasta and a Caesar salad in the fridge."

"Perfect," she said. "And, Richard, I do understand."

We walked most of the way back to Blue-Ridge in silence. Having accepted that I wanted and needed to be with Sophie was one thing, my conscience and the guilt that went with it, was another.

Two months was too short a period to come to terms with losing Belinda. Right up to an hour before she died, she had a smile for me, it was a weak smile but it was still there. Holding her when she had so little time to live was awful: she felt warm, her head rested against my shoulder, everything should have been normal. It is only now that I will admit to myself, but never to anybody else, that I had helped her die. The morphine drip muted the pain, and the nurse who showed me how to operate it and change the bottles, also told me that I could increase the dose if Belinda became too uncomfortable. Although she didn't say so in as many words, she was telling me what to do when Belinda told me it was time.

Belinda and I understood.

I had been to have a shower and had brought Belinda a cup of warm sweet tea when the look in her eyes told me 'it was time'. I will never forget the way her tearful eyes pleaded with me to understand, the weak smile telling me she would always be there for me.

I sat on the side of the bed and she took my right hand in hers. "Kiss me,' she said, her voice very weak. The lips I kissed were the same lips I had kissed so many times over the previous twenty years, but knowing this would be the last time was too much.

"I can't do it," I whispered. "I just can't do it." My own tears were streaming down my face.

"It … it will happen very soon anyway, please let me die free of pain, Richard. Please help me."

Her eyes were still pleading with me, but I could see the pain was already there. Without taking my eyes from hers, I reached for and touched the button to increase the dose. I pressed the button four more times.

"Thank you," Belinda said, "and thank you for a wonderful life and two marvellous children. Please hold me; we mustn't say goodbye because I will always be there with you and when you talk to me I will answer you. I love you, Richard."

I went round to my side of the bed and got in next to Belinda. She snuggled up to me as she always did and I told her that I loved her, and she was right, she would always be with me.

There were thirty people standing at the graveside but I felt very alone. Standing there, holding hands with the twins, and with Elizabeth and Charles only feet away, everything became a blur.

At that moment, I knew I had to get away, to be on my own. I didn't think I would ever come to terms with losing Belinda but I needed the solitude to allow my mind to put the future in perspective with the past. I had to be there for the twins and for Elizabeth and Charles.

When I was a few days into my isolation, I decided I wasn't naïve enough to believe that there would never be anybody else for me, but time was a factor that had to be considered. Time, and the right amount of it, would add decency to and belief in a new relationship. I imagined what people would say if I got it wrong. "He didn't waste any time, did he? Do you think anything was going on before Belinda died, poor girl?" and then maybe if I got it right, "We see Richard has found someone to love, poor dear. He deserved to find love again, he has mourned Belinda for too long."

Who these *people* were I had no idea. I suppose they were people who really mattered to me: Isabelle, David, Elizabeth and Charles. The twins would resent me finding somebody else because I was trying to replace their mummy; Elizabeth, but maybe not Charles, would think I was replacing their daughter.

If time and what other people thought mattered, why was I walking up the hill towards my house with Sophie? Why was I contemplating an evening … a night … with somebody I hardly knew? Did I feel that I was under some form of obligation because she had told me she was in love with me? I shrugged and hoped that Sophie hadn't noticed. She was walking silently beside me, her hand resting on my arm. The shrug had been deliberate but the shudder was involuntary.

After everything that had occurred and in such a short space of time, and with some of my promises already broken, my only immediate concern was that it was too soon for me to be considering a relationship with another woman. The twins were due home in a matter of days for their summer holidays. Charles and Elizabeth had seen me with Sophie and no doubt were discussing what their scoundrel of a son-in-law was up to so soon after burying their daughter.

All of their feelings needed due consideration. It wasn't only me who would be affected by my decision.

The click of her shoes on the road, her hand resting in the crook of my arm, her hip every few steps brushing against me, her silence: they all added up to a need that I wouldn't admit to myself was there. She would know what I was thinking, the way my mind was going round in circles.

We both knew that by the time we reached Blue-Ridge I would have to make a decision.

It wasn't a case of offering her somewhere to sleep. She wasn't a friend who had come to stay for a few days. If I invited her in for more than a drink before she drove back to wherever she had driven from – I assumed it was London – then I would have made a commitment. Sophie had said that she didn't want a commitment from me, but my definition of a commitment differed from hers. For me, by accepting that I needed her, I was making a commitment and breaking a promise.

We turned the last corner before Blue-Ridge and I hesitated. It was where Belinda and I had stopped so often to admire the house, and then look over our shoulders at the view towards the village and the valley. It was *our* view: it had been one moment of many moments that were extremely personal.

I had made my decision.

Sophie took her hand from my arm, and crossing the road she was the one now looking at our view. For a few seconds I didn't see Sophie, I saw Belinda before she turned with that smile on her face that told me why I was blissfully happy.

I joined Sophie at the fence.

"I know I'm stalling, Sophie," I said, "but unless I get this right it could finish up as a rather embarrassing mess. I have got others to consider, not only myself."

She didn't look at me as she spoke. "I hope you are including me when thinking of other people. You haven't said anything since we left the pub, your silence could mean anything."

"I think you know where I'm coming from."

"Do I? I know that we are two adults who are free and find each other more than just attractive. I know our backgrounds are different. I'm the product of an unpleasant divorce and you lost your wife, to whom you were obviously devoted, under the most tragic of circumstances." She placed her hands on the top of the fence in front of her but still she didn't look at me. "I didn't set out to fall in love with you, or anybody else. In fact, it was the last thing I was looking for, but it happened. I'm here because I want to be near you, I want to be with you. I have never wanted to be this close to anybody before but if you would prefer that I wasn't then all you have to do is say exactly that."

"It's not that –"

"Richard, we're not heading back towards the flattered bit again are we, because if we are, I would prefer to be told to go."

I took her hands from the fence and gave her little choice but to look at me.

"Sophie, my mind is still in a complete muddle. It's not you I am fighting against, it is my conscience and at the moment it is stricken with guilt. A little more than ten weeks ago it was Belinda here with me, she wanted to look at this view one last time. I had to carry her because she didn't have the strength to support her own weight – which by then was less than five stone."

"Richard, I –"

"No, Sophie, let me finish. We stood here and cried together, and for me it will always be yesterday." I took a deep breath. "If you can put up with knowing how I felt about Belinda, and that as we pass this spot and many others, I will be thinking about her, then … then … Look, if I let you walk away now, I doubt if I will ever see you again. If we had met in six months' or a year's time I hope there would have been no hesitation on either of our parts. We can't control how we feel about someone, and as you feel about me, I feel the same about you, and have done since … before Cave beach."

Sophie face broke into a smile. "Are you telling me in a roundabout way that that you are in love with me?"

"Yes, Sophie, I am in love with you and have been since you walked out of the bathroom in the hotel after we'd been to Mama Wong's."

Her brow furrowed. "That will take some explaining," she said.

Smiling, I said, "And I will."

"Richard, I respect everything you have said about Belinda, and I love you even more for saying it." She paused. "Can you now tell me what should happen next?"

"I suggest we go back to the house and you unpack the weekend case I guess you have with you, and well ..." I said.

Her eyes widened in mock disbelief. "Are you suggesting, Mr Blythe, that I should not only stay in your house tonight but also share your bed?" She fluttered her eyelids.

"Yes, I think I probably am," I replied.

Perhaps I already believed there was a strong possibility that I would regret my decision but Sophie didn't strike me as the sort of person who would go into hibernation until I was ready for her. Rightly or wrongly, she had forced me into a corner and only I could decide which way I wanted to leave it.

I started to turn away but Sophie held onto my hands.

"I didn't resign from my job because of you. That was a decision I took some time ago. I suppose I needed a helping hand. I have no regrets about coming to Medbourne to find you because one of us had to take the initiative. If I had left it to you, maybe you would never have found me. I knew where you lived, don't forget. You wouldn't have known where to start with me." She smiled. "Before we walk through those gates," she added, indicating the entrance to Blue-Ridge, "I want you to know that I will stay for as long as you want me to, but I will also walk away if ... I am not, and will never be, a substitute for Belinda. I can see she was her own person, but so am I."

Chapter Twenty-Nine

The next twenty-four hours didn't go the way I anticipated. Once through the front door of Blue-Ridge, we both seemed to abandon all sensibility and the strong feelings of guilt miraculously disappeared.

Sitting in the conservatory with a drink, or making small talk anywhere else in the house, would have been an unnecessary diversion from what we both knew was going to happen.

I followed Sophie up the stairs carrying the over-night bag she had retrieved from her car, and opened the door to the main bedroom. She looked round the room and headed straight for the bathroom, emerging a few minutes later dressed in nothing but a man's shirt.

She stopped just inside the room and looked at me. "I feel a little embarrassed," she said softly, "and you look as though you're still going to play a round of golf."

The only words I can use to describe what happened next are total abandonment of responsibilities, consciences and thoughts for other people. It certainly wasn't what I expected. We were like two animals – apart for too long, and when eventually we were put into the same cage, nothing and nobody acted as inhibitors.

I have no idea how long it was before we mutually agreed that we needed a rest but, as we lay on the bed, Sophie's head resting on my shoulder and one leg draped across mine, I could not believe the way she had made me feel.

The faint pink lines on her thighs were a reminder of our pasts. There were other lines running below her navel and hips. Letting the tips of my fingers move lightly down the blemishes, I said, "I'm not sure I know what to say."

"Is there any need to say anything?" Her breath was warm

against my shoulder, her hair soft against my face.

"I suppose not but we can't lie here in silence."

"I'm warm, satisfied and happy," she said. "I feel like falling asleep."

Moreover, that's exactly what she did. Her breathing became slower and within minutes, she was fast asleep. I looked around the room expecting suddenly to be overcome with remorse but it didn't happen. There were photographs of Belinda, the twins and me on everywhere, but I simply looked at them and smiled. The way other items in the room were arranged hadn't been changed: I had left them exactly as Belinda liked them to be. Some of her everyday necklaces and bracelets were hanging from the mirror support on her dressing table above the bottles of lotions and potions. I looked at them and smiled again. One of the wardrobe doors was slightly open and I could see some of Belinda's dresses and tops.

I looked at them and smiled.

I didn't know what magic the woman lying next to me possessed but whatever it was it had worked. She had been gentle, caring and persuasive. She had guided my hands and fingers to areas that she particularly liked to be touched, while at the same time ensuring that she gave more than she received. It hadn't been simply two frustrated people using the other for satisfaction: there was a chemistry that I never thought would exist with another woman.

When the phone rang Sophie was still asleep. I checked my watch as I reached for the receiver. It was seven o'clock in the evening. Sophie gave no sign that the phone had disturbed her, and leaving one arm round her shoulders, I balanced the receiver next to my right ear.

"Hello," I said in almost a whisper.

"Daddy," shrilled Isabelle at the other end. "Is it really nearly the holidays?"

"In less than a week," I told her, trying to keep my voice low. "You don't normally ring at this time."

"I know but I'm getting excited ... I thought I would ring to make sure all was okay."

"Why wouldn't it be?" I was aware that I probably didn't sound that receptive. With Isabelle talking in one ear, and a naked female resting her head against my other shoulder, I felt a little uncomfortable.

"No reason," she replied. "Are we going away?"

"You mean have I booked anywhere yet?"

"Well, yes. I thought we'd agreed that we would go somewhere." It hadn't slipped my mind but the opportunity hadn't really arisen. We had talked about taking a villa on one of the Balearic Islands but as it was only late June I was sure we would find something still available.

"We did and we will. I thought it would be fun if we all looked together, maybe next week."

"That would be great. What time will you be down on Friday?"

"What time will you and David be ready?"

"If you're coming to Mass it starts at eleven o'clock. We can leave soon after that."

"I'll be there for eleven o'clock. Is there any other news?"

"No, not really." Her voice had dropped.

"What about exam results?"

"We get them tomorrow. I think I've passed them all. Daddy?"

"What about David?" I asked.

"He says he's happy. Daddy, are you all right?"

"Yes, what makes you think I'm not?"

"You sound a bit strange, sort of distant. You're whispering."

"I'm fine, Bella, just a little tired maybe."

"How's Grandma?" I had told them during the last exeat

about Elizabeth's stroke.

"Much improved. Have you rung her?"

"Yes of course, but you can't really tell anything when you can't see the person you're speaking to." I was rather pleased my daughter couldn't see her father at that moment, she most definitely would not have understood.

Belinda had given the twins phone cards at the start of the term, but I was sure David had sold his on – at a profit – because he never rang of his own accord. It crossed my mind that Belinda had touched the card Isabelle was now using.

"I saw them this afternoon. Grandpa was taking her out for a drive and she was fine."

She seemed satisfied. "Got to go, Daddy," she said in a rush. "We've got our end of term party this evening."

"Well have a lovely time and I'll see you on Friday."

"Okay."

"And when you see David tell him the same will you?"

"Will do. Bye."

"Bye, Bella."

Trying not to disturb Sophie, I replaced the old-fashioned receiver in its cradle.

"Was that your daughter?" a sleepy voice asked next to me.

She had been awake all the time. "Yes," I replied to the top of her head. "Just checking on arrangements for Friday."

Adjusting her position, Sophie twisted onto her stomach and looked at me. "I pick Emma up on Friday as well."

"Where is she at school?"

"Crawbury College," Sophie said running her tongue over her lips. "It's between Chipping Norton and Burford."

"I think I know it." We hadn't looked at it for the twins but I remembered one of my colleagues from Astek saying that his daughters went there. Crawbury College was exclusive and therefore expensive.

Sophie tucked her hair behind her ears. She looked tired. The phone call from Isabelle had probably woken her from a deep sleep.

"Are you ready to talk?" she said.

"About what?"

"Stop being evasive, Richard," she scolded me, but with a smile. Lifting herself up, she knelt beside, and put a hand on my chest. She had a lovely figure and Abby had been right: it was as good out of a swimming costume as it was in. Suddenly thinking of what Abby had said seemed a little incongruous and insensitive under the circumstances, but at least it brought a reciprocal smile to my lips.

"What are you smiling for?"

"I was enjoying what I was looking at, that's all."

Sophie took her hand from my chest and moved her fingers along the pink lines on her thighs and then on her stomach. "I don't think these will ever go, regardless of what I was told."

"Maybe in time, they have already faded."

"I know and I suppose whenever I see them it'll remind me of what you did for me."

I put my fingers on her cheek and stroked her face. "I told you at the time, I did no more than anyone else could have done."

"Are there any decent restaurants in Market Harborough?" Sophie asked, opening her eyes and holding my hands in hers.

"A couple."

"Shall we give your pasta a miss this evening? I feel that we should celebrate."

"Yes," I said smiling, "I think we should."

"In that case, and as it'll take me only a few minutes to get ready, we have time to work up an appetite."

It was over an hour later that we drove away from Blue-Ridge and headed down the hill towards the village. At the bottom of the hill, I was about to turn left for Market Harborough, when Sophie suddenly said: "No, not yet. Can you go and park by the ford?"

I did as she asked but with a quizzical expression on my face. We got out of the car and, taking my hand, she led me to Belinda's grave. She knelt down at the end of the grave and put her hands together.

"Belinda, I have already told him, and now I am here to tell you, that I have fallen in love with Richard. I do honestly believe that I can make him happy. I know how much he loved you and still does, but I know I can bring him some of the happiness he lost in April. I also know we have a lot to go through. I know we are going to have to cope with a lot of wagging tongues but most of all I know that people are going to say that it is too soon. Can you put a time limit on when people should or shouldn't fall in love? The children – I have a daughter, Emma, who is the same age as Isabelle and David – aren't going to find what we have to tell them easy to accept but, given time, I am sure they will learn to accept us both. I have already met, albeit briefly, your mother and father, and they too will need some convincing that I'm not a frustrated divorcee looking for security with another man.

"Richard has been through a lot recently and I don't know what he has already told you, but I'm sure he will come back to see you on his own. It is important that I am not here when he tells you the circumstances under which he and I met. Belinda, I'm not stealing your husband, I am asking if I can share him with you. I am sure I can make him happy again, and I promise you I will look after him. I am sure you will agree that he isn't the sort of man who should be left on his own.

"Belinda, thank you for listening. I didn't know you but from what I have been told and seen in Blue-Ridge, you were a lovely, lovely person. I felt I could come and talk to you and, if you don't mind, I will come back and talk to you again."

Sophie bowed her head, closed her eyes and said a few words I couldn't hear. Leaning over Belinda's grave, she picked up a couple of small sticks that had fallen from the adjacent tree. She then stood up and walked over to me.

"Don't say a word," she told me.

She took my hand again and led me back towards Pooh Bridge. Once we were standing in the middle, she gave me one of the sticks.

"I'm not going to even try to replace Belinda, Richard. I couldn't, but over the last couple of hours you have given me more happiness than I have ever had before. I want that happiness to continue for both of us. Each time we come back here and play Pooh sticks, I am really saying thank you not only to you but also to Belinda for giving me the opportunity to be happy."

She dropped her stick over the side of the bridge and I did the same with mine.

We watched the sticks bobbing in the water as they floated away, and I realised that perhaps I could cope with what we were going to have to face, because when Sophie Mackintosh knelt in front of Belinda's grave and started talking to her, I felt the conscience that had haunted me for so long, fade away.

The End

About the Author

Nigel Lampard was a Lieutenant-Colonel in the British Army and after thirty-nine years of active service he retired in 1999. Trained as an ammunition and explosives expert, he travelled the world and was appointed an Order of the British Empire for services to his country.

As a second career he helped British Forces personnel with their transition to civilian life, and finally retired in 2007, when he and his wife Jane moved to Leigh-on-Sea in Essex. Married for over forty years, they have two sons and four grandchildren.

Nigel started writing after a tour in Berlin in the early 1980s – he fell in love with what was then a walled and divided city. After leaving Berlin, the only way he could continue this love was to write about it. By the time he completed the draft for his first novel he was already in love with writing.

Made in the USA
Charleston, SC
14 April 2015